TOGGENBURG – BOOK 2
Edelweiss

Michaela Francis

TOGGENBURG – BOOK 2
Edelweiss

FICTION4ALL

Chapter One

On the day that Frau Fritzl finally released Sarah from service at the Hotel Toggenburg, Sarah and Daniela climbed the mountain. The ascent had its genesis in a number of apparently unrelated coincidences. To begin with, Frau Fritzl decided that she could not, with any degree of financial justification, require Sarah's services for a few days. However much Frau Fritzl wished to encourage the relationship between the two girls, she was, nevertheless, forced to admit that, with her workforce back to full strength following Magdalena's full recovery and with a sadly quiet period of business looming, it simply made no sense to continue to employ Sarah. Frau Fritzl could, of course, have justified Sarah's continued employment on the grounds that she was still enjoying the benefits of Daniela's presence in the hotel but this was a woman of far greater sensibility than that. Perhaps she realised that Sarah and Daniela had reached an impasse in their relationship; a pause in development dictated by Sarah's working routine. In a sense, she could kill two birds with a single stone. Sarah needed a break. It would be highly gratifying if that break included Daniela.

Toward the end of her shift, therefore, Frau Fritzl called Sarah across to the table where she was adding up the day's earnings. "Sarah," she began, "Now that I've a full staff back up and running and we've got nothing on for the next few days, why don't you take a break?"

Sarah blinked. "Oh don't you need me tomorrow?"

"I can always use you Sarah but you've just worked three weeks without a break and all work and no play makes Jill a dull girl. Now we've got damn all doing for the next few days so why don't you get off and get out somewhere? I'm sure we can manage a few days without you."

"I'm not tired of working Frau Fritzl. I've been enjoying it." Sarah looked uncertain.

"I know Sarah and I'm pleased that you've been working for us. I'm very grateful for your efforts. You've been marvellous as usual. But Sarah, you need to get out of the place for a few days. I know it gets on my nerves after a while if I can't get off and relax somewhere." Frau Fritzl paused. "I know," she said, as if the thought had only just occurred to her, "Why don't you take your young lady out hiking for a couple of days? You've been saying for days how you'd love to show her the mountains. Here's your chance."

Sarah blushed. Daniela was by now firmly entrenched as Sarah's "young lady" in Frau Fritzl's terminology. "I... I don't know. I don't know if Daniela would like that."

Frau Fritzl put her head back and roared with laughter. "Oh Sarah! Daniela would enthusiastically embrace the idea of a day trip to Hell if you were the guide." Frau Fritzl recovered her composure and leaned forward seriously. "I think it's a good idea." She said quietly. "Take her for a little trip up the mountains. I'm sure she'd love it."

Sarah swallowed and nodded. "Well we have talked about taking a proper hike one day."

"Well there you go. Take the girl out and show her the mountains. Show her..." Frau Fritzl paused with a tongue in her cheek. "Show her where you live."

As Sarah finished up her duties for the evening, waiting for Daniela, the idea grew on her. She had long wanted to introduce Daniela to the high mountains she so loved and it was a perfect opportunity. She knew instinctively that Daniela would be thrilled by the experience and she longed to witness Daniela's reaction to the true wonder of her mountains. She had only taken Daniela up the Chaserugg until now and that in a cable car. She wanted Daniela to feel a real mountain beneath her boots now however and that meant, to Sarah, the

Santis and the wild wastelands of the Toggenburg's most majestic peak. The more she thought about it, the more excited she became and her face was flushed with exuberance when Daniela came to pick her up dutifully at ten o'clock.

The other major factor influencing Sarah's sudden endorsement of the idea was the unexpected absence of Nicole. Just that morning, Nicole had been obliged to make her apologies at the Hotel Hirschen and take her farewell of Sarah to drive away to attend upon her mother. Nicole's mother had had an accident and broken her ankle. That, for the purposes of the narrative, is putting it simply. There were however few matters concerning Nicole's mother that could be described as simple and it is worth taking a brief moment to take a look at the remarkable woman who had, some twenty years ago, produced such a singular daughter as the fruit of her loins. Nicole's mother was a middle aged woman and one might have expected her accident to be the misfortune of a mundane mishap concerning, perhaps, a loose stair in her house or perchance an unfortunate slip on an uneven flagstone. It was, of course, none of the above. In fact she had sustained her injury following a bad landing whilst para-gliding!

It could be argued (and many of her more conservative neighbours *would* argue) that a woman of her mature years ought to have known better than to be jumping off mountains, with a parachute on her back, at her age. We are, however, talking about a woman that had inflicted a minor back injury on herself the previous year whilst bungee jumping in the nude to protest the exploitation of animals in the fur trade. Nicole's mother was a madcap eccentric; an unrepentant rebel that the growing years of age had failed utterly to tame. She was Nicole... only more so and even Nicole was apt, on occasion, to wince at her mother's latest lunatic escapade. Nicole's father was devoted to his impossibly wayward wife and he had stoically endured all her misadventures

7

through nearly thirty years of marriage with a long suffering, tranquil patience that Job himself would have admired. It was a legend in the family that he had quietly and, without fuss, proposed to her the day he had had to bail her out of jail following her public misconduct during an anti-military demonstration in Bern. Sarah knew Nicole's mother well. She adored her.

It was true, however, that Nicole's mother would be somewhat demanding of attention in her current disability and, with Nicole's father away on business, it was Nicole that was obliged to jump into the breach to care for her during her incapacitation. It meant that Nicole would be absent for two or three days and it gave Sarah the opportunity to escape with Daniela without the uncomfortable questions she might face in front of Nicole.

Frau Fritzl allowed her away early and Sarah almost snatched Daniela's hand impulsively as she dragged her away from the hotel. "Come on let's go for a drink at the Schwendi before you drive me home. I have an idea." she said. Daniela looked bemused by Sarah's sudden flushed excitement and she allowed herself to pulled away with pleasure. Sarah would say nothing until they had crossed the short distance between the Hotel and the Schwendi restaurant and Daniela bit her lip in eager anticipation. Once in the Schwendi Sarah ordered drinks for them and grasped Daniela's hand to pull her outside to the garden. It was quite cool, although not intolerably so, and they had the garden to themselves.

Uncharacteristically, Sarah grasped Daniela in a hug and kissed her. Daniela seemed delighted by the unexpected, impulsive gesture of affection. She laughed. "Come on Sarah! What's eating you?"

"Danny. Have you got anything on for the next couple of days?"

"Well yes actually."

Sarah looked deflated. "Oh! What?"

"Well I was hoping to spend them with my adorable Sarah."

Sarah grinned. "Stop it Danny! Look if you've nothing on do you fancy coming for a walk?"

Daniela raised an eyebrow. "Do I presume that we are not talking about a stroll around the Schwendiseen?"

"Yes. Look Frau Fritzl's giving me a few days off. Do you want to hike up the Santis?"

"Whew! The Santis? You mean the big one?"

"It's the biggest we've got around here. Ok it's no four thousand meter peak but it's a serious mountain and it's wonderful. Are you up for it?"

Daniela looked uncertain. "I don't know Sarah. I've never climbed anything as serious as that before. I don't know if I'm ready for it."

"You'll be fine Danny. We'll take our time. It takes about four and a half hours for an experienced hiker to get to the summit from the Alpli but we don't have to do it that fast. Assuming we start early enough we've got all day to get up. We'll just go at your own pace I promise."

Daniela grinned caught up in Sarah's enthusiasm. "Ok if you think I can do it."

"You can do it Danny. I'm sure of it. Please say you'll come. I so want to show you the Santis."

"You've sold me. Come on what's the plan?"

Chapter Two

With Daniela's agreement secured, Sarah grinned and grabbed a menu off the table and a pen from her uniform to take notes. "Ok it means an early start. I want to be away by seven o'clock in the morning at the latest. Is that a problem?"

Daniela shook her head vigorously. "No, no. But why so early if it only takes four and a half hours?"

"Because I don't know how quickly we'll go Danny. You're not used to hiking so I have to reckon that we'll take a good deal longer than that. Then there's the weather. It's predicted to be hot tomorrow so it's best to get the hard climbing at low altitude out of the way while it's still cool in the morning. It'll be cooler higher up so it won't matter so much later on. But we have to reach the summit by mid-afternoon."

"Why?"

"Thunderstorms Danny. In hot weather the thunderstorms close in around the mountain around the late afternoon and you need to be in shelter before that. Trust me. You do not want to be peeing around on an exposed mountain side with lightning hitting the rocks around you. First adage of mountain hiking; start early; finish early. Now do you have a problem with an early start?"

Daniela shook her head once more. "No. I presume we'll start from your side of the valley. I can drive over in the morning. Can I leave my car at your place?"

"Yes of course. Ok we'll take the direct route up from Alpli to Tierwis. That's easy enough and we can take a break at Tierwis."

"How far from the summit is that?"

"Well I can make the summit in about an hour and a quarter from there but you might take a bit longer since you've not done it before. In any case, as long as we're on schedule, we've loads of time to gain the summit."

"What happens when we reach the summit? Do we set off back down?"

Sarah grinned happily. "No. We stay the night at the Santis hut on the summit."

"Together?"

"Well of course together."

Daniela clapped her hands in pleasure. "This sounds worth climbing a mountain for. It gets better all the time."

"Behave Danny! We'll only be staying in the Massenlage."

"Massenlage?"

"The dormitory in the mountain hut."

"Can we share a bunk?"

"They aren't bunks Danny. They're sort of wooden shelves where you might be sleeping a dozen people in a row. They look a bit like the barrack rooms in the less salubrious prison of war camps from world war two."

"I'll deal with it Sarah. If it's the only chance I get to sleep with you, I'll slum it."

Sarah giggled and slapped Daniela's hand affectionately. "Stop it! We're planning a serious alpine excursion not a dirty weekend on a mountain."

"Pretty primitive these mountain refuges are they?"

"Oh hell yes. I mean I'm used to them but I hope you won't find them too basic."

"Oh I think I'll enjoy it. It will be just like being back in the Girl Guides again."

Sarah pulled a mock frown. "In view of your past record with Lord Baden Powell's honourable young ladies' healthy, outdoor movement I'm not sure I feel reassured by that."

Daniela stuck her tongue out and grinned. "Ok we spend the night on the summit. Then what?"

"Well, if you're up to it, I thought we could hike the next day over the Lysengrat to the Rotsteinpass, have a bite to eat in the hut there and then climb up the Altmansattel."

"You're talking Cantonese Sarah. I can barely pronounce those words let alone know what they refer to."

"Ok the Lysengrat is the ridge from the Santis summit across to the Rotsteinpass, or red stone pass, which separates the Santis from the mountain Altmann. After that you have about a forty five minute climb, up a big cliff, to the ridge that leads to the Altmann summit. We'd pass the summit to the west and then drop down to the Fahlensee; a beautiful alpine lake and spend a second night there. On the last day we'll climb back up through the Zwinglipass and drop back down to the Obertoggenburg by way of Gamplut."

"My God Sarah! Are you sure I can handle this?"

"Yes, or I wouldn't ask you to do it. If there's a moment you can't do any more then there's loads of places we can bug out with an easy descent or by cable car. Trust me Danny. I've taken loads of people up around this mountain. I won't ask you to do anything you can't deal with."

"So it's a three day adventure."

"Yes if you're up for it."

Daniela took a deep breath and smiled gloriously. "I wouldn't miss it for anything. Take me to your mountain Sarah."

Sarah bit her knuckle in excitement. "Good. Now we have to talk about the stuff you have to bring with you. You said you had proper mountain boots."

"Yes, I bought them when I came to the Toggenburg. The guy in the shop ensured me that they were top quality."

"Excellent. The boots on your feet are by far the most important item you'll have with you. What about a rucksack?"

"Again no problem. I've got a brand new one I've never used. I bought a few things when I first came here

12

with the vague idea that I'd like to do some hiking. Of course I didn't know what hiking in the mountains entailed then and I found it a bit intimidating when I realised it wasn't just a ramble in the countryside."

"Ok then. Now since we're taking a three day hike you'll need clothes for three days. I'd say two pairs of jeans, two shirts or T-shirts, enough underwear for three days and at least three pairs of hiking socks. You need always at least one full change of dry clothes in case you get caught in weather. Oh yes... don't forget to pack at least one warm pullover too. It might look warm down here in the valley but trust me it can get chilly up on the tops even in summer. Oh and pack a waterproof jacket as well if you've got one." Sarah was scribbling notes for Daniela on the back of the menu.

"What about a skirt Sarah?" asked Daniela uncertainly. "I mean would that be appropriate if we were hiking in hot weather?"

"Oh sure; or a pair of shorts. I was going to take a short skirt myself because the forecast is for some seriously hot weather. You can always bring something skimpy to keep you cool just don't forget the warm clothes in your rucksack. You can always peel off clothes when it gets warm but you can't put clothes on you haven't got when it cools down. Just don't bring too much stuff though. Remember you have to carry all this on your back. Oh and another thing; if you do bring shorts or a short skirt and a sleeveless top or something make sure to pack some sun cream. Actually, come to think of it, I'd better bring that. Most people don't use strong enough sun blocker when they go hiking in the mountains. I always carry a bottle of full strength, alpine standard blocker. It would be a good idea would be to bring a hat or a cap to keep the sun off your face as well."

Daniela smiled. "You seem to be inordinately concerned with my complexion darling."

Sarah shook her head seriously. "No Danny. I'm serious. The air's thinner at high altitude and the ultra violet rays cut through much more strongly. You've got to protect any exposed skin. Even in winter you can burn to a crisp up in the mountains. It's dangerous Danny. You can seriously damage your skin."

"Ok I've got the message. I've got a cap somewhere although I'm not much of a girl for head gear. I wore a silly hat to go to the races in a couple of years ago and I looked a complete prat in it! I suppose ponceing around on a mountainside wielding a girly parasol would make me persona non grata at this year's Alpine Club Ball wouldn't it?"

"You might end up being the first person ever to get laughed off a mountain Danny."

"I shall resist the temptation then. What about clothes in the mountain huts?"

"Oh I wouldn't worry too much as long as you've got dry clothes to change into. Mountain huts aren't exactly trendsetting locations for haut couture you know. You won't even need shoes because they've normally got slippers you can pull on so you don't drag half the mountainside in with you on your boots."

"Do I need to bring a pair of pyjamas?"

"Oh yes and a hot water bottle, a woolly bed cap, your cocoa mug, a copy of Grimm's Fairy Tales and your Teddy Bear."

Daniela threw a beer mat at her. "Stop making fun of me. I'm serious. What are we supposed to wear to bed in these dormitories?"

Sarah shrugged with a grin. "Oh I just usually make do with a T-shirt and a pair of knickers. If it's likely to be really cold I might pack a track suit bottom but there's always plenty of blankets."

"Isn't it a bit well... public to be flouncing around in your underwear?"

"Oh it's acceptable dress code in a mountain hut Danny. Everybody's used to it and people are too polite to stare."

"I don't believe a word of it. If you tell me that the two best looking tarts in the Toggenburg are going to strip down to their undies and nobody will look then I'll start to believe in porcine aviation."

Sarah giggled helplessly. "Well some people might sneak a little peep. It never bothers me though. I mean I'm usually quite shy about undressing in public but the general atmosphere and camaraderie in the mountain huts is different. You're all in the same boat together and it just seems silly being unduly modest. It's not as if there's much in the way of titillation about it. I mean the general odour of sweaty bodies and pongy hiking socks tends to take the erotic edge off things."

"All right then I shall bow to the conventions of acceptable dress. I give you due warning though. If I start to get cold in the middle of the night I'm going to crawl in with you and cuddle up."

"It wouldn't be the first time. I've often shared blankets with a friend in the massenlage. I even used to crawl in with Peter when we stayed overnight somewhere. He was always a perfect gentleman about it though blast him." Sarah pulled a wry face, "I should have realised that something was amiss then."

"I might have less sense of propriety than your Peter."

Sarah wagged a finger, "I forbid you to start any hanky panky in the massenlage. Behave yourself you hear."

Daniela poked her tongue out. "Meany! Ok what else do I need?"

"Bring a water bottle. The Santis is limestone mostly and there are virtually no springs on it anywhere, at altitude, because all the water seeps underground. It's incredibly dry on the mountain and it can be thirsty work climbing."

15

"What about food?"

"Bring something to nibble if you want but don't bother bringing a sodding great packed lunch. We'll never be more than a few hours away from the next mountain hut and food and drink. Oh if you bring chocolate, be damn sure you pack it separately in a plastic bag. I've had past experience of opening my rucksack to discover that my change of clothes is now liberally smeared in melted chocolate. It's a good idea, in any case, to pack all your spare clothes in plastic bags before putting them in your rucksack. That way they'll stay dry even if we get caught in heavy rain."

"I thought you said that the weather forecast was for hot weather."

"Doesn't mean a damn thing Danny. You've no idea how fast a thunderstorm can spring up in the mountains. In fact the hotter the weather the more likely it is often that you'll get late afternoon thunderstorms. This is why we try to finish the day's hike before the latter part of the afternoon. We could still get caught however. The weather's fickle in the mountains."

"Ok anything else? Do I need to hire a couple of Sherpas and a yak for instance?"

"Well bring some toiletry stuff with you. Don't go overboard however. Mountain huts don't exactly provide en suite bathrooms for a nice leisurely soak at the end of the day. On the Santis we'll probably have to make do with an enamel bowl of cold water to perform our daily ablutions in. They're always short of water up on the summit. It'll be better at Bollenwies because they've plenty of water down by the lake but I'd put a hold on the hope of a nice bubble bath until we get home. Oh yes and bring your mobile too."

"I was hoping I could leave the damn thing at home."

Sarah shook her head. "No it's better to have it with you and fully charged Danny. If we get into trouble we'll need some way to call the rescue team out. I'll carry mine too so we've got back up in case of emergency."

"God! Is it really that dangerous?"

"It's a *mountain* Danny. It's *always* dangerous. Anything can happen on a mountain. You have to treat them with respect and take every precaution. People get killed on the Santis every year Danny. Most of the time it's their own fault because they didn't treat the mountain with the respect it deserves. Even the most experienced and careful climbers can still come to grief however. Mountains are inherently dangerous places. I've been climbing on that mountain ever since I was a kid but I'm still wary of it. It's like a having a lover you adore but you can never quite trust to be faithful to you. You're just an insect on the mountain. It can swat you in an instance."

Daniela looked sober. "I'll bear it in mind Sarah."

"Then there's money Danny. Don't forget to bring money and, by money, I mean the folding stuff. They're going to look at you like you've lost your marbles if you try to pay your bill with a card in a mountain hut. Do you have a walking stick?"

Daniela opened her eyes in surprise. "A walking stick?"

"I didn't think so. Well never mind I have a spare one you can use."

"Why the blazes do I need a walking stick Sarah? I know I'm not an experienced alpinist but I'm not exactly geriatric you know."

"You don't need to be decrepit to use a stick Danny. A lot of experienced hikers use them. You'll find that they save a hell of a lot of wear and tear on your legs especially on steep descents when you can use them to cushion the stress on your knees. I usually take one for long hikes. I'm old fashioned though and I like the old style of wooden alpenstock but I've got a more modern telescopic metal one you can have. It's lightweight and it folds down to fit in your rucksack for the parts when you

17

need both hands free. Don't be coy about using one Danny. You'll thank me for it by the end of three days."

"Ok as long as you don't expect me to use a Zimmer frame."

Sarah looked down at the list she'd compiled. "Well I think that more or less covers it from your point of view. I'll carry the extra gear we need."

"What extra gear?"

"Oh just some short ropes, harnesses, carabiners and so on."

"Ropes and harnesses? Do we need them?"

"I hope not. But I'd just like to be on the safe side."

"Jesus! It's beginning to sound like an assault on K2."

"Am I starting to make you have second thoughts?"

"No way! I can't wait to get started."

Sarah glanced at her watch. "Well if we're up for an early start we'd better wrap this up. Can you drop me home?"

Daniela drove Sarah back to the Alpli. They paused outside Sarah's house and, after a quick kiss, Sarah began to get out of the car. "Seven o'clock now. Don't be late."

"I won't. Is Nicole home then?"

"No she left today to go to her parents."

"Hmmm..." Daniela was looking thoughtful and a strange smile was visible on her face in the lights from the car dashboard.

"What's the matter Danny?"

"Oh something that just occurred to me Sarah. How many times have you climbed that mountain?"

"More times than I can remember."

"So it would probably take you just a few minutes to pack your things wouldn't it?"

Sarah paused uncertain about the direction the conversation was going in. "Well yes I'm pretty used to it."

"So it would have been a more practical logistical operation for you to come back to my place, supervise my packing and stayed the night. We could have driven down here first thing to pick your things up and set off then couldn't we?"

Sarah swallowed. "Er well I suppose so."

"Sarah that mountain doesn't frighten you so why are you so scared of *me*?"

"I... I don't know Danny."

Daniela leaned over impulsively and kissed her. "Forgive me Sarah. I don't want to upset you. I'll climb your mountain tomorrow Sarah. One day perhaps you'll climb mine. Now get along with you. I'll be here at seven sharp."

Sarah watched the lights of Daniela's car fade into the darkness of the Alpli and sat down on the little stone wall outside the house. The house behind stood empty and Sarah felt suddenly alone.

Chapter Three

It was just gone half past six in the morning, the next day, when Sarah heard the sound of Daniela's car in the quiet of the Alpli. The Ferrari had a distinctive feral growl to it that was unmistakeable. Sarah often reflected that the powerful automobile seemed in such contrast with Daniela's gentle nature and her natural modesty that it was little wonder that she was uncomfortable with it. She only really drove it because it had been a present from people she cared about and Sarah was beginning to learn that devotion to other people ruled Daniela absolutely. Nevertheless, it was true that the striking red car jarred against Daniela's personality as much as it stood out in the quiet rural background of the Toggenburg. For all her fame, Daniela was a person who would be happy enough to fade into the background although, even without her celebrity status, hers was an arresting beauty that would have brought her to attention anywhere.

Sarah was in the kitchen packing a few last items into her rucksack. She glanced up at the clock. Daniela was early. As the car pulled up at the side of the house, she stepped to the kitchen door, to wave and beckon Daniela in. Daniela eased out of the car and picked up a bulky looking rucksack from the passenger seat beside her. Sarah frowned. That rucksack looked as if it could do with some trimming down. She smiled when she saw Daniela however. Daniela had obviously interpreted Sarah's instructions as to suitable alpine wear in a fairly liberal fashion. She was clad in a ridiculously short, white skirt and a blue top. Her hair was tied back in a pony tail and the tail tucked through the gap in the back of a baseball cap. She did however have her feet clad in thick woollen socks and mountain boots. It was the first time that Sarah had seen Daniela wear anything other

20

than elegant feminine footwear. Even in a pair of jeans Daniela seemed to contrive to match them with pretty sandals. The sight of her in decidedly inelegant hiking boots was almost incongruous but Sarah noted, with satisfaction, that the boots were of good quality and from a respectable maker.

Daniela seemed in a fine humour. In fact she looked as excited as a child at Disneyland and her face glowed with animation as she embraced Sarah. "You're early." Sarah told her.

"I couldn't wait to get going. Is that coffee I can smell brewing?"

"Yes I was just making some. Do you want a cup?"

"Please."

Daniela eased her rucksack to the ground. Sarah regarded it acerbically. "How much bloody stuff have you brought? I told you to cut down the weight."

"It's not as heavy as it looks Sarah. It's mostly spare clothes and they don't weigh much."

Sarah picked the rucksack up and discovered that Daniela was telling the truth. It wasn't excessively heavy. In fact it was somewhat lighter than Sarah's. Sarah felt a shape in a side pocket. "You've brought a book."

"Yes I brought the Alpine flower guide you gave me. I was looking through it last night and I was hoping to find some of the flowers in it. There's a lovely flower called "King of the Alps" I'd love to see."

Sarah laughed. "You didn't read the text properly. King of the Alps only grows on acidic rocks and screes between two and a half and three and a half thousand metres. Since all our mountains locally are alkaline limestone and only just manage to reach two thousand five hundred metres, I think you're on a hiding to nothing there."

"Oh." Daniela looked deflated. "So we won't see it then?"

"I've never seen it in the Toggenburg. I have found *Queen* of the Alps locally but it's pretty rare."

21

"Is that similar?"

"No. Doesn't look a bit like it. It's an entirely different family. It's an umbellifer; a member of the carrot family. It's not even a particularly pretty flower."

"Well I've got my own personal Queen of the Alps to admire."

"I'll get the coffee!"

They sat at the kitchen table to sip coffee and Daniela looked around the kitchen in pleasure. "This is the first time I've ever been in your house Sarah. It looks just like I imagined it to be. This is a lovely old house."

Sarah smiled in pleasure. She too loved the old wooden farm house with its wooden walls, uneven floors and solid wooden beams and the little windows framed with lacy net curtains. "Yes it's a nice old house. It's over two hundred years old. It's a bitch to keep clean though."

"It looks spotless to me. You and Nicole must be good housekeepers."

"That's mostly me." Sarah confessed. "Nicole would have the place looking like a bomb site in no time if I didn't keep on top of her." Sarah looked at Daniela. "Are you sure you're going to be warm enough dressed like that?"

"Oh sure. It's actually not cold out. The sun's already up and feels warm. I've got a feeling it's going to be a scorcher by mid-morning."

Sarah glanced out of the window. "Yes I think you could be right. Maybe I'll wear my tennis dress again. I found it was actually quite practical for hiking in hot weather in; light and non-constraining."

"Oh go on please. We'll see if we can set a record for an ascension of the Santis whilst wearing the least amount of clothes."

"We wouldn't be in the running I'm afraid. There was a mad German naturalist couple two years ago that scandalised the whole valley by insisting on climbing the Santis in hiking boots and bugger all else. They had to send a policeman up from Schwagalp to tell them off and make them put some clothes on and he was a young lad from Appenzell who couldn't stop blushing. Apparently it was the funniest scene on the mountain anyone's seen in years."

"Well I'm game if you are."

"Behave Danny. We've probably started enough stories about us so far without exhibiting ourselves with public indecency."

"Hmmph! Let them twitter."

Eventually, carried along by Daniela's enthusiasm, Sarah did change into her tennis skirt and they shouldered their rucksacks picked up their hiking sticks and left the house. Sarah regarded Daniela's car. "I think it will be ok here Danny. I don't think anyone will nick it."

"See if I care if they do. It's insured anyway. They're welcome to the bloody thing."

Daniela was right. The morning, although cool, was warming rapidly as the sun rose and began to dispel the shadows in the vale. The Alpli side valley stretched back far from the main Toggenburg valley below and right to the foot of the Santis itself. They walked hand in hand along the tarmac road, winding between the meadows and belts of woodland with the air full of birdsong; the twittering of finches, the thin calls of tits, the fluty songs of Song Thrushes, the monotonous repetitive song of the little Chiff Chaffs, the yelping calls of woodpeckers and, the most evocative of all, the far carrying, mournful cries of cuckoos. There were few people abroad at this hour but nature was out in full cry. There were White Wagtails and Black Redstarts busy around the barns and houses, crows in the meadows and House Martins and Swallows on the wing. At one point, Sarah stopped and pointed out something to Daniela. The sun touching the flanks of the Stein, an offshoot of the Schaffberg to the east, had evidently already produced some rising thermals of warm air for, high in the air, a large brown predator was circling. Daniela peered at the distant speck uncertainly. "Is it an eagle?"

"Yes it's a Golden Eagle." Sarah lifted her binoculars to her eyes. "It's a second year bird, not fully adult. They don't really reach full adulthood until their third year. It'll be off to find its own territory next year."

"How can you possibly tell all that from this distance? It just looks like a speck from here."

Sarah laughed. "Oh I know every eagle in the Toggenburg Danny. It's not hard. There are only two nesting pairs; one here that nests on the Schaffberg and another over by Voralpsee. This bird is the offspring of our local pair raised two years ago. They didn't successfully raise any young last year." Sarah handed Daniela her binoculars. "Here take a look."

Daniela was thrilled as she watched the soaring raptor. "I've never seen one before. Oh I've seen buzzards and so on but not something I knew was an eagle. It's amazing."

"Yes it's hard to avoid old worn clichés like majestic and regal when you talk about Golden Eagles but they are pretty spectacular birds of prey. There's only one bird you might be lucky enough to see in the Swiss Alps that beats it when it comes to the wow factor."

"What's that?"

"Ah I'm keeping that for a surprise because we've got a chance of seeing one up at Rotsteinpass tomorrow."

Reluctantly Daniela handed the binoculars back to Sarah. "That's the next thing on my shopping list." she noted. "I have to get myself a pair of those. They seem really good."

"They should be. They're Zeiss Ikon and cost over two thousand francs a pair. My Dad bought me these on my sixteenth birthday. For years I never left the house without them."

"It sounds as if your father knows you better than your mother does."

Sarah laughed, "That's true enough. Come on let's leave our eagle. We've got a fair way to go yet."

Towards the end of the Alpli, the valley narrowed between high cliffs. With the forests behind them, the alp was just a series of grassy meadows dotted with a few last barns. The little tarmac road finally ended here where a few Crag Martins were swooping low to catch the early insects. Beyond, a little path wound across the last meadows and then steeply ascended up the grassy flank of the mountain. Sarah adjusted the straps on her rucksack and turned to Daniela. "Ok Danny. Are you ready for some hard climbing?"

"Lead on Fraulein Tenzing. I'll take up the rear. That way I can see up your legs. It'll be like a carrot to a donkey."

Sarah laughed and pushed Daniela playfully. "You're just incorrigible."

"I always believe in remaining true to my own self."

Sarah glanced up at the path weaving its way up into the distance above. "I'm afraid this stretch is the most mind numbingly tedious bit we'll have to do throughout our three days Danny. It's just a long monotonous haul up to Tierwis and it's arse paralysing. Just plug away at it and take your own time. It will get better at Tierwis. The fun starts at over two thousand metres."

"Well I suppose it's best to get the uninteresting bits out of the way early." Daniela looked up at the steep trail winding up the mountain. "Mind you if this is the boring part I hate to think what the exciting bits are going to look like."

Sarah grinned. "Come on! Let's take the mountain."

Chapter Four

And so they climbed. It was not a demanding climb other than through sheer physical effort for, as Sarah had noted, it was really just a long, tedious slog up the mountain. The mountainside here was mostly steeply sloping, grassy meadow; occasionally dissected by low limestone terraces. Sarah herself would have preferred a more interesting route; for instance an approach from the western flank around the side of the Silberplatten, but that was a longer and more arduous route, taking in a long haul across a massive boulder field and she was conscious that she was carrying a beginner with her. This was probably the easiest route to the Santis summit and quite enough for anybody not used to the mountain. Sarah set a pace slower than her normal rate, to allow Daniela to keep up, and she watched her friend carefully.

To her gratification, Daniela seemed to be handling the task admirably. She breathed deeply and a slight sheen of perspiration appeared on her forehead, as the morning grew warmer, but she climbed steadily without complaint and she was always ready with a smile. She was clearly enjoying herself and Sarah realised that she was fitter than most people would have credited her with being. She may have looked delicate and fragile but, in fact, she was tougher than appearances suggested and her perfect slender legs concealed wiry muscles that kept her steadily moving upwards. Sarah was pleased by their progress. It was far better than she had hoped. In fact, Sarah was enjoying herself immensely. Daniela was proving to be a perfect companion on the mountain. Even while panting with the exertions of the climb she was always ready with some teasing banter or funny quip and when she grew serious it was only to look around the unfolding vista with wonder, quite clearly awed by the scenery.

At last Sarah called a time out. "Ok let's take a break."

Daniela eased her rucksack off and flopped down onto some short grass before rummaging in her pack for her water bottle. She pulled off her cap and untied her hair to shake it loose and wiped her forehead with her wrist. "It's getting warm." she observed.

"It'll be a bit cooler higher up."

"How high are we anyway?"

By way of an answer, Sarah reached into her bag and pulled out a small plastic instrument and consulted it. "Around one thousand eight hundred and fifty metres Danny."

"What is that thing?"

"Oh it's an altimeter; a pocket altimeter. I often carry one to record the exact altitude of any species of animal or plant I find on the mountain. It's useful data to gather. There're many species whose altitudinal ranges are only poorly understood."

"How does it work?"

"By air pressure. The pressure reduces as you climb in altitude. Of course air pressure is variable according to weather so you have to calibrate it to a known altitudinal point each day otherwise during a low pressure system for instance you might find it telling you that you're apparently hovering a couple of hundred metres over the summit of the mountain you're standing on. I set it this morning before we set off."

"I see and our first base camp, this Tierwis you keep mentioning, is how high?"

"Two thousand and eighty five and after that we've a little over another four hundred metres to reach the summit."

"It feels plenty high right here. I understand now what you were saying about feeling like an insect on the mountainside. This is just colossal! I've never felt so insignificant in my life. I've never felt so alive either. Just look at that view."

"How are you doing anyway?" asked Sarah.

"Good. I hope I'm not holding you back."

"No you're doing brilliantly. You're a lot fitter than I thought you were."

"I work out a lot Sarah. I'm a dancer don't forget. I have to keep myself fit."

"Well I'm impressed. You'll easy make the summit I would have thought."

"I'll get up there if it kills me."

"Don't say that Danny! It's bad luck to taunt the mountain."

"Sorry Brown Owl. It's a lot less scary than I thought it was going to be though."

"Er this is the easy bit Danny. The real challenges come higher up."

"I'd sort of figured that. Still it's gratifying that the only real hazard I've faced so far is the imminent danger of planting my boot in a nice juicy cow pat. I didn't think there were going to be this many cows up here."

"Oh this area is quite extensively grazed by cattle in the summer months. A lot of the flowers you see around you are actually more lowland species that are invasive up her. They can reach up to this altitude because of the nitrate enrichment of the soil through generations of cow poo. We'll see a more pure alpine flora higher up."

"The flowers are just gorgeous anyway. Are those yellow things Spotted Gentians?"

Sarah smiled. "I see you've been doing some homework. Yes they are and blooming quite early for this altitude. There are Great Yellow Gentians a bit lower down as well and those big purple things we saw just before that last terrace are Monkshood. You see that big plant with the spike of little white flowers over there?"

"Yes."

"Well don't eat it. It's False White Helleborine and it is seriously poisonous."

"Why on earth would I want to eat it?"

"Actually people do get poisoned by it. The problem is that, before it's in flower, it looks just like non-flowering Great Yellow Gentian which is picked to make a sort of schnapps with. If you don't know what you're doing it's easy to mix the two up."

"Isn't it dangerous for the cows?"

"No they know it. They just graze around it. Often you'll see a meadow that's been grazed and the helleborine just standing there isolated."

"My God! This place is a paradise. What's this little yellow thing growing by my foot?"

"That's Alpine Birdsfoot Trefoil. It's very common. It's a member of the pea family related to clovers."

"It's just bewildering. I've never seen so many different wild flowers."

"This is nothing Danny. This is not a particularly rich zone for alpine flowers. Wait till you see some of the other places we're going."

Daniela grinned hugely. "I can't wait. Come on let's have a quick photo and then push on."

They took some snapshots with Daniela's camera and began to climb once more. There was a moment of comic relief when Daniela found herself hemmed, in a small gully passing through a limestone terrace, between two cows who obstinately refused to move out of the way and regarded her ineffectual protestations and flapping arms with the dumbly stoic incomprehension of the bovine race. "Shoo! Shoo!" she yelled at them. "Move out of the bloody way you great useless lumps of beef steak!" She paused to regard Sarah with exasperation. "Stop laughing Sarah."

Sarah had collapsed helplessly to the ground holding her sides at the sight of Daniela's predicament. "I... I can't help it!"

"You're *not* helping. What am I supposed to do?"

"Use your stick. Smack them around the rump you muppet! They'll soon shift."

"Oh great! Now you want me to start a fight with two blasted great horned beasts massing around twenty times my weight between them. Now why didn't *I* think of that?"

Eventually Sarah was obliged to rescue Daniela by driving the cows away with a few well aimed blows to their nether portions and Daniela was able to negotiate the rest of the gully safely but with tattered dignity. Sarah couldn't stop laughing. Hiking with Daniela was fun.

In spite of this minor hiccup they made fine progress and, well before noon, they crested the shoulder of the mountain to see a great extensive limestone terrace stretching before them. To Daniela's eyes, this terrace looked like a lunar landscape of bare rock pitted with crevices and yawning potholes but, in the distance, was the little mountain hut of Tierwis perched on the ridge beyond with a Swiss flag dancing merrily in the breeze on the pole by the hut. "Well there's base camp one Danny." Sarah told her. "We've done really well so we can have a nice long stop here."

Daniela pointed to the rugged terrain separating them from the welcoming hut in the distance. We have to get across this crap first Sarah."

"It's easy. We just follow the red and white marks painted on the rocks and there's an easy path across."

"Who marks these trails?"

"Oh the mountain guides, the owners of the huts, all the people who keep open the hiking trails on the mountain. I've done it myself. Hiking up the trails and refreshing the marks with a pot of paint. It's tedious work but it has to be done. They're colour coded of course. Yellow trails are low level rambling routes for casual walkers. The red and white marks denote mountain trails for serious hikers properly equipped. You might also see red and green marks but they're only for experienced alpinists and they're not trails marked on general hiking maps."

"Are we taking any red and green trails?"

"Only if you fancy taking a detour up the Altmann tomorrow. I think we'd better skip that. You've got enough challenges facing you."

Sarah was right. The route across to the Tierwis hut was straightforward. The hut was a welcoming little house of stone, painted grey and with a side building off to one side, perched precariously on the ridge of the mountain. Outside the hut were several wooden tables surrounded by benches and Sarah heaved her rucksack off by the side of one. Beyond the hut the ground fell away steeply and Daniela walked over in curiosity to investigate. "Er I wouldn't go too close to that edge if I was you Danny." Sarah warned.

Daniela ground to a halt at the edge. "Holy shit!" From the ridge of Tierwis the mountainside plunged down to the north over a serious of terrifying precipices to the green vale of Schwagalp over seven hundred metres below. It was a mind boggling chasm and Daniela stepped back hurriedly. "Jesus! I never expected that."

Sarah laughed and approached the edge of the ridge. "Come over here and look. It's a bit safer here and the view is worth it."

Daniela approached hesitantly and squatted down by Sarah behind a rock overlooking the abyss below. "What are those buildings down there?" she asked.

"That's the cable car station and restaurant." Sarah put her binoculars to her eyes and examined the terrain far below. "It'll be busy on the summit today. There're loads of cars in the car park."

Daniela took the binoculars and perused the scene. The big car park in the alp was indeed full of cars and she could make out the tiny specks of people walking about in the alp. "Good grief there's loads of people. Are they all coming up the mountain?"

"Not all of them. A lot will just be spending the time in the Schwagalp which is a beauty spot in its own right with the Santis towering overhead. Still I should imagine quite a lot will take the trip up."

Daniela shook her head. "It seems downright silly that we're taking most of the day to get to the top of the mountain and those people just drive up, jump in a cable car and they're up in a few minutes."

"They don't see the mountain as we do."

"No that's true. It seems a shame that the top of the mountain is desecrated as a tourist destination."

"Yes but it's only the summit. Few tourists wander away from the restaurants on the top. Anyway by six o'clock the cable car stops running and then we'll have the mountain top to ourselves and anybody else that got there under their own steam."

"It's weird. I mean we haven't seen another soul all morning and then there are all those hoards."

"Well the route we came up is not a very interesting one but it has the advantage of being a quiet one. We'll probably start to bump into more people along the trail now."

"Why?"

"Because the path up from Schwagalp joins us just over there beyond the hut. It's a popular hiking route in the summer."

"You're not seriously telling me that there's a path up this bloody face."

"Oh yes. It's steep but perfectly manageable. It's statistically the most dangerous route on the whole mountain but that's more a reflection on the heavy usage it gets than its inherent dangers although it can be hazardous from rock falls."

"Christ!"

Sarah laughed and patted Daniela affectionately on the bottom. "Come on let's get a drink. The hut here has a speciality I'm waiting to introduce you to."

They took a seat at one of the wooden tables and a lady emerged from the hut to serve them. "Hoi Sarah. You're early."

"Gruezi Frau Schoop. Yes we made better time than I expected."

The lady regarded Daniela with obvious interest and it was clear she recognised her. Sarah was starting to get used to the reactions to her famous companion and she smiled. "This is my friend Daniela, Frau Schoop."

Daniela held out a hand politely. "I'm pleased to meet you Frau Schoop."

The lady took Daniela's hand, obviously bursting with interest but too polite to ask intrusive questions. Sarah put her out of her misery by ordering for them. "Can we have two Pflumli Schumlis please Frau Schoop?"

"Yes... yes of course." She scuttled back indoors to prepare their drinks.

"Early?" asked Daniela. "She said you're early. Was she expecting us?"

"Yes of course. I phoned up this morning to say we were coming and our estimated time of arrival."

"But why? I thought we were staying on the summit, not here."

"We are. I've phoned the hut on the summit as well to let them know when we expect to be there. Simple alpine precautions Danny. You call ahead to inform people that you are on the mountain and on which route you're heading for them and when you expect to arrive. If you've a mobile you leave your number too. If you don't turn up as expected they can give you a call to make sure you're all right. If you're in trouble or can't answer they know which route to send out the search parties along. Of course I didn't anticipate anything happening to us on the way up here but I'd be shirking my responsibilities if I didn't take elementary precautions. I've never acted as guide to such a famous national star before. I'd have to leave the country if I let anything happen to you."

"Would they call out the mountain rescue teams to extract my alpenstock from your fanny because you're going the right way to find out?"

Sarah giggled. "I'm sorry. I'll stop teasing you. Are you hungry?"

"I could eat something yes."

"Well it won't be haut cuisine but I'm sure we can rustle something up here. How about some bread and cheese?"

"Sounds fine to me."

Sarah stood. "I'll go tell Frau Schoop."

Inside the hut Sarah found that Frau Schoop had nearly finished their drinks. "I'll take those out Frau Schoop." Sarah volunteered. "I wondered if we could have some bread and cheese and maybe some pickles."

"Yes, yes, naturally." The lady was obviously in an agony of inquisitiveness. "Sarah your... your friend... she isn't... I mean...."

Sarah smiled. "Yes she is Frau Schoop."

"I knew it! I recognised her from the papers. How do you know her Sarah?"

"She lives in the Toggenburg Frau Schoop. She's well known locally." Frau Schoop and her family hailed from the other side of the mountain. They lived in Appenzell.

"My word! And is she a friend of yours?"

"Oh yes, a good friend, although I only met her for the first time this summer."

"Goodness! What's it like having such a famous friend?"

"I don't really notice to be honest Frau Schoop. She's such a nice girl I forget that she's so famous."

"Well it's a surprise. Do you think she'd let me take her photo for our wall?"

On one wall was a board containing dozens of photographs of well-known people or locally known personalities that had graced the hut with their presence over the years. Until now the most renowned were respected alpinists, local politicians, mountain guides and the odd ski instructor. There was a photo of Sarah when she'd been fourteen with her father in the collection. Sarah smiled. "I'll ask her for you Frau Schoop. I'm sure she wouldn't mind."

"Thank you Sarah. Here are your drinks. I'll see to your food."

Sarah carried the drinks out into the bright sunshine. Daniela had evidently made the acquaintance of the hut's cat during Sarah's absence for she was bending down to stroke the little black animal who was purring luxuriously under her ministrations. "I see you've met the cat."

"He scared me to death Sarah. He came up behind me and brushed against my leg. I nearly jumped off the mountainside."

"Well watch that one. He's a villain. As soon as you take your eyes off him, he's up and licking the cream off your coffee."

"He's sweet."

"Do you like cats?"

"I should hope so since I've got four of my own."

Sarah was surprised. "You have four cats?"

"Yes Sarah and if I can ever prevail upon you to venture inside my humble abode I'll introduce you to them."

"Who's looking after them?"

"Oh my cleaning lady. I'm away a lot and she always takes care of them although they're a pretty independent bunch."

Heavens! Somehow I didn't think of you as a cat lover."

"I love all animals Sarah. I've always kept pets when I could. I'd love to have a dog but it wouldn't be fair to it because I'm so often away and dogs need more attention."

"What kind of cats are they? I mean are they pedigrees; Persians or Siamese or something?"

"Oh no! Just common old garden moggies. I love them though!" Daniela pointed to the two glasses. "Come on then. What is this?" The drinks were glasses full of dark brown liquid liberally topped with a generous head of whipped cream sprinkled with chocolate.

"Pflumli schumli!"

"What, in the name of all the atrocities inflicted on the human ear by the Swiss German dialect, is frigging pflumli schumli?"

"Hot sweet coffee laced with plum schnapps topped off with cream."

"It sounds like another dietician's nightmare."

"Don't worry. We'll work the calories off you on the mountain. Go ahead. Try it."

Daniela took a hesitant sip. "Whew! I thought you said it was coffee laced with schnapps not raw spirits that somebody's waved a coffee bean over. A couple of these and I'll fly up the rest of the mountain."

Sarah laughed. "I think we'll limit it to one. We don't want to turn up at the Santis hut rolling drunk." She paused nervously. "Oh listen Danny. I hope you won't mind, but Frau Schoop wants to have your photograph." Quickly Sarah explained about the photographic visitor's board in the hut.

Daniela nodded. "And you're on this board too?"

"Oh yes."

"Well in that case I won't be ashamed to join such illustrious company. If she really wants she can have my photo. It won't be very glamorous of course. I mean I've just hiked a thousand metres up a dirty great mountain and I probably look like something the dog found dead in a ditch."

"You look gorgeous as always."

"Well she can have my photo on one condition."

"And that is?"

"That you're in the photo too."

"What the hell for?"

"Because I want you to be."

"Oh hell! All right then."

They lingered long over their food and drink and drank in the incredible scenery around them. Daniela smeared mustard on her nutty Appenzeller cheese with pleasure. "Before I came to live permanently in Switzerland," she noted, "I would have thought that anyone putting mustard on cheese had come adrift of their marbles. Experience has taught me wisdom however. It's a delicious combination." She ate the good wholesome bread with the slab of cheese and creamy fresh, salted butter with deep satisfaction and gazed dreamily into the distant view. Away to the south, the line of the Churfirsten mountains were like a row of sharp teeth on the far side of the Toggenburg and, beyond them, lay line after line of towering peaks dwindling, seemingly endlessly, into the hazy blue distance. Behind the, hut the line of the ridge curved around crested by jagged outcroppings all the way around to the mountain Silberplatten and beyond. To the east of them lay the bulk of the Santis itself. They could see the summit clearly from here with the top dominated by the modern buildings at the end of the cable car and crowned by the large red tipped communications mast poking into the clear blue sky. "God it's heavenly here!" Daniela breathed. "Do you ever stay at this hut?"

"Oh yes. I stayed here last summer in fact. I got caught in bad weather trying to get to the top and I retreated and spent the night here instead. I was the only person in the massenlage."

"How long do you reckon it'll take us to the top from here?"

"I'm figuring about an hour and a half the way we're going. We can always drop back though if you can't manage it."

"Why the hell would I come this far to bug out at the last hurdle?"

Sarah grimaced. "Well there's a bit of a sting in the tail Danny." She confessed. "Before we reach the summit we have to negotiate the Himmelsleiter."

"Oh, oh! That sounds ominous. If my rudimentary German hasn't let me down, that translates as Heaven's ladder doesn't it?"

"That's right. It's a steep climb right at the very top up a sloping rock face. It's not as dangerous as it looks but it can be a bit intimidating if you're not used to it."

"And how long does this face take?"

"About a quarter of an hour. Don't worry though. If you're too scared to attempt it we'll just drop back down and stay here. There's no shame in saying you can't face it Danny. I don't want you to do anything you're not comfortable with. If you like I can rope you up to go up it. That way you'd feel more secure."

"Well let's wait and see shall we. I might have another of those flummy things for Dutch courage mind."

Chapter Five

At last they felt rested enough to tackle the last stage of the mountain. Sarah had been right about one thing; there were more people around for several parties of hikers appeared, as if by magic, over the, apparently, precipitous cliff face down to Schwagalp. Some paused for a drink at the hut whilst others turned and marched resolutely onward toward the summit. Sarah was less than impressed by some of these hikers. "Look at those idiots!" she snorted at one small group. "They've come up here in shorts and trainers. Trainers for God's sake! One stumble and their ankles gone and they either fall off the mountain or somebody has to airlift them off with a helicopter. No wonder there're so many accidents on this mountain. Some people have no bloody sense."

Daniela grinned at her outrage. "Go and tell them off Sarah. Sarah Fuchs, mountain patrol, wishes to take issue with your footwear."

"I'm sorry Danny. It just makes me mad."

"Sarah people will be people and not always very clever about it. Stupidity and ignorance must have *some* survival value to the species or it would have been weeded out by Darwinian selection long ago. Just be grateful that you're one of the smart ones. I know I'm grateful for having a smart girl like you to look after me on the mountain."

"Flatterer! Come on let's finish this job off."

Beyond Tierwis, the terrain of the mountain changed markedly. Now they were scrambling over bare rock with just the occasional tufts of flowers peeking from the crevices. They passed under the cable car and close to the pylon holding the cables that jutted at an alarming angle out from the side of the mountain. Sarah explained that you could take the steps up the pylon, ring a bell and the gondola would stop to pick you up. "If you don't fancy the Himmelsleiter we can always retreat to here and take the cable car up the rest of the way." she assured Daniela."

"I'd feel like I'd cheated."

The route got steeper and soon they had packed their sticks away in their bags so that they could use both hands to scramble up the rock. Daniela was enjoying herself. "This is fun." she declared. "I'm starting to feel like I'm really climbing a mountain and not just walking up a particularly big, particularly steep hill."

"It gets worse." Sarah warned her.

But Daniela seemed to have come alive and, at one point, she even took the lead climbing steadily above the bemused Sarah. She reached the top of a small cliff and came to a dead halt in shock. Stood facing her was a large brown goat. It wasn't just the size of the goat that arrested her however but rather its horns. Daniela had never seen a pair of horns quite like them. They were huge; great curving things, so long that the animal could have tilted its head back and scratched its own backside easily. The animal was regarding her coldly.

Sarah saw her pause from below. "What's the matter Danny?"

"Sarah! There's a bloody great Billy Goat here staring at me. I don't like the look of it."

Sarah grinned. She'd anticipated a similar encounter at some point. She emerged at the top of the cliff and regarded the animal with amusement. "Don't get your knickers in a twist Danny. It's only a Steinbock. Perfectly harmless."

"Harmless! Look at the bloody horns on the thing!"

"Yes it's a buck. The females have much smaller horns."

"I didn't know they herded goats up here."

"Oh Danny you do-nut! It's not a domestic goat. It's an Ibex, an Alpine Ibex, they're wild animals."

"Seriously? My God! Why doesn't it run away then?"

"Oh they're as tame as anything Danny. They're protected so they aren't frightened of people and they see a lot of people up here. We've got a lot of them on the Santis. We're lucky to have them Danny. They were hunted nearly to extinction in the nineteenth century, apart from a last remaining herd in the Gran Paradiso in Italy which were protected by King Emmanuel II. All the Ibex we have now are all descendants from that one remaining herd which have been reintroduced to the Alps. I think there are over forty thousand of them in the Alps now and around fifteen thousand in Switzerland. They've become so numerous that they've allowed some limited hunting for them again."

Daniela stared in disbelief. "They'd hunt this? How the hell is that sporting? The damn thing hasn't even the sense to run away."

"You'll find they get a lot more wary during the hunting season Danny. They normally only shoot the old bucks anyway. I know it's not nice but it's better than not having them at all. It's actually one of the few success stories we can boast of bringing an animal back from the point of extinction."

"So they're not dangerous?"

"Well I wouldn't mess with one if it decided to contest your path on a steep slope Danny. They're incredible climbers. I've seen them on the side of rock faces you wouldn't have thought a monkey could keep a grip on. Actually they're most dangerous when they're on a cliff face above you. They have an endearing habit, which they share with Chamois, of kicking rocks down on any enemy they perceive climbing up after them. I'm always a bit wary if I've got them on a slope above me."

Daniela shook her head. "What an amazing animal."

"Oh yes. We're proud of our Ibex. I suppose they're as close as it comes to a national animal of Switzerland although there is no *official* national animal."

"I'm just thrilled to have seen one."

"I doubt if it'll be the last Danny. We've a lot of them on the Santis. Come on. Let's push on."

"Oh let me just take a photograph of him!"

Sarah smiled at Daniela's pleasure in the wild creature. "Ok Danny. No rush. We're doing well."

The slope got steeper as they climbed and it was a job for both hands hauling up over the ledges of rock but it wasn't until the final hurdle that Daniela saw the nature of the remaining task and she didn't like the look of it at all. They'd crested out on a sharp ridge which ran for a few metres before dipping into a small gully. From this gully rose a smooth rock face towering above them. Clinging to it high above, apparently like flies on a wall, was a group of hikers who had overtaken them back at Tierwis. To Daniela's fevered perception the wall looked, to all intents and purposes, vertical although that was actually an illusion of perspective. In fact the rock slab tilted at about seventy degrees and was far easier to scale than first appearances would suggest. Daniela nevertheless regarded the feature with abject horror. "Oh God! Please don't tell me that we have to go up that."

"Yes Danny. That's the Himmelsleiter."

Daniela had turned white. "Sarah I... I don't think I can do this."

Sarah put a hand around her waist. "Honestly Danny it's not nearly as bad as it looks. Look there's a cleft cut out of the rock with fixed steel cables on both sides to hold onto and pegs and iron rungs set into the rock for your feet. As long as you hold on you can't fall. It's less dangerous than climbing a ladder. You just have to hold on, put one foot in front of the other and work your way up. Just make sure that you always have three points secure at any one time. In other words always have two feet and one hand in contact with the ladder or two hands and one foot. Make sure that all your other three points are steady and secure before you move a limb. We'll be at the top before you know it."

"I... I'm sorry. I'm a coward Sarah. I'm not a very brave person I'm afraid."

"Bullshit! You walk out on stage and perform in front of thousands of people. I couldn't do that. I'd shit myself!"

"I suffer from terrible stage fright Sarah."

"But you do it anyway. That takes courage. My dad always used to say that courage isn't being not frightened of something, but being frightened of something and doing it anyway. Listen Danny I wouldn't ask you to do something if I thought it was really dangerous. The only times I've ever seen anyone get into trouble on the Himmelsleiter is when people have just been too frightened to move any further and have to be helped up. Now I'm going to be there to help you. What I'll do is attach a harness to both us and I'll secure a rope to mine. I won't rope you up unless you really don't feel you can go any further at which point I'll just clip the rope to your harness and you'll be secure."

"But if I fell I'd pull you off too then."

"No you wouldn't because I'd attach myself to the cable. The worst that could possibly happen is that we'd slip a couple of feet and look like a pair of idiots. We wouldn't even dangle on the rope because the angle of the slope is mostly twenty degrees off the vertical. I know it looks sheer but trust me it isn't. You can do this Danny. I know you can."

"I'm sorry to be such a pussy Sarah. Every time I think about it though my brain wants to jump out of my skull and run around in circles gibbering."

"Look sit down for a few minutes and catch your breath. There's a party of hikers coming up behind us. We'll let them go up first. When you see how quickly they go up you'll see that it's not as difficult as you imagine. When you're ready we'll have a go."

Daniela nodded and sat down on the stony ridge wringing her hands in anxiety. Before the party of hikers behind could catch up, however, they became aware of

43

somebody descending the Himmelsleiter above. Daniela regarded the approaching figure with disbelief. It was an old man well into his seventies and clearly a veteran on the mountain for he was dressed in the standard peasant's costume of green felt trousers and jacket over an open necked shirt decorated with Edelweiss. An old battered trilby hat adorned his head and a traditional farmer's pipe jutted out from his grizzled beard. He was humming tunelessly to himself as he descended rapidly as though out for a stroll to the post office. It wasn't this elderly gentleman that so astonished Daniela, however, but rather his companion for, swarming down the ladder before him, was a scruffy little black and white animal that Daniela's senses perceived, in the face of all that rational consideration would suggest to the contrary, could only be a dog.

Daniela blinked incredulously. She wouldn't have credited the possibility of any animal not possessed of the arboreal attributes of a primate, and possibly a prehensile tail, negotiating that cliff. The dog didn't seem to have read the manual saying that it was physically impossible for a four legged canine to walk head first down an apparently vertical rock face. It didn't seem at all worried about it either. It was wagging its tail.

The dog, which Daniela now saw was a small collie, reached the bottom of the ladder and sprung joyfully up onto the ridge to dash over to Sarah to greet her with a wet sloppy tongue. Sarah grinned delightedly and ruffled the little animal's fur. "Hoi Shep!" she greeted the dog in pleasure. The scruffy little collie was evidently possessed of a courteous nature for after exchanging greetings with Sarah he rushed over to sniff at Daniela and lick her hand as she stroked his head in wonderment.

"Do you know him?" asked Daniela in wonderment.

"Oh sure. Shep and I are old friends. We always stop for a chat when we meet each other on the mountain."

The little dog's master clumped up onto the ridge and adjusted the weathered old backpack on his shoulders. He took his pipe from his mouth and nodded at Sarah. "Hoi Sarahli."

Sarah rose politely to her feet. "Gruezi Herr Handelsmann." She turned to Daniela who had also risen. "This is my friend Daniela."

The old man nodded at Daniela. "Gruezi Fraulein." He obviously didn't recognise her. Herr Handelsmann was not big on the celebrity pages of popular journals. He tilted his head back in the direction from which he had come. "Going up?"

"Yes Herr Handelsmann." Sarah told him. "We're staying at the hut for the night.

Herr Handelsmann nodded sagely. He was obviously a man of few words. "How's your father Sarahli?" he asked at last.

"Oh, he's very well Herr Handelsmann. Thank you for asking."

The old man grunted in satisfaction. "Well tell him I asked." Then with a final nod and a mumbled farewell he waved his dog on its way and left them with Shep dancing merrily down the mountainside in front.

Daniela sat down heavily on the rock. "I just don't believe I just saw that. How the hell can a dog come down that?"

Sarah laughed. "Shep's a real mountain dog. He's been running around on this old hill ever since he was a puppy."

"What are they doing up here?"

"No surprise there. Herr Handelsmann is a shepherd. I think he's got his flock over the other side of the Silberplatten. He often pops up to the Santis for his lunch."

"You mean he just felt a bit peckish so he just slipped up to the summit for a quick bite to eat."

"Yes he does it most days when he's up the mountain."

"Jesus!"

"He's a real old mountain character Danny. I've known him ever since I was a kid."

"Doesn't say much does he?"

"Hey that was quite a protracted conversation for old Albert. He must have been pleased to see me."

"I still can't believe that a dog could climb down that face."

"I keep telling you. It's not as bad as it looks."

Daniela's fears were further undermined by the party of hikers that arrived on the ridge behind them. They were a family group and Sarah would have approved of them for they were well equipped and quite obviously serious about their pastime. After exchanging the customary greetings with Sarah and Daniela, the father took the lead up the Himmelsleiter and the mother formed the tail end. Sandwiched between the two, and roped to her father above for safety, was a little girl with flaxen hair who could not have been more than eight years of age. She was dressed in a pink top and shorts and stomped about in great self-importance in her hiking boots and her pink rucksack with a bunny rabbit embroidered on it. She was evidently having the time of her life for her eyes were shining and Daniela could hear her giggling and chattering incessantly as she swarmed up the Himmelsleiter behind her father like a little mountain monkey. "God! She's so young." Daniela observed in amazement.

Sarah pulled a gentle smile. "I was younger than she is when I first came up this mountain Danny."

Daniela took a deep breath and rose to her feet shouldering her rucksack. "Come on then Sarah! If a dog and a little girl can do it I'm going to look a complete prat if I bottle out. Let's take this bloody mountain."

Sarah grinned hugely. "That's my girl. Let's go for the peak."

Before they were a quarter of the way up Sarah had decided that she wouldn't need to rope Daniela to her, for her friend was moving steadily up the ladder behind her, biting her lip and carefully grasping the steel cables. She was somewhat quiet but when Sarah glanced back concernedly to see how she was doing she managed a feeble smile. "You're doing great." Sarah encouraged.

Daniela panted "I tell you something I've realised Sarah. It's bad enough climbing up this bloody thing but I bet it's a bitch to come *down* it."

Sarah nodded with a smile. "Yes. I know it's a cliché but it helps not to look down Danny. Just keep your eyes on the foot and handholds in front of you."

But of course Daniela did glance nervously behind her on occasion and it was a result of one of these anxious glimpses that the only real crisis of the ascent occurred. "Sarah!" Daniela hissed urgently. "There's a bunch of guys coming up quickly behind us."

Sarah looked back. "It's ok Danny. They're holding back. I don't think they'll want to overtake us."

"I'll bet they bloody won't."

"What's the matter then?"

"Oh never mind. Just keep going all right."

Eventually, gloriously, they heaved themselves over the last of the ladder and onto a broad ledge just below the summit of the mountain. Daniela flopped down onto the rocks and buried her face in her hands. To Sarah's alarm she was shaking violently. In concern Sarah rushed to her and placed an arm about her shoulders. "Are you all right Danny?"

"I don't believe I just did that." Daniela choked and in shock Sarah realised she was shaking with laughter. Daniela lifted her face and her eyes were full of tears of mirth. "Why did we do it?" she intoned pompously. "Possibly because we're fucking stupid!" she added as an afterthought.

"Language Danny! Remember your public."

"I think we've given the public enough of a demonstration today Sarah. Has it yet occurred to you that we've just climbed up a frigging great rock face

47

with four young lads behind us staring straight up our skirts? No wonder they were in no hurry to overtake us. It's a good job we remembered to wear knickers."

Sarah clasped a hand to her mouth and burst into laughter. "Oh God! I never thought about that."

The two girls leaned against each other and laughed helplessly. When the four young men emerged at the top, wearing huge grins on their faces, they provoked another storm of mirth from the two young ladies, who were giggling like a pair of adolescent schoolgirls. The four young gentlemen obviously thought the two girls had lost their minds for they passed on into a small tunnel with nervous greetings. Finally Daniela wiped her eyes. "Oh God Sarah! If those lads are staying at the mountain hut tonight we won't be short of male company. I hope to hell they weren't carrying cameras."

"Stop it! You'll start me giggling again."

Daniela leaned against Sarah and rested her head on Sarah's shoulder. "We did it Sarah. We climbed the bloody mountain."

"We sure did."

"I've been a good girl and brave Sarah. Do I get a kiss?"

"Of course."

The kiss was the longest they had ever exchanged and for long seconds they held each other and nuzzled at each other's lips in great contentment. Finally Daniela sprang to her feet, took off her cap, shook her hair loose and hauled Sarah up by the hand to embrace her. "Let's go Sarah. I've got a thirst you could cut with a knife. Let's find this bloody hut and have a celebratory drink."

Chapter Six

The exit from the Himmelsleiter to the summit of the mountain was through a short tunnel. It was dark in the tunnel, after the bright sunshine outside, and Sarah had a word of warning. "Watch it Danny. Let your eyes adjust. I once had an accident in here. I came straight out of the sunshine and walked smack into a wall and bashed my head."

But the tunnel was only a few yards long and they emerged on a track over a slab of rock that rose a few feet to a gate in a fence surrounding a concrete terrace. After the rocky wasteland of the mountain slope beneath, the top of the mountain was a different world. It was almost entirely artificial with paved walkways and sun terraces around the cable car station and large self-service cafeteria. Stairways led up to viewing terraces and there were benches scattered around for tourists to admire the view from. There were stone plinths set with interesting information for the day trippers and panoramic relief maps showing the names of the mountains around them. There was a souvenir shop by the cafeteria and even a children's playground. It was like finding a theme park in the middle of a wilderness. And, all over this jarring artificiality, swarmed hundreds of tourists; young people, elderly couples and parents clutching the hands of young children, all dressed in summer clothes, incongruously jarring atop the summit of a mighty mountain.

Amidst all these people that had done nothing more strenuous that day than climb aboard a cable car, Sarah and Daniela felt curiously isolated, like some strange alien beings that had somehow emerged from the uncharted primeval badlands below. As they stood there, oddly alone among the crowds of tourists, Daniela realised that there were two populations of people on the mountain; those that had ascended by the cable car and those that had made their way on their own two feet and there was a barrier, invisible but unmistakeable, between them. "My God!" she breathed, "What *have* they done to this poor mountain?"

Sarah frowned. "Yes it's bloody crowded. Come on let's go round to the hut. It'll be quieter there."

Sarah set off at a quick pace along the pathway that led around the summit to the back of the mountain where the alpine hut stood. She had not gone far before she realised she was alone. Puzzled she turned to see where Daniela was. Daniela's isolation had not lasted long. She was over a hundred metres behind Sarah and surrounded by excited tourists who were pressing pens and pieces of paper on her. She was signing autographs resignedly and trying to look congenial about the obligation. Sarah raced back to rescue her and steer her through the protesting crowds. "Well!" she commented wryly, "Of all the delays I expected on our route today, a horde of autograph hunters was the last I anticipated."

"Give me a break Sarah. What could I do?"

"Nothing at all." Sarah grinned wickedly. "I thought it was very *brave* of you."

"Do they have toads on this mountain?"

"Unlikely at this altitude. Why?"

"Because I had half a mind to put one in your bedclothes tonight."

"I thought you had another half a mind to *share* my bedclothes."

"Hmm that's a thought. Oh well I'll think of some other suitable retribution." Suddenly she stopped. "Oh look at that little bird!" Just in front of them walking about on the path, quite unconcerned by their presence, was a handsome small bird a little larger than a sparrow. It was grey with darker speckling on its back, a white speckled throat and rufous streaks to its flanks. "Is it ill Sarah do you think?"

"Why should it be ill?"

"Well why doesn't it fly away?"

"It's an Alpine Accentor Danny. They're often really tame. I've even had one walk between my legs before."

"It's a gorgeous little thing. Are they common?"

"Common enough up here. They're birds of the high mountain slopes. You'll rarely see one much lower than the tree line in summer although they do tend to winter further down. There's quite a few species of birds that are exclusive to the high alpine zone. Later on, when all the tourists bugger off and it's a bit quieter, we'll take a turn around the mountain and see if I can't show you some Snow finches. They're lovely birds."

They were turning the corner of the mountain around to the hut and Daniela pointed out the parties of Alpine Choughs wheeling about in the sky by the hut. "I see our old friends are here." she noted with pleasure.

Sarah nodded, "Yes but they're not overly popular up here. They're real bandits on the Santis. They literally fly down and steal the food off people's plates when they're eating out on the terrace. You wouldn't believe how cheeky they are. The family that owns the hut have been in a state of undeclared war with them for years."

"I don't care! I love them. The fact that they're audacious pirates just adds to their charm."

"Well don't let Hans or his wife catch you feeding them. They don't encourage it."

It was still busy around the Santis hut although markedly less so that the more modern built up areas of the mountain top. The Santis hut was the oldest man made construction on the summit of the mountain and it retained its elderly charm. The old stone building was perched on a ledge overlooking a huge shadowy basin saddled between two radiating arms of the main mountain. The most formidable of these was the most southerly of the two; a jagged knife edged ridge stretching away toward the curious dome topped mountain Altman in the distance. It was a series of intimidating looking precipitous cliffs topped by impossibly narrow spikes plunging down dizzyingly into the gloomy looking basin beneath where snow still lingered in the frigid wasteland below. Daniela paused to regard the feature with awe. "God look at that horrible ridge!" she intoned in a horrified voice. "It makes my spine tingle just to look at it."

"Yes that's the Lyssengrat. There's a trail over it."

"You mean there are misguided idiots that actually climb over that thing?"

Sarah grinned and snaked an arm around Daniela's waist. "You'll be one of them tomorrow Danny dearest. That's our projected route in the morning."

Daniela gaped in horror. "You're taking the piss! We can't walk over that. It looks like one of the less inviting shield walls of Mordor."

"Ach no! Just a nice stroll in the high places. You can do it with your eyes shut. Piece of piss!"

"I have this ambition Sarah to be buried in a nice graveyard; somewhere where my fans can come and lay wreaths without risking becoming chough fodder."

"Certain Tibetan monks lay their corpses out on the mountainside to provide food for the vultures Danny."

"Well that's very eco-friendly of them Sarah but I am not a Tibetan monk and I fear I would find little vocation for spending a lifetime of frugal austerity sat on a mountain top, spinning prayer wheels and surrounded by hungry looking birds all wondering when I was going to kick the bucket. Anyway I look terrible in orange." She stared at the ridge again. "Seriously though, we're not really climbing over that tomorrow are we?"

"Honestly Danny it's not as....."

"If you say, "it's not as bad as it looks" I'll slap you!"

Sarah laughed. "We'll worry about it in the morning Danny. Come on let's go in the hut. I could do with a beer."

The terrace of the hut was crowded but the girls had spent enough time in the sunshine that day and they were content to enter the old and charming stone building which had graced the rugged mountain top since 1846, long before any cable car had come to open the summit to more general tourism. Again Daniela had the odd feeling of isolation, as if the little guest house was an archaic anachronism, stubbornly clinging on in some reflection of an older age of alpine adventurism in the face of the modern world now so firmly entrenched on what had once been its splendid lofty solitude. It was notable that the majority of the people eating and drinking on the terrace were those with worn clothes, scuffed hiking boots and rucksacks. The Santis hut was their natural environment and they regarded the panorama about them or consulted maps on their tables with the eyes of people whose thoughts were already drifting away to distant peaks or hidden valleys. If you had hiked up the Santis, the modern cafeteria, souvenir shops and museum were not for you. This was where you came.

Inside the hut, the girls eased their rucksacks off by a rough wooden table by the window. Daniela looked around her in contentment. The dining room of the mountain guest house was classic rural simplicity of montane Switzerland with bare wooden tables, on a bare wooden floor, ringed by simple chairs. There was an old upright piano in one corner and the wooden walls were decorated with old photographs of the hut from the days when it had been the only building on the mountain. There were also black and white photos of old alpinists, pictures of Ibex and small embroidered tapestries with poems in Swiss dialect upon them. There were polished wooden planks and tree boles decorated with naive Appenzeller art, depicting cows and cowherds amid the alpine landscape and there were the inevitable decorated cowbells displayed on the walls. On a shelf there were stuffed marmots and Ptarmigan and other trophies of the hunt included the horns of Chamois mounted on wooden shields and an enormous pair of Ibex horns resting over a doorway.

A young girl of about fifteen, dressed in a black skirt and a blue smock, whose lapels were decorated with embroidered Edelweiss and Alpenrose, came to greet them. "Hoi Sarah!" she called gaily. She looked excited. Evidently Daniela's presence had not gone unnoticed among the hut's staff.

"Hoi Elsa. Is Hans around?"

"Yes he's in the kitchen. Do you want to see him?"

"We'll have a drink first and wait till he's got more time Elsa. I can see you're busy."

"Oh yes! It's crazy today. We haven't stopped all day."

"Be a darling then Elsa and bring us two beers."

The young girl had a haunted look. "One for you and one for er Miss.... Miss..."

"This is my friend Daniela Elsa."

"*Daniela Devin*?" the young girl blurted out impulsively.

Daniela held out a hand with a smile. "I'm pleased to meet you Elsa."

The young girl grasped her hand unbelievingly and switched to English. "I am pleased to meet also you Miss Devin. You have walking up the mountain today?"

"Don't I know it. Sarah here has been putting me through the mill."

"Oh sorry my English is not good."

"I mean yes we have climbed up today."

"And you are staying here tonight?"

"Yes that's the plan."

"Oh perhaps you are singing us some songs tonight Miss Devin. My sister and me, we are big fans."

"I'm not very good at yodelling Elsa. If I'm not too tired later on though I might play you a song or two on that piano if it's in tune."

"Oh thank you! My sister and me we try play some of your songs sometime."

"Elsa." interrupted Sarah in German, "We're really thirsty. How about those two beers?"

"Oh yes! I'll fetch them right away. I'll tell grandpa you're here."

The young girl scuttled away excitedly and Sarah and Daniela took a seat at the table gratefully. "Elsa's one of the owner's grandchildren." Sarah explained. "Half of Hans' clan work up here during the summer months. They're a big family." Sarah shook her head in wonderment. "I still can't get used to the way that everywhere we go everyone knows you."

Daniela laughed merrily. "You know Sarah I was thinking just the same thing about you. I'm sure if I came upon some reclusive hermit living in an inaccessible cave somewhere on this mountain it would turn out that he dandled you on his knee when you were a child. Do you know *everybody* on these mountains?"

Sarah rubbed her chin ruefully. "Pretty much I guess."

Daniela regarded her seriously. "You're a lucky girl Sarah. People know me just because I'm a singer and I get my name in the papers or on television. Round here though you're the real star. People love you for who you are. I'd swap my fame for yours any day."

"I'm not famous Danny."

"You are here. There's even a photo of you on that wall over there. I saw it as soon as we came in."

Sarah stared at the picture. "Oh God! I'd forgotten that was here. I must have been about eight years old when that was taken. How did you recognise me?"

"Let's just say that your face has become familiar to me. Is that your family with you?"

"Yes that's my father and mother. The older girl is my big sister and the boy is my brother."

"Your mother is a fine looking woman Sarah. You look a lot like her."

"Yes a lot of people say that. We hiked up here as a family on that occasion. Mum used to come walking with us quite a bit when I was younger. Not any more though. You wouldn't catch her dead in hiking boots now."

"You've inherited her looks Sarah. She's a beautiful lady."

"Oh I'm not as beautiful as my mother. She was a model when she was younger and she's still a strikingly beautiful woman. She's very elegant and feminine. I'm hopeless compared to her. I've got too much of my dad's character. Both my brother and sister take after my Dad in appearance but they've both got a streak of my mum's character. I look more like mum but I'm closer to my father in most other respects. I was the youngest and always Dad's favourite. He spoiled me rotten when I was a kid."

"You sound as if you had a happy childhood Sarah."

"Oh I did. I had a golden childhood Danny. My parents were wonderful to me. I know I have my disagreements with my mother now but she was always a good mother to me." Sarah stared out of the window wistfully. "Perhaps that's why I feel such a louse for the moment. My parents expect me to marry Alan and I don't know if I want to any more. They've always done the best for me and always given me all I could have wished for so why am I now thinking of defying their wishes? I've never defied them before."

"In the end you'll do what's best Sarah. Your parents obviously love you. In the final analysis they'll accept whatever makes you happiest."

Sarah nodded but before she could answer Elsa returned with two bottles of beer and two glasses on a tray. Trailing in her wake and wiping his hands on his apron was the guest house's proprietor; Hans who was grinning in pleasure. Sarah jumped to her feet to embrace the elderly gentleman and his eyes regarded her fondly as she pecked him on the cheek. Sarah was a great favourite of his. As Elsa excitedly poured the beer Daniela rose politely to greet their host. Sarah introduced Hans to her illustrious hiking companion. "This is Daniela Hans; my friend."

Hans took Daniela's hand courteously. "Gruezi Fraulein. You honour us with your company. It's not often we get such famous people up here."

Daniela graced Hans with the gentle warm smile which made her irresistible to people. "Thank you Mein Herr but I'm just trotting along after Sarah today."

"And you've hiked up?"

"Yes, all the way from Alpli."

"Do you do much alpine walking?"

Daniela grinned. "Good heavens no! This is the first time I've ever really climbed a serious mountain. Sarah's been putting me through the mill. I've got muscles aching that I didn't even know I had."

"She's done really well Hans." Sarah interjected. "We made really good time up to Tierwis. I thought she might have a few problems on the last stretch but she flew up here with ease."

Daniela threw back her head and laughed. "Take no notice of Sarah sir. She's being overly kind to me and telling you fibs. I didn't fly up at all. I nearly peed myself on the last bit."

"She didn't Hans. Oh she was a bit nervous when she saw the Himmelsleiter but once she was on it she swarmed up with no problems other than the fact that she was worried that the people coming up behind could see up her skirt."

Hans chuckled deeply. "So you young ladies are staying the night then. What's your route in the morning Sarah?"

"We're heading over to Rotsteinpass and then up over Altmannsattel and dropping down to Bollenwies."

Hans raised an eyebrow. "That's quite a hike for a young lady without experience Sarah. Are you sure your friend here can manage it?"

"I'm sure of it Hans. She's a lot better than she thinks she is. I'll make an alpinist out her yet."

"Well take good care of her on the Lysengrat Sarah. There's not much snow left on there but it can still be tricky for someone not used to it."

"I'll rope her up on the grat Hans. She'll be fine."

"Well look after her Sarah. We don't want to lose anybody famous do we? Do you want to put your stuff in the massenlage?"

"We'll have drink first Hans. Are you busy tonight?"

Hans shook his head. "No it's mostly trippers today. Once the last cable car goes down we'll be quiet. We've only got a handful of guests staying. You'll have plenty of room. Anyway I'd better get back in the kitchen. We'll talk later Sarah and you Miss; welcome to the Santis."

The evening passed pleasantly. The girls dined on big pork sausages in onion gravy with a mound of rosti and, when the last tourists had left the mountain top, they took a short walk around the summit. It was eerily quiet once the crowds had departed and the calls of the choughs echoed loudly in the still evening air. Sarah found a flock of Snowfinches for Daniela and she was enchanted by the little mountain sparrows. They found a flock of perhaps a dozen of them on a large gently sloping slab of rock on the northern side of the summit. The birds seemed to disappear into the background at a distance as they scuttled around furtively among the rocks but as Sarah and Daniela approached them they all took to the air where their strikingly marked black and white wings made a startling spectacle. Finally they were close enough to observe the birds on the ground and Daniela was amused by the odd, slightly goofy high stepping gait of the birds almost as if they were trying to imitate marching storm troopers. The sun was sinking low as they returned to the hut and the basins of the mountain below them were wreathed in shadow. They pulled their jackets about themselves tightly for the temperature was falling fast. Even the choughs seemed to have ceased their incessant wheeling around the mountain and settled down for the night. The silence of the mountain was only broken the occasional calls of the Ptarmigan in the rocks below and the sound of human voices from the interior of the hut.

The company in the hut stayed up later than was usual in an alpine guest house whose occupants faced early starts and a day of hard hiking on the morrow. The reason for this, of course, was that the Santis Hut had rarely had such a celebrated guest as Daniela Devin before. Sarah and Daniela found themselves seated in places of honour at the big Stammtisch; the large oval table that was reserved for regulars and friends. The conventions of the Stammtisch were suspended for the evening as all the guests in the house pulled up chairs to gather around their famous new comrade. In addition to the hikers staying at the hut, the company was fleshed out by several workers at the Swiss Telecom and weather stations who were summering on the mountain, the guest house's staff and Hans, his wife and such members of their extensive family as were currently present. It was a merry evening of much camaraderie and laughter. Elsa and her sister played and sang some songs shyly on the piano conscious that they had one of Switzerland's most accomplished and famous musicians listening to them. Daniela was impressed by them however and applauded warmly.

Of course, after that, it was incumbent on Daniela to take to the piano herself and sing a few songs for the company. The gathering at the Stammtisch grew quiet as Daniela sang a short collection of her more romantic compositions. Sarah listened to the hauntingly beautiful voice with emotions that hovered between deep pride in her remarkable friend and strange feelings that quickened her heart in unfamiliar fashions. She glanced around the other listeners and saw enraptured eyes glistening in bewildered enchantment as Daniela wove her special magic over them. In one of those moments in which one sees a crucial crux in the turning of one's life Sarah realised that this amazing woman would be a part of her life forever. A deep up-swelling of emotion seemed to grip her throat and leave her incapable of speech. She glanced around and saw that Hans was looking at her curiously. He nodded at her in some depth of understanding. "She's a fine lady, your friend." he murmured and Sarah drew a breath, wondering if he meant more than his simple words conveyed.

Slowly the guests drifted away to bed and Sarah and Daniela found themselves alone with Hans who smoked his pipe in deep contentment. "We'd best get to bed." Sarah told Daniela.

Daniela rubbed her eyes. "That sounds like a good idea. I'm shattered!"

They made their way to the massenlage after a rudimentary toilet with a bowl of cold water. It was pitch dark in the dormitory and they groped their way to the ladder that led them to the uppermost shelf of the layered sleeping bunks. They had earlier laid out their blankets and pillows on the uppermost tier close by the little window that looked out on the mountain vista. The mattresses were thin coverings over the bare wooden boards of the upper shelf and the blankets were of coarse wool but at least their fellow guests occupied the lower tiers and they had the upper shelf to themselves. They undressed in silence, the stillness of the dormitory only broken by the soft snores of the people on the tiers below, and folded their clothes carefully by the pillows at their heads. Sarah stripped down to her knickers and a T-shirt whilst Daniela wore just a pair of knickers and a chemise to sleep. It was cool in the massenlage and they pulled blankets over themselves gratefully.

Sarah, closest to the window, glanced out. The moon was rising over the mountains and illuminating the peaks in pearly whiteness. As she lay on her back

Daniela suddenly squirmed closer, folding her blankets over Sarah's, and throwing an arm across her. Sarah held her breath as Daniela moulded her body against her. "It's cold." Daniela murmured as she nestled against Sarah.

"It's not cold at all." Sarah whispered in protest but Daniela just chuckled softly and wrapped herself more closely to Sarah. Sarah felt the tickle of Daniela's hair as she laid her head on her shoulder and the smoothness of her bare legs as they enfolded her own. Daniela's hand found the sliver of bare flesh between her knickers and her T-shirt and Sarah bit her lip to stifle the sigh of arousal the touch brought to her. Daniela's body was warm against her and Sarah's heart was beating wildly; torn between fear and desire. She lay for long minutes dreading that Daniela would escalate the sexual tension between them and at the same time yearning for her to do so.

Daniela, however, seemed content to simply hold her and as the minutes passed Sarah felt the need to say something; something that would somehow express what she had felt throughout her day on the mountain with the astonishing woman who lay in her arms. "Danny," she whispered at last. "I don't know what to do. I've never met anyone like you before. I've never felt like this before. I... I think I'm falling in love with you."

There was no response. Sarah glanced at Daniela. The moonlight was now shafting through the windows illuminating the dormitory with pale light. Daniela's face was soft and tranquil on Sarah's shoulder. With relief, Sarah realised that Daniela had not heard a word that she had said. The hard day of toil in the fresh mountain air had taken its toll. Daniela was fast asleep. With a tenderness that she was at a loss to explain, Sarah bent down and kissed the lovely face at her side. She hugged Daniela close to her side and lay long awake daring to dream the unthinkable.

Chapter Seven

A shaft of morning sunlight lanced through the little windows in the massenlage and Sarah, as she emerged sluggishly to awakening, heard somebody from the tiers below moving about and dressing. She lay quietly and listened. Whoever was abroad was evidently well advanced in their morning preparations for, within a minute or two, Sarah heard the sound of the dormitory door and it closing behind their receding footsteps. She held her breath and let her ears attune to the silence in the dormitory. Apart from the gentle breathing beside her the silence was complete and Sarah realised that she and Daniela must be the last people to rise and were completely alone in the massenlage. She was completely wrapped in Daniela's arms and with a blush she realised that they must have slept like that all night. She wondered nervously if anybody, upon rising, had happened to look up at the top shelf of bunks and what spectacle she and Daniela must have presented in such intimate close contact. Extracting an arm from beneath Daniela's head she reached behind the pillow for her watch. She blinked in surprise. It was nearly a quarter to nine which was almost an indecently late hour to rouse oneself in a mountain hut.

She looked at Daniela fondly. It was not the first time that she had had occasion to regard her friend in slumber at leisure but it was a sight that brought her pleasure for Daniela looked peaceful and sweet asleep. There was even a soft smile on her features as if her spirit wandered in beautiful dreams. Sarah felt a great wave of tenderness overwhelm her and an odd feeling of protectiveness. Daniela might be an awesomely talented and capable woman but she seemed as vulnerable as a child as she lay in Sarah's arms. With a shock Sarah realised the extent to which this woman was becoming part of her life and what she was beginning to mean to her. She tried to imagine Alan alongside her in bed but his features seemed distant and hazy. Only Daniela, murmuring softly in her sleep with her hair tickling Sarah's bare arm, seemed real. Her own words that she had whispered in the quiet of the night to the sleeping Daniela came back to haunt her. It would be so easy; so perilously easy to fall in love with this astonishing woman.

Sarah stroked Daniela's hair for a moment or two and then she shook her gently. "Danny. Danny wake up." Daniela stirred and murmured uncertainly. "Come on Miss Sleepy Head it's getting late."

Daniela's eyes flickered open and she looked blearily at Sarah as her vision stirred into focus. "What time is it?"

"Time we were up and about. Everybody else has already left."

In response Daniela closed her eyes again and snuggled closer to Sarah. "Can't we just lie here all day?"

"No we can't. We've got a long way to go and if we want to have a wash and get some breakfast and still have something of the morning left we're going to have to get our act together soon."

Daniela nuzzled in the crook of Sarah's neck and sighed. "Just five minutes Sarah. It's heavenly to just lie here with you like this."

"Five minutes then; no more. Then we have to move."

Daniela chuckled softly. "I suppose a morning kiss would be out of the question."

"You're impossible." Sarah protested with a smile but she did turn her face to accept the kiss. It was very nearly a mistake. Daniela had awoken in a languorously amorous mood and she grasped Sarah close to her and possessed her mouth hungrily. Her hand slid up under Sarah's T-shirt to caress her back and Sarah felt her

63

quickening with rousing passion. "Danny stop it!" she hissed. "Somebody might come in."

"I don't care."

"Please Danny. I... I'm not very comfortable with this."

Daniela looked at her with a smile and raised a finger to stroke Sarah's bottom lip. "I know honey. I'm sorry but I can't help myself. You are so beautiful and I want you. I love you Sarah. You must know that by now."

Sarah swallowed. "Danny please! This isn't right. I have a boyfriend. I don't sleep with girls."

"You always say that Sarah but then when I touch you your face flushes with arousal, your mouth opens to be kissed, your breathing quickens and your pupils dilate." Daniela chuckled deeply and her hand moved quickly to stroke a finger across Sarah's left nipple. "Even your nipples become erect. You tell me one thing and your body tells me another. You want me Sarah don't you? You want me as much as I want you. That's the truth isn't it?"

"Danny! I can't."

"Can't what Sarah? Admit the truth that is staring you in the face? One day you'll have to because you're a poor liar Sarah. You can't lie to yourself indefinitely and you can't lie to me forever either."

"I haven't lied to you."

"Yes you have." Daniela disagreed with a sleepy laugh. "You must think I'm simple if you think I don't know that this guest house has private rooms as well as dormitories Sarah. For a few francs extra we could have spent the night alone. Now there's a dangerous thought isn't there?"

"Danny please! I'm not ready for this."

"I know you're not sweetheart. I just hope you're ready sometime soon because life is too sweet and too short and a day without you in my arms is a day wasted." She kissed Sarah a last time and raised herself to a seated position shaking out her hair. "Come along then darling. Let's see what Hans can rustle up for breakfast."

Breakfast in the Santis hut was the usual frugal repast of bread and butter smeared with jam and mugs of coffee. Hans however was prepared to defer to the tastes of his beloved Sarah and her famous friend and thus he provided Sarah with some tart cheese as well and even a couple of soft boiled eggs for Daniela. They ate quietly by the window, both dressed in jeans and blouses in deference to the cool morning air on the mountain top. Daniela's eyes strayed often to the frightening looking ridge that Sarah had told her was the route for the day. Is it going to be really rocky?" she asked nervously.

"Oh it'll be rocky all right. Not much else but rocks up here."

"I meant rocky in the more metaphorical sense Sarah. I mean is it going to be pee in my pants standard scary?"

"Oh you'll be fine Danny. Trust me. I've taken a lot of people across the Lysengrat and I've never lost one yet."

"I'm still aching from yesterday. I'm not as fit as I thought."

"You'll be ok once we get moving Danny and loosen up a bit. Actually, physically speaking, we've got an easier day than yesterday because we're mostly descending. We're just following the ridge over the Lysengrat and then we drop down to the Rotsteinpass. That'll take us about an hour and a half if we don't hang around and then we've got the only real climb of the day from there up to the Altmannsattel. That's a short but steep climb but we should do it in about forty five to fifty minutes. That's about the highest we'll go today and after that it's just a long hike over the tops and a descent to the Fahlensee. It's a beautiful route. You'll like it."

"Aren't we starting a bit late?"

"Yes but I'm not too worried about that today since we're losing altitude. The chances are that we'll be well down in the valley by late afternoon should we get caught in weather."

"Well I'm up for it. I slept like a baby."

Sarah looked at her quizzically. "That's unusual Danny. Most people take some time to get acclimatised to sleeping at high altitude. I thought you might have a restless night but you went out like a light as soon as we hit the pillow."

"I could sleep through an earthquake Sarah." She reached over and touched Sarah's hand briefly "Especially with such a gorgeous bed partner."

Sarah blushed. "I was talking to you but I don't know if you heard me."

"Never heard a thing. What were you saying?"

"Oh nothing much."

"Damn! You were whispering sweet nothings to me and I didn't even hear you."

"It wasn't anything Danny."

Daniela leaned forward teasingly. "What were you saying to me Sarah? Come on tell me."

"I... I can't remember. I think I was a bit drunk. That last Kaffee Krauter was a bit much."

"So you don't remember?"

"No."

Daniela looked at her carefully; a smile on her face and the impossible big blue eyes mocking her gently. "Liar!"

"Were you awake?"

Daniela shook her head. "Nope. Can't remember a thing. You'll have to repeat yourself sometime." She grinned at Sarah's discomfort. "You can tell me tonight. Right now let's have another cup of coffee and then I suppose we'd better face this bloody Lysengrat of yours!"

Hans was sorry to see his two beautiful young guests leave and he emerged from his kitchen, where preparations for another anticipated busy day were already under way, to see them on their way. To the girl's surprise Hans' grandchildren were also there to see them off and Elsa approached shyly with a parting gift. The two girls had thoughtfully prepared a packed lunch of cheese sandwiches, apples and chocolate for Sarah and Daniela. Sarah thanked them warmly with a kiss and carefully stowed away the offering in her rucksack as Daniela signed autographs for them.

At last, however, they departed from the hut and took to the trail away from the summit. Their first obstacle of any note was a ledge cut into a cliff just off the mountain summit. It was well constructed, reasonably broad with handholds in the form of a steel cable secured to the cliff face for security and not particularly dangerous. It was, however, quite frightening for there was a long drop below it and Sarah observed Daniela carefully. She crossed the obstacle without apparent trouble however although her face was set grimly and she was breathing heavily by the end of it.

Beyond this was a small shoulder of very short grass and rocks decorated with exquisite high alpine flowers. Daniela adored the little tufts of small pink flowers set in cushions of densely packed tiny leaves. Sarah told her it was called Moss Campion and Daniela thought it well named for the dense tufts did indeed resemble patches of luxuriant moss surprisingly dotted with pink flowers. She kneeled down on the short turf to admire the plant at close quarters and to take a photograph. "It's a pretty common flower locally." Sarah told her. "We've got something a bit rarer over here look." This turned out to be another plant forming small dense cushions growing among the rocks. In this case, however, the leaves were even tinier and more densely packed and they were distinctly greyish in colour. The flowers were tiny too; enchanting little white blooms scattered among the grey green leaves. "This is a high alpine species Danny." Sarah informed her, "It's Swiss

Rock Jasmine and you'll rarely see it much under two thousand metres."

"It's so tiny."

"Most of the high alpine species are pretty small Danny. You've got a pretty short growing season up here. Plants don't have time to grow tall."

The lovely little flowers put Daniela in a fine humour which was just as well for shortly after they came upon the Lysengrat proper. Daniela sat down on a rock and regarded the feature before her in abject horror. "Sarah." she said seriously. "I don't think I can do this."

Sarah sat down beside her and placed an arm about her waist. "You can Danny! Trust me."

"But look at it!" It was not a pretty sight. From their position onward the track degenerated into a tiny thin ledge traversing a vertical rock face. The ledge descended slightly across the face to about half way across before rising again and disappearing into the rocks beyond. At no point did the ledge seem to be more than two feet wide and, in places, about half that. Handholds were provided by way of another steel cable set into the cliff face about waist high above the ledge and secured there by steel pitons. In truth, had you reproduced the feature in a children's playground a couple of feet above the ground, you would have seen no difficulty whatsoever in it. You would have traversed the cliff with ease and wondered what the fuss was about. But it wasn't set in a children's playground. It was perched terrifyingly above an awful abyss; a sheer face plummeting hundreds of metres into the gloomy col below. The technical difficulties of crossing that wall were slight. The psychological problems were immense. The mind simply refused to contemplate that terrible yawning chasm below. Daniela bit her lip; her heart was hammering in her chest. "I'm sorry Sarah. I'm a coward."

Sarah shook her head. "No Danny. There's only one coward between us on this mountain this morning."

"What do you mean? You're no coward Sarah."

"Yes I am. I bottled it this morning Danny; in bed." Sarah waved her hand at the cliff before her. "Oh this sort of thing doesn't worry me at all but this morning I had another sort of cliff to climb and I didn't have the courage for it."

"What are you trying to say Sarah?"

Sarah sighed. "Last night when I was a bit drunk I said something but you were asleep. This morning when you asked me what I said I was too pusillanimous to tell you. I'm not proud of myself."

Daniela reached up to touch Sarah's face. Her eyes were wide and serious. "What was it you wanted to say Sarah?" she whispered.

Sarah choked and lowered her head. "I... I just wanted to say I love you."

Daniela nodded and took Sarah's hand gently. "Thank you Sarah. You could not have said a better thing to me."

"I... I was frightened to say it Danny."

"You just did Sarah!"

"But I'm still frightened."

"So am I. I'm frightened of that fucking rock face!" Daniela let her eyes drift to the cliff. "Fear." she noted. "That's all it really is isn't it Sarah? Fear to take the hard path; fear to step boldly forward whatever the prize beyond. That's what really holds us back isn't it? We lose sight of the glories ahead because we dare not take that first step on the dangerous path and look instead for the easy way. I could stop now and we could go back to the summit and take the cable car down. But then I'd never see the mountains beyond or the beautiful lake in the alp you've promised me. And I'd never walk beside that lake with my Sarah's hand in mine." Daniela paused in contemplation. A single tear rolled down her cheek. "Thank you Sarah. Thank you for telling me now. You've crossed your cliff now I'll cross mine. We'll cross this one together and when we reach the other side

69

we'll turn back and poke our tongues out at it and laugh at it and walk forward into the future together."

"We've still got the Altmannsattel after this Danny. There are more cliffs ahead."

"There always will be Sarah. We'll climb our fears together."

Sarah nodded unable to speak for a moment. The she became business like and opened her rucksack. "I'm going to rope us up Danny for extra safety." From her rucksack Sarah produced two climbing harnesses. They were full body harnesses comprising of a sit harness with a waist band and two legs bands combined with a chest harness worn over the shoulders. "Take your rucksack off Danny." Sarah ordered and then she spent some minutes easing Daniela into the harness and adjusting the straps. "You're not pinching anything are you?" she asked in concern.

Daniela laughed. "I don't think so. I didn't expect this though. If the paparazzi find out that I've been trying out bondage paraphernalia at two thousand three hundred metres they'll have a field day."

Sarah laughed. "It's going to get worse." She quickly donned her own harness and then took two short lengths of rope with carabiners attached to each end and clipped them to the waist bands of their harnesses passing them through a ring on the chest strap for extra stability. "You have to clip the free end onto the cable Danny." She explained. "Now each time you come to a piton you'll have to hold on with one hand and unclip the loop, pass it over the piton and re-clip it on the other side."

"But then I'd be unattached while I was doing it."

Sarah shook her head vigorously. "No because I'm going to take this longer rope and attach it at each end to our harnesses. That way you'll always be fastened to me and I'll always be roped to the wall when your clip is undone. The same goes for you. Always keep your harness fastened to the cable whenever I have to lift my clip over a piton. That way we always have at least one secure attachment to the wall and we can't fall. We *can't.*"

"Would that cable take the weight of two of us if we fell?"

"Danny those pitons are driven so hard into this rock you could dangle a bus on them."

Daniela picked up her rucksack and took a deep breath. "Ok let's do it."

Sarah's elaborate preparations were almost entirely psychological. With the security of the ropes holding her to the wall Daniela's fears were greatly reduced. Also comforting was Sarah's close presence for they were never more than a few feet apart as they edged gingerly across the traverse. Daniela realised that she was in the hands of a very competent young woman and her confidence grew by the minute. Her fears were in her mind after all. Sarah would never let her fall. They forged a bonding on that horrifying face with their boot heels teetering over the void below. They placed their lives in each other's hands and though they may remove the rope that held them together once the hazard was passed Daniela knew in her heart that the rope would always be there tying them together forever. As Sarah negotiated a passage over one of the metal spikes holding the cable to the cliff Daniela realised in shock that Sarah trusted her to keep her attachment to the cable as she unfastened her own spring clip. For brief seconds Sarah's life was held by a rope to Daniela and Daniela found her breath taken by the trust Sarah held in her.

It seemed like an age crossing that traverse although, in reality, they were over in a few minutes. At the end they scrambled up a cleft through the rocks and found themselves in an extraordinary place. From any distance the peak of the Lysengrat looked like a jagged saw-toothed edge falling away precipitously to either side. In point of fact however the sharp edge was notched. A groove several metres long ran the length of the edge and within the groove you were surrounded on both sides by flat walls of rock and entirely cocooned from the cliffs on either side. It was an unexpected sanctuary; a safe haven of security in this bizarre alpine wilderness.

The two girls flopped to the ground in this cleft exuberantly. "We did it." Sarah declared triumphantly and Daniela laughed aloud. She began to understand the thrill of these mountain challenges. It was almost the same exhilaration you felt after walking from the stage after a successful concert with the adrenaline coursing through your veins and feeling as though you could do anything.

Daniela leaned against the rock and laughed. "I don't believe I just did that." she declared. "Part of me is telling me that I'm mad and the other part wants to go back and do it again just to prove I can."

Sarah giggled. "You were great Danny. She eased her rucksack off and began to unfasten her harness. "Well that's the worst thing I'm going to ask you to do today. We won't need all this clobber now."

They divested themselves of their safety apparatus and Sarah began to pack it away in her rucksack. She coiled up the longer rope that had secured them to each other and was about to stow it away when Daniela stopped her. "Is that expensive?" she asked.

Sarah paused in consideration. "No not really. You can buy decent quality carabiners for about thirty francs each. This is a professionally prepared safety line but it won't cost you much more than a hundred francs or so."

"Are we going to need it again on this trip?"

"I doubt it."

"Well then may I have it? May I have it as a souvenir of what we just did? It would mean a lot to me Sarah."

Sarah pondered for a moment thoughtfully. "Well it'll cost you."

"Name your price."

"A kiss!"

Daniela laughed and grasped Sarah to her. "It's a pleasure doing business with you my lady Sarah!"

Chapter Eight

The rest of the Lysengrat was easy for it was merely a scramble up and down the clefts in the rock and, after that, there was just a steep descent to a broad grassy shoulder that descended more gently to the Rotsteinpass. This shoulder was ample reward for their exertions on the Lysengrat for it was a piece of paradise set among the astonishing scenery of the surrounding mountains. The whole mountainside at this point seemed to be ablaze with colour for the south facing slope was awash in a bewildering variety of alpine flowers. The slope gleamed with golds, whites, pinks, reds, blues and violets set among a verdant green as if some particularly excitable impressionist artist had taken leave of his senses and daubed the mountainside with every colour he could find on his palette. Nature had gone slightly mad here and indulged itself extravagantly, swathing the meadows and rocks in vivid hues. They walked slowly through this floral wonderland, breath taken by its richness and clutching each other's hand, barely daring to speak less their words somehow sully the glory of the beauty around them. The sun was high by now and the butterflies were on the wing; skippers, whites, browns, gaudy fritillaries, big Apollos, jewel like blues, tortoiseshells and clouded yellows; so many of them and in such a variety of colours it seemed as if the flowers of the meadows were taking wing.

They paused often to examine the flowers and at one point Sarah became excited about a butterfly. She dropped her rucksack to the ground and reached inside its apparently bottomless depths. She pulled out the last thing that Daniela expected her to. Daniela blinked in puzzlement. At first glance the object appeared to be a badminton racket. Then she took a closer look. It was in fact... a badminton racket. It was heavily modified however. In place of the strings Sarah had fashioned a long, fine-meshed, muslin net. "My butterfly net." She explained. Then she reached into her rucksack once more and produced a jam jar containing a few twigs.

"What the hell else have you got in there?" asked Daniela with a laugh. "It's like the bloody Tardis your rucksack. I half expect us to stop for a picnic and you pulling out a bloody barbecue grill or something."

Sarah laughed but then suddenly jumped to her feet. "Oops there's one!" With that she dashed off over the slope wielding her butterfly net. Daniela sat on a rock and watched her with deep affection. After a hot pursuit Sarah captured her butterfly and transferred it from her net to the jam jar.

"Are you going to kill it?" asked Daniela as Sarah retraced her steps to where Daniela was sitting.

"No of course not. I just need to identify it. The differences between some species of butterfly are so small that you need to examine them at close quarters to tell them apart. So I just trap him in the jar for a minute or two. I always put a few twigs in there so that they'll stop flapping about and settle on one so I can take a good look."

Daniela peered at Sarah's capture. It was a relatively drab, brown butterfly with pale orange markings on its wings. "Well!" she declared, "That looks just about the most uninteresting butterfly on this mountainside. I'll bet you're about to tell me that it's anything but though."

Sarah nodded delightedly. "Yes it's quite a rare species Danny and generally very localised. Actually the lack of features on it is almost a feature in itself. This is a male so he has two tiny nearly invisible dark spots on each of his forewings. In the female they'd have white centres."

"So what is it?"

"It's a Mnestra's Ringlet Danny; *Erebia mnestra*. I've known about this colony on this slope for years now.

75

They tend to be very local and attached to one small area. This is the only colony I know of in the Toggenburg-Alpstein region but, because they're difficult to identify at a distance, I may have overlooked others. It's a bit high for their altitudinal range here because we're over two thousand metres but I think it's because this is such a sunny slope that they can reach higher here. I think colonies of them are commoner in southern Switzerland; the Valais in particular. They're a rarity so far north."

"Who else knows about them here Sarah?"

Sarah scratched her head in puzzlement. "Why I don't know that anyone does Danny. It's not exactly the sort of thing that you normally discuss with people."

Daniela shook her head. "That's criminal Sarah. All your years on these mountains amount to an encyclopaedic knowledge of their fauna and flora. You ought to share that knowledge Sarah. You might be carrying around a priceless body of data on the natural eco-system of this region. You ought to write it all down."

"Well I keep field diaries."

"Then you ought to publish them. You may be carrying completely unknown knowledge in that pretty head of yours. God only knows what you know about the plants and animals around here."

Sarah grinned. "I know. Sometimes it's amazing what turns up. A few years ago an amateur naturalist was messing around on the Chaserugg. That's the mountain we went up on the cable car. Well he discovered a species of grasshopper entirely new to science. In all the world, that grasshopper is only known from the Chaserugg and the mountain next to it; the Gamserugg. It's never been found anywhere else! It scares me sometimes to think what we might be missing that's lurking around in these mountains somewhere." Sarah smiled ruefully and opened the jam jar. "Let's let this little fellow go." The butterfly flew quickly away over the meadows and disappeared over the brow of the slope.

They watched it go in pleasure. Sarah jumped to her feet and held out a hand to help Daniela up. "Onwards to the Rotsteinpass Danny. I'm hoping you'll get to meet Rudi."

"Who is Rudi?"

"Ah now that's a *big* surprise."

They dropped down the last of the shoulder and the little mountain hut at Rotsteinpass came into view nestling in the deep pass between the shoulder of the Santis and the steep cliffs that towered above towards the Altmann. As they approached the hut Daniela yipped in excitement. "Look Sarah! There are some of those goats; what did you call them; Ibex."

Sarah perused the small herd with her binoculars. "Yes it's a party of males Danny. The sexes tend to segregate sexually outside the rutting season with the bucks forming their own herds and the does and dams with the kids in separate herds."

"I always thought that you called males and females Billy and Nanny goats."

"Well you can do. Generally though, the two terms are interchangeable. Mostly you call domestic breeds by those names. I prefer to use the more formal term for wild animals."

"There're a lot of them Sarah. There must be nearly twenty of them in that herd."

"Twenty three actually. I just counted them. I like to keep tabs on the numbers."

Daniela laughed delightedly. "You're something else Sarah." They walked on toward the hut. "Do you think they're open Sarah?" asked Daniela.

"Yes they've got the flag flying outside. We can grab a coffee here if you like."

Daniela snorted. "They'll probably be grateful for the custom. They can't be doing much business. We haven't seen a soul on the trail since we left the Santis."

"Oh they do alright. They can get quite busy in the high season. There are four separate hiking trails that meet up on this pass."

The Ibex seemed totally unconcerned as they approached the hut and merely drifted away down the pass. Sarah and Daniela dumped their rucksacks on the floor by the wooden tables and benches outside the hut gratefully. Daniela regarded the towering cliff face in front of them acerbically. "I'm making a shrewd guess that we're going to be climbing that sod shortly."

"Yes that's the Fliswand; the way up to Altmannsattel."

"I'll make a further guess that you're about to tell me that it's not as bad as it looks."

Sarah giggled. "That's right."

Daniela shrugged with a grin. "Oh the hell with it! I'm feeling so happy that if you told me we were going for a light stroll up the Eiger Nordwand I'd probably go along with you."

Sarah laughed. "It'll be easier than the Lysengrat believe me. It's a funny wall. The only hairy bits are near the bottom. It gets easier and safer the higher you get." She looked around. "There doesn't seem to be anyone around. I'll go in and see if I can find someone. What do you want to drink?"

"I'll have a beer. I know it's still early but I've got a hell of a thirst and I'd love a cold beer."

Sarah glanced at her watch. "Well it's nearly twelve o'clock so it's not that disgraceful. I think I'll have one too." Sarah disappeared into the hut. She couldn't find anyone and assumed that the proprietor and his staff must be out doing some maintenance on the trail. She helped herself to two beers from behind the counter and scribbled a quick note, leaving the money on top. As she re-emerged into the sunlight she saw Daniela gesticulating wildly and pointing at something behind the hut.

"Sarah!" hissed Daniela, "Look! It's a bloody great eagle!" Perched on a rock a little behind the hut was an enormous dark bird of prey, well over a metre long, clutching what appeared to be a bloody bone in its talon. It regarded them suspiciously with curiously beady white eyes set in its almost primitive looking head and opened its wings briefly; enormous great wings fully three metres in span. Daniela was regarding the creature with awe. Sarah put down the beers with a satisfied smirk.

"So you've met Rudi then?"

"Rudi? Is that what you call him? He just appeared from nowhere! Scared the shit out of me. I thought it was fucking Pterodactyl or something. Is it an eagle?"

Sarah shook her head. "No Rudi's not an eagle. He's a vulture. To be more precise he's a Bearded Vulture."

"Am I losing the plot Sarah? Surely we don't have vultures in the Swiss Alps."

"We do now Danny or rather we do again. Bearded Vultures were once common in the Alps but the farmers and shepherds regarded them as vermin and persecuted them. They exterminated the last at the beginning of the twentieth century. I think the last one was shot in 1913."

"So what the hell's this beast doing here?"

"It's a re-introduced bird Danny. Some years ago they started a project to reintroduce Bearded Vultures to the Alps at four sites in Austria, Switzerland and France. They were raised in captive breeding programmes in various zoos and released as young birds in National Parks. They've released over a hundred all told up until now. Rudi here was originally let loose in the Swiss National Park in the lower Engadine. He's just over two years old and still not fully adult which explains his all dark plumage although I note he's getting a bit lighter on his breast. The full adult birds are handsome creatures. In captivity they have a pale yellow breast but in the wild they bathe in iron oxide rich pools and stain their under-parts a deep rusty red. Rudi wandered over here last year. He sort of hung around a while and then drifted away. He kept coming back to visit however and he's been here at the Rotsteinpass for a few weeks now, presumably because the owners feed him. They shouldn't really."

"Why not?"

"Well the birds are hand reared in captivity Danny and what you're really hoping is that they learn to be independent and find food for themselves when you release them into the wild. They try to wean them off dependency on human beings. So it's a bit naughty to keep feeding Rudi although I suppose we don't have a lot of options around here."

"Why's that?"

"Well I guess we're just too tidy. The Alpstein is a watershed providing drinking water for all the communities around it so the authorities tend to be ultra-cautious when it comes to leaving dead carcasses lying around. Any dead animals get cleared away as soon as they're seen which might be fine for our peace of mind when it comes to the purity of our water but it's bad news for vultures."

"So they eat carrion?"

"Oh yes. All vultures are essentially carrion eaters. Bearded Vultures are a bit special though. Most of the carcass they ignore. They just eat the bones. Ninety percent of their diet consists of bones."

"Oh come on Sarah! That can't be true. How can a bird however big it is eat bones? It's not as if it's got teeth or anything."

"It's true Danny. Some older guides say they just eat the marrow out of the bones but it's not true. They eat the whole lot. Their stomach acids can digest bone."

"How the hell do they get them down?"

"Ah that's one of the bits of magic about them. They pick up the bones in their talons and fly up in the air and drop them on rocks to smash them into small pieces. Once it's broken up they just swoop down and gobble up the bits."

"Incredible! So this bird keeps coming back here because he gets fed?"

"Yes. Oh there are initiatives in Switzerland now to leave animal carcasses alone. Dead animals are after all part of the food chain. I think we're being overly paranoid about cleaning up corpses. In the Swiss National Park any animal that dies is left where it falls which makes it ideal for the vultures. I don't suggest for a minute that it would be acceptable to leave carcasses lying around in stream beds or whatever but you've seen how dry the mountains are in this region. Most of the water is well underground and ninety nine times out of a hundred the risks of contamination are minimal."

"Did the people that run the hut call him Rudi then?"

"No that was the name he was given before he was released. Every bird in the re-introduction program is given a name and marked with distinctive white stripes in its tail or wing feathers so it can be easily identified and monitored after release. Rudi's mostly moulted out of his marked plumage by now but he's pretty much well known. Still he's going to have to shift before he gets much older or he won't find a mate since he's the only vulture in the region so far. Vultures aren't exactly known for promiscuity. They breed slowly. I think there were only about a dozen identified breeding pairs out of the introduction last year and in at least five cases they were unsuccessful."

"Do you think he's going to fly up and drop that bone he's holding onto something?"

"I hope so. I've never seen one do that although I've seen a few now. My father took me to see some of the earlier releases in the Swiss National Park when I was a kid. We had one soaring on a thermal above us. They're a fantastic sight in the air with that huge wingspan and their diamond shaped tails. There's a story that in warmer countries they even pick up wild tortoises to drop them and crack them open to eat. I don't know how much truth there is in that though. There's an old legend that the Greek playwright Aeschylus was killed by a tortoise dropped on his head in 458 BC by what was said to be an eagle but some people now think must have been a Bearded Vulture."

"I think they're amazing Sarah. I've never even heard of a Bearded Vulture before."

"Well make sure you remember the name. Ignorant English birdwatchers often call them Lammergeiers which is a terrible misnomer."

"Why?"

"Well it's a German name but not the accepted one. Actually it's an old peasant's name for them. Geier means vulture and Lammer means lambing or lamb killing so the word translates most closely as lamb killing vulture. It grows out of the ignorant misapprehension that the vultures killed lambs and it was for that reason that they were shot or poisoned to extinction. Of course lambs die all the time in the mountains for all sorts of reasons and when they do the vultures will feed on the carcasses. Naturally, therefore, when some old shepherd saw a vulture eating one of his precious lambs he assumed that the bird had killed it. They don't of course. They're carrion eaters but it's the sort of bad name that caused them to be so persecuted. Nowadays it is the ultimate ornithological political incorrectness to call them Lammergeiers. I don't know why English birdwatchers persist in referring to them by such an archaic, discredited German name when there's a perfectly acceptable English name for them. They'd soon be pissed off if someone called a Goshawk a pheasant killing vermin. If they insist on calling them a German name then why don't they use the correct name which is Bartgeier. Bart means beard so the exact translation of Bartgeier is Bearded Vulture. It's also more closely a translation of the Latin name for them which is *Gypaetus barbatus.*" Sarah paused with a laugh. "I'm sorry I'm starting to rant."

"I'll buy you a soapbox when we get home."

Sarah grinned and pushed a bottle over to Daniela. "Come on drink your beer before it gets warm. There was no one in the hut so I left the money on the counter."

They sat and drank in contentment watching the enormous raptor picking at its bone in a desultory fashion. Daniela produced her camera to take some shots of it. She was rapidly accumulating a fine photographic record of alpine fauna and flora. Finally, when it appeared that Rudi was in a lethargic mood and unlikely to put on a performance for them they set out once more; this time to conquer the imposing Fliswand that towered over the pass.

Despite its foreboding appearance Daniela found the Fliswand relatively straightforward after the scary Lysengrat and they crested out on the saddle high above in a little over fifty minutes. Whilst technically not very demanding it was nevertheless hard work for the sun was now hot on the mountain flank and the girls were perspiring freely by the time they reached the high saddle. Daniela wiped an arm across her brow. "Whew that was quite a climb. How far did we just come up?"

Sarah flopped down on a handy rock and extracted her water bottle from her rucksack. "Well the Rotsteinpass is around two thousand one hundred and twenty metres in altitude and we're at two thousand three hundred and sixty eight here so we've just done about two hundred and fifty metres straight up."

Daniela nodded towards the dome like peak further along the saddle before them. "And that's the Altmann is it?"

"Yes. It translates as old man in English. When it's got snow on it it's supposed to look like an old man's face. I can't see it myself."

"How high is it?"

"Two thousand four hundred and thirty five."

83

"So we're less than a hundred metres in altitude from the summit?"

"Oh yes. We could probably take the summit in less than an hour from here. I don't think you'd enjoy it though. It's basically just a scramble up a smooth slippery rock face with a nasty sting in the tail right at the top where you have to edge over a horrible little rock bridge. It's only really worth doing just to be able to say you have. I think we'll leave that one for another day."

"Suits me. I'm knackered after that climb and I don't think I've got anything else to prove today. Which way are we heading now then?"

"Straight along the ridge and around the Altmann. After that we drop down through a gully onto a lovely series of terraces and grassy shoulders. It's a beautiful region. I thought we could stop for a picnic there with our packed lunch. From there it's a straightforward descent to the Fahlensee."

Sarah was right. Beyond the grey stone wall of the Altmann they dropped down into a region of such captivating beauty that Daniela was instantly enchanted. They found a little hollow sheltered among the limestone rocks that seemed just perfect in its charm. It was covered in short grass so verdant and velvety that it seemed like a manicured lawn dotted with tiny alpine flowers. It was the perfect place to stop for lunch and they dropped their rucksacks in delight. "My God! This is gorgeous!" exclaimed Daniela and she literally twirled in pleasure with her arms held wide.

Sarah took out their lunch and laid it out on the short turf as Daniela eased off her boots and socks and enjoyed the luxury of the grass on her bare feet. "How are your feet?" Sarah asked.

Daniela sat down to rub them carefully. "Not bad actually. I expected to be half crippled with blisters by now but those boots are really comfortable and, apart from being a bit whiffy, there's not a thing wrong with my feet." Daniela tossed off her cap and shook her hair loose. "I tell you one thing though. I'm getting bloody warm. I'm going to change into something a bit cooler." With that she fumbled in her rucksack and extracted a little cotton white dress and shook it out. "Hmm a bit crumpled but perfectly alright considering we're hardly needing to conform to social conventions up here."

Sarah laughed at her. "And to think you made fun of the contents of *my* rucksack. Are you carrying your whole summer collection in there?"

"At least I'm not humping about an entire entomological field laboratory with me. Be a darling Sarah and chuck me one of those sandwiches and an apple."

Sarah complied and Daniela took a bite of bread and cheese and began to peel off her shirt and jeans. It seemed that when Daniela determined to change her clothes she intended to do the job properly for she slipped out of underwear too and kneeled down to fold and pack her discarded apparel back in her rucksack. Sarah blinked in shocked embarrassment. "Danny! What are you doing? You haven't got a stitch on!"

Daniela glanced down at herself as if only just realising that she was completely naked. "So? Nobody here but us chickens right?"

"You can't just disport yourself naked on a mountain top Danny. What if someone comes hiking over that ridge?"

"Sarah dear, sometimes in concerts I've had to change costumes as many as five or six times. You've no idea how fast I can jump into a set of clothes." Daniela leaned back on her elbows and luxuriated in the caress of the breeze on her naked skin. "Hmm heavenly."

Sarah caught her breath. The vision of Daniela naked and reclining on the short green alpine grass surrounded by flowers and her hair loose in the breeze was heart-breakingly beautiful. She looked like some mythical, golden haired, mountain nymph; wild and free in some fantasy world of a bygone era. Sarah realised she had been staring. She blushed and turned her face away. The motion did not go unnoticed by Daniela. She chuckled softly. "You *can* look at me Sarah you know."

"I... I'm embarrassed Danny."

"What? By my naked body? Why on earth should you be? Am I hideous?"

"You know you're not."

"So you don't actually find my naked body repulsive?"

"You... you're beautiful and you know it."

"Well if you think I'm beautiful why don't you look at me? You have no such inhibitions about looking at a beautiful flower. I don't mind you looking at me. On the contrary; call me vain if you will but I revel in the fact that you think I'm beautiful and I love you to look at me and enjoy the sight."

"Danny you're impossible."

"Oh no Sarah. I'm all *too* possible. Come on look at me. Take a really good long look. I dare you." Reluctantly Sarah lifted her head and looked at Daniela bashfully. Daniela was smiling. "There now that wasn't so bad was it? I'm just a girl without her clothes on. Nothing earth shakingly terrible there is there?"

"Except that you just happen to be the most beautiful girl I've ever seen without her clothes on."

Daniela smiled seductively. "Why thank you Sarah." She stroked a languid hand across her bosom. "Do you like my breasts?"

"Stop it Danny! You're teasing me."

Daniela threw back her head in laughter. "Of course I am." Then she looked at Sarah soberly. "Seriously though Sarah you mustn't feel shy to admire my body. I look at yours all the time."

"You're a wicked, ruthless seductress."

"But obviously not a very good one since after three weeks of my best efforts I still haven't got you into bed alone."

Sarah threw a sandwich wrapping at her. "Behave yourself Danny and put some damn clothes on."

Daniela poked her tongue out. "Shan't! I'm enjoying the wind on my body."

"Seriously Danny you shouldn't expose your skin too long to the sun. You can burn to a crisp up here."

"Well if you're that concerned about my dermatological health you could always volunteer to smear me all over with protective sun cream."

Sarah shook her head with a laugh. "You're just incorrigible."

Daniela looked at her wickedly. "Ok take your clothes off Sarah."

"*WHAT?*"

"I said take your clothes off. I want to see you naked."

"You are stark, staring barking mad!"

"Come on Sarah. You've seen me undressed. Now it's my turn. I want to see you without your clothes on."

"I... I can't do it."

"Now *there's* a familiar expression. I seem to have spent the last two days saying that, every time you've asked me to tackle some bloody cliff face when every rational sense in my body is telling me to run away screaming in the opposite direction. Well I found I could do it after all and so can you. And after all I'm not asking you to risk your life, just a few moments of embarrassment. That's not much to ask for."

"I... I'm shy."

"Oh Sarah I've seen you undressed before. I had you stripped down to your knickers the first afternoon you got free from the Hotel Toggenburg. There's not a lot of you I haven't seen yet. Come on just for a minute. I dare you."

Sarah swallowed. "Oh all right. Just for a minute though."

"That's my girl." Sarah stripped out of her clothes shyly and Daniela never took her eyes from her. Sarah finally sat on the grass naked, holding her arms protectively in front of her and blushing furiously. Daniela wasn't satisfied. "Put your arms down. Let me see you properly."

"I can't believe you've persuaded me to sit as naked as the day I was born at two thousand three hundred metres up a bloody mountain Danny." Sarah grumbled but she complied nervously.

Daniela sat back on her heels and gazed at Sarah in shockingly open admiration. "You are so, so, so beautiful Sarah." She sighed in deep satisfaction. "Will you do something for me Sarah?"

"What?" asked Sarah suspiciously.

"Will you let me paint you one day; paint you just like you are now; naked and free in the garden of your mountains?"

"Oh bloody hell!"

"Please Sarah. Pretty please."

"I... I'll think about it."

"Thank you." With an unexpected fluid motion Daniela rose and crossed the gap between them to kneel in front of Sarah.

Sarah started and backed away a little nervously. "What are you going to do?"

Daniela snaked out her arms and placed them around Sarah's neck. "I'm going to kiss you. No harm there is there? I mean I thought we'd crossed this bridge some time ago. We have kissed before."

"Not when we're both stark naked we haven't."

"Well then we've been denying ourselves the pleasure of it haven't we?" Daniela leaned forward to touch her forehead against Sarah's "Just a little kiss Sarah." she murmured. Sarah was lost. Daniela's naked closeness was intoxicating and her head felt light and dizzy as she turned her lips to be embraced. The kiss started light and gentle but quickly escalated into urgency. Daniela teased Sarah's lips apart with her tongue and her hand slid to Sarah's back to pull her close.

Sarah felt the swell of Daniela's breasts against her own and she was shocked when she involuntarily moaned with rising desire. She had nothing left. She knew that within seconds Daniela would gently push her onto her back among the soft grass and the flowers and she would not be able to resist. The heat in her body was betraying her. Daniela had her at her mercy.

Then Daniela glanced over Sarah's shoulder and froze. She leaned forward to whisper into Sarah's ear. "Turn around really slowly and look behind you Sarah."

Sarah stiffened with alarm. "Is someone coming?" she hissed.

"No, no. It's a bird; a funny bird. He just walked out from the rocks behind you."

Sarah turned slowly to look. A dark brown grouse with white wings and under parts and a red crest over its eye was stalking carefully along in the short turf a few metres behind them. Sarah let out her breath. "It's a Ptarmigan Danny; a sort of high mountain grouse. There're loads of them on the mountains. I was wondering when we'd see one. There was one calling from the scree slopes just under the Altmannsattel earlier and we had loads around the Santis calling last night but they wouldn't show themselves. He's a male in summer plumage. In winter they're completely white apart from that red mark over their eyes."

"He seems very tame."

"Oh as long as we don't make any sudden movements he'll probably ignore us. Sometimes they react to a threat by freezing on the ground and blending into the background until you're right on top of them. You wouldn't believe the number of times I've nearly had a heart attack when one's exploded from under my feet a second before I trod on it."

Daniela was watching the bird intently. "Hmm. I wonder."

She slowly disengaged herself from Sarah and eased over to her rucksack. She reached in and withdrew

89

her camera. Sarah covered herself with her arms in agitation. "If you dare to take a photograph of me like this I'll... I'll..."

"Keep still! I'm trying to photograph the bird, you muppet." The bird was most cooperative and Daniela took two or three photos before it unconcernedly disappeared once more among the rocks. Daniela put her camera away in satisfaction and picked up her sandwich to take a bite. "Pass me the water bottle Sarah please."

Sarah reached over for the bottle marvelling at her sudden escape. Daniela had switched off the sexual tension with the suddenness of a light switch. She was munching away at her sandwich unconcernedly and apparently quite oblivious to the fact that, a minute before, they had been within seconds of consummating their passion in the grass. Sarah felt conflicting emotions of relief, frustration and bewilderment. Daniela had released her; released at the very moment she had had her totally at her subjugation. Sarah didn't understand it. Daniela's mercurial mood changes baffled her. She passed the water bottle to Daniela with trembling hands. Daniela took it with a thank you and finished off her sandwich. She picked up the crisp green apple and polished it on the side of her arm and then, because she needed two hands to unscrew the bottle, she jammed the apple between her teeth.

Sarah suddenly giggled. "You look just like a pig."

Daniela glanced at her sharply and removed the apple from her mouth. "What? Did you just call me a pig?"

"With that apple in your mouth. You looked like a suckling pig ready for roasting."

Daniela regarded her sourly. "Well this will make an interesting call to the mountain rescue services won't it? "Can you come quickly please? There's a naked girl lying injured on the Altmann. I think she's been beaned by a Granny Smith's."

Sarah giggled helplessly. "You looked funny." They ate contentedly, naked on the grass and for the first time Sarah found herself at ease in her nudity. It was true that the breeze felt refreshing on the naked skin and Daniela made no further advances but chattered away as if it was the most natural thing in the world to be sharing a picnic completely naked. Daniela was so uninhibited about her nakedness and so relaxed in her flesh that Sarah was quite disarmed and soon she barely noticed her undressed state. Even when Daniela prevailed upon her to rub some sun lotion on her shoulders, the act was more one of caring friendship rather than sensual. Daniela's ability to manipulate the mood from sexual immediacy to affectionate but platonic intimacy was almost frightening. She was an absolute artist in the creation of mood Sarah realised. This was a woman that could hold large audiences spellbound and tied to her will and emotion. Sarah felt like putty in her hands.

At last Daniela brushed the crumbs from her breasts and picked up her short dress. "You're right Sarah. We'd better get dressed. My skin is turning pink already. I'll put some cream on my legs. Why don't you put your little white dress on? It's hot."

"Yes I think I will." Daniela pulled her own dress over her shoulders and tugged it down to her calves before packing her previous clothes in her rucksack. She squatted on the ground to pull on her socks and boots. "Danny!" Sarah cried accusingly. "You forgot to put your knickers back on."

"Och dinna fash yerself the noo wee bairn. The lassies in the Highlands gan aboot wi naught beneath their tartan in the Glens. I'm just wantin' ter feel the wind under ma kilt."

"You're not wearing a kilt, you fake Scot you. You're wearing a flimsy little dress. There'll be more people down by the Fahlensee and if the wind gets under that thing there'll be some funny looks going around."

"Nobody will know a thing Sarah." Daniela paused to wink. "Apart from you that is."

"You're the most impossible woman I've ever come across."

"You keep saying that. I don't know why you should think I'm so unattainable."

"You know damn well what I mean."

Daniela laughed and rose to her feet. "Come along Sarah. Get dressed. You'll catch your death of cold walking about like that up here."

"Oh! You... you..."

"Hurry up Sarah. I want to see this lake you keep telling me about."

Chapter Nine

After Sarah had donned her tennis dress, they descended from the mountain. Sarah was not normally a fast hiker. Of course she was fit enough to set a good pace when the need was there but she was always so interested in the alpine world around her that she often lingered to enjoy it or to spend some time observing the nature about her. That said, however, she could rarely have spent a longer time descending a simple route than she did that day. They didn't exactly loiter but their progress was blissfully slow, as if they resented every footstep that took them away from their solitude in the mountains toward the trappings of civilisation below. Remarkably not another soul seemed to be on the trail that day and they walked in peace and tender intimacy, pausing often to admire the surroundings or simply each other; punctuating their languorous steps with gentle touches and stolen kisses. On the flatter parts they walked hand in hand and Daniela would rest her head on Sarah's shoulder and sigh with gladness. Sometimes they placed an arm around the other's waist and, at one point, Daniela let her hand rest on Sarah's bottom as they walked and Sarah felt the touch like a tingling heat through the thin material of her dress.

There were a few steep sections to negotiate through rocky gullies and one of these afforded them amusement for the hem of Daniela's dress caught upon a rock as she slithered down and, had anyone else been present, her modesty would have been irreparably compromised. It was another gully, however, that proved that their blessings of the day were not over. They had just scrambled down a little rocky cliff. To their left a large wall of rock towered above. Sarah gasped suddenly and snatched Daniela's arm and pointed. "Look up there! Just by that big rock sticking out."

Daniela followed her pointing finger. Just discernible against the grey of the rock a tiny bird almost the same colour of the rock was scuttling about, clinging to the vertical wall. "What is it?" she asked.

Sarah grinned in delight. "Now you've *really* been lucky." she told Daniela. "That's the first one I've seen all year."

Daniela peered intently. "I'd have never have spotted that bird if you hadn't pointed it out. It's so well camouflaged that if it didn't move it would just disappear into the background."

"Wait a minute. Let's see if he flies. You'll get a shock then." within a minute the bird did flutter to a position a little lower down.

Daniela gasped in wonder. The little grey bird had suddenly sparkled with bright vermilion wings, edged with black with white spots, like an unexpected jewel detaching itself from the rock face. "My God!" breathed Daniela. "Lend me your binoculars Sarah. I want to see that again just to reassure myself I wasn't hallucinating."

Eagerly Daniela perused the little bird with childlike delight. "Oh God! He's gorgeous. I can just see the red in his wings. How is he clinging on to that rock face? Oh look he's opening his wings again. Oh wow! He's beautiful. What on earth is it Sarah?"

"It's a Wallcreeper Danny; one of the most elusive of all our high alpine birds. It's the bird that every naturalist wants to see when they visit the Alps and just about one of the most difficult there is to find. They need a huge territory of rock face to live in and as you've seen they can be incredibly difficult to spot. They just blend in with the colour of the rock and you're trying to spot one from a couple of kilometres away on a cliff face the size of half a dozen big cathedrals dumped on top of one another. It's always lucky to see one. I bumped into a couple of English birdwatchers on holiday when I was working at the Toggenburg last summer. Frau Fritzl told them to talk to me because I knew where most of the alpine birds were. They were moaning that they hadn't seen a Wallcreeper yet. I don't know what they were thinking. They seemed to think that the mountains must be crawling with them. I wish. If I see three in a year it's been a good year. You've no idea how lucky you are to see that."

"I feel truly blessed. He's beautiful. Oh damn! He's flown away."

Sarah laughed and slapped Daniela on the rump. "Let's be going then."

"Ouch! That hurt."

"Well you should wear more protection on your bottom then. Your scandalous behaviour today merits a good spanking."

Daniela assumed a comical face of childish contrition. "Yeth Tharah." she lisped, "I've been ever thuch a naughty girl. Pleath put me over your knee and thpank my bottom."

Sarah pushed her away with a laugh. "You're hopeless. Come on we're nearly down to the valley. Let's push on."

Before long they were walking along a flat valley bottom along a broad track. The valley floor was carpeted in white and golden buttercups and a few cows grazed on the far side of the alp; their bells and soft lows carried on the breeze across the flowery meadow. There was water here too for a little stream bubbled over gravelly beds beneath little timber bridges by the stone huts of the cowherds. The meadow was marshy in places and lush with green and the stream meandered across it before seeping out in a little delta into the deep alpine lake; the Fahlensee, nestling between the arms of the mountain which plunged down into its tranquil depths. Daniela grasped Sarah's hand and held it to her breast so tightly that Sarah could feel her heart beating. For a moment she seemed lost for words. "Oh Sarah." she breathed at last. "Did we die on the Lysengrat? Are we walking together in paradise?"

"It's lovely isn't it?"

"I've never seen anything like it. Thank you Sarah. Thank you for bringing me here."

Sarah felt a thrill she had never known before. Daniela's eyes were gleaming with joy and her mouth hung open in wonderment. Daniela's reactions were everything Sarah had hoped for. She seemed to regard every new splendour presented to her as a precious gift. Sarah had shown many people her favourite places in the mountains over the years but nobody whose soul seemed so touched by them as Daniela's was. It was sheer pleasure to watch her appreciation; a joy to lay each captivating spectacle before her. Sarah's eyes were everywhere hunting new pleasures to bestow upon her beautiful friend. She touched Daniela's elbow and pointed at the grassy mountainside above. "Look up there Danny. We have visitors."

Daniela peered uncertainly. "Where?"

"Just left from those rocky crags about half way up. Can't you see them?"

"Oh yes! God you must have eyes like laser beams Sarah. I'd never have seen them. Are they Ibex?"

Sarah shook her head. "No Danny they're Chamois. Here take my binoculars and have a look." Daniela took the glasses and scanned the small herd of animals. "See how they've got small black curved horns and dark stripes on their faces? They're in their summer coats. They're much darker in winter; almost black."

"They've got young ones with them Sarah."

"Yes it's a group of females with their kids. The males are usually solitary outside the rutting season. I make it four does and three kids. Is that right?"

"Yes. My word you've got incredible eyes. Are they a sort of goat as well?"

"Yes they're related to goats. There's two species of them in Europe; the type species and the Pyrenean Chamois. Our Swiss chamois are actually a sub-species; the Alpine Chamois; *Rupicapra rupicapra rupicapra*."

"That's a nasty stammer you've got there Sarah."

"I can't help it. That's just the Latin name they've got dumped with."

Daniela handed the binoculars back. "I can't believe the amount of wildlife up in the mountains. I always had the feeling they were rocky barren sort of places."

"Oh God no! Wait till this evening. There's one of my favourites I want to show you. I haven't managed to see any today yet but there's a colony of them near Bollenwies I know of not far from the guest house we're staying at."

"What are they?"

"It's a surprise!"

Daniela laughed. "You love this don't you? You love showing me your mountains."

"Yes. Yes I do." Sarah simpered in pleasure. "Come on there's something really special just along the trail I want you to see."

The path wound around the side of the still lake on a broad ledge and the sunny scrubby sides of the track were riotous with alpine blooms; so many sorts that Daniela's head swam in bewilderment. Sarah was hunting something special however. She paused by a large out cropping of rock and dropped her rucksack to the ground and scrambled up the rock examining the ground intensely. Daniela watched from below in puzzlement. Sarah yipped in triumph. "Found one! Come up here Danny. I want to show you something." Daniela divested herself of her rucksack in amusement and climbed up to join Sarah. Sarah was gleefully stooped over a little flower and holding it gently for Daniela to see. "Look what I've found." she declared exuberantly.

Daniela stooped to look. The flower was a greyish white tiny plant with silvery grey leaves. The flower itself consisted of numerous hairy white petals around a greenish cluster of inner sepals. Daniela gasped. "Oh God! It's Edelweiss isn't it?"

Sarah nodded gleefully. "Yes it is. Do you like it?"

"Of course I do. I've never seen it in the wild before. Did you know it was here?"

"Oh yes. I've known about this little colony for years. A lot of the time Edelweiss grows in pretty inaccessible places. That's usually because it grows mostly above two thousand metres in rocky places. I rather suspect however that it's less common in easily accessible places because people pick it."

"Let me get my camera." Daniela slithered down the rock to return with her camera and snap some photos. Sarah seemed racked with a dilemma. Daniela regarded her curiously. "What's the matter Sarah?"

"I want to do something Danny; something very naughty; something I've never done before in my life."

"And that is?"

In answer Sarah took a deep breath and bent down to select one of the little flowers. Carefully she plucked it and held it out for Daniela. "For you." She said.

Daniela took the tiny bloom gently. "Why is this naughty Sarah?"

"Because it's a protected flower Danny. I shouldn't really pick it at all. I've never done that before."

"Then why did you do it Sarah?"

Sarah blushed deeply. "Do you know the significance of the Edelweiss here in the Alps Danny?"

"Enlighten me."

Sarah swallowed uncomfortably. "It's the ultimate flower of love Danny. Because it grows in high places it was dangerous to collect, so young men would risk their lives to go into the mountains to bring their lady friends Edelweiss to prove their love for them. To give a person Edelweiss is a declaration of love."

"Oh Sarah!"

Sarah shook her head with a rueful laugh. "God I don't know why I did that. I... I never did anything like that before in my life."

Daniela touched her. "Sarah I'm going to put this carefully in a pocket in my rucksack. I have a little box I can use. When I get home I'm going to press it, preserve it and then mount it in a frame to hang on my wall so I can look at it and think of you."

"For God's sake don't tell anyone *I* picked it. I'm forever berating people for picking protected flowers."

"It will remain precious to me Sarah. I promise you."

"You keep making me do things I never thought I would Danny."

"Well long may the trend continue my love." She stood and helped Sarah to her feet. "Come darling. Let's walk on. We have an evening and night of magic to look forward to and then another day of wonder tomorrow and beyond that.... well we shall see. Let's walk on my love. Every step we make takes us further into adventure. The future lies at our feet."

Chapter Ten

The final walk to the mountain guest house at Bollenwies was bliss. It was not a bliss of exuberance or unfettered exhilaration but more a deep satisfaction; a completeness of being; a serenity of wholeness as if there was no other place in the world you would rather be or any other person with whom you would wish to share this moment. For the most part, they walked in silence. Words enough had been said. It was now the time to enjoy the fact that they had been said; to walk hand in hand with peace between you and know that you were not alone. To the right lay the tranquil waters of the Fahlensee; the breeze barely rippling its surface as it mirrored the peaks surrounding it in its placid quietude. On the left the mountain flank rose high above them but, in the scrubby banks that abutted their path, the mountain flowers shimmered in the sunlight, dominated in places by the yellow foxgloves of which bloom, they might have considered, was extracted the drug digitalis; efficacious in the regulation of the heartbeat of one's life.

There were other people on the trail here for the Fahlensee was well known and loved. Sarah clung to Daniela's hand on the broad trail and, for the first time, she was not timid to do so. That other people saw her so closely joined, worried her not. On the contrary; she was proud of the woman that walked beside her; revelled in her visible presence. Let people look. Let them see that this was an extraordinary woman and let them see that she belonged to her. Perhaps it was a momentary illusion; a fantasy of the mountain world in which they walked but they surrendered to the fantasy; gloried in it and cared not what anyone else in the world might think.

But realities impinged upon them nevertheless. As they came closer to the guest house at Bollenwees, the beautiful wooden building set upon a rocky terrace at the far end of the lake, it was obvious that there were many guests at the house. Daniela's fame threatened the solitude of their companionship so, with a sigh, she pulled her baseball cap low on her head, tied her hair in a ponytail and donned dark sunglasses. The disguise was crude and improvised but it seemed effective for nobody recognised her as they walked up to the guest house and took a seat on the sunny terrace overlooking the lake.

Daniela lifted her skirt and lowered herself onto the wooden bench at their table opposite Sarah. She squeaked comically and rose quickly. "Eek! That bench is cold."

Sarah leaned across to castigate her in an exasperated whisper. "I've no sympathy Miss Devin. I told you to put some knickers on."

Daniela poked her tongue out and fumbled in her rucksack, emerging with a light blue angora wool pullover which was presumably her interpretation of cold weather wear in the mountains. She folded the pullover carefully, placed it on the bench and sat on it. "That's better." she declared smugly before wriggling mischievously. "Tickles a bit mind."

"You're a disgrace." Sarah told her.

"Stop telling me off Sarah. I've told you what to do if I've been naughty."

"Hmmph!" Sarah looked around. At least three quarters of the tables on the terrace were occupied. "I'd better go and let the owners know we're here Danny. They look like they're kind of busy. You stay here with our gear and I'll see if I can find them. I might as well get a drink at the same time. Do you want a beer?"

"Yes please. It's my round though. You got the beers at Rotsteinpass."

"Yes but you paid for nearly everything on the Santis last night so put your money away."

"Sarah I've got the stuff to burn."

"Then burn it Danny. Just stop giving it to me."

Daniela looked at Sarah seriously. "I'm not trying to buy you. You don't think that do you?"

"No Danny. I don't. It's just that... well I feel uncomfortable living off your money. Oh know you're rich Daniela but I don't want to feel like a kept woman or something. I'm not impoverished Danny. I can pay my own way. Call me silly if you will but it's a matter of pride."

Daniela grasped Sarah's hand. "Sarah if that's what it takes to win you I'll sell all my possessions and give all my money away to charity. We'll go and live in a little bedsitter somewhere and I'll go and sing in the local pub to make ends meet. I've been broke before Sarah. It doesn't frighten me. We'll cook together on a two ring gas stove and share a single bed and I'd consider myself the richest woman alive."

"Dreamer! It couldn't happen and you know it. You're already famous. You can't turn the clock back."

Daniela lowered her head sadly. "I know but it's nice to dream sometimes."

Sarah stood up. "I'll go and find the owners."

"I suppose they're expecting us."

"Of course. I phoned up from the Santis last night to tell them to expect us and our projected route."

Berggasthaus Bollenwees was another family run affair and Sarah quickly located the proprietor's wife who was dispensing drinks over the counter to a pair of overworked looking waitresses who were ferrying them out to guests on the terrace. Her eyes lit up when she saw Sarah approach. "Hoi Sarah. You got here then?"

"Gruezi Frau Manser. Yes we made it all right although we're a bit late. We took our time over the tops."

"Well it's good to see you Sarah. My word it must be more than a year since the last time you were here. How are you keeping?"

They exchanged pleasantries for a minute or two before Sarah broached the subject that was concerning her. "Er you seem to be quite busy Frau Manser."

"Damn yes! We're rushed off our feet at the moment. I can't think where all these people have come from. Don't worry though I've enough room in the matratzenlage for you and your friend. You did say you were coming with a friend didn't you?"

"Yes that's right."

"Where is this friend?"

"Oh outside on the terrace with our rucksacks. Er it's about them I wanted to talk to you."

"Yes?"

"Well I know that I told you that we needed two places in the dormitory but there might be a problem there. I was wondering... er... if you had any double rooms left."

Frau Manser raised an eyebrow. "Are you with the boyfriend Sarah?"

Sarah shook her head vigorously, knowing she was blushing. "No, no! My boyfriend's still in America. I'm with a friend, a girlfriend... I mean a girl I know and it's just that... well it would be more convenient for us not to have to share with other people."

Frau Manser frowned and rubbed her chin. "Well I wish you'd let me know beforehand Sarah. Most of my single rooms and family rooms are taken. I've just got the one double room with a shower left but it's seventy two francs a head with breakfast Sarah."

"That's all right Frau Manser. We'll take it."

"Why have you suddenly decided not to sleep in the matratzenlage Sarah?"

Sarah steeled herself. "Well it's like this Frau Manser. My friend, the lady I'm with, is a singer, a pop singer and she's very famous. Yesterday on the Santis we got swamped with autograph hunters and while she doesn't mind that she still likes a little bit of privacy as you can imagine. I just thought she'd prefer not to have to share with a load of other people."

"My word! What's this diva called?"

"Her name's Daniela Devin."

"Good God! You've brought Daniela Devin here?"

"Yes. She's a friend of mine."

"Heavens! We don't often get people as famous as that here. No wonder you want a private room and there's me worried that you might find the room expensive. She must be worth a fortune."

"*I'm* paying for the room Frau Manser."

Frau Manser was flapping excitedly. She didn't seem to have heard Sarah. "Will she be wanting anything special for dinner Sarah? I mean Theo's a good cook but we're not really set up to cater for celebrities. You should have let me know Sarah so we could put something special on. What about wine as well? Oh God I hope she doesn't want champagne. I don't think we've got any!"

Sarah groaned in exasperation. "I'm sure the food will be just fine Frau Manser. As to drinks well I came in to get two bottles of beer if I may."

"Of course, of course! I'll bring them out personally, straight away."

"Really Frau Manser. That won't be necessary. I can carry them out myself."

"No, no, no Sarah! I insist! We don't get many celebrities up her. It's the least I can do to make sure we make the lady welcome."

Realising with a sigh that further protest would be futile, Sarah thanked her and retraced her steps to the terrace. She paused at the doorstep with another groan. Daniela's feeble disguise had already come undone. She was surrounded by eager guests from the other tables seeking autographs and snapshots. Sarah pushed through the crowd to the table with a polite "Excuse me."

The admiring crowd regarded Sarah's arrival with interest. A young girl having obtained Daniela's autograph pushed a piece of paper and a pen at Sarah obviously under the misapprehension that Sarah must be famous simply because of her association with Daniela. Sarah stared at the piece of paper blankly, completely unsure how to react. Frau Manser was hard on Sarah's heels bearing two bottles of beer. She glared at the crowd around the table. "What do you all think you're doing?" she demanded furiously. "Shoo! Shoo, the lot of you! You're a disgrace. Leave Miss Devin here in peace. I'll not have my guests harassed in this fashion. Miss Devin has come up here for some peace and quiet and the last thing she wants is to be bothered by you lot. Go back to your own tables and leave the lady alone. If there's any repetition of this behaviour I'll put you out of the house and you can hike back down to Samtisersee for the night." Frau Manser bristling on the warpath was an intimidating adversary and the crowd melted away abjectly. Frau Manser was fawningly apologetic as she laid down the beers. "I'm terribly sorry Miss Devin. I can't think what gets into people sometimes. You'd think they'd never seen anybody famous before." Sarah grinned to herself. She'd been thinking much the same about Frau Manser. "Now then Miss Devin," Frau Manser continued in a business-like manner, "You needn't worry about having your privacy disturbed tonight. Sarah here has explained the circumstances and so I've reserved the best room in the house for you two young ladies." Daniela glanced at Sarah out of the corner of her eye and raised an eyebrow sardonically. Sarah blushed much to her disgust. "I'm afraid it won't be a suite at the Palace in St Moritz." Frau Manser was saying. "We're a bit rustic here but I hope you'll be very comfortable."

"I'm sure it will be delightful Mein Frau. "Daniela reassured her. "I wasn't expecting a private room at all." Daniela turned to look at Sarah but Sarah had her nose buried in her beer glass and was avoiding Daniela's eye.

"Well now if there's anything, anything at all I can get, you just shout out won't you and I'll attend to it personally. If anybody bothers you just let me know and I'll deal with them. I want you to have a nice pleasant stay with us."

Daniela opened her face in a wide lovely smile and turned the full wattage of her charm on Frau Manser. "You are most kind Mein Frau but please don't make any special efforts on our behalf. We're just a couple of girls out for a few days hiking in the mountains. Sarah assures me that your hospitality is second to none in the Alpstein and I'm sure that we will be more than content with the high standard that you afford to *all* your guests."

Daniela, on full charm offensive, was irresistible and Frau Manser simpered visibly. "Why thank you Miss Devin. We do pride ourselves on making all our guests feel welcome. However we're not often privileged to have such a famous young lady among our clientele and I must say we are honoured that you have decided to make a short visit to our humble house." Sarah was beginning to wonder if Frau Manser was going to drop down on one knee and kiss Daniela's hand. But the lady instead clasped her hands together and regarded Daniela with pleasure. "However I'll leave you alone for the moment and send one of the girls out with the key to your room. What time will you be dining at? I'll make sure you get a nice quiet table away from the crowd."

"Oh we don't know Frau Manser." Sarah chirped in, wondering if Frau Manser had forgotten her existence, "We were going to have a drink and freshen up and then see."

"Well just let us know and I'll see what we can do. In the meantime welcome to Berggasthaus Bollenwees Miss Devin."

"Thank you Frau Manser."

Frau Manser turned and left. Sarah glanced at her watch. "I'll give her between ten and fifteen minutes

106

before she's out again to see if there's anything else we require. I've never seen her so star-struck."

"I thought she was being rather sweet Sarah."

"Sweet? Frau Manser? She's an ogre! She rules this establishment with a rod of iron. I used to be terrified of her when I was a kid. Once, when I was thirteen, I stayed a night here and drank a coke in bed against all the rules. I spilled some on my duvet in the dormitory and she gave me a hell of a telling off. I thought she was going to take me into her office and spank me."

"Well for heaven's sake don't repeat your sinful past Sarah. I'd hate to have to start tomorrow standing in a corner of her office with my hands on my head, my knickers round my ankles and my backside smarting because of your reprehensible behaviour."

"Oh pooh to you! At least you might actually have some knickers on to wear around your ankles in the morning. I wonder if Frau Manser would have been quite so enamoured of her glamorous guest if she'd known that the above was walking around like a shameless hussy with no underwear on. Don't bring my past sins up. My behaviour has been beyond reproach compared with yours today."

"Oh yes? Such as booking us into a double room for the night perhaps? What bullshit did you tell her Sarah? Something about my delicate soul wanting some respite and privacy from the baying hordes was it?"

"It's not bullshit! I genuinely thought you'd be happier if we didn't have to stay in the dormitory."

"Oh I'll be happier all right."

"Behave! It is better if we stay in a private room seriously Daniela. I mean you *are* famous and it's not acceptable that you are exposed to the risks of such close proximity to a lot of people. I mean there are nutters with fixations on famous people; stalkers and the like. It's bad enough just walking around in broad daylight Danny but actually *sleeping* among a load of strangers... well I thought it safer. It wasn't too bad up on the Santis because the hut was quiet but here, when the place is three quarters full, I decided it was a risk we shouldn't take."

"So all of this is entirely to do with my well-being and safety is it and the fact that you blushed to the roots of your hair when Frau Manser announced that she was giving us what amounted to the honeymoon suite was entirely coincidental?"

"Stop it Danny!"

Daniela leaned on her elbows, touched her fingertips together and raised her eyes to heaven in amusement. "I wonder how Frau Manser would have interpreted your innocent concerns for my privacy and safety had she known that only a few hours earlier you'd been carousing with me naked on the flanks of the Altmann."

"I was *not* carousing!"

"Hmm! I think that had anyone happened upon us at that instance you might have had a hard time convincing them of that."

"One word; one more bloody word and you can have that double room to yourself and I'll go and sleep in the dormitory."

"My lips are sealed sweetheart."

"I'll believe that when I see it." Sarah took a sip of her beer. "Anyway there's one good thing. At least we can have a shower today." They had been obliged to attend to their toiletries with an enamel bowl and a large jug of hot water on the Santis.

"We have a shower?"

"Oh yes; en suite as well."

"Oh heaven! I wasn't expecting one and I whiff like an old buck Ibex. We'd better go and jump in it at some point. Of course we'll have to share. I've become very conscious and aware of the need to conserve water in the high mountains on this visit."

"That was on the Santis you disgraceful strumpet. There's no water shortage here. In case it's escaped your notice, there's a bloody great lake full of the stuff just over there."

Daniela sighed comically. "Damn you're hard work Sarah."

Sarah looked at her suddenly serious. "I'm not hard work Daniela. Don't tease me. You know I'm not."

Daniela became serious in her turn. "What do you mean Sarah?"

Sarah swallowed. "I... I wasn't hard work on that mountainside was I Danny?"

Daniela's great blue eyes were unfathomable as she regarded Sarah slowly. "It depends on what you mean."

"I... I was yours on that mountainside Danny and you knew it. I... I'd given in. You could have done what you wanted with me. Why did you stop?"

Daniela smiled slowly and took a deep breath. "Sarah my sweet on these mountains you are the Queen; frightened of nothing; fazed by nothing and in complete control of your destiny. When it comes to the arts of love however you are an innocent virgin. That's not a criticism. I wouldn't have it any other way but you are a sitting duck for anyone with a mastery over the guiles of seduction. I could have done what I wanted with you, as you put it, a dozen times over by now. If I really wanted to seduce you, you wouldn't have an earthly chance of resisting me."

Sarah blinked in surprise. "Then you don't want me?"

"Of course I want you. I can think of nothing more in the world that I want. Every time I look at you I am possessed by a deep yearning desire to have you. I am no innocent Sarah. I am a woman with a past but I have never felt like this about anybody in my life before. In a sense my past is of no assistance to me in this instance. I'm in new territory. I'm treading paths I've never trod before and looking for signposts to help me navigate. All I know is that that which I most desire in all the world is sat in front of me dribbling beer down her adorable chin."

Sarah wiped her mouth hastily. "But it doesn't make sense Danny. If you wanted me so much then why didn't you take me when you had the chance?"

"Why didn't you take *me* Sarah?"

"You're changing the subject."

"No I'm not. It's a pertinent question. All this time it's about you "giving in" to me, me doing what I want with you; your surrender to my will. You're the one frightened about being overwhelmed by me. I'm the seductress; the one who wants her wicked way with poor little innocent Sarah. You're even buying into that yourself. You quite deliberately laid yourself open to attack tonight. You took a double room for tonight knowing full well that if in the night I roll over to your side of the bed it will take a simple kiss or a gentle caress and you'll surrender yourself to me. If we became lovers like that Sarah what will everybody say; that a famous pop singer carried the head of a young, naive, star-struck rural girl and used her for her personal gratification? You would have been unfaithful to your boyfriend; might alienate your family and friends and have sullied your reputation. I'm a terrible risk to you Sarah. You know that and that's why you're so afraid of me."

Daniela fingered her beer glass sadly. "You know Sarah, my career has been wonderful to me. It has given me the most enormous satisfaction in doing something I love. It has given me more money than I know what to do with and it has made me famous. But with fame comes burdens and responsibilities. With fame comes always the nagging thought, at the back of your mind, that people treat you in a certain way because you are famous. I came to live in the Toggenburg because the people there are so polite and so considerate of a person's privacy that, once the novelty had died down, I could lead an almost normal life; walk the streets

110

without drawing undue attention. Even there though I'm still, and possibly always will be, the woman who's a famous pop singer. I can never just be an ordinary person that happens to live in the valley. I'll always be treated a little differently and, furthermore, I'll be expected to behave differently. Every time I talk to somebody, I know that, in some subtle way, however much they would wish otherwise, they'll always see a pop diva and not just the person in front of them. Take Frau Manser there. Do you think she'd have been the same to me if she'd never heard of me; if I'd been just an ordinary girl out for a hike in the mountains? Of course not."

"What's this got to do with me Danny? You're surely not suggesting that I'm really just with you because you're famous."

Daniela shook her head. "No Sarah I'm not. I don't even know why not. I've asked myself if you would really want to know me if I wasn't famous of course but I honestly feel that you're one of the very few people I've ever met that honestly couldn't give a toss about my fame. Oh it impinges itself on our relationship; of course it does. But you don't want to bask in it. You sometimes even seem embarrassed by it. When you look at me you look straight at me and not at the image of me as a pop singer." Daniela shook her head with a laugh. With a shock Sarah saw she was blushing. "Can I tell you something strange Sarah?" she asked.

"Of course."

Daniela bit her lip. "When we were walking back today along the lake, I was looking at you. Nothing odd there. I usually look at you a lot. But you had a strange look to your face; a sort of radiance about it. I couldn't figure it out to begin with then it dawned on me. It was pride. You were proud of me. It wasn't pride because I was famous or a singer in a rock and roll band; it was just simple pride in the woman whose hand you held. I don't know why you were proud of me Sarah but you've

111

no idea what that meant to me. I felt so desperately in love, my heart felt as if it would burst."

Sarah bit her lip. "You're right Danny. I was proud of you. I still am. You're right too that it's nothing to do with you being famous. I just think you're an amazing person and beautiful. I wouldn't be right in the head if I wasn't proud that someone like you wanted to be with me."

"Then you feel exactly the same as I do Sarah because I've been proud of you from the first moment you consented to be my friend. I feel overwhelmed with pride every time I see you; every time you let me take your hand; every moment you spend in my presence. I want the world to see that this incredible woman belongs to me." Daniela dropped her head in melancholy. "But she doesn't."

"I'm sorry?"

"I said you don't belong to me. You see you're famous too. Here on the Alpstein and back in the valley you're famous. You're the Toggenburg's favourite daughter; known by all; beloved by everyone. You're no pop star; you haven't sold millions of records; you haven't been on television but you are the *real* star in the Toggenburg. The valley would never forgive me if I stole their darling away."

"That's nonsense Danny."

"Is it? I'm not so sure. I think you know it too. I think you know the risks that becoming my lover would entail. We'd be isolated Sarah. When your family, your friends, your boyfriend and the valley turn their backs on you because you let some two bit pop singer with notions above her station steal you away would you ever feel the same about me again?"

"You're being ridiculous Danny. My business is my own business."

"No it's not Sarah. That's the price of fame."

"Well in that case nobody has a right to their own business. Everybody is known and has responsibility to others."

"Those are true words Sarah. Fame isn't actually a unique condition. It's just a matter of magnitude; the normal condition of human existence amplified by the number of people. You could almost draw an equation couldn't you? The number of people that know you is inversely proportional to the degree of privacy you can expect in your life and directly proportional to the burden of expectation upon you. We both are known by a lot of people Sarah."

"Is this why you stopped on that mountain then; because you're worried about my reputation, or yours, or both?"

"I'm just trying to point out the risks Sarah. I know what risks I pose to you and, madly in love with you as I am, I would still be irresponsible if I were not aware of them. That's all I'm saying."

"And the risks to you?"

"I'm a pop star Sarah. We're almost expected to live risky lives. I sometimes think my fans are quite disappointed that I don't have to go into rehab regularly for a drug habit, trash the occasional hotel room or indulge in wild sex orgies. I'm pretty boring for a rock singer."

"You're still evading the question Danny. I still don't understand why you stopped. You said you could have seduced me anytime. But you didn't. You say you want me more than anything but you are not taking the steps to possess me even when you say you know you can. Why Danny? It can't be just that you're concerned about my reputation."

"No it's because *you're* concerned about your reputation."

"Me?"

"Sarah listen to me. This is a moment for truth. You desire me; you have done from the moment you first saw me. Isn't that the truth?"

Sarah hesitated and then nodded. "You're the most beautiful woman I ever knew Danny."

"Have you ever slept with another woman before Sarah?"

"No. You know I haven't."

"So all of a sudden comes along this woman and for the first time in your life that you'll admit you desire another woman. The trouble is that, if you succumb to that desire, it has consequences far beyond the mere gratification of that desire doesn't it? For one thing it means that you have to reappraise your entire sexuality. You've never considered yourself lesbian and neither has anyone that knows you. You know how shocked everybody will be. You are, after all, very nearly engaged to be married. Your friends and all the people in the valley will be appalled. Your family will be shaken to its roots. Once you cross that line there's no going back Sarah. You'll never be quite sweet little Sarah again. You've declared yourself to be something strange and threatening. You told me about your friend Peter. Can you imagine how difficult it must have been for him to openly declare his sexuality to you Sarah and you're one of his best friends? What's it going to be like for you Sarah? I'm too well known and so are you to be able to keep it secret for long. It'll be all round the valley in no time that we have something other than a shared interest in botany together. You could lose everything; the respect of everyone you know; your family; your marriage; even your best friends Sarah. This is why you're frightened of me Sarah. You desire me and yet you're terrified of surrendering to that desire. That's why I asked you why you didn't take me. You've desired me from the beginning and I left you in no doubt that that desire was reciprocated. You could, at any time, have expressed that desire; told me unequivocally exactly

114

what you felt. You could have taken me whenever you wanted Sarah. You still can but you won't. As yet the risks still outweigh the rewards. I said on the Lysengrat that I needed to take the risk; look fear in the face or I would never see the shining beauty of the world beyond you wanted to show me. This is your Lysengrat Sarah. I can help you. I can encourage you but ultimately you are going to have to have the courage to step onto that cliff face."

"I was ready to do that today."

"No you weren't. You were simply overwhelmed by physical desire. You weren't ready for the real cliff Sarah. You were just giving in. You were not making a positive step. You don't win a battle by surrendering Sarah. You win the battle by achieving the aims you set out for. You win the battle by conquering and by conquering you reap the rewards."

"What are the rewards Danny?"

Daniela leaned back on the bench and looked at her gently. "Nothing much Sarah. Just me; the woman in front of you with all her faults and foibles; the woman who loves you. Nothing more than that. I have nothing else to offer."

"Oh Danny!"

"I'm greedy you see Sarah. I don't just want your body, gorgeous and desirable though it is, I want all of you. I want your heart, your soul, your mind; I want your love. It gets worse too. I not only want all that of you but I want to give all that of me to you as well. I don't just want to own you Sarah, I want you to own me. So far you haven't seen it like that. It was always about you surrendering to me. Well I was waving a white flag too Sarah. Love isn't a person surrendering to another. It's a mutual capitulation. It's easy to surrender Sarah. The hard part is accepting the other person's submission. I can't accept your surrender while you reject mine Sarah. That's why I stopped on that mountainside today Sarah. That's why I'll not take you as my lover tonight. It's because you're not ready to take *me*. At the moment, all you see are a few hours of fearful ecstasy. You don't see the shining valley beyond; the house that would be our house, the garden we would tend together, the bed we would share and the life that would be ours. That's what I want Sarah. If that's not enough for you then let's walk back over that mountain together in the morning, kiss, say goodbye and leave that dream as a sweet echo to reside among the flowers in the mountain meadows forever."

"Danny! Stop it! You're making me cry."

"I'm sorry Sarah. I love you. Perhaps it would have been better for you if you had never met me."

"Don't say things like that."

"I can't help it Sarah. You're not the only one frightened on this table. I love you! I am so frightened of losing you."

Sarah wiped away a tear and reached for a tissue in the pocket of her rucksack. "Oh Danny! I don't know what to do." She blew her nose loudly. "Please don't say goodbye to me tomorrow Danny. I don't think I could bear it! Will you be patient with me? Will you give me time?"

"All the time you could ever wish my darling. Please don't feel pressurised into a decision. That's not what I wanted to do. I'll be here when you feel ready for me." Daniela glanced up. "Dry your eyes quickly Sarah. I see Frau Manser is looming up on the horizon."

Chapter Eleven

When they had finished their beers, they took their rucksacks to their room. The room was simple with wooden floor, walls and ceiling in plain polished spruce. A row of small windows decorated with lace curtains overlooked the lake and there were a couple of pictures on the walls but otherwise the room lacked any ornamentation whatsoever. The wooden bed was, in fact, two solid wooden single beds pushed together with two separate mattresses on them but there were large warm looking duvets on each bed with floral covers on them and matching pillows. A pair of bedside lamps sat on a little tables at each side of the bed. They appeared to be the only form of electrical illumination in the room. Daniela turned one on out of interest. "Where do they get the electricity from in these places Sarah?" she asked.

"Well a lot of the more remote huts don't have any Danny. Some of them use solar panels for basic lighting and so on, as they do at Rotsteinpass for instance. Any other power sources such as gas bottles, and so on, have to be airlifted up by helicopter. Some of the rougher ones just use gas lamps or even oil lamps. There's electricity on the Santis of course because the whole summit complex is linked by way of the cable car pylons to the grid in Schwagalp below. This guest house is connected to the Appenzell electricity grid as well although it wasn't always the case. So we've got full electrical power here."

"Have you seen this?" Daniela asked in amusement, indicating a small table which, apart from a single chair and the beds, bedside tables and a simple wardrobe, was the only other furniture in the room. Reposing on this table, was a vase containing freshly cut yellow wild flowers, a bowl of fruit, a little dish of chocolates, a bottle of wine and a welcome card.

Sarah picked up the card with a grin. "It looks like Frau Manser's laying on the VIP treatment for you Danny. I bet she had one of her girls frantically preparing this while we were sat outside."

Daniela sniffed the flowers. "Hmm nice."

"They'd have been a lot nicer if she'd left them in the alp where they were growing."

"They're not protected are they?"

"Well no they're just Arnica but you shouldn't really pick them anyway. Don't eat them by the way. They're poisonous."

"It's not usually my habit to snack on the ornamental flowers in hotel bedrooms when I feel peckish during the night Sarah."

Sarah was exploring the tiny little adjoining bathroom. "My God this is small. I'm afraid your hopes for a sybaritic orgy are going to run into logistical problems here Danny. You couldn't swing a cat in here."

"You'd be amazed at the size of a space you can fit two human bodies into Sarah if they're prepared to get friendly enough."

"Well do you want to use the shower first?" asked Sarah.

Daniela's eyes fluttered in mock coyness. "Only if you promise not to jump in after me. I'd hate you to take advantage of me when I'm so vulnerable."

Sarah picked up a pillow and threw it at her. "Go and get in the bloody shower!"

Sarah sat on the bed whilst Daniela showered. Daniela liked to sing in the shower it appeared. The little shower closet could scarcely have been graced by a more beautiful voice before. Eventually Daniela emerged from the shower with a towel wrapped around her looking glum. She lifted up a lock of her wet hair. "Now there's something we didn't think to include among our basic alpine survival kit." She observed, "A sodding hair dryer."

Sarah managed to look smug. "You didn't look far enough. There's one in the cabinet over the washbasin."

"You're kidding me."

"Nope I saw it earlier."

"My God! A five star mountain hut. You'll be telling me they have room service next."

Sarah laughed. "I'm sure Frau Manser would be willing to oblige. Anyway if you're finished in there I'm going to shower." Sarah luxuriated under the stream of hot water for a long time. She could still hear Daniela singing to herself in the other room as she dried her hair. She sounded happy. Sarah thought about that for a few moments. A little while earlier a twinge of sadness had come between them. Sarah realised that that sadness had its roots in the fact that they had dared to think of the world beyond; the world that included the people of the Toggenburg, Sarah's friends; Nicole, Peter, Sarah's family, Alan and all the rest of the real world. Tomorrow they would have to come down from the mountain and face that world. Life with Daniela seemed like a dream divorced from reality. But it was a happy dream. Sarah, whilst with Daniela, had never felt so happy in her life. She wanted to stay up the mountain forever.

The towels provided were thick and soft; plain white but with borders of embroidered blue flowers. Sarah towelled herself down and wrapped the towel around her. She emerged from the bathroom to find Daniela sat on the side of the bed drying her hair. It took a good deal of drying. The thick, honey gold tresses absorbed a considerable amount of water. Sarah squatted down on the bed beside Daniela and took the brush from her hand. "Here let me." she murmured in a hoarse voice. Daniela smiled and handed her the hair dryer. It was awkward for the dryer's cable was short and the only power socket was the one from which the bedside lamp took its electricity but Sarah gloried in the task of brushing out the rich, wavy, luxurious mane that adorned Daniela's head. She was astonished how heavy it felt, how soft was its texture and how lustrous its sheen. "You have beautiful hair." She told Daniela.

"Thank you honey. Don't mess it up though or my insurance company will be well pissed off."

"You're joking! You're seriously not telling me that your hair's insured."

"I'm a performing artist Sarah. Not only my voice but also my looks are my working assets. Lots of artists insure the things they depend on to make a living. I knew one country and western singer who insured her tits for millions."

"Please tell me that yours aren't."

Daniela laughed. "Well yes they are but I guess that just comes under the general heading of bodily damage. Seriously though, my appearance is part of my performance too. If I was seriously disfigured it would impair my ability to perform live or in front of camera badly and with consequent loss of earnings. So I'm insured against the possibility. My agent would consider it criminally irresponsible of me if I wasn't."

Sarah sighed. "Sometimes I just can't get used to the fact that you're so famous. Here I am brushing your hair and it's probably worth its weight in gold and all I can think about is what a lovely colour it is."

"Thank you. It's my natural colour too as I'm sure you observed this afternoon on the Altmann."

"Have you ever dyed it?"

"No. Oh I've put highlights in from time to time but I like my hair the colour it is. If it ain't broke don't fix it. I'm just a dizzy blond and perfectly happy to remain so for the rest of my days."

Sarah finished drying Daniela's hair and then submitted happily as Daniela returned the favour. "Your hair ain't shit either Sarah." Daniela told her, with pleasure, as she brushed out Sarah's long brown hair with its chestnut sheen. "It was one of the first things I found attractive about you."

"Don't tell me that. You'll make me vain."

"I don't believe it. Vanity is not one of your weaknesses."

Daniela finished her task with a kiss to Sarah's shoulder and stood up to discard her towel and rummage among her belongings for clothing. Sarah stared at her naked body with admiration. It was so perfect it seemed. And yet it wasn't perfect; not quite. Barely visible on her admirably flat stomach were the faintest of marks. Sarah hadn't noticed them that afternoon but here, so close to her, she could make them out. Daniela felt her gaze upon her and turned. "What are you looking at Sarah?"

"Oh... nothing."

"You were staring at my stomach."

"I... I'm sorry. I didn't mean to." Sarah lowered her eyes.

Daniela smiled and came close to Sarah sitting on the bed. She stood before her and lifted her chin up. "Go ahead and stare Sarah. I told you this afternoon that there is nothing of me that you're not allowed to look at."

"You... you have marks... marks on your tummy. I didn't notice them before."

"Your eye must be getting keener. I thought they were barely visible anymore."

"But they look like..."

"They're just stretch marks Sarah. I've thought of having them removed surgically but they're not really intrusive and they're easily covered cosmetically when I have to show my belly. It's not worth the hassle of removing them."

"But that means..."

"I have a daughter Sarah. She lives in California with my parents."

"Oh God! I'm sorry. I never knew."

"Why should you? It's not even something that gets in the paper much. My parents are pretty protective of her."

God how old is she?"

121

"Nearly ten Sarah. I was very young. It's an old story; a boy at school and a silly young girl who didn't have the sense to keep her legs closed. I'm not proud of it but my daughter is healthy and happy. My parents raised her more than I did. She goes to a good school where she does well and has lots of friends."

"Don't you miss her?"

"Of course I do but she's happier where she is. The life of a performing artist is no place to bring up a child. I fly over to see her three or four times a year. I love her and she'll never want for anything if I can help it but I wasn't able then to be a real mother to her and she's better where she is. She's spoiled rotten mind. My parents dote on her. My mother nearly died when she had me and she was never able to have any more children. She was only nineteen when they told her that and she so desperately wanted more children. Becoming a surrogate mother to my daughter at the age of thirty five was a new lease of life to her."

"God you were only fifteen."

"Yes. You can't even look after yourself at that age let alone a child. I was very young and foolish. Are you shocked Sarah?"

"No! Well a little bit I suppose. I... I never thought of you as a mother."

"I'm not really except in a biological sense Sarah. Oh my daughter knows that I'm her mother and she's always happy to see me when I visit but my mother and father are her real parents in that it's they who are bringing her up. I get letters and photos most weeks and I only have to see the photos of a bright happy child to know that I did the right thing. It's hard to be separated from your child but sometimes when you love somebody you have to sacrifice your own desires to do what is the best for them. I placed my daughter in the best possible circumstances for her and as a side effect I brought great joy to my parents too. My own feelings are irrelevant in the face of those facts."

"I think you'd be a wonderful mother Danny."

"Thank you Sarah. One day perhaps."

"One day? But..."

"But what Sarah?"

"I mean you... you're...."

"I'm what? Lesbian? I'm a bit more complicated than that Sarah." Daniela took a seat on the bed alongside Sarah. "Did you know I was married?"

"Oh my God! No. I didn't."

"There spoke a girl who never read a tabloid newspaper gossip column in her life. My marriage and subsequent divorce is hardly a secret Sarah especially since my ex-husband is one of my best friends and the lead guitarist in my band."

"Oh God! Every time I think I'm beginning to know you then you come up with a surprise like this."

"I'm sorry Sarah. I told you I had a past. I come with a bit of baggage attached I'm afraid."

"I didn't want to pry into your private affairs Danny. I'm sorry. You just never talk about these things."

"That's because when I talk to you Sarah all I want to see is the future not the past."

"How long were you married?"

"About three years Sarah. I was only nineteen. I did a lot of foolish things when I was younger. He was a part of my first band and we were touring all over England and sleeping most of the time in the back of a camper van. It just seemed natural to come together. We got married in a snotty little country hotel between gigs. I think we both knew almost straight away that it was a mistake but we soldiered on and tried to make the best of it. I suppose we ran out of steam after about a year and separated after eighteen months. The separation was amicable. We just weren't cut out for each other and my being gay didn't help. I recorded my first solo album just after we split and after I moved to Switzerland. Paul came out to join me on tour and he fell in love with the girl who was my keyboard player at the time. So I let him go and wished him well and we finalised the divorce. In the tabloid version you'll hear that I ran off with one of my backing vocalists. That's a load of rubbish. She is a very good friend of mine and we did sleep together on occasion when I needed someone but now she's in a steady relationship with my bass guitarist who is sensible enough to tolerate and forgive her occasional deviations from the path of fidelity. The band's a bit of a complicated tangle of relationships Sarah. Just one big happy family of messed up love affairs. I spend half my life just trying to sort out my band's convoluted emotional problems. I even acted as matchmaker between my husband and his new wife. They married last year. I was a bloody bridesmaid at the wedding for God's sake and they took me to bed on their wedding night to thank me for bringing them together."

"Oh my God! Seriously?"

"Yes but for fuck's sake don't tell anybody I told you that. The papers would have a field day."

"You've had a hell of a life."

"Not really Sarah. Since my marriage I've not been in many other relationships. Oh I'm no angel. I've had lovers but I've never had a really steady relationship since. The band are always worrying about me. They think I'd be happier with someone but I never found anyone to fall in love with.... until now."

"You're right. You're complicated."

"I suppose so Sarah but, when I'm with you, things seem a lot simpler."

"Do you want more children?"

"Oh yes! I adore children. I'd love one day to have another child."

"Wouldn't that be difficult? I mean if you were with another woman?"

"There are all sorts of ways around that problem Sarah as I'm sure you can figure out."

"You mean with test tubes or something?"

"Why go to all that clinical bother? What's wrong with just inviting a good friend around for dinner one night? If everyone was mature enough about it then where's the problem?"

"God! I believe you'd do it too."

"I wouldn't have a problem with it. What about you? Don't you want children?"

Sarah blushed. "Well it's not something I think about a lot but yes, I suppose I do."

"I'd never stand in your way if you wanted children Sarah. I know from personal experience the heart break of frustrated motherhood. If you wanted to invite the postman in for tea and cakes, I'd slip out to the shops for an hour. We could bring up our children together. It would be marvellous to have a real family."

"Oh my God! I'm out of my depth here."

"You'll want children someday Sarah. You're a woman. It's wired into the system. You're supposed to be getting married at the end of summer. You must have thought about children."

"I'm having a hard enough time contemplating being married at all let alone being a mother Danny."

Daniela leaned forward and kissed her playfully. "If I have our first daughter sweetheart I'm going to call her Sarah. I know it'll be complicated having two Sarahs in the house so we'll have to allocate nicknames."

Sarah pushed her away with a laugh. "Stop it Danny! You make us sound like a married couple."

"In my dreams!" Daniela stood up suddenly and shook out her hair. "Come on darling let's get dressed and go down for dinner. The mountain air gives you an appetite. I'm starving."

Dinner was simple but wholesome; sliced lean veal in a creamy mushroom sauce served with homemade butter rosti and a fresh, green side salad. The food was good and Frau Manser proved good to her word, for they were placed at a table well away from the other diners although their presence still attracted interested glances.

The overall sense of privacy however was somewhat spoiled by the somewhat over solicitous attentions of the guest house's staff. Both Frau Manser and her husband were frequent visitors to their table and Herr Manser insisted upon pressing free liqueurs on them at the conclusion of their meal. Then there was a seemingly, ceaselessly vigilant shuttle of waitresses that appeared, as if by magic, at their table if they even remotely looked as if they were in need any further service. Even the chef emerged from his kitchen, in a clean white apron, to nervously inquire if the food was agreeable to their palates and withdrew, visibly relieved by their reassurances.

After their meal, the girls sat out on the terrace to watch the sun sinking low over the surrounding mountains. The sky was clear and the temperature fell rapidly so they donned warm pullovers over their shirts and jeans. Daniela wore the same angora wool pullover she had earlier used as a cushion. Sarah frowned and sniffed it suspiciously. "What are you doing?" asked Daniela indignantly.

"Just making sure your jumper doesn't pong of your private bits."

"How would *you* know what my private bits pong like? I haven't exactly noticed you snuffling around down there yet, although I live in hope."

"I have a sensitive nose."

"Well use it to some good purpose then instead of merely turning it up in disapproval of my conduct."

Sarah laughed. She enjoyed the flirtatious banter with Daniela. "It'll be dark soon. Do you want to go for a short walk along the lake?"

"I'd love to. Let's go for a walk under the stars. The stars will be glorious tonight."

Chapter Twelve

Daniela was right. As they walked away from the lights of the guest house, as darkness fell, the heavens opened in a glorious vista above them. Few people were privileged to see the starry firmament away from the lights of the city and under the clear skies of the mountains. The spectacle was breath-taking. The whole velvety dark background seemed to glow with distant luminescence; glittering with the remote radiance of mighty stars; humbling you with the vastness of the cosmos beyond your cosy little world. Dividing the sky was the ethereal band of the Milky Way; the very disc of the majestic galaxy of which the sun and all the worlds that orbited it were but insignificant motes of dust in the magnificence of it. And yet that galaxy itself was a mere note; a single harmony in the greater orchestration of the cosmos.

The two girls sat upon a rock beside the lake shore. Daniela sat behind Sarah and wrapped her arms about her while Sarah leaned back against her, feeling comforted by the warmth of her in the chill of the night. Their eyes were fixed upon the radiance above. "It's incredible isn't it?" whispered Daniela as she nestled Sarah's head on her shoulder. "I don't think I ever really looked at the stars properly until I came to live in the Toggenburg. I spent too much of my time in cities. It was one of the first things I noticed when I came here; just how incredible the night sky was in the mountains. Sometimes I can sit outside my house for hours and look at it."

Sarah nodded. "My father and I often used to sit outside on dark nights when I was a child. He's got an interest in astronomy and he used to teach me the names of the constellations and stars. We had an astronomical telescope in the back garden then and I used to peer through it for hours. My mother used to go mad with me. She told me that I'd catch my death of cold staying outside at night so long. I guess she just never could believe that it was something little girls should be interested in."

"You know the names of the constellations?"

"Oh yes! I've lived under this sky most of my life."

"What's that beautiful one like a great cross there on the Milky Way?"

"That's Cygnus the swan Danny. If you use your imagination it actually looks a little like the outline of a great swan flying along the galactic plane with the two short arms of the cross its wings, the shorter head of the cross its tail and the longer its neck. Apparently, in some ancient cultures, people thought that birds migrated along the Milky Way. If you follow the direction of the swan's flight along it the next big constellation is Aquila the eagle. Do you see the bright star in the tail of the swan?"

"Yes."

"Well that's quite a remarkable star Danny. It's called Deneb which is derived from the Arabic for tail. It's a blue white super giant approximately sixty thousand times more luminous than our sun. It's huge too. Its diameter is thought to be over two hundred times that of our sun. If you placed it where our sun is then its outer edge would extend out to the orbit of the earth."

"Jesus!" Daniela chuckled softly in Sarah's ear. "I might have known that if I asked for a name I'd get an in depth lecture on the subject."

"I'm sorry. I'm being a geek again."

"You're being as wonderful as ever." Daniela cuddled her in satisfaction. "Come on then little Miss Geek what's that one up there like a big W?"

"That's Cassiopeia, the upside down queen."

"What Cassiopeia from the Greek legend?"

"Yes. Do you know the legend?"

128

"Of course I do. I may not be much on astronomy but I have a sound classical education Sarah. That story's one of my favourites." Suddenly Daniela gripped Sarah tightly. "That's it! Perfect! I have a name for you."

"What? Cassiopeia?"

"No, no! Cassiopeia is your mother. You're Andromeda the chained maiden."

"Is this some sort of bondage fantasy?"

"No Sarah. Be serious. Think about it. Cassiopeia is the vain queen whose vanity is punished by having her beautiful daughter Andromeda chained to the cliffs as a sacrifice to Cetus the sea monster who will come up out of the sea and gobble her up, except in this instance he'll be flying up out of the sea in a 747 jet and carrying you away to his dark lair in a Zurich suburb to devour you. I'm Perseus flying in on my winged steed Pegasus to rescue you."

"Pegasus was white Danny, not red and, in any case, the prancing horse logo on your Ferrari doesn't have wings."

"Details, details. Hmm now where can I get a Gorgon's head from? There's an old harridan who lives in a cottage near the Gade that might pass for Medusa."

"That's a horrible thing to say. I know her. I know she's a funny old stick but she's perfectly harmless. Anyway you don't need a Medusa's head to slay Cetus. In the original story Perseus only used Medusa's head to turn his rival for Andromeda's hand to stone at the wedding feast. He never used it to turn Cetus to stone. That's a later corruption of the story."

"Well if I use Medusa's head to kill off Cetus or Phineus it's the same isn't it? Either way, I get to win the girl. You're definitely Andromeda. I'll call you Andy when you're being brunette and sensible or Annie when you're in blond mode. How's that?"

"Does this mean I have to call you Percy?"

"Not unless you want your bottom smacking."

"Well your analogy is hopeless Danny. For one thing I'm not a princess."

"Purely a matter of opinion my dear."

"And for another thing Andromeda lived in a kingdom by the sea which hardly describes Switzerland. Andromeda was chained to the sea cliffs. I've never even *seen* the sea."

"I beg your pardon."

"I said I've never seen the sea."

"You're pulling my leg."

"No honestly. Oh I think my parents took me to the sea when I was a baby in England but I can't remember it."

"You told me you went on holiday in Italy last year."

"Yes I did. We went to Lake Como."

"And you never got to see the sea?"

"No. I've not really travelled much outside Switzerland Danny."

"I don't believe this. I cannot believe that in your whole life you've never seen the sea."

"I'm sorry. It's true. I'd like to one day though."

Daniela gripped her closely in excitement. "Promise me something Sarah."

"What's that Danny?"

"Promise me that you won't go to the sea without me. I want to be the first person to show you the sea. Let me take you to the sea Sarah. Please let me."

Sarah laughed, warmed by Daniela's sudden enthusiasm. "All right Danny. I promise. I won't go to the sea until you take me."

Daniela kissed her. "Thank you Sarah."

"Where are you going to take me?"

"Ah somewhere special."

"Go on... tell me."

"No way! I want it to be a surprise."

"Meanie."

"Look Sarah! A shooting star." The streak of light arrowed down across the sky. "Make a wish Sarah."

Sarah laughed. "Ever seen the Perseids Danny?"

"What the hell are they?"

"Well if you're going to be Perseus you should see them. After all they're named for the descendants of Perseus. It's an annual meteor shower that peaks around the 12th or 13th of August Danny. I try to see them every year. You'll make a lot of wishes then. I've counted as many as ninety five shooting stars in an hour during their peak. They're called the Perseids because their radiant point appears to be in the constellation Perseus close to a feature known as the double cluster; a pair of open star clusters; NGC 884 and NGC 869, if I remember correctly. The radiant point is the point, that if you drew a line from each meteor train, backwards they would all meet at the same point so you say that's where they all radiate out from. They're actually the dusty debris from the tail of the comet Swift-Tuttle. Each year the earth's orbit intersects that of the comet's dust trail in between the end of July and the end of August with the densest concentration around the middle of August and that's what causes the meteor shower. The Catholics call the shower the Tears of St Lawrence because his martyrdom is celebrated on the 10th of August. One of the biggest showers with the highest Zenithal Hourly Rate was in...."

"Sarah do you think if we see another shooting star it will grant me my wish that you shut up talking?"

Sarah laughed again. "All right! I'll shut up."

A pearly iridescence painted the sky above the eastern sky above the mountains and the tips of the higher peaks to the south lit up in silvery light. "The moon's coming up," Daniela observed. "And I'm getting cold. Let's walk back." As they ambled back along the lake shore, the moon rose above the mountainside and bathed the steep sided little valley in pale luminescence and glittered in reflection in the still waters of the lake. A tawny owl hooted from the patches of forest near the guest house and they walked in a dreamlike state with the night air chill on their breath. Daniela sighed in profound satisfaction. "Every time I think I've seen all the magic this day can bring it pulls another whammy on me." She murmured waving a hand to indicate the ethereal vista of the vale under the soft illumination of the moon. "This just feels unreal. I feel as if I stepped inside a fairy story." Sarah nodded. She had seen the mountains under the light of the moon more times than she could recall but she never tired of the view of it and nor had she ever seen it with Daniela's hand about her waist and her head resting on her shoulder to bless the vision with perfection.

It was cold in their room back in the guest house and they made a hasty toilet in the tiny bathroom before crawling quickly under the big duvets on the bed in their underwear. Daniela snuggled up close to Sarah for warmth and hugged her in pleasure. "So what's the plan of action for tomorrow Sherpa Andromeda?" she asked.

"We just cut up to Saxe Locke and from there we turn up the valley on that side and climb up to Zwinglipass. It's an easy hike. The gradient is pretty gentle."

"And after Zwinglipass?"

"Then it's just a long descent down the other side back to the Toggenburg and home."

"Let's take our time about it Sarah. I want these days to last as long as possible before we have to go back to Kansas."

"Ok Dorothy! We'll take our time."

Daniela was true to her word. She made no move to beguile Sarah into sexual intimacy although it would have been no difficult task for Sarah's senses were responding to the warmth and softness of Daniela's body against her. Instead Daniela turned on her side away from Sarah but held her arm closely about her and nestled her body into the curve of Sarah's. Her propensity for instant hebetude was shortly apparent for her deep breathing told Sarah that she was fast asleep. Sarah lay awake and lay against her. Daniela's rump was pressed against her groin and their bare legs touched beneath the duvet. Sarah felt the rising heat of desire and knew that her vulva was swollen and moist. Her breath deepened and her body tingled. The moonlight was filtering through the windows in the room and casting its rays on Daniela's recumbent figure. With her great mane of hair lying like a fan on the pillow and her face tranquil and childlike in sleep, she looked achingly beautiful and Sarah yearned with longing for her. But she hardly dared to move and held her breath to still its urgency and the wild racing of her heart. She lay there unfulfilled and willed calm upon herself. He hand was close to Daniela's breast. Fearfully, in case she should rouse the sleeping woman beside her, and very, very carefully, she moved her hand to cup Daniela's breast gently. The orb was firm beneath her touch and she could feel the nipple, erect in the cool air of the room, beneath her fingertips under the thin material of Daniela's chemise. She lay like that for a long time her breath taken away by her audacity and yet content to hold Daniela's breast so. Daniela stirred in her sleep and covered Sarah's hand with her own, holding it to her breast and Sarah felt a small triumph in the success of her daring. It was sufficient for the time being and as far as Sarah's courage would extend for the moment. The long hard day in the mountains finally took its toll and Sarah fell asleep clutching Daniela's breast and dreamed of naked mythological sirens dancing naked among the flowers in the mountains.

Chapter Thirteen

The final day of their excursion in the mountains dawned bright and clear and, although cool under the first rays of the morning sun, there seemed little doubt that the day would be another hot one. They rose early and did not discuss the night before. Both young women knew how close they had come to being lovers. They almost felt like lovers without the final consummation that would truly make them so. That consecrating act had now become the watershed upon which they knew their relationship now hinged. It had become of over-riding significance. Both of them were fully aware that any sexual escalation between them now would carry its own momentum and drive them completely into unknown territory. Such an escalation had no possibility of reversal. It would be a flat statement of intent; a commitment to a future both dangerous and uncertain. There was no question that such an act would be casual or inconsequential. The intensity of the feelings between the two girls precluded that. There *would* be consequences.

Only the awareness of those consequences explained why they, on this bright morning, still hovered on the edge of the lake of those consequences and yet hesitated to plunge in. By all good sense, having slept alone together the night before, they should have, by now, finally bowed to the forces driving them together and taken each other in the little room in the guest house. But they had not yet taken that fatal step. It was still possible, although only just, to argue that they were good friends and not something more. They had gone to the edge and stepped back. It was, paradoxically, both a great danger narrowly averted and a golden opportunity sadly squandered.

The girls were oddly subdued over breakfast and it was this paradox that preyed on their minds. Something of the magic of the preceding day had been lost. That such a day should have rightly ended in the sweetness of physical love and had not, left the memory of it slightly tarnished; unfulfilled. And now they were running out of time. Tonight there would be no little guest house nestling in a cleft in the mountains to lure them once more into bed together. Today they were going home. They would pass through a cleft in the mountain's shoulder and into an adjoining valley and from there climb up to a high pass. That pass represented almost an ending for, from there, there would be merely the long drop down out of the mountains to the Toggenburg valley below. At Gamplut they would cut across the alp at the feet of the Schafberg and from there descend through the forest to Alpli and Sarah's house where Daniela could reunite herself with her car and drive home. The dream like world they had experienced since setting foot on the mountain would end there. It would require some re-creation of the dream beyond that.

They lingered long over breakfast as if they were reluctant to begin the journey to bring them back to reality. They justified their tardiness on the grounds that there were a lot of people setting out from the guest house that morning and that it was better to let them depart so that they would have more solitude on the way. It was a tenuous excuse. Neither of them wanted to go home. They wanted to linger in the garden of the mountain where they had so truly found each other and delay as long as possible their return to a world that might yet tear them apart. It was only with deep sighs of resignation that they finally paid their bills, shouldered their rucksacks and took once more to the trail. It was a not a departure that went unnoticed for the entire staff and family of the guest house emerged to wish them on their way and to press small gifts of food and drink on them for their journey. They climbed the short slope beyond the guest house and paused in silence, clutching hands, to look back at the entrancing little steep-sided valley with the lake shining the clear blue of the sky above and perhaps to wonder if they'd ever walk back together that way again.

"Why do I feel that we just a part of us behind in that valley?" asked Daniela at last; ever the one to express their feelings with chosen words.

Sarah choked. "We'll come back someday." She managed at last.

"I hope so Sarah. Come on this is breaking my heart. Let's move on."

And so they did. The climb from Saxe Locke up to the pass was an easy one; a gentle climb through the high meadows of the valley strewn here and there with rocks and alive with Water Pipits, Wheatears and Linnets. Sarah took Daniela aside to show her one of her favourites among the fauna of the high mountains. They hid behind a rock to watch the Alpine Marmots; the fat ground squirrels that burrowed among the meadows and boulders in these high places. Daniela was entranced by the dumpy little animals with their cumbersome lope and spent long minutes trying to photograph them. The animals were vigilant however, often rearing up on their haunches to spot for danger and warning their comrades with sharp piercing whistles. "They're so cute!" gushed Daniela anthropomorphically and Sarah groaned.

"Oh Danny! You sound like a tourist."

"I *am* a tourist. Anyway they *are* cute. They're so fat."

"That's nothing. Wait till you see them at the end of summer and the beginning of autumn when they're fattening up for hibernation. They can barely move then. They must be the laziest animals in the world. They spend at least half of the year, if not longer, asleep."

"I'm guessing that's because of the winter conditions up here."

"Sure. They really live in pretty much arctic conditions. They burrow deep under the ground and under the snow in winter. They go into hibernation as early as October and don't emerge until April or even May. A big adult can weigh as much as eight kilos when they hibernate. They're the biggest species of squirrel in Europe."

"You mean they're related to the squirrels I have in the trees at the back of my garden?"

"Yes. It's a family referred to as Sciuridae and it includes tree squirrels, marmots, chipmunks, ground squirrels, sousliks, prairie dogs and flying squirrels."

"I always thought we had just two sorts of squirrels; red ones and grey ones. That can't be right though because the ones in my garden are black!"

"They're just black forms of the Red Squirrel Daniela. You'll find that a lot of the red squirrels in coniferous forest are actually black. My theory is that it's more suitable for camouflage for them in dark coniferous forest than red. The browny red colour of the red form is much better in autumnal deciduous forest. I don't know if there is any scientific evidence to back that up but it's marked how much the two forms seem to be differentiated in colour according to their environment. The Grey Squirrel is an American species introduced into the British Isles. To be absolutely accurate it's the Eastern Grey Squirrel; *Sciuurus carolinensis*."

Daniela solemnly placed two hands on either side of Sarah's head. "Nope! Doesn't seem to be any bigger than normal heads. Where do you put all this stuff in there Sarah? Are you just another sort of squirrel?"

"Stop it Danny!" Sarah laughed, "I can't help being a bore."

"You're not boring me darling. I find your head fascinating."

One type of animal they found less than welcome on the route up to the pass was the number of hikers on the path. Whereas yesterday they had seen hardly anybody until descending to the Fahlensee, today there were a number of parties both before them and behind. The glorious weather it seemed had attracted many people into the outdoors and the route was an easy and popular one with casual hikers. It was by no means crowded but there were enough groups of people to deprive the girls of the solitude they craved. This lack of privacy added to the growing sense of melancholy they felt as their mountain adventure came closer to its end. Finally they reached the top of the pass and Sarah could stand it no longer. She flopped down to the ground and wriggled out of her rucksack. "Let's take a break Danny." she said.

Daniela wiped her brow. "Suits me. It's getting bloody hot." Daniela sat down, extracted her water bottle from her rucksack and drank thirstily.

Sarah took her mobile phone from a side pocket of her pack and regarded it sourly. "Blast it!"

"What's the problem Sarah?"

"My phone's out of charge. I knew I should have brought my charger. Have you still got charge on your phone?"

"Should have. It's been switched off most of the time. God knows how many messages there'll be on there by now."

"Well as long as we've got one working phone between us in case we have an accident."

"Is that important? I mean there're so many people on the trail, I'd have thought we'd never be far from assistance."

Well that's what I was going to suggest Danny. We can just follow the path straight down from here or we can take the path there to the right and come around by the high route. It's a prettier route but the descent is a lot steeper at the end. Still it would get us away from all these people."

"Let's go for it Sarah. Anything that gives us a bit of peace and quiet is worth it."

The decision was an inspired one. Not only was the high path far more scenic but they had it to themselves and at last regained the reclusion they had been missing. They lingered long on this trail enjoying the peace of the mountain and pausing often to admire its rugged beauty. They sat for a long break on a tiny alpine meadow set among great pitted terraces of limestone with the Altmann to their back and the long ridge toward the Schafberg before them. Sarah had a new choice to make. They could press on to the Schafberg and drop down the eastern flank of it to come to Gamplut. But Sarah knew that that descent was a painfully steep scramble down a crumbly dry sandy track and would be torment in the hot weather. The decisive factor in her decision however was the lateness of the hour. They had loitered so long along the route that it was by now well into the afternoon and the hot weather was turning muggy and ominous looking clouds were beginning to form around the peaks. She could smell thunder in the air. She considered it imperative to lose altitude as quickly as possible. She decided, therefore, to take an earlier descent through an alpine scrub zone; the same route in fact she had taken from the Zwingli hut earlier that summer to where she had fled following her first dinner date with Daniela.

The zigzag track down through the scrub was tough on the knees and Sarah noted with satisfaction that Daniela made good use of the walking stick she had leant her. Nevertheless, despite her short dress, Daniela looked hot and tired although by no means unhappy. In fact with her hair tied back under her cap and a sheen of perspiration on her skin she looked radiantly attractive. Sarah was coming to accept the fact that she found Daniela physically attractive and that it was acceptable to admire her openly. She looked at Daniela's slim but shapely legs with pleasure as she descended behind her.

Daniela was of course always conscious of Sarah's attention. "Are you staring at my legs Sarah?"

"I just noticed you've got a streak of dirt on your right leg." Sarah smiled as Daniela bent down to examine the offending blemish. She didn't find it a desecration; indeed it was quite endearing.

Daniela was less amused. "Damn it!" she muttered.

"A bit of dirt won't hurt you Danny. Actually I've never seen your legs looking anything less than perfect before. It's quite...." Sarah paused to grin wickedly, "It's quite *cute*!"

"Is there a stream down in this valley Sarah?"

"Yes. Why? Do you want to wash your leg?"

"No! I want to throw you in it."

Sarah grinned again. "I don't think I'd object at the moment. It's bloody hot isn't it?"

"Yes it is. Have you got any water left in your bottle? I drank the last of mine back up on the pass."

"Only a mouthful I'm afraid but you're welcome to it."

"Can we fill our bottles in the valley here?"

"Well I wouldn't drink from the stream Danny. Further up it's alright but down this end of the valley there's a lot of cows grazing so if you don't want your drinking water flavoured with assorted bovine excretions I'd give it a miss."

"Oh hell! I've got a hell of a thirst."

"I've got a couple of oranges from Frau Manser's fruit bowl if you'd like one."

"Yes please. It's better than nothing."

Sarah found the oranges and tossed one to Daniela who peeled it rapidly and sank her teeth into the juicy pith greedily. "Anyway Danny," said Sarah reassuringly, "We're nearly down on the valley floor and then we've only a short hike to the restaurant at Gamplut. We can get a drink there."

"What happens after Gamplut?"

"Well we could take the cable car down to Wildhaus but that wouldn't help us much because we'd still have to get down to Unterwasser and climb up to the Alpli. So what we'll do is cut across the alp and walk down through the forest to Alpli after we've had a drink."

"Is it far?"

"No not at all. It's less than an hour from Gamplut to my house."

"I've got a better idea. Let's get a drink at Gamplut then turn around the way we came and do it all over again. In fact why don't we just stay up here for good and spend the rest of our lives wandering about on the mountain. I could phone up and hire a helicopter to airlift us some provisions and clothes whenever we needed them. In years to come they'd tell stories about the two strange women that walk about on the mountain and wonder where they were going. When we're too old to walk any more we'll jump off a cliff together and leave our bones for your Bearded Vultures to feast upon."

"You're just a hopeless dreamer Danny."

"I know. But it's good to have dreams." Daniela looked sad. "Somehow I'm dreading returning to the real world. It feels like an ending. It shouldn't do but it does. I just want to walk with you in these mountains forever."

"Danny we have to go back sometime."

"Yes I know. What shall I do with this orange peel?"

"Throw it on the ground Danny. It's perfectly biodegradable litter. The ants and bugs will make short work of it."

"Ok then." Daniela tossed the peel aside. "Let's move along then. At least we've got a drink at Gamplut to look forward to."

They descended on to the valley floor and crossed the meadows towards the stream. A herd of cows regarded them stoically and lowed gently. Daniela suddenly stopped. "Don't move Sarah," she warned. She pointed. "There's a sodding great bull there!"

Sarah laughed. "Oh it's only old Lucy."

"*Lucy?*"

"Short for Lucifer Danny. He's an old friend. Come on let me introduce you." Sarah marched across the grass in the direction of the huge animal.

"Are you stark staring, barking mad Sarah?" asked Daniela in a horrified voice.

"He's harmless honestly Danny." Daniela watched appalled as Sarah calmly walked up to the great beast who ambled toward her looking, if it were possible for more than a thousand pounds of male bovine to do so, kittenish. He closed his eyes ecstatically as Sarah scratched him behind the ears and Daniela regarded the scene in open mouthed astonishment. "Come and say hello Danny." Sarah urged.

"Are you sure he's safe?"

"Absolutely Danny. He won't hurt you."

Hesitantly Daniela approached the animal. Once at Sarah's side she dared to reach out and stroke its head. Lucifer reacted with a deep rumble of contentment and nuzzled at her arm. "My God!" she declared. "He's a big pussy cat."

"That's old Lucy alright. I've known him since he was a calf. He's nearly ten years old and he's sired hundreds of calves. He's past his prime now of course. The farmer says he keeps him on because he can still produce high quality offspring. He's an award winning pedigree Brown Swiss after all. Personally I think he's more of a family pet than anything and they can't bear the thought of him going to the knackers. He'll probably spend the rest of his natural days coming up here to loaf around in the summer."

"How long do cows live anyway?"

"Well of course they're mostly slaughtered long before their natural life span but if they're not they can live anywhere between fifteen and, in extreme cases, twenty five years. I used to come and play with Lucy when I was a young girl. I'd like to think that in another ten years I'll still be able to come up here in the summer and say hello. Lucy's an old friend."

Daniela regarded her with wonder. "You're an extraordinary woman Sarah."

"Stop it Danny. I'm not really."

"Oh but you are." Suddenly Daniela jumped. "OW!" she yelped. "Something just bit me on the back of my leg."

"Turn around and let me look."

Daniela turned obediently. There was a small trickle of blood from a tiny puncture on the back of her thigh. "Jesus that hurt!"

Sarah examined the wound critically. "Hmm I thought we might run into this problem down here."

"What the hell was it?"

"A cleg; a horsefly. The weather's turning thundery and that always makes them more active especially if there're cattle around. They're endearing little creatures. They come up silently behind you and stick their proboscis in to suck your blood. They're nature's own stealth weapon. You don't hear or see them until you feel an excruciating lance of pain in the back of your leg. I can put some ointment on if you want but with this hot muggy weather closing in it's likely that it won't be the last bite you'll have to suffer before we reach Gamplut."

"Oh Christ! Maybe I ought to put my jeans on."

"Well if it makes you feel better. It won't stop the horseflies though. They can bite through a cow's hide so a pair of denims isn't going to faze them."

"Oh charming! And just when I was beginning to like the fauna of the mountains."

Sarah laughed. "Nobody said *all* of nature was *cute* Danny."

"Just wait until we're in the privacy of some isolated little cowshed Miss Fuchs. I'm going to put you

143

over my knee and paddle your arse till you squeal for mercy."

Sarah giggled. "I think I might quite enjoy that."

Daniela snorted. "Hmmph! Let's go Sarah before some other of the native *Insecta* fauna decides to use me for a light afternoon snack."

They walked on down the valley and, by now, it was plain that the weather was closing in for thunderheads were forming around the peaks behind them and what little breeze there was died away leaving an ominous silence around the valley. Sarah regarded the sky with anxiety. "Are we in any danger Sarah?" asked Daniela nervously.

"Oh no. We're well off the peaks and we'll be at Gamplut very shortly. The worst that can happen is that we get caught on the way down to Alpli and get soaked. Hopefully we can shelter at Gamplut until the worst is past."

The impending malevolence of the thickening weather did not improve the two girls' humour as they walked towards Gamplut. There was a sinister feeling in the air that reflected the depression they both felt at the nearing of the end of their journey together. Sarah felt that it was ending wrongly; unsatisfactorily with too much left undone or said. They were walking in silence now; aware that each step took them closer to a parting and a parting that neither wanted. Sarah felt a quiet desperation at the thought of that parting; a premonition of loss filling her with an aching void. It seemed impossible to imagine any more a moment without Daniela at her side. The thought of going home and sleeping alone tonight, whilst Daniela returned to her house at Oberdorf was suddenly unbearable. Daniela broke the silence between them with a mundane question; so mundane it broke Sarah's tolerance. "What we're you thinking of doing this evening after we get home?" she asked. Daniela started in surprise as Sarah suddenly grasped her by the arms. "What's the matter Sarah?"

"Stay with me tonight Danny! Come back to my house and stay tonight. I... I don't want you to go home. Nicole's away at her mother's and we'll have the house to ourselves. I'll cook you dinner and we can.... we can..."

Sarah's eyes were haunted and desperate. Daniela looked at her intently. "Sarah! Are you sure? Do you really want me to stay?"

"Yes! Please stay Danny. I... I can't bear to let go of you yet."

"Then of course I'll stay Sarah. Thank you. I would love to spend the night with you."

Sarah blushed and glanced up at the gathering clouds. "Well we'd better get a move on then or we're going to get caught in the rain."

"Ever danced naked in the rain Sarah?"

"Not since I was a little girl Danny. It was wet and cold."

"That's my Sarah. Ever the romantic."

"I think sensible is the word you're looking for."

Their steps quickened after this new resolve. Their stride lengthened with renewed urgency. The leaden pace toward some intolerable parting was lifted from its melancholy. There was now a reason to hasten; another night to spend together and, if the darkening clouds accumulating in the valley behind them were not enough to spur their efforts, then the anticipation of the unspoken promise in Sarah's invitation was ample enough to hurry them forward in eagerness. It was a promise doomed by circumstance.

It was not until the final drop to Gamplut that their hopes received some inkling of the disaster about to overtake them. They crested a small rocky prominence sparsely sprinkled with stunted conifers and looked down onto Gamplut; the broad sunny alp of verdant meadow where the little restaurant rested at the top of the cable car line which brought the small gondolas up from Wildhaus. They had hoped for a secluded drink at

145

the restaurant; a little period of rest and peace before the final leg of their hike down to Alpli. The first intimation that such a hope was bedevilled was the sound of music wafting up from the alp. They stood and regarded the scene below with amazement and dismay. Around the restaurant there appeared to be dozens of people milling around. There was a marquee erected alongside the restaurant and there were extra collapsible tables and benches around small beer tents and barbecue grills. There was music from a band under a covered stage and people were dancing in a cleared space before it. The sound of laughter and the scents of food drifted up to them through the air which was becoming ominously still and heavy as the storm clouds gathered over the mountains.

"Damn!" remarked Daniela, "It looks like there's a hell of a party going on."

Sarah grunted with resignation. "It's an alpfest. A lot of mountain huts and guest houses throw a fest during the summer months. Maybe that's why there were so many people coming over the pass today. I'm sorry Danny. I didn't know there'd be a fest on at Gamplut today."

"Well there goes our chance for a quiet drink Sarah."

"Yes we can't go in there. You'd be swamped in no time. I guess we'd better cut past and just head across the alp and down to Alpli."

"Damn it Sarah! I was really looking forward to a drink. I'm parched."

"I'm sorry Danny." Sarah looked deflated. "But if we go in there you're going to have everybody and their grandma crawling all over you. I... I wanted you to have a little privacy."

"I'm used to the attentions of a lot of people Sarah."

"I know Danny but... but well I wanted you all for myself."

Daniela smiled and touched Sarah lightly on the arm. "Darling we'll have all the time in the world to ourselves. Right now though, I could do with a drink."

Sarah thought for a moment. "Perhaps you could wait here and I can slip down, grab us a couple of drinks and then we can push on."

Daniela shook her heads with a wry grin. "Sarah sweetheart. When are you going to understand that I'm not the only person here with a monopoly on the condition of fame? I'm guessing that that party down there is going to be full of people from the Toggenburg. That means it's going to be crawling with your friends, sundry acquaintances and other diverse members of the Sarah Fuchs fan club. You haven't a hope in hell of walking in there, grabbing a couple of bottles and shoving off without mortally offending half the inhabitants of the valley."

Sarah agonised over the truth in Daniela's words. "Well what the hell are we going to do then?"

"Let's just go down and have one drink Sarah. We'll put in a token appearance, pay our condescending respects to the peasantry and then push off with abject apologies concerning the pressing requirements of urgent necessity."

"Are you sure Danny?"

Even as Sarah articulated her doubts a long, reverberating crash of thunder echoed off the mountains around them. They glanced back to see an evil looking black cloud enveloping the peaks behind them and rolling down the valley toward them. Daniela nodded gloomily. "I think that more or less makes our decision for us Sarah; Noblesse oblige or Cumulonimbus. We can walk into that party as star guests or walk down to Alpli like half drowned rats."

"Oh the hell with it then. Let's go get a drink. Hopefully that thunderstorm will pass over quickly."

Once they had made the decision they crossed the intervening space quickly. Crashes of thunder were becoming frequent now and they saw the agitation from among the people at the party as barbecues were being hastily relocated under shelter and awnings being erected over the stage and makeshift bars. In the consternation excited by the approaching weather front Daniela and Sarah's arrival on the scene went largely unnoticed. Their anonymity was fleetingly ephemeral however. There was a piercing and all too familiar whistle. Sarah glanced up in shock. Hurrying toward them was a small figure clad in a black flimsy top and a scandalously short orange pettiskirt resembling a ballet tutu. "Oh shit!" murmured Sarah, "It's Nicole."

Chapter Fourteen

Sarah approached Nicole warily, almost guiltily, conscious of the fact that Nicole was quite within her rights to attach the worst possible interpretation onto Daniela's presence alongside her. Indeed Nicole, who had stood to approach them was looking ill pleased and her eyes were darting between them suspiciously. Sarah forced a smile onto her face and tried desperately to look nonchalant and innocent. It only succeeded in making her appear more guilty than ever. Drama had never been one of Sarah's strong subjects at school. Nicole's suspicions deepened and Sarah would have to concede that they were not without foundation. "Hi there Nicky!" Sarah greeted her brightly but her voice sounded brittle even to her. "I... I didn't know you were back yet."

"I'd already figured that." Nicole turned to Daniela. "Hello Daniela." she said with ill-favoured grace.

Daniela's performance was far more polished than Sarah's and she held out a hand with a dazzling smile. "Hello Nicole. It's good to see you again." Daniela's greeting was so full of natural warmth that even Nicole's barely concealed animosity melted somewhat under it and she took Daniela's hand reluctantly. Sarah realised with inner resignation that she would never be able to match Daniela's easy charm and grace. Daniela didn't seem at all fazed by Nicole apparently catching her with her fingers in the jam jar and there was nothing whatsoever in her manner to suggest that she was not delighted to see Nicole. In fact Daniela genuinely liked Nicole, she knew, and was even, on occasion, to accord her foibles more sympathy than Sarah.

Sarah seemed to think that explanations were in order. "Er Daniela and I have been hiking Nicky." She ventured tentatively. She could have kicked herself immediately. Since both she and Daniela were after all on a mountainside clad in hiking boots and bearing walking sticks and hefty looking rucksacks it was an unlikely assumption that they had just spent the day shopping.

Nicole regarded her sourly. "*Really*!" she replied and Sarah reflected that she had rarely in her life heard so much sarcasm, disbelief and accusation squeezed into a single word.

Daniela intervened smoothly. "What's the party all about?" she asked.

Nicole regarded Daniela with incredulity. "You mean you don't *know*?"

Daniela blinked; caught by surprise by Nicole's suddenly furious demand. "No. I'm sorry. I have no idea."

Sarah glanced around nervously suddenly aware that she was missing something important. "What's happening Nicky?"

Nicole was staring at her in disbelief. "You didn't get the letters or the messages then? You actually had no idea what was going on?"

"Well er no Nicky. I... I just thought...."

Before Sarah could flounder out of the quagmire of recriminations that seemed to be enveloping her a booming voice arrested her. "At last! The star's finally arrived." She turned in shock to see Peter approaching with his arms held wide. "I know the star is always late Sarah but you really kept us dangling this time. Nicky here didn't think you were going to turn up at all."

Sarah staggered in bewilderment. "Star.... turn up... what the hell are you talking about?"

Nicole placed her hands on her hips and turned to Peter in disgust. "She didn't even *know* Peter. She obviously hasn't got any of our messages or other communications. She's been fannying around up a mountain for the last few days and quite obviously hasn't a clue what's going on."

"Oh Christ! Seriously? Oh my God! I must have left a dozen messages on your phone Sarah. When I couldn't get a reply from you I left messages with everyone I could think of to contact you; even Alan and your parents. I thought somebody must have contacted you."

"No Peter. My phone's been uncharged for the past day or so. I don't know what the devil all this is about."

"You don't mean that you just turned up here by accident?"

"Yes of course. Daniela and I have been hiking. We were just on our way back and thought we'd drop in here for a drink."

"Oh Jesus!" Peter looked devastated.

"Amazing isn't it?" declared Nicole contemptuously. "After all the effort you put in as well Peter."

"Well at least she's here now." said Peter brightening somewhat. "Better late than never." He paused to hold out a hand to Daniela. "You must be Miss Devin miss. Forgive my rudeness in not saying hello. My name's Peter. I'm a friend of Sarah's."

Daniela turned on her full charm and took the hand warmly. "Hello Peter. I'm pleased to meet you at last. Sarah has told me much about you."

"Good things I hope."

"Oh yes. Nothing but good things. Sarah admires you a great deal sir."

Peter rubbed his chin sheepishly. "Well I don't know about that. Anyway thank God you two ladies decided to hike back this way or we would have been facing a major embarrassment."

Sarah suddenly stamped her foot angrily. "Will somebody please explain what the bloody hell is going on!"

Nicole took her arm. "You'd better come with me Miss Fuchs. All will become apparent in due course."

Peter jumped about in agitation. "Wait Nicky! Let me go inside and make the announcement first."

A rumble of thunder warned once again of the approaching storm. "Well hurry up Pete." Nicole urged. "It's going to piss it down in about two minutes."

"Two minutes then. Just wait here." Peter dashed off into the marquee where it seemed most of the party goers were gathering to shelter.

Sarah was nearly weeping in frustration and nervousness. "Please Nicky. Tell me what's happening."

Nicole was unmoved by Sarah's plaintive bleating. "You can wait and find out."

They waited for a few minutes but then a rushing sound on the alp behind them warned that their self-possession was about to be sorely tested by the weather. The Schafberg had already disappeared behind a great black cloud and a rolling sheet of rain was racing down the alp toward them. Nicole hurried them under the shelter of the marquee.

Sarah recognised the big tent. The restaurant at Gamplut often used it for big outdoor parties and the smaller tents, hastily erected to house outdoor bars and barbecues. Inside the marquee, Sarah blinked in astonishment. It was packed with people she knew and her entrance elicited an enormous cheer. She gazed around completely stunned. Her name was everywhere; on the bunting hanging from the walls, on the myriads of balloons that were all over the place and on the great banner hung above the stage, where a popular local band was mustered in front of a wooden dance floor. Sarah stood white faced as people crowded around her to hug her and kiss her, as Nicole relieved her of her rucksack. The lead singer of the band; an attractive girl in her early twenties stepped up to the microphone. "Ladies and gentlemen! The star of the show has finally arrived. Let's all hear it for the Toggenburg's one and only Sarah." There was another raucous burst of cheering and then the band launched into an obviously prearranged ballad from the 1980's with heavily modified lyrics.

"Go now don't look back we've drawn the line,

Move on it's no good to go back in time,

We'll never find another girl like you, for happy endings it takes two
We're fire and ice, let the dream come true

Sarah, Sarah, storms are brewing in your eyes
Sarah, Sarah, no time is a good time for goodbyes

Danger in the game when stakes are high
Branded; our hearts were branded while our senses stood by

We'll never find another girl like you, for happy endings it takes two,
We're fire and ice, let the dream come true,

Sarah, Sarah, storms are brewing in your eyes
Sarah, Sarah, no time is a good time oh
Sarah, Sarah, storms are brewing in your eyes
Sarah, Sarah, no time is a good time for goodbyes

'Cause Sarah we love you, like no-one ever loved before
And Sarah, it hurts us like no-one hurt us before
And Sarah, Sarah
And Sarah we'll love you evermore

We'll never find another girl like you
We're fire and ice, let the dream come true

Sarah, Sarah, no time is a good time oh

Sarah, Sarah, storms are brewing in your eyes
Sarah, Sarah, no time is a good time for goodbyes

Sarah, Sarah, storms are brewing in your eyes
Sarah, Sarah, no time is a good time, no

153

Oh Sarah, don't let it, don't let it, don't let it all fall apart."

A huge round of cheering accompanied the end of the song and Sarah stood in utter bewilderment, amid the chaos, with tears streaming down her eyes. Peter was at her side grinning. "This is your party Sarah. The valley's big send off for our very own Sarah."

"What... what do you mean Peter?"

"Alan called a few days ago Sarah. He's coming back to Switzerland in two weeks and then he's taking you away. He wants you in the Ticino when he gets back so we had to put this all together in a hurry. We wanted to give you a big send off so a few of us got together to hire the Gamplut for the day and throw a big party. We've got the place until midnight and they're going to run the gondola until then so everyone can get back. I've been trying to get hold of you for two days now. Nicky didn't think you'd come at all but I thought we'd find you sooner or later. Have a good time Sarah. This is your big night."

Sarah was crying. "Oh Peter! You... you immortal idiot! Why have you done this?"

"Just a surprise Sarah. I just wanted to let you know how much we all think about you."

Nicole was pushing her way through the crowd surrounding Sarah. "Come on everybody. Give Sarah some room and let her get her breath back." She took Sarah's arm. "Come on Foxy. Let's get you a drink."

"Where... where's Danny... I mean Daniela?"

"Just over here. I've kept a table free. Now what do you want; beer, wine; something stronger?"

"A beer please. Christ!" Sarah's blasphemy was understandable for the tent suddenly shook to a gust of wind and the sound of hammering rain on the roof.

"Ok one beer coming up. What does er... Daniela want?"

"I think she'll probably have a beer too."

Nicole nodded. "Ok I'll just bring a case!" She looked at Sarah sideways. "You and me have to have a serious talk Miss Fuchs. You have some bloody explaining to do!" Nicole departed with a grim face.

Sarah dabbed her eyes and composed herself. She wended her way through the crowd to the table where Daniela was sitting alone. She paused in concern. Daniela had her face buried in her hands and she was shaking. For an awful moment Sarah thought that Daniela was distraught but then she realised that her friend was in fact laughing helplessly. Sarah slid onto the bench next to her. "What's so bloody funny?" she hissed furiously.

Daniela gasped for breath and wiped her eyes. "Oh Sarah! This is priceless. There you were worrying that *I'd* be the centre of attention. My God!" Daniela collapsed in another paroxysm of laughter. "God I've never been so upstaged in my life. You should have seen your face when we walked in here. You were absolutely precious."

"Stop it Danny. It's not funny. I could kill Peter for dropping this on me."

"Go with the flow sweetheart. This is the price of fame. I guess we can forget about a quick drink and a swift diplomatic departure now."

"Oh God! I don't know. Maybe we'll be able to get away."

"Dreamer! Your public will never allow it. Grin and bear it darling. You're stuck here for the duration. Put on a brave face and try to look pleased."

"I'm sorry Danny. I had no idea this was going to happen. I suppose I'll have to stay now. You don't have to though."

"I wouldn't miss it for the world honey. Anyway I haven't the faintest idea how to get back to your place from here on my own."

Sarah groaned comically. "Oh God! I nearly died when they played that song for me. Where the hell did that come from?"

"It's a 1986 hit song; "*Sara*" from "Starship" which was a spin-off from the old Jefferson Starship, Sarah. It was on their album "Knee Deep in the Hoopla" released in 1985 which also featured their hit single "We Built this City". It was written by Peter and Ina Wolf and sung in the original line-up by Mickey Thomas. It's been covered a lot of times since; I think quite recently by Shania Twain. That band did quite a slick version of it, I thought, although they changed the lyrics considerably."

"Now who's being a geek?"

"You know your natural history Sarah. I know my music."

Sarah sighed. "Oh God! Why did this have to happen? I know it's sweet of them to have arranged this party for me but I wanted to be alone with you. Everything's ruined now."

Daniela placed a hand on Sarah's bare leg just below the hem of her short skirt and leaned forward to whisper in her ear. "There'll be other times my sweet."

"Ahem!" Sarah jumped and pulled away from Daniela. Nicole was standing by the table bearing beer and looking at her curiously.

"Oh er... thanks Nicky." Sarah took the beer; her face flushing crimson.

Peter came up in Nicole's wake looking pleased with himself. "Are you ladies hungry?" he asked. "We've managed to get the barbecues out of the rain."

"I certainly am." Daniela declared. "We had a bite up on the Zwinglipass but, apart from an orange, I've had nothing since. Shall we go grab something off the barby Sarah?"

Nicole intervened in an aloof tone. "Perhaps Peter can accompany you to the barbeque Miss Devin. I'd like a quick word with Sarah if you don't mind. Alone!"

"Why of course I'll take Miss Devin to the barbecue." Peter volunteered. "It would be my pleasure."

Daniela seemed to be having a hard time keeping a straight face but she rose politely and wickedly placed a hand in the crook of Peter's arm. "Why thank you kind sir. That is most gallant of you. But please call me Daniela or better yet just Danny."

As soon as they had departed Nicole sat down firmly at Sarah's side and regarded her with a determined look on her face. "Right then Miss Fuchs. Start talking. You have some bloody explaining to do."

Sarah glared at her. "I can't see anything I have to explain Nicky."

"Oh no? Well let's start with how it is that you've just spent the last three days having a cosy little affair with Daniela bloody Devin."

"I have *not* been having an affair. We went hiking in the mountains; that's all. She wanted to see the high mountains so I told her I'd be her guide. Why are you being so rude and hostile to her?"

"Are you sleeping with her?"

"We stayed in the dormitory Nicky. If sharing a room with her and a dozen or so other assorted hikers counts as sleeping together then I suppose I am."

"You know damn well what I mean Sarah. You were holding hands with her when you were walking across the alp."

"She's a good friend Nicky. She's an affectionate person. There's nothing sinister in two girls holding hands."

"Hmmph! Just sisterly affection then was it? You're not exactly known for tactile contact with your good friends Sarah. You never hold *my* hand."

"That's different."

"Oh yes I know. I'm not a drop dead gorgeous, filthy rich, famous rock star."

"I don't know what you're trying to insinuate Nicole but I won't have it. I like Daniela and I don't give

157

a damn for her money or fame. I won't have you being so uncivil to her. She's a nice person and she doesn't deserve to be treated like that. If you can't find anything pleasant to say to her, then hold your tongue."

"Well just what is your relationship to her?"

"She's a dear friend Nicole although I don't see what business it is of yours."

"Of course it's my business Sarah. I'm your oldest friend remember. We share a house together. Naturally it's my business if my best friend is going off for three days and making a fool of herself with some female rock star. You're not cut out to be a groupie Sarah."

"That's a monstrous thing to say!"

"Peter's been going mental wondering where you were. He phoned me up at my parents yesterday and told me about this party he was throwing for you but he couldn't get hold of you anywhere. I tried to phone you without success and then *I* was worried. Peter asked me to come back and help locate you. I didn't need much urging. Mum was sat around, with her leg in plaster, being a bloody drama queen. I drove back this morning and picked up Peter in Unterwasser and we drove up to the house. The first thing we see is a bloody great red Ferrari parked in the drive and the neighbours tell us it's been planted there for the last three days. There was no sign of you in the house and no indication that the place had been occupied for the last three days. Well we kept trying to phone you and we must have left at least a dozen messages on your phone telling you about the party and asking you to get in touch. I thought at least you might check your messages once in a while. Peter was frantic. He'd gone to all this trouble to arrange this party for you and it looked like we might have to cancel.

We phoned up everywhere we could think of. We even phoned Frau Fritzl at the Toggenburg and she hadn't seen you either. She did say however that you were talking about going off hiking. Well I checked your room and sure enough your hiking boots and rucksack were missing. So we started phoning around the mountain huts. Finally I got hold of Hans on the Santis and he told us that you'd been there the day before but you'd left in the morning to head for Rotsteinpass. So then I phoned up Rotsteinpass and they said they hadn't seen you."

"There was nobody around when we got there but I left a note."

"Well Peter was beside himself at this point and it was all I could do to stop him from calling out the mountain rescue service. I urged him to be calm and sat down and thought a bit. It's only an hour and a half from Santis to Rotsteinpass so maybe you never stopped there. I phoned up Schafboden in case you'd cut down from Rotsteinpass in that direction but no joy there. Then it occurred to me that you might have climbed up over Altmann and so I phoned up Samtisersee and finally Bollenwees. There I hit pay dirt. Frau Manser was most informative. Yes you'd been there last night; sharing a double room with no less a personage than Fraulein Daniela Devin. She didn't mention anything about dormitories and the dozen other hikers you were sharing with Sarah. It sounded all very domestic to me.

"Anyway she said you'd headed off over Zwinglipass toward Gamplut and we naturally assumed that you must have got the messages after all and that it was your plan to make it to the party so we decided to go ahead. It would have been too late to cancel in any case by then. The band and the barbecues were already up here and invitations had gone out to just about everyone in the valley and then some. We'd have looked like complete berks if you'd decided to take another route home. It's going to take some diplomatic niceties to explain Daniela's presence with you in any case. God knows what the scandal would have been if it had become known that you missed a party thrown in your honour because you were out gadding about with your new girlfriend."

Sarah blushed but she was honest enough to concede that Nicole had some grounds for grievance. "I'm sorry to have worried you Nicky. My phone's been dead for the last day or so and I forgot to take my charger. I had no idea that Peter was throwing a party for me."

"Why the hell didn't you let someone know where you were going?"

"I did! I phoned Hans up to let him know we were coming."

"Why didn't you phone up and tell *me*?"

"I.... I didn't think you'd understand."

"Damn right I don't. You deliberately never phoned me didn't you Sarah? You quite blatantly waited until I was out of the house for a few days so you could go off with your girlfriend without having to tell me. You were being deceitful Sarah. What the hell's happening to you? You've never tried to deceive me before. Then you breeze in here and brazenly tell me that you and Daniela are just good friends. I don't believe a word of it Sarah. You wouldn't have been so sly and duplicitous if she was just a pal you were going hiking with. You're having an affair with her aren't you? Don't try to deny it. You've got guilt written all over your face."

"Nicky I haven't slept with her honestly. Yes it's true we took a double room last night but that was because there were so many people at Bollenwees and it's bad enough for somebody as famous as she is just to share a dining room with a lot of people let alone sleep in the same dorm with them. But nothing happened Nicky I swear it."

"Nothing? Nothing at all?"

"We... we haven't.... haven't had sex Nicky if that's what you mean."

"So you've just been holding hands."

"Well I.... I've kissed her."

"Aha!"

"It's just a kiss Nicky; perfectly innocent. I've kissed girls before. I've kissed *you* before."

"Yes but you've never turned as red as a beetroot whilst confessing it before."

"Oh it's just a kiss Nicky."

"Just the one kiss was it Sarah; just a friendly little peck on the cheek was it?"

Sarah lowered her head. "Well no.... I suppose not."

"So these innocent kisses are getting a little beyond the requirements of sisterly affection aren't they Sarah? Not to put too fine a point on it one might even say that your drawers are hanging on your hips by the flimsiest of threads."

"Do you have to be so vulgar?"

"You don't deny it then. If you hadn't come to this party and I was still away what were your plans for tonight Sarah?"

"We were going to have dinner together."

"In a restaurant or at home?"

"Well I said I was going to cook for her."

"I see! And after that? A nice cosy game of backgammon perhaps?"

"I wasn't planning to jump into bed with her if that's what you mean by these insinuations!"

Nicole put her beer bottle down with deliberation and looked Sarah straight in the eye. "Sarah, tell me the truth. There *is* something going on between you and her isn't there? Ok so maybe you've not been sleeping with her but that's not for the want of her trying is it? When I brought the beers back she was pawing at your leg and looking at you with smoky, come to bed eyes. She's wrapping you around her little finger Sarah."

"What do you mean?"

"Oh Sarah! Don't be naive. This is a powerful woman; a consummate seductress and predatory. She probably gobbles up silly little star-struck girls for breakfast. She's a worldly and sophisticated female Sarah. You might have a university degree Foxy but when all's said and done you're still a simple country girl at heart. You've no chance against the Daniela Devin's of this world. She'll swallow you and spit you out. She's got her pick of thousands of young girls slobbering around her feet. What makes you think that *you're* anything special? She'll soon get tired of you once she's had her way with you."

"You're being horrible Nicky! You're wrong about her. She's not that kind of person."

"Are you attracted to her Sarah? Be honest."

Sarah blushed and swallowed. "Yes," she whispered at last, "Yes I am."

Nicole shook her head sadly. "This is all going to end in tears Sarah. What the hell's happened to you? Until you met this woman you've never shown the slightest inclination to be attracted to your own sex. Now you're going to throw it all away; your reputation, your marriage, your friends and family all over some starry-eyed infatuation with a bloody pop star. You're a grown woman Sarah, not a bloody teenager. Come to think of it, you had more sense when you were a teenager. Maybe you just deferred your maturation. I don't know. All I know is that you're heading for one almighty great heartbreak. I can't let you do it Sarah. I can't sit back and watch you blow everything with a late resurgence of adolescent adulation. You should have exercised this sort of crap when you were sixteen Sarah; not now. You've too much to lose now."

"You're being hateful Nicky! I can't believe you're talking like this about me."

"You've never acted like this before."

Sarah's eyes flashed dangerously. "Well you're wrong Nicky! Oh I can see why you might think these things about me but you're wrong. You're wrong about me and you're wrong about Daniela. Yes I'm attracted to her but it's not because she's a celebrated pop star. It's because she happens to be a wonderful kind and gentle woman the like of which I never met before. She's shown me more affection and consideration in a few weeks than my so-called future husband has managed in three years. Ok maybe I *have* grown up a bit late. I've let my family determine my future for too long. I've let them bulldoze over my own feelings and bind me to a marriage that makes my stomach turn over every time I think about it. Well now I am growing up Nicky. I'm growing up enough to know my own mind. I've learned things about myself Nicole since I've known Daniela; things perhaps that I never was able to admit to myself before. I've found more happiness with Daniela in a few weeks than ever I knew with the men in my life. So does that make me wrong? Maybe you'll condemn me for being lesbian. Maybe you'll think that you'll be tainted by association; that people will say you've been sharing a house with a lesbian and it'll cast doubt on you. I don't know Nicky. I don't want to do anything to hurt you. I didn't want this to happen. My mind is all in a turmoil Nicky. I need your support, not your criticism. Nothing like this ever happened to me before. I'm at a crisis point in my life Nicole and all you can do is accuse me of being immature. I'd hoped for better from you." Sarah buried her face in her hands and sobbed. "You just don't understand do you?"

Nicole placed an arm around Sarah's shoulder in concern. "Sarah I *am* trying to understand honey. I just don't want to see you get hurt." Nicole sighed heavily. "I had a long talk with Peter about you today Sarah."

Sarah lifted a teary face. "Oh God! What were you saying about me?"

"Peter told me all about what happened between you in Winterthur. I told him that you came home that night in tears. I don't think he realised just how devastated you were when he told you he was gay. He feels terrible about it. He was the real love of your life wasn't he Sarah? He was the man you really wanted and then it turns out he's gay and he's snatched away from you. The next thing we know you've fallen into the arms of another woman. Peter thinks it's all his fault."

"Oh my God! Is this what you think? Do you think I've just rebounded on Daniela because of my unrequited love for Peter?"

"I don't know *what's* going on with you Sarah. All I know is that all of a sudden I don't recognise the girl I've known ever since we were kids. You've always been the steady sensible one and I was the one that was always the volatile one. Now look at you. You're an emotional mess. You've been on a roller coaster ride ever since you got home from uni and I don't know where your head's at any more. I want to help you but I don't know how."

"So what am I supposed to do Nicky?"

"Do? Do what you always used to do Sarah. Take a time out; stand back and take a good long appraisal of things. Chill this thing you've got going with Daniela and stand back and take a good look at it. Let the sensible Sarah take the upper hand again."

"I'm sick of being sensible Nicky. Being sensible roped me into a marriage I don't want."

"Is that it Sarah? Is suddenly turning lesbian a way of worming out of marriage to Alan?"

"Give me a break Nicky! I was dreading marrying before I even knew who Daniela was."

Nicole took a deep breath and stared at Sarah with tragically wide eyes. "Sarah! Please don't tell me that you've fallen in love with this woman."

"Well what if I have? Is that wrong?"

"Yes it is. It's the worst possible thing that could have happened."

Sarah glared at her and would have replied but at that moment Peter and Daniela returned with plates of food. Hastily Sarah dried her eyes but knew it was futile. Daniela was surveying the two of them piercingly and Sarah knew that she would see instantly that she'd been crying. "Are we interrupting?" Daniela inquired in a neutral tone.

Sarah shook her head miserably and Nicole sighed and said, "No I think we're all done."

Peter placed the food on the table. "We've brought some munchies. I hope it didn't get too damp. We had to make a dash from the barbecue and it's peeing it down out there."

They ate in an awkward silence. Sarah turned her attention to her food with a devotion that the rather simple repast of grilled meats, sausages, burgers and salads didn't particularly deserve. It was merely a way of avoiding Nicole's eye which was fixed on her piercingly and full of unspoken accusation. Peter looked thoroughly discomfited and he kept glancing at Sarah concernedly. The only person not looking uncomfortable was Daniela. Sarah was aware that there was a steel core; an inner strength to her friend that had its roots in personal experience; the sort of wisdom that came with having seen it all before. It would take more than an embarrassing encounter to faze Daniela. She kept her silence at the table with what Sarah could only describe as serene tranquillity.

There was a little more to it too for Sarah, who was beginning to recognise the subtle nuances in her complex friend's character, could detect just a hint of amusement in Daniela's demeanour; a sort of wicked enjoyment of the situation that tickled her sense of the absurd. She could not have been more diplomatic however. She had quickly seen that any remarks from her would be inappropriate at this juncture and so she kept her peace, responding only to Peter's polite remarks and inquiries. Peter was becoming more and more uncomfortable with the fact that Nicole, by avoiding talking to Daniela, was being unnecessarily rude if not downright hostile. Whatever Peter might think about Daniela's relationship to Sarah he was nevertheless a courteous man and he could see no justification for not treating her with respect. Most of what little conversation passed therefore was between him and Daniela. "Is this the first time that you've hiked on the Alpstein then Daniela?" he asked.

Daniela nodded warmly. "Yes but it certainly won't be the last. It was beautiful in the mountains. I've had a wonderful three days."

This last remark elicited a barely concealed snort of disgust from Nicole. Peter glared at her but ploughed on bravely. "So you'd like to do some more hiking here then?"

"Absolutely. There are a lot of places I still want to see." Daniela paused and curiously looked straight at Nicole, who was avoiding her glance, before continuing. "I don't think I'm ready to go off on my own however. I'd certainly need to be accompanied by..." she let the phrase hang for a second, "by a companion." Nicole stabbed her fork into a piece of grilled steak with undue venom and Daniela turned her attention back to her own food with a tiny smile. Sarah frowned thoughtfully. Daniela was playing a mischievous game with Nicole. Nicole might accuse Sarah of being out of her depth when it came to dealing with Daniela's manipulations but it seemed evident to Sarah that Nicole was likely to be no match for her either. She hoped fervently that open hostilities would not break out between them.

After a pause the band started to play again and began to lure people out onto the dance floor. The tensions around their table became defused as more and more people arrived at the table to pay their respects to Sarah. For once Sarah didn't mind the attention for it deflected the focus away from the potentially explosive situation. Of course the party was in Sarah's honour so naturally she was at the centre of this attention but she was well aware that Daniela's presence made her company doubly attractive. Most of the people at the party were from the Toggenburg and, by now, they had become accustomed to the presence of Daniela in the valley. Many of them had seen her around or even talked to her. Nevertheless there was still novelty in her attendance for few of the guests at the party had had the chance to speak to her socially and there were also other people from further away, including many of Sarah's old school friends, who had never seen her in person and were eager to meet her.

Daniela dealt with the attention with the grace and easy charm that Sarah was beginning to find characteristic of her. Nicole was somewhat less graceful for she was furious that Sarah was seemingly being upstaged at a party thrown especially for her. Peter, to his credit, was more understanding and tried, as well as he could, to divert guests away from Daniela out of respect for her privacy. He possibly had ulterior motives for this consideration of course. It had not escaped his attention that Daniela's close association with Sarah had all the makings of a monumental scandal in formation. He was fighting a rear-guard action against the inevitable wagging tongues.

Gratifyingly the thunderstorm proved to be relatively short-lived and the clouds dissipated from the mountain tops and the evening sunshine returned to grace the alp and to lure people to the outside of the tent to the open air bars to enjoy their drinks under a glorious sunset. The ground dried quickly although it was too late for some guests who had, in a moment of misplaced enthusiasm, gone out to dance in the rain and were now soaking wet. The party was good natured and Sarah, once she had resigned herself to its inevitability, began to enjoy herself. There were friends whom she had not seen for years and she gossiped happily with them whilst airily brushing aside inquiries about her glamorous companion. A steady flow of drinks appeared before her but she seemed oblivious to the impending peril of her intake of alcohol.

The band was good. They were hardly an innovative outfit for they had few songs of their own and most of their performance was in covering popular songs and golden oldies. In spite of this they were slick and professional in the execution of the songs; very competent musicians and the lead singer had a fine voice. They were certainly not limited by musical style for they offered up a wide selection from rock and roll to country and commercial pop songs to popular ballads. They had a seemingly inexhaustible repertoire and had a little of something for everyone. They were what they said on the packet essentially; just a good professional dance band and just the sort of line-up you would want to hire for a party of this nature. They even had a few traditional folk dances and carnival tunes which were efficacious in filling the dance floor and adding to the good atmosphere of the proceedings. Daniela approved of the band; an approval that found a sympathetic note in her memories of her own humble musical beginnings when she and her band had travelled from gig to gig crammed into a Transit van and played to audiences in dingy nightclubs or at wedding receptions. There was one underlying note of tension however. Among the band's stock of popular tunes were two or three of Daniela's own compositions and the band dared not play them whilst the illustrious author of them was present among the audience.

With so many of the guests succumbing to the music and venturing out to dance, the crowds around Sarah's table thinned out and they enjoyed a few minutes of comparative privacy. Sarah was becoming uncomfortable that she was hardly having a chance to talk to Daniela and it seemed a golden moment. Peter however surprised her. The band began a slow ballad and Peter rose and held out a hand. "Would you like to dance Sarah?"

Sarah blinked at him in surprise. "Dance? You? Dance?"

"I do dance occasionally Sarah."

"I've never seen you."

"I've been taking lessons. Now do you want to dance or not?"

Sarah glanced around with a haunted expression to Daniela who seemed to be having trouble keeping a straight face. "Er will you be all right on your own for a few minutes Danny?" She glanced at Nicole who was sat with a set face.

Daniela grinned. "I'm a big girl Sarah. I can look after myself. You go ahead."

Sarah rose reluctantly pausing only to shoot a sharp look at Nicole, who remained impassive, and allowed Peter to lead her onto the dance floor. Peter took her carefully in his arms for the dance and Sarah could detect bitterly the brotherly way in which he held her, devoid of any sensual content. It was the way in which her father might have danced with her. "What's all this about Peter?" she demanded suspiciously.

"All what Sarah?"

"This! You dancing with me. You've never asked me to dance with you before in your life."

"Sarah you're my best friend and this is your night. I just wanted to dance with you."

"If this is a ruse to get me away from Daniela so that Nicky can have a go at her I'll be well pissed off Peter."

"Sarah please. I have no ulterior motives whatsoever. I just wanted to dance with you. I wanted to talk to you."

"I refuse to discuss my private life to the accompaniment of the theme tune from "Titanic" Peter."

"I just wanted to know that you've forgiven me is all Sarah."

"Forgiven you?"

"Yes; forgiven me for hurting you. Nicole told me how much I hurt you. She said you were shattered after we met in Winterthur. I just wanted to say how sorry I am Sarah."

Sarah sighed resignedly. "It's fine Peter. I've done my crying. I'll get over it."

"Sarah I just wanted you to know that... well that if I was otherwise inclined I'd... well I would have wanted to marry you. You're the only girl I could ever have married. But I couldn't Sarah. It would have been a lie. I... I never realised just how much I meant to you. I'm so sorry Sarah. I'm gay. I can't help that. I didn't ask for things to be that way. It's just the way I'm wired up Sarah. I didn't have a choice about it."

"Where is Simon anyway Peter?"

"At home."

"Why isn't he here?"

Peter hesitated. "We... we thought it best he didn't come."

"Why Peter? You can't hide it forever you know."

Peter nodded miserably. "I know Sarah. I... I just need a little time. This is not an easy time for me at the moment Sarah. It took enough guts for me to tell you, my best friend, and even that caused enough heartbreak. Only a handful of people know. My parents have no idea and I'm dreading telling them."

"It's best they find out from you Peter and not through the grapevine."

"Yes I suppose so. You haven't told anyone else have you; I mean apart from Nicole?"

"I couldn't hide it from Nicky Peter. She's my closest friend."

"You're avoiding the question."

"All right Peter. Yes I have. I've told Daniela."

"Daniela? Why?"

"Because she's the only other person I know who would understand Peter. You need have no fears Peter. She's very discreet and wouldn't dream of disseminating anything I told her in confidence; especially something of this nature. She was very sympathetic to you Peter; probably more than I was. I was... well I was upset but she told me to be more understanding; said that you were

170

probably having a hard time and needed my support. She helped me to put things into perspective. I've forgiven you Peter. There was nothing to forgive really. Things are the way they are. We can't change that. Daniela helped me to see that."

"Sarah were you in love with me?"

"Yes I suppose I was Peter. I'm sorry."

"Sarah I'm *gay*."

"I *know* Peter."

"You don't understand Sarah. You were in love with me. Alan thinks you're in love with him. I'm gay Sarah. You're not."

"What are you trying to say Peter?"

"Daniela. That's what I'm trying to say."

"So that's what's bothering you."

"Damn right it is."

"Maybe people change Peter."

"They don't change in the space of three weeks Sarah. Three weeks ago you were torn between the two men in your life that you loved and now you're out flirting with a known lesbian. It doesn't add up Sarah. What's going on with you?"

"I'm not flirting Peter."

"Well it looks like it."

"It's not a flirtation Peter. It's far more serious than that."

"Oh God Sarah! What are you trying to say?"

"I don't know Peter. You ask me what's happening to me. Well I can't tell you. I just don't know. All I know is that you're not the only one going through a rough time in their personal relationships at the moment. I need your support too Peter. I'd have thought that, given your own personal situation, you at least would understand. I know I can't expect much sympathy from Nicky but I thought that at least you could empathise."

"You have more sympathy from Nicole than you realise Sarah."

"Well she's not doing a good job of showing it Peter."

"Nicky's the way Nicky is Sarah. Don't be hard on her. She cares deeply about you and she doesn't want to see you get hurt."

"Does she want to see me happy though?"

"Everybody wants to see you happy Sarah."

"Do they? You know Peter everybody has strong opinions about what is best for me but nobody actually ever seems to ask me if I agree with them." The song came to an end and the lead singer announced that the band was taking a short respite. The couples drifted away from the dance floor in search of drinks and Sarah paused to say. "Thank you for the dance Peter. I shall treasure that."

Peter grasped her by the arms strongly. "We have to talk Sarah; we have to talk seriously."

"Not tonight Peter. I have too many things to think about. Not tonight."

"Tomorrow then! I'll call around tomorrow."

"If you wish Peter. Now let's join the others."

If Peter had had no ulterior motive in removing Sarah so that Nicole could have words with Daniela then Nicole at least had no such compunctions over the opportunity afforded for, as soon as Sarah was strategically removed from the equation, she turned to Daniela determinedly. "What are you doing to Sarah?" she demanded heatedly.

Daniela's poise remained calm and unruffled. "I'm not doing anything to Sarah Nicole. Why ever would you think that I'm "doing" something to her?"

"Are you sleeping with her?"

"I'm sure Nicole that you've already asked Sarah the same question. I'm sure she's told you the truth."

"She denies it."

"Well then why are you questioning her veracity?"

"I want to know the truth!"

"Then why do you disbelieve it when you are told it?"

"Sarah's my best friend Daniela. I'm not just going to stand by and watch her get hurt."

"I'm very pleased to hear it Nicole. Your concerns are admirable. I would not want to see her get hurt either."

"She'll get hurt with you Daniela."

"I'm sorry if you think that Nicole. It certainly isn't my intention to hurt her."

"Is she one of your groupies Daniela?"

Daniela held up a hand with a flash in her eyes. "Nicole there is no need to be offensive. I don't *have* groupies and I certainly don't regard Sarah as such. She is very dear to me and I am offended that you should refer to her in such a derogatory fashion. You may insult me as much as you wish but I won't tolerate you speaking of someone dear to me in that fashion. If she is truly your best friend then I think you ought to afford her the respect due to her. I won't hear you talk about her like that."

Nicole backed off, shocked by Daniela's sudden flash of anger and realising that she had overstepped the mark. "All right I'm sorry. Maybe that was a bit over the top. But you still can't keep seeing her like this. You've got her all confused and it's going to end in tears."

"Sarah is a grown woman Nicole. I would let her make up her own mind about things."

"Sarah can't make up her own mind. She's out of her depth."

"So am I Nicole."

"What do you mean?"

"I mean Nicole that I'm floundering just as much as Sarah is. I know you think that I'm some predatory siren come to steal Sarah away but that's not the truth Nicole. I'm not in control over what happens between Sarah and me. I'm as much a victim of events as she is."

"I don't believe it."

173

"I'm sorry you feel that way Nicole. I don't want there to be animosity between us. I like you and admire you. I know that your hostility to me comes only from a deep wish to protect Sarah and I applaud you for that sentiment and I can't hold it against you. I know what Sarah means to you."

"You've no idea what Sarah means to me."

"Oh but I do Nicole. I know what Sarah means to you better than Sarah knows what she means to you."

"What do you mean?"

"Only that I'm sorry Nicole. I truly am. I hope one day that you will forgive me and we can be reconciled. In the meantime, let me at least offer this reassurance. As long as I live I will endeavour never, whether intentionally or otherwise, to hurt Sarah."

"Then leave her alone."

"I'm sorry Nicole. I really am sorry but it's too late for that. I can't leave her."

"What about her marriage?"

"Ultimately she will decide that herself Nicole. It is not my part to speculate on that. Something interests me though. Why do you perceive me to be a threat to Sarah and her fiancée not? Why is it acceptable to you for her to be tied in a marriage to a man she does not love yet it is so unthinkable that she might fall in love with another woman? I'm not asking you Nicole for that is your business but I can't help but wonder."

Daniela was gazing at Nicole steadily; her eyes searching. Nicole swallowed. "What makes you say she's in love with you?"

"I didn't Nicole. But I rather suspect that you think she may be."

"Sarah's not a lesbian. Why would she go with another woman? She's never been with another girl before!"

"She's been with one girl I can think of most of her life Nicole."

"What are you talking about?"

174

"Nothing really. Just idle thoughts. Let's at least declare a temporary truce Nicole. I don't want to fight with you and this is hardly an appropriate occasion for us to fall out. Can we not just declare a cessation of hostilities for the moment and try to be civil to each other? We could be friends."

"Why would you want to be friendly with me?"

"Because Sarah loves you and that makes you special to me."

Nicole choked and struggled for words. Before she could find any the song had come to an end and Peter and Sarah returned to the table. Sarah glared at Nicole fiercely, aware that they were interrupting what could only have been a charged conversation. Daniela rummaged in her rucksack for a small handbag and rose easily to her feet. "If you'll excuse me ladies and gentleman I need to use the ladies."

As soon as she had left Sarah rounded on Nicole furiously. "What have you been saying to Daniela Nicky?"

"We've just been talking."

"Bullshit! You've been having a go at her haven't you?"

"I said my piece and she said hers Sarah. That's all. We agree to differ, so let's drop it."

Sarah jumped to her feet to follow Daniela. "If you've upset her Nicky I'll never forgive you." She stormed off in pursuit of Daniela.

Peter caught his breath. "God! What's happened?" He looked at Nicole and paused in shock. Nicole had her head buried in her hands and she was weeping uncontrollably.

Chapter Fifteen

Sarah caught up with Daniela in the ladies lavatory in the little restaurant, a few yards away from the party tent. She was brushing out her hair before the mirror looking solemn; her face tinged with sadness. "Oh Danny!" Sarah began, "I'm sorry. I don't know what's the matter with Nicky. She's got no right to be so mean to you."

Daniela smiled sadly. "Sarah honey we knew that this would happen. We had to return to the real world and people would put the worst possible interpretation on things. I did warn you that this would happen."

Sarah frowned angrily. "It's too bad of her Danny. She's being a complete bitch. If she's upset you I swear I'll never talk to her again."

Daniela spun around so sharply that Sarah was caught off balance. Daniela grasped her wrists so tightly that it hurt. "Don't say that Sarah! Don't *ever* say that! Nicole is your best friend. Don't ever lose her because of me. Friends like that Sarah are too precious to lose just over some silly little disagreement. Withdraw that remark!"

Sarah blinked, taken aback by Daniela's sudden vehemence. "I... I'm sorry Danny. I... I was just a bit angry."

Daniela's eyes were piercing in their intensity. "Listen Sarah! Listen carefully. Nicole is too important to you. Never lose her. Never cast her aside and never let me come between you. Nicole has not upset me Sarah. She's made me a little sad perhaps but not for the reasons you might think. I feel for Nicole Sarah. She might hate me but I sympathise with her. You should too. This is not easy for her."

"But why should she hate you?"

Daniela lowered her head sadly. "Oh Sarah. I love you to bits. You're the most wonderful girl I ever met but you can be really dense sometimes."

"What... what are you talking about?"

"I love you Sarah. I love you so much it is like a great ache in my heart. Every minute that I'm not with you is a minute wasted; a constant pain of your absence. I can no longer imagine a life without you. It would be so desolate and devoid of joy. If I feel like that after just a few short weeks how must that feel to Nicole?"

"What do you mean?"

"Nicole has loved you longer than I have Sarah. I'm Jenny come lately; the woman who stole her girl."

"Th... that's crazy!"

"Is it Sarah?"

"Of course it is. Nicky has never been jealous of Alan or Peter and she knows that I've thought of marrying one of them."

"Yes Sarah but they were men and men that she knew that, deep down, you didn't really love in the same way you love her. Now I come along Sarah and she sees that you are falling in love with me. She thinks that you are giving me that part of your heart that she always considered belonged to her and she's frightened. This is the worst thing that could happen to her. She couldn't lose her Sarah to Alan but she fears terribly that she could lose her to me."

Sarah pulled away and leaned against the wall. "Oh God! That can't be true."

"I'm sorry Sarah. I feel terrible about this. I wish it could have been otherwise but there it is. Perhaps I should walk away; leave you to her. I'm rich and famous Sarah. How unfair it must seem to her that I, who has so much, must take away the one thing she really has."

"Stop it Danny! You're not taking me away."

Daniela sighed profoundly. "I don't know if I can Sarah." The big blue eyes were damp with tears.

Sarah rushed across to her and grasped her. "Kiss me Danny! Kiss me now."

"Sarah darling! You've had too much to drink and so have I. Somebody could walk in."

"I don't care! Kiss me."

Daniela embraced her sweetly but there was a sadness between them; a sadness rooted in reality; the sort that happens when the cold facts of life impinge upon magic. Sarah felt herself desperately clinging to a dream; a dream that was slipping away like a dancing will o' the wisp fading into the alpine meadows; elusive and unobtainable as if she was awakening on a cold clear morning still trying to hold on to the last fragments of a beautiful dream that slipped further from her grasp with every waking moment. She held Daniela's body against her as if the physical warmth of it could somehow allow her a tangible hold on that dream and that the walls of the ladies' lavatory might fade into transparency and they would find themselves once more on the high mountain meadows with the gentians about their feet and the butterflies on the wing. "Oh Danny what do I do?" she whispered in quiet despondency.

"I don't know Sarah. You're asking the wrong person for advice. I follow the imperatives of my heart. I always do the thing that it tells me I must and that isn't always the thing that I should. I'm frightened of losing you Sarah but I don't know how you can reconcile me to the rest of your life. Cold logic says that you should walk away from me now and pretend I never happened and every fibre of my soul screams the wrongness of that. I'm not a good guide in this Sarah."

Sarah took Daniela's hand. "It's stopped raining Danny. Let's sit outside a while."

The benches at the tables outside were damp from the downpour but they found a sheet of cardboard from a box that had served as a receptacle for the food being served at the barbeque and laid that down on the bench to sit on. The light was fading now and the air was cooler but they huddled close enough to warm each other with the heat from their bodies. They held hands but they sat in silence for the most part, listening to the music from the marquee and the laughter of the guests inside. "We'll have to go back in soon Sarah." Daniela noted at last.

"I know. I just wanted a few minutes with you Danny." Sarah cast her eyes down sadly. "I love you Danny. Is that wrong?"

"A lot of people will tell you it's wrong Sarah. Do you think it's wrong?"

"I... I don't know. I've never been here before. All my life I've assumed that one day I'll marry a nice man, have a big white wedding, have my own home and children. Then you come along and I don't know what I want any more. Nicole is right. I've never been inclined towards girls before. I've never even thought about it before. What's happening to me?"

"I can't help you there Sarah. I'm not a good person for rationalising my emotions. You'll have people telling you that it's just a phase you're going through; a momentary blip; an adolescent infatuation or whatever but ultimately it is you who will have to decide what it is. Me; I'm a person that runs with the flow. If my heart tells me that something feels good and wonderful, I don't question it. I just throw myself in. I can't advise you to do the same. My past record hardly indicates some sort of infallibility when it comes to making right decisions."

"Nicole wants me to be sensible. She says I'm always the sensible one."

"I always thought that the word "sensible" was an interesting one. On the face of it, it means prudent, level headed or rational yet the word sensibility means appreciative or the ability to feel. Sensible people have well-tuned senses it would seem. Who knows? It may be "sensible" to follow the dictates of your heart rather than the cold logic of your brain."

"There's nothing logical about my brain at the moment Danny. I've never felt so confused." Sarah paused in vexation. "Oh Christ! Why did Peter throw this bloody party for me? Things were so much simpler when we were just alone in the mountains together."

Daniela nudged her and nodded at a figure emerging from the marquee. "Talk of the devil. Here comes Peter now."

Peter approached them uncertainly, his eyes flitting nervously. "Oh here you both are. I thought we'd lost you."

"We just wanted to take a time out for a moment Peter." Sarah told him. "So we thought we'd sit outside for a few minutes."

Peter nodded started to speak but changed his mind. Eventually he cleared his throat and addressed Daniela. "I'm sorry Daniela. I don't want to impose on you or anything but the guys in the band have been asking me if they could meet you. Apparently they're great fans of your music and they're terribly keen to meet you. I said I would ask you but if you want some privacy then I'll tell them that they must respect that."

Daniela smiled. "Thank you for your discretion Peter. Of course I'll have a word with them. I would be delighted." She rose to her feet.

Sarah stood up as well. "I'll go and get some more drinks while you talk shop with the band then Danny." Then with a sudden flash of defiance Sarah leaned forward and kissed Daniela full on the lips before tossing her head with a flourish, shooting a mutinous look at Peter and marching off toward the bar in the restaurant.

A number of old friends were milling around the bar in the restaurant and Sarah found herself caught up in conversation. It was a long time before she could drag herself away and return to the outside marquee. When she did so the band were about to start playing again and there was no sign of Daniela at the table. Sarah put the drinks down in puzzlement. "Where's Danny?" she inquired.

Nicole replied haughtily. "You girlfriend has condescended to sing a song for the peasantry."

Peter glared at Nicole in annoyance. "Shut up Nicky. I thought it was very sporting of her to volunteer." He turned to Sarah. "The band asked Daniela if she'd sing a number with them Sarah and she's graciously agreed. I thought she was really nice about it."

Sarah glowered at Nicole sourly. "She's actually a very nice person Peter; a fact that some people around here can't seem to get into their thick skulls." Nicole turned her face away looking sulky.

The lead singer of the band appeared at the microphone. She looked flushed and excited. "Ladies and gentlemen!" she announced, "We've got a bit of a treat for you now. We've got a guest star appearance from somebody I think you all know. Let's have a big hand for Miss Daniela Devin." The crowd rose to its feet in appreciation and Daniela walked up on to the stage with a warm smile. She was still wearing the little simple dress she had hiked in all day but Sarah noticed with amusement that she'd removed her hiking boots and she walked out barefooted. She looked stunningly beautiful. The band's singer held up a hand to still the applause. "Thank you for showing your appreciation ladies and gentlemen. Daniela's agreed to sing a couple of numbers with us but since we've obviously never played together before you might have to be a little forgiving if it's not up to Daniela's usual concert standards."

Daniela took the second microphone. "I'm sure we'll be just fine." she assured with a laugh. She turned to the audience and gazed out, instantly captivating everybody with her electrifying stage presence. "The band's asked me to sing one of my own numbers ladies and gentlemen but before I do we'd like to do something else." Daniela held out a hand in the direction of Sarah and smiled at her. "As we all know this is our friend

Sarah's special night so we'd like to sing a song especially for her." The crowd applauded wildly and Sarah blushed crimson. "This is an old Fleetwood Mac song," Daniela continued and I hope you'll all forgive me if I take a few liberties with the lyrics." Daniela nodded to the band and the song began quietly to just the accompaniment of the keyboards. She seemed lost in thought as she listened to the opening bars before raising the microphone to her lips.

"Wait a minute baby, stay with me awhile

Said you'd give me light but you never told me 'bout the fire

The first haunting lyrics hung in the air before the drums crashed in and the bass and guitars took up the rhythm propelling the song into a faster tempo. Daniela's vocals were a pure thrill over the admirably professional backing and her voice rose from deep sultriness to soaring high notes wavering with her natural tremolo as she threw herself into the song. Sarah sat and stared, mesmerised.

"Drowning in the sea of love where everyone would love to drown

But if it's gone, it doesn't matter what for

When you build your house then call me... Home

And it was like a great dark wing, within the wings of a storm

I think I had met my match, she was singing and undoing and undoing the laces, undoing the laces

Said, "Sarah, you're the poet of my heart, never change, never stop"

And if it's gone, it doesn't matter what for

But when you build your house then call me.... Home

Hold on, the night is coming and the starling flew for days

182

I'd stay at home at night all the time
I'd go anywhere, anywhere, anywhere
Ask me and I'll be, ask me and I'll be, 'cause I care

In the sea of love where everyone would love to drown
And when it's gone, they say it doesn't matter any more
If you build your house then please call me Home
Sarah, you're the poet in my heart, never change, and don't you ever stop
If it's gone, no, it doesn't matter any more
When you build your house, I'll come by. Don't let it go Sarah, Don't let it go, don't let it go Sarah

Crazy, well, but there's a heartbeat that never really died, they said it never really died Sarah
Oh would you swallow all your pride, would you speak a little louder Sarah
Oh Sarah. Sarah
All I ever wanted was to know that you were dreaming........ Sarah.... Oh Sarah"

Daniela let the refrain of Sarah drift out in the closing beats of the song leaving Sarah's name fading into the high distance. The crowd was on its feet but Sarah bit her knuckles and tears streamed from her eyes. Daniela had delivered a stunning performance for her and done so publicly. It had been tantamount to a public declaration of love and Sarah was deeply moved by it. Nicole was staring at her hauntedly. Sarah found herself unable to watch the rest of Daniela's short performance and she fled outside, out beyond the terrace of the restaurant and among the damp grass beyond where the sweet tones of her friend's voice carried to her from the tent in the darkening alp and she was able to bury her face in her hands and weep freely.

She stayed there for a long time with her heart aching and she barely heard the gentle footsteps approaching. Daniela hadn't replaced her boots. She stood barefoot in the wet grass on the alp. "You ran off Sarah." she noted sadly. Sarah was unable to speak but she grasped Daniela and possessed her mouth with wild kisses. Nicole came in search of Sarah and found them clutched in one another's arms and it broke her heart asunder.

Chapter Sixteen

It was not the best awakening for Sarah the following day. For one thing she woke up in her own bed in the cottage in the Alpli and, if truth be known, she had only the faintest of recollections as to how she had got there. Secondly she woke up alone. In the preceding two days she had awoken twice to find Daniela peacefully asleep alongside her and it was something she had enjoyed and cherished. Now she was manifestly alone and it felt wrong. Thirdly, and of more immediate importance to her quality of life for the day, she felt distinctly unwell. This malaise was of a common type she had once heard described by the coined term "veisalgia" which apparently had its etymological roots in the Greek word "algia" for pain and grief and the Norwegian word "kveis" which translated as unease after debauchery. The illness was more commonly known as a hangover and it only took a few fearful blinks out from beneath the duvet at the bright morning sunshine flooding her bedroom to tell her that this one was a stinker. Her head was pounding, her throat was dry and tasted foul, her body felt weak and shivery and there was a hint of nausea in the pit of her stomach.

With a groan she buried her head beneath the duvet, cursing herself for the amount of alcohol she'd consumed the previous night and trying to reconstruct some semblance of memories of events in the latter part of the evening. She knew that it had been very late before the party broke up and she'd drunk steadily throughout the night. She vaguely recalled being half carried out and loaded unceremoniously into a gondola on the cable car and she had a notion that there'd been a car at the bottom into which she had been deposited but the details were elusive. She was pretty sure that Daniela had accompanied her in the gondola but she couldn't, for the life of her, remember when she and Daniela had parted company which, given Daniela's obvious absence now, they must have done. Nicole must have accompanied her home because, out of the disjointed recollections of the night, she could remember Nicole helping her to be sick by the roadside just outside the cottage. Where was Daniela though?

Gingerly she raised her head to peer uncertainly at the clock beside her bed. It told a sorry tale for it was nearly lunchtime. She could hear Nicole downstairs and she realised that sooner or later she was going to have to face her. She wasn't looking forward to the encounter. Her memory of the night might be incomplete but she had a fair idea that her conduct had not been exemplary and it was more than possible that she was in disgrace this morning. Tentatively she eased out of bed and crept abjectly to the bathroom. At least she had managed to undress it seemed for she was naked and, whilst she was not wearing her pyjamas, it was nevertheless a relief to discover that she had not slept in her clothes.

She took a quick shower which freshened her a little and brushed her teeth to remove the impression that some small unclean animal had died in her mouth during the night. She pulled on fresh underwear and a pair of jeans and a clean white blouse before daring to glance at her reflection in the mirror. She was gratified to note that she didn't look half as bad as she felt which, she reflected ruefully, would have been impossible without a complete physical breakdown. Finally satisfied that her appearance was about as good as it was going to get today she went downstairs to face the music.

Nicole was busy in the kitchen. "Morning Sarah!" she greeted her with what Sarah thought was an unnecessarily loud and cheery voice. "Heard you getting up so I've got coffee on. What do you want for breakfast?"

Sarah slumped down in a chair at the kitchen table. "I'm not hungry." She muttered.

"Rubbish! You ought to eat something even if it's just a piece of toast."

"Honestly Nicky I can't manage anything. I feel terrible. My head's in pieces."

"Well, when you go to the shop to have it put back together, see if they'll do you a two for the price of one deal and do a repair job on your reputation while they're at it."

"Please don't start on me this morning Nicky. I'm not in the mood."

Nicole shrugged. "As you wish. Let me pour you some coffee."

Sarah took the cup gratefully and nursed it in both hands. "How did we get home anyway?" she asked hesitantly.

"Peter's boyfriend picked us up at the gondola station in Wildhaus and drove us back. Don't you remember?" Sarah shook her head miserably. "Well he drove us back here and, after you'd thrown up outside, Peter carried you upstairs."

"Carried me?"

"Yep! He's a strong guy Peter. He just threw you over his shoulder like a sack of grain and humped you upstairs. I thought it was hilarious. At long last Peter has carried you manly away to a bedroom but his boyfriend is downstairs and you are too unconscious to know anything about it."

"Oh God! Did he undress me as well?"

"No I did that and a bloody pain in the arse you were being too."

"You... you undressed me?"

"Yeah. I wanted to try and get you into your pyjamas but you weren't exactly being cooperative so I just tucked you up in your birthday suit and hoped for the best."

"Where... where is everyone else?"

"If you're worried about the girlfriend, Simon dropped her off at her place in Oberdorf before he brought us back here. You wanted to stay with her but Peter his foot down and managed to prise you loose. You were hopelessly drunk and maudlin by then, weeping and bleating and wanting to be sick."

"But... but where's her car?"

"Still outside in the driveway. I assume she'll be picking it up today. I hope so. Not only is it taking up my parking spot but its presence is already the source of endless conjecture locally and, after last night's debacle, I should imagine that the speculation will rise even more. The sooner we're rid of it the better."

"Was I really out of order last night?"

"Let's put it this way Sarah, if there's a person in the Toggenburg this morning that doesn't know you spent most of the latter part of the evening yesterday snogging with Daniela Devin at the back of the marquee then they're either a hermit recluse or dead. I suppose you have no recollection of sitting on her knee and slobbering all over her face."

"Oh God!"

"Do you remember dancing a slow dance with her? You had your mouth so firmly clasped to hers I thought you were trying to clean out the drains. I was about ready to throw a bucket of water over the pair of you to break it up."

"Oh God! This is worse than I thought."

"It's not good Sarah. Your reputation is in ruins this morning. If I was you I'd keep a low profile until you go off to the Ticino and I'll try and do some damage control in the meantime."

"God! Why did I get so drunk?"

"Yes well your girlfriend was pretty tanked as well although not as bad as you. I just hope to hell the press doesn't get hold of the story or we'll have bloody paparazzi crawling around the place and that'll be a nice surprise for your parents when it hits the headlines in the "Blick"."

"Oh God this is awful!"

"Well I'd keep your head down Sarah. People are going to be talking."

Sarah buried her head in her hands and moaned. "Oh Nicky I've been such a fool."

Nicole looked at her compassionately and drew up a chair opposite. "Sarah, Foxy honey. We all do stupid things from time to time. God knows I've done enough. I guess I'm just not used to *you* going off the rails. You're usually the one with your head screwed on. I always thought you were a bit too good to be true because you never seemed to fuck up like other people. Well now you're only human after all. Ok you were pretty damn stupid last night but you *were* very drunk and with a bit of luck people will have forgotten about it by the time you get back from Ticino. Just keep a bit low and for God's sake chill this idiocy with Daniela. This isn't any old person you've had a mad infatuation with Foxy. This is an international celebrity. Ok so your reputation has taken a knock locally but that's nothing to what it'll suffer if this thing goes national."

Sarah grimaced. "Maybe I ought to emigrate. Mars seems like a good idea."

A car pulled up outside the cottage and Nicole stood up to see who it was. "Hello. It's Peter and Simon Sarah."

Sarah groaned comically. "Oh great! All my auxiliary consciences turning up. Doubtless I'm going to get an ear chewing from Peter as well."

"I should imagine that will be the case Sarah. He was looking disappointed in you last night."

"Oh brilliant! My gay boyfriend pissed off with me because I flirted with another woman. If he starts lecturing me on morality, I'll bean him with the bloody coffee pot."

Peter and Simon walked in at the back door which, as usual, was unlocked. Peter looked troubled but Simon was smiling and looking devastatingly handsome. He was a fine looking young man with the sort of dark

189

soulful eyes that would have had any young lady of heterosexual orientation cursing the fact that he was gay. Despite his ruination of Sarah's fondest hopes, Sarah liked Simon and the feeling was mutual. He greeted her with a warm brotherly kiss in contrast to Peter's awkward embrace and he was the only person in the kitchen not looking judgemental. "There's fresh coffee brewed boys." Nicole informed the guests. "Anybody want a cup?"

Peter hesitated but Simon took a seat at the kitchen table easily. "I'll take one if you please."

Peter frowned but sat down politely. "How are you today Sarah?" he asked hesitantly.

"She's a total mess." Nicole interjected. "I was thinking of throwing her out with the garbage."

Sarah glared at Nicole before replying. "I've had better days."

"Yes well you did drink a hell of a lot last night. I was surprised at you."

Sarah held up a hand in warning. "Peter I've already had an earful from Nicky regarding my conduct last night. I don't require another one from you."

"Well I hope she berated you for making a disgraceful exhibition of yourself with Daniela Devin in front of the whole Toggenburg."

Sarah's eyes flashed angrily. "You're not my keeper Peter. If I choose to be seen in public with a girlfriend then that's my business." It was a telling stroke. Peter was guiltily aware that he had deliberately concealed his boyfriend from public view.

Peter blushed but fought back bravely. "She's not your girlfriend Sarah. You're practically engaged to be married."

Sarah's hangover was putting her in an irritably defiant mood. "So maybe I want to live a little before the bloody vicar sounds the knell of doom and bangs me up for life in sodding marriage."

"There won't be a marriage Sarah if Alan finds out you're seeing a woman."

"Good!"

"Sarah stop it! I've never known you like this before. It's not like you. Your life doesn't end with marriage. On the contrary it's only just beginning. Alan is a fine man. He will make you a fine husband and a wonderful father to your children. I don't know what game you're playing here Sarah but you're doing Alan a dishonour with it. If he learns that you're out carousing with some female pop star he'll be devastated."

"Oh you mean he would he be less distraught if I was sleeping with a farmer's daughter?"

"Stop being facetious Sarah. You know what I mean."

"I'm afraid not Peter. I hardly think that my companion's professional career is at all relevant to the discussion."

"Of course it is! Now don't get me wrong. I think that Daniela is a very nice person. I like her. However there's no getting away from the fact that she is famous. It would be bad enough if you were just messing around with anybody but with somebody as well-known publicly as she is would be terrible. Think of the scandal. If you don't care about your own name being dragged through the mud you could at least consider what it would do to Alan. He doesn't deserve this Sarah. He has never given you any cause to treat him like this. I don't know what's happening to you Sarah but I'm begging you to come to your senses before you bring everything down in ruins."

"So you're only concerned about Alan's reputation then? What about *me* Peter? Is anybody considering my feelings?"

"You don't know your feelings from your arse at the moment Sarah. I know you're frightened of getting married. I know I hurt you by telling you I was gay. It's no wonder you're confused but you can't just let it all go to pieces and suddenly start seeing a dangerously prominent woman. You've never shown any interest in girls before so why now? Think about it Sarah. You're *not* gay."

Simon put down his coffee cup and looked at Peter steadily. "I think Sarah ought to be the judge of that Pete."

Sarah blinked, caught by surprise at sympathetic support from such an unexpected direction. Peter was taken aback. "What do you mean Simon?"

"I mean Peter how would *you* know if Sarah is gay or not?"

"I've known her all my life."

"So? She's known *you* all your life. Tell me... did she know you were gay before you told her in Winterthur that afternoon?"

"Well... well no."

"So why should you be any better a judge Pete. People aren't always what they seem. If Sarah has feelings for this woman then who are we to judge her for it? So it might cause a scandal. So what? That comes with the patch Pete. Anytime somebody comes out and declares them self to be gay there's going to be scandal. I know that and so do you. You of all people should know that. Perhaps Sarah loves this woman Peter and all you're doing is lecturing her about it. When we told Sarah in Winterthur that we were in love I didn't hear Sarah telling us a load of moralistic bullshit about scandals and our obligations of duty to become faithful husbands to women we had no feelings for."

"Simon butt out. You don't know Sarah."

"No I don't Pete but I *do* know what it's like to realise that you're gay and how scary and confusing it is. Maybe it could be that Sarah here needs our sympathy and support Pete and not being chewed out over feelings she has no control over. So she got a bit pissed last night and let everybody know how she feels about Daniela. So what? We ought to try doing the same and then maybe we wouldn't have to pussyfoot around pretending that we're not an item to the world. We can't condemn Sarah for having the guts to do something that we're too scared of. You ought to cut Sarah a bit of slack here. This could be a hard time for her."

"Simon it's different."

"Oh? Like how?"

"We're in love Simon. Sarah's not in love with Daniela. She can't be. She hardly knows her."

"Why don't you ask her Pete? Go on ask her. You're very quick to make judgements about how she should or shouldn't feel. Have you thought to actually to ask her how she feels?"

Peter bit his lip in uncertainty and it was Nicole, unable to keep her peace any longer, who interceded. "Tell us it's not true Sarah. Tell us you're not really in love with her."

The question could have hardly come from a worse direction and Sarah grasped her coffee cup fearsomely, unable to speak for a moment. Eventually she spoke. "Please let's drop this subject. I... I don't know any more. Please leave me alone. I don't want to talk about it."

Peter saw that Sarah was close to tears and awkwardly he tried to mollify her. "Well Sarah it's up to you. I've said my piece and I'll let it rest there. I didn't want to upset you. I'll not tell Alan what's happened I promise. What's happened is between you and him and no business of mine." Peter glanced at his watch. "I'm going to have to get going shortly. I have to drive into town."

Sarah glanced up. "Why did you call round Peter? Was it just to express disapproval of my behaviour?"

"No Sarah I was just dropping Simon off here. He's supposed to be picking up Daniela's car for her."

Sarah blinked in astonishment. "Danny's car?"

Simon nodded. "Yes, last night when we dropped her off she was worried about how she was going to get her car back so I volunteered to come round and fetch it today if she'd lend me the keys. Otherwise she'd have to walk right across the valley to fetch it."

Nicole snorted. "So what's wrong with her legs? Is walking too common for her?"

Sarah bridled angrily. "That's not fair Nicky. She spent the last three days walking which is a sight more exercise than you've done recently. If you can't find a civil thing to say about her, then hold your tongue."

Nicole retreated sulkily. "All right. Don't snap my head off! I get the picture. The girlfriend's off limits. Pardon me for speaking."

Sarah felt immediately contrite about her anger with Nicole but she bit her lip and turned to Simon. "Danny's got a big powerful Ferrari Simon. Are you comfortable with driving that?"

Simon grinned. "I'm a semi-professional sports car and rally car racing driver Sarah. I'm not scared of fast cars."

"Oh! Oh I'm sorry. I never knew."

"Don't worry about it. I'm not exactly well known. It'll be a while yet before you see me at Monaco or Le Mans. But don't worry about your girlfriend's car. I'll take care of it."

"So you're driving it up to her place?"

"Yes. She said there was no hurry as long as she had it back sometime today. It's quite a hot car. I'm tempted to take it for a run before I deliver it back."

"I know nothing about cars. I'm scared to death of that thing though."

"It's a F430 Spider convertible Sarah with a 4.3 litre V8 engine generating 490 horsepower. She'll top three hundred klicks an hour with your foot on the floor. That's a serious machine."

Sarah smiled. Simon's eyes had come alight at the thought of Daniela's car. It was obviously no onerous imposition for him to deliver it back to Daniela. "Well try to get it back to her in one piece."

"Oh God yes. I doubt she paid a penny less than a hundred and seventy thousand euros for that baby. If I bend it I'm on the first flight out to the remoter part of the North West Territories."

"Can I come with you? Not to the North West Territories I mean but when you go up to Danny's. I want to see her."

Peter jumped in instantly. "Is that wise Sarah? I mean after last night don't you think it might be better to let the brouhaha calm down for a few days?"

"So I just ignore her because of your concerns Peter?"

Nicole had her pennyworth to say. "Foxy she hasn't phoned you today yet. She soaked up quite a bit of booze herself last night. If she hasn't phoned it probably means she's not even out of bed yet."

"Well maybe I'll phone her first then." Sarah said sullenly.

Nicole threw her hands up. "Oh God! Talk some sense into her Peter."

"I don't think she's listening to me Nicky."

With an almost uncanny sense of timing, the telephone in the kitchen chimed. Sarah looked triumphant. "That's probably her now."

With a sigh Nicole picked up the receiver. "Hello. Toggenburg Sanctuary for Wounded Hearts and Sexual Identity Crisis here. May I be of assistance?" Sarah glared at her furiously but before she could protest Nicole froze on the phone. "Oh hello sir! I'm sorry. Just an in joke. Yes. Yes of course she's here. Just one moment sir." Nicole covered the mouthpiece with a hand. "Foxy it's your dad!"

Sarah took the hand piece in surprise. "Hello Daddy."

"Hello Sarah. Was that Nicole on the line?"

"Yes daddy."

"Is she all right Sarah? She was babbling some nonsense about wounded hearts and sexual identity."

"I'm terribly sorry daddy." Sarah glared straight at Nicole. "No Nicole's not al; right. She's stark staring, raving bonkers. Has been for years. Hopefully her upcoming pre-frontal lobotomy will sort the problem out." Nicole poked her tongue out at Sarah.

Sarah's father chuckled. "Oh dear. Are you two girls having a girly domestic today?"

"Something like that daddy. It's lovely to hear from you. Are you calling for any particular reason?"

"Yes I am actually. What are you doing today?"

"Er I don't have any specific plans daddy."

"Good! I'm round your way and I was wondering if you'd like to meet up for lunch. I have some things I need to talk to you about."

"Lunch? Where?"

"Well I thought about the Sternen in Unterwasser. Would that be all right?"

"Yes. Yes of course. That would be lovely. Er what time?"

"Shall we say in about an hour honey?"

"Yes. Yes fine."

"Good then. Do you want me to pick you up?"

"No, no daddy. I'll get down to Unterwasser. I'll meet you at the Sternen."

"Good I look forward to it. See you then."

"See you daddy." Sarah hung up. "Oh God! My father's here. He wants to meet up for lunch in an hour in the Sternen in Unterwasser."

Peter nodded. "Well you won't have time to go up to Oberdorf now."

"There's no need to look quite so smug Peter."

Nicole looked agitated. "Come on Sarah. If your dad's wanting to take you out to lunch there's not a minute to spare. You've got to get changed and smarten up sharpish."

"How am I going to do that Nicky? It's a long walk to Unterwasser and your car is still at Wildhaus. I'll have to set off as I am."

196

"You can't go out to lunch with your dad looking like that Sarah; not in those grubby old jeans."

"They're not grubby!"

"Your dad will want to see his little baby girl looking pretty Sarah. You've got to get changed. A pretty summer frock and some nice shoes are a minimum requirement."

"How am I supposed to walk down the hill by way of Thurfall in good shoes Nicky?"

"Peter can give you a lift."

Peter held his hands up. "Can't help you. I'm late as it is and I have to get going. I haven't the time to wait while you get tidied up Sarah."

"I'm not in a hurry." volunteered Simon. "I can wait and drive you down in Daniela's car."

"Brilliant!" yipped Nicole.

"Wait a minute." protested Sarah. "How am I supposed to explain that to my father? Don't you think he might be suspicious seeing me driven up in a red Ferrari by a handsome young man? I mean I know that Simon's gay but dad doesn't know that."

Nicole snorted. "Hmmph! It'll be easier to explain than some other items of your recent conduct. Stop griping Sarah and shift your arse. We've got to find you something to wear."

Peter rose and informed the company that he had to leave. Simon was abandoned with a cup of coffee as Nicole dragged a futilely protesting Sarah upstairs. Sarah's wardrobe had improved markedly through her association with Daniela and Nicole found ample resources to smarten Sarah up to meet her father. There was the lovely white silk blouse that Daniela had bought for her in Buchs and a little pleated skirt in emerald green and white which matched it well. Daniela had given her a sweet pair of white, high heeled, open sandals one day when they had met for Sarah's afternoon break whilst working at the Toggenburg that perfectly complimented the outfit. There were even little green ribbons decorating the shoes as if Daniela had been picking out matching accessories to dress her beloved Sarah. Nicole was delighted and even insisted on painting Sarah's toenails in emerald green to complete the ensemble. Of course there was one accessory that was perfect for Sarah's appearance. It was the white gold necklace with the brilliant emerald that Daniela had given her the night that they had dined out at the Gade. Feeling that she might as well be hung for a sheep as a lamb, Sarah took her moissanite earrings from their box and hung them from her ears. Nicole fussed over her make-up and hair before standing back to clap her hands in satisfaction. "Perfect! You look great."

Sarah pulled a face. "Dad's going to think I've lost my marbles. I don't suppose he's ever seen me dress up like this before."

"You look brilliant Foxy. What's wrong with looking your best for your dad?"

"Nothing I suppose." conceded Sarah reluctantly, although she wryly reflected that virtually her entire costume that day was a result of Daniela's influence in her life. Still, as she admired herself in the mirror, she was forced to admit that she had rarely looked better. Her ensemble was both reserved and yet alluring; grown up and mature in appearance with just a hint of flirtatiousness about it. The short skirt was flattering to her long legs with their deep tan accumulated during the past few days on the mountainside. There was something slightly sophisticated about her dress; a young woman about town rather than a simple country girl with some growing up to do. Sarah winced as she regarded her reflection. Her father always made her feel like a little girl. Somehow this cool womanly appearance seemed at odds with that.

Nicole refused to listen to her protestations however and hustled her downstairs to where Simon was beginning to regard his wristwatch with increasing disbelief. He smiled as he looked at Sarah. "You look wonderful." he told her. "You could almost tempt me into going straight."

Nicole rolled her eyes to heaven. "Brilliant! Now we have a closet heterosexual on our hands. What's going on? People are switching sides faster than Italian politicians."

Sarah ignored her. "Do you want dad to drop me off in Wildhaus so I can pick your car up Nicky?"

"No thank you. The first thing you'll do is drive up to Oberdorf and, before I know it, people will be saying my car was parked outside Daniela Devin's front drive. I don't want everybody to start questioning *my* sexual orientation as well."

"Considering the fact that over the last five years you've slept with half the single male population of the valley Nicky I don't think that's really an issue. Oh well it was just an offer. You can go and fetch your own bloody car. Come on Simon we'd better get going."

Sarah and Simon discovered that the interior of Daniela's car had reached a furnace like temperature under the rays of the hot sun and Simon, demonstrating admirable familiarity with the mark, lowered the roof to allow a cooling breeze to create a more tolerable environment within the car. Simon slid into the driving seat with a gleam on his eyes and stroked the controls lovingly. Sarah regarded him with amusement reflecting on the contrast between his attitude to the automobile and its owner's who never seemed to be entirely comfortable with the machine. Before Simon could begin to croon anthropomorphically over the car, Sarah interrupted his new infatuation with a gentle thank you. "Simon," she said. "Thanks for that. I mean thanks for saying what you did when Peter was laying in to me. You're the only person who's shown any sympathy and support for me."

Simon leaned on the steering wheel and pursed his lips thoughtfully. "Don't mention it Sarah. Just try to be equally understanding with Pete. I love him to bits Sarah but I know he can come across as a pompous ass sometimes. You've just got to be patient with him. He's had a difficult time coming to terms with his own sexuality. For some reason, that makes it difficult for him to be sensitive to other people's own struggles. I know that he's very fond of you Sarah. I think perhaps that's why he was being such an arsehole with you. I think he can't bear the thought of his little Sarah having to endure the same agonies he's had to go through. He feels very protective of you. I guess he thinks of you as his kid sister and he's never really grasped the fact that you're a grown woman."

"Do you think he's right though Simon? I mean do you think that it would be a terrible mistake to fall in love with another woman?"

"Sarah, falling in love isn't something you can make a conscious decision about. Of course it's always a risky business and even more so when the person you love is the same sex. You can't help falling in love though. Of course it's dangerous. It always is. You'll risk everything but that's true with whoever you fall in love with. You gamble your life on love Sarah. The risks are enormous and we wouldn't take them if the rewards weren't so incalculable."

"I'm not sure I'm ready to gamble so much Simon."

"You avoided the question back there in the house Sarah. Do you love this woman?"

"Yes I do. I've never felt this way about anybody before."

"Then you might *have* to gamble Sarah. Not taking the chance carries its own risk. You risk waking up one morning twenty years from now and hating yourself because you threw your life away for folding your hand when you were holding a pair of aces and you were too frightened to up the ante. I'd go with your feelings Sarah. Love is always going to present you with impossible choices. There isn't a rational way of dealing with it.

Love is never a sensible option. It's always a form of madness. That's what makes it so exciting and lunatic."

"You're a wise person for your years Simon. I... I'm pleased Peter has found someone like you."

"I'm not wise Sarah but I know what you're going through because I've been there and bought the T-shirt. I'd say you're in for a tough ride Sarah but if it's any consolation then remember that there'll be two of you sharing the ride together and that's a hell of a lot better than facing the roller coaster alone. You'll find other support as well and sometimes in places where you least expected it. You can count on my support anyway."

"Thank you Simon."

Simon grinned. "Anyway, talking of tough rides; enough of my worldly advice; let's gun this engine and see what this honey can do."

Simon drove Daniela's car with what Sarah was forced to concede was far more skill and confidence than Daniela ever seemed to manage. Daniela always seemed to be slightly frightened of the growling beast beneath her as she gingerly steered it around. Simon on the other hand threw it into the corners of the narrow roads leading to Unterwasser with controlled glee nearly purring with pleasure as the powerful car responded to his deft touch. Sarah felt the wind whip in her hair as Simon rang through the gear changes and allowed the car its head. Simon chortled almost maniacally as he drove and declared. "I've just got to get myself one of these." The run to Unterwasser was all too short.

They pulled up outside the Sternen hotel in flamboyant fashion. "Thanks for the lift Simon." Sarah told him "That was exhilarating."

Simon smiled. "I thought I noticed a bit of a bump on the downshift into third gear. I'd better take the car for a quick test run to make sure Daniela doesn't have a problem there."

"Liar! You just want an excuse to put the car through its paces." She touched his arm fondly. "Go ahead and enjoy yourself. I'm sure Danny wouldn't mind. Just get it back in one piece."

"I'll treat her like my own baby." He leaned forward and kissed Sarah lightly on the cheek. "You take care of yourself Sarah and you take care of that girl of yours too."

Sarah hesitated. "Simon," she ventured, "I... I was upset when Peter introduced you to me as his boyfriend but I'm not any more. I... I think you're a fine man. I'm sorry if I might have misjudged you."

"Sarah think nothing of it. For the record I think you're a pretty wonderful girl too. If it all gets a bit hairy and difficult you have a friend here. Don't let them take your life away from you Sarah. That girl of yours is a hell of a woman! Don't lose her because of other people's notions of antiquated morality. Look take my card. It's got my phone number on it. If you need any friendly advice just call me whenever you want ok."

Sarah placed the card in her handbag. "Th... thank you Simon." She stepped out of the car and stood back to acknowledge Simon's wave as he revved the engine hard and leapt away with a squeal of tyres and roared off down the village street.

Chapter Seventeen

She saw her father straight away. He was sitting at a table on the front terrace of the hotel with his favourite newspaper, the International Herald Tribune, in front of him and looking thoughtful. She stepped up onto the terrace and dashed toward him with pleasure. Sarah adored her father but her feelings were slightly tinged with guilty shame. To put it simply, Sarah's father was the man that Sarah had looked for all her life without success. He was tall and of admirably slim build with nary a hint of middle aged paunch about him. His face was perhaps weathered a little with age but still retained the craggy good looks that could melt a woman's heart and if his dark hair was somewhat peppered with grey it only added to his aura of distinction and matched his grey eyes that always seemed calm, kind and reassuring in their gentle wisdom.

Sarah had never known him lose his temper or even much of his patience and tranquillity which, given his long marriage to Sarah's mercurially testing mother, was an extraordinary achievement in itself. He was a bedrock of stability; the calm water at the heart of his family's occasional turbulent upheavals. Few people could have tamed Sarah's quicksilver mother but this gentle man had managed the feat effortlessly for over twenty five years. He was by no means subservient however. Sarah retained an old memory from when she had been a small girl when her mother had been particularly fractious and difficult. Her father had sighed resignedly and led her mother away to the sanctuary of their nuptial bedroom where, judging by the loud slapping sounds and agonised squealing from behind the bedroom door, he had placed her firmly over his knee and spanked her bottom for her soundly. She'd been like a little kitten for days afterwards and there'd been peace in the house. Sarah still had guilty thoughts about the memory. In her deepest and most private of inner sanctums Sarah knew she was attracted to her father and somewhat jealous of her mother.

Her father rose from his table and enfolded her in strong arms to kiss her. Sarah felt slightly weak and flustered at the contact. He held her at arm's length the better to regard her. "My word Sarah!" he exclaimed. "You look absolutely wonderful. I see that you've been putting the extra allowance I sent you to good cause. You look beautiful. New clothes; new jewellery; a whole new look; your mother will hardly recognise you."

Sarah blushed guiltily. It was hardly the moment to mention that her entire ensemble consisted of gifts from a girlfriend. Instead she lowered her eyes demurely and said, "I'm pleased you like it Daddy."

"I do indeed. I just hope that your new look was just a way to make your poor old dad feel even more proud of you than ever."

"What do you mean daddy.?"

Sarah's father looked at her shrewdly. "Who was the boy that dropped you off Sarah?"

"Just a friend daddy."

"A friend? Is that all Sarah? Seemed a good looking chap to me and driving around in a very flash car too. Are you telling me he's just a friend?"

Sarah smiled ruefully. She'd anticipated her father's suspicions on this score and was thankful that he was unaware of the real threat. "Daddy! Believe me he really is just a friend. Anyway he's gay so he's hardly likely to be anything *but* a friend. That's not even his car in any case. He's borrowed it."

Her father seemed mollified. Sarah was a poor liar but the one person who she could reasonably rely upon to fog the vision of with half-truths and prevarications was her father, whose image of her was hopelessly tainted with the rose tinted spectacles of a man who doted upon his favourite daughter. He nodded with a smile. "I see. I'm sorry my little mumurli." Murmuli was a diminutive for murmultier; the German word for the alpine marmot; the alpine ground squirrels of the high mountain slopes and her father's affectionate nickname for her. "Come along," he continued, "Take a seat and a drink. We have to talk." Sarah nodded gravely and took the chair her father offered gracefully. "What would you like?" he asked.

"Er just a mineral water please daddy."

Her father raised his hand to draw the waitress' attention. His was a commanding presence and a waitress was at their table instantly. "I'll take another coffee and a mineral water please," he told her. "Oh yes and can we look at your lunch menu please?" The waitress simpered visibly under Sarah's father's charm and rushed away to comply. He turned to Sarah seriously. "I'm sorry if I was a little too hasty to jump to conclusions about your companion Sarah. I should have known that you were completely innocent. I'm just under orders to keep an eye on you. Your mother is worried to death about you."

Sarah bristled. Her mother's unwarranted intrusions into her private life generally tended to place her on the defensive. "Why? What's the matter with her?"

Her father clasped his hands together on the table in front of him; a characteristic mannerism of his whilst marshalling his thoughts and pondering the most diplomatic way to express them. "Well Sarah," he said at last, "I don't want to seem as if I'm nagging you, but your mother is concerned that you're not taking your upcoming marriage seriously enough."

"Is that why you're here?" asked Sarah with her dudgeon well up.

"Sarah I was passing through the area and your mother asked me to have a word with you that's all. Now don't get all spiky with me. I would have wanted to see you in any case. Nevertheless your mother has a point. You... well you seem less enthusiastic about your marriage than you have previously Sarah and naturally we're concerned."

Sarah grimaced and stared at the table in front of her. "What marriage is this daddy? I wasn't aware that there was one in the offing."

Sarah's father looked surprised. He took a deep breath. "Please don't tell me that you're having second thoughts Sarah!"

"Daddy I haven't even been canvassed on my *first* thoughts. Why are you and mum assuming I'm marrying Alan before he's even had the wherewithal to ask me if I *want* to marry him? Before being shipped off into holy matrimony daddy I would appreciate the common courtesy of being *asked* first. I'm not a chattel in some third world arranged marriage daddy. Until I am formally proposed to and agree to that proposal then as far as I'm concerned there is no marriage."

Her father shook his head with a smile. "You're as stubborn as your mother Sarah."

"Why? Just because I would like some say into my future daddy?"

Her father regarded her seriously. "Sarah honey. You'll always have some say in your future. But there are times when you have to make decisions about that future. You know as well as I that it has been an unspoken understanding for a long time that Alan will formally ask for your hand in marriage. I'm sure that Alan wanted to ensure that he would have career opportunities that would ensure that he was able to support a wife and family and that it would be unethical of him to make a formal proposal until such time as he was able to give those guarantees. I think that has been a very sensible and, in fact, a very admirable consideration of his. I know that he is aware that I would have expected nothing less before granting him permission to marry my beloved daughter. I know also that he is very eager to marry you but, to his credit, he has demonstrated enormous patience and a willingness to forego his eagerness in order to put a marriage plan into being that will ensure the future prosperity of your marriage. I realise that you may have become impatient with his caution but I'm certain Sarah that it stems from nothing else than his complete commitment to making your marriage a success. I know he has worked very hard and with admirable dedication to make sure that you will not want for anything in your marriage and I think you ought to give him credit for that."

"I don't want for anything now daddy. I can look after myself. I've worked hard too. I worked hard for three years at university to get a degree. Is that hard work meaningless now because Alan will be looking after me for the rest of my life?"

"I know you've worked hard honey. I'm proud of what you've achieved at university. Of course it's not meaningless. I hope that you'll continue to maintain an interest in your academic pursuits but, at the end of the day, an academic degree in history isn't going to put bread and butter on the table and it isn't going to feed your children either. You're not a young girl any more Sarah. It's time to start thinking about the children you'll raise. A lot of women have to put their personal ambitions to one side to think about their children. There's nothing new about that. Motherhood is a full time occupation Sarah. That's why men exist. We do the crappy work to bring the bacon in so that you can concentrate on what's truly important; bringing up the future generation. That's not sexist Sarah; it's just the way life is and has been since the stone ages. It's your job; your responsibility to build the nest; your task to ensure that you have a good husband; a good father and a good provider for your children. Your children won't be impressed that you have high university grades in history Sarah. They need a mother. Being a mother is the hardest challenge you will ever face. This is what growing up means Sarah. Now I think you will be a fine mother but it's time to put childhood to rest Sarah. Yes we all go through these agonies when it's time to grow up and take up our responsibilities. We all lament the loss of our childhood but we all know or come to realise that this is what is truly important in life."

"You make it sound so horrible."

"No Sarah. I don't mean to make it sound so onerous. There's a great joy in it too. I gave up many things to marry your mother and I'd do it again. Nothing of what I gave up could possibly compare to the joy I've taken from my marriage and the love I have for my three wonderful children. Yes it's been difficult at times but that's the joy and the heartache of it. That's what you do to be truly fulfilled in your life."

"You love mum?"

"Of course I do. I couldn't imagine life without her. I know she can be difficult and sometimes she drives me crazy but I couldn't live without her."

"Does Alan... does Alan love me?"

"Of that I am certain Sarah. If I were not certain I would forbid him ever to come near you again. I know that he only wants to make you happy. A father always looks at a suitor for his daughter with a bit of a jaundiced eye but he has persuaded me that he only wants the very best for you. That pleases me. I only want the best for you too and I think that Alan is a good man and can provide that. If I didn't I'd never let him in the house again."

"So when is he going to make a formal bid for me?"

"Ah well I was coming to that. Alan is returning home to Switzerland in ten days. I believe he has exciting news for you and I think that now he is ready to formally ask for your hand. In ten days he'll be in the Ticino and we, your mother and I that is, are throwing a party, together with his family, for his homecoming. We want you to be there Sarah. It will, I believe, be your formal engagement party and we're going to make it a big do. We're not anticipating a long engagement so there'll be a lot of planning for the wedding to do as well.

I'm looking forward to giving you away Sarah. I'll be the proudest man on earth when I escort you down that aisle."

Sarah blanched. "Ten days!"

"Yes but you can come earlier if you want. In fact I'd recommend it. We have a lot of logistics to sort out. Everybody is very excited about it. It'll be the wedding of the year in Ticino."

Sarah lowered her eyes. "Yes daddy."

Her father picked up the menu. "Now come on. Let's order some lunch!"

Sarah gulped. "I'm not very hungry daddy."

"Nonsense! You always have a good appetite."

"Nicky and Peter threw a... well a going away party for me last night. I'm afraid I drank too much."

"Well you can manage something light. Now come along. What about a nice salad?"

Sarah sighed and frowned thoughtfully. "Daddy would you marry me?"

Her father's eyebrows rose dramatically. "What an odd thing to ask Sarah."

"I mean hypothetically. If you were a young man and not my father obviously would you marry a girl like me?"

"Like a shot Sarah. You're a beautiful, intelligent and warm hearted girl. Any man would be proud to be your husband. Alan is a lucky man and doesn't he know it. I think the pair of you will make a fine couple and your children will be extraordinary. Come on now. I'm hungry. Let's get some food."

Sarah shrugged resignedly, knowing she was defeated at last. "Well perhaps just a salad daddy. I have to watch my waistline if I'm going to fit into my wedding dress."

Chapter Eighteen

"So what are you going to do?" asked Nicole. She was sat at the kitchen table with Sarah in their shared cottage. Sarah's meeting with her father had lasted over two hours and Sarah had returned home disturbed and depressed.

"I don't know. What can I do?" Sarah wrung her hands miserably. "I've promised dad that I'm going to be in Ticino for Alan's return. They've planned it all as my big engagement party. Everybody's going to be there; all my family; all Alan's family; even all the friends of the family and Alan's. I can't squirm out of it. Alan's going to make the engagement official and there's no way on earth I can turn him down without causing a huge scandal and alienating my entire family. Dad was telling me that they've got people coming from all over Switzerland to the party and even people from outside. Alan's even got relations flying in from Australia for God's sake. Dad says there'll be over two hundred people at the party and my mum's putting on a huge outdoor buffet and barbecue to feed them all. They've even got outside caterers in to provide food and drink and a bloody six piece band for entertainment. The highlight of the entire event however will be the official announcement of my engagement and the announcement of the wedding date. Presumably official invitations will be issued as well. God! Mum's even apparently bought the bloody dress. I'm not even allowed to choose my own wedding dress. She's even drawing up shortlists for the sodding bridesmaids. I thought it was usually the bride who gets to choose her bridesmaids among her friends. Not this bloody wedding though!"

Nicole grimaced. "Well at least that lets *me* off the hook. I'll be lucky if I even get an invitation to the wedding."

"Oh yes! Mum's got complete control of the guest lists. All her friends will be invited. She presumably thinks I haven't got any."

"Christ Sarah! You can't let her shanghai your wedding like this."

"Have you ever tried thwarting my mother when she's got her mind set on something?"

Nicole nodded grimly. "Yes she's not a woman that takes no for an answer. So what's the schedule? I mean when are you going down?"

"Well the party is in ten days. Dad wanted to me to get there at least four or five days early but I put him off telling him I had things to do. I'm going down on the day of the party or maybe the day before. I think they're expecting that to be a more or less permanent move until the wedding so they'll expect me to turn up with a huge pile of luggage and someone will pick me up in Bellinzona. I'm supposed to be winding up my affairs here and have my belongings ready to be moved to Zurich following the wedding."

Nicole looked sad. "I... I'm going to miss you."

"I'm not doing it!"

"What?"

"I mean I'm not packing all my stuff up yet. Why should I have everything packed in anticipation of a proposal that hasn't happened yet? It'll only take me a few days once the wedding date has been announced anyway. They can spare me for that. I mean it's not as if my presence is absolutely essential for the wedding plans, is it? Mum's doing just fine on her own blast her! I could probably send a stand in along for the ceremony for all anybody would notice."

"You could still turn Alan down."

"Oh right! In public with everybody watching? It's no good Nicky. They've got me trapped."

"They can't just bully you into marrying."

Sarah rested her head in her hands miserably. "They don't see it that way. They think they're doing the best

211

thing possible for me. I don't think they even credit me with enough sense to know what's best for me. Dad as much as told me to grow up and accept my responsibilities. You know what's stupid? Two weeks or so after this shindig I'm supposed to be in Bern for my graduation. Nobody has even thought about that. When I mentioned it to Dad he frowned and said that might be inconvenient. Inconvenient! I spend three years hard sweat at university to obtain a degree and they can't even spare me to go to Bern to pick up my diploma. Dad says that they'll send me it by post and there's no real need to go to the graduation ceremony. He's proud that I'm going to marry Alan but not the fact that I'm clever enough to earn a degree it seems. All anybody wants to see is me in a bloody wedding frock not a cap and gown. I even sent Dad a copy of my final dissertation and he's never got round to reading it. My brains don't count for anything; only my decorative value in white, wearing a tiara and carrying a bloody bouquet. I might just as well have not bothered going to university at all. Dad said that a degree in history wasn't going to put bread and butter on the table and hinted that he thought my studies amounted to nothing more than a childish hobby that I'd have to put aside for the serious business of raising his sodding grandchildren. I feel like a fucking brood cow!"

"There was a time you wanted kids Sarah." Nicole pointed out.

"Yes but on my own terms, in my own time and with whom I choose."

"Until this summer I thought you'd chosen Alan."

"It doesn't seem as if I had any choice at all in the matter."

Nicole cleared her throat and hesitated. "Er Daniela called while you were out."

"Oh God! What did she say?"

"Nothing much. Just wanted to see how you were and talk to you."

"Why didn't she call me on my mobile?"

"She *did* call you on your mobile. You left it on the kitchen top when you went out, you doughnut!"

"Oh! Oh shit. I'd better call her."

"I wouldn't bother. She says that she has to go off for some important business meeting this afternoon and evening. She says she'll try to call you later or, failing that, tomorrow."

"Did she get her car back?"

"Yes Simon had just delivered it. It sounds like he must have gone for a run in it before taking it back because it was a good hour and a half since he took off with you."

Sarah nodded. "I can believe it. He was like a kid at Christmas when he got his paws on that machine. I hope he had the decency to fill it up again after thrashing it around the countryside for an hour and a half."

"What are you going to say to Daniela?"

"Oh God! I don't know."

"You'll have to finish with her."

"Damn it Nicky! I haven't *started* with her." Sarah lowered her head abjectly. "No, that's not true. I have started with her I suppose. I haven't slept with her.... well technically I have... but I haven't had sex with her. Nevertheless I am tangled up with her. What the hell am I going to say to her?"

"Just tell her that you're getting married and that your future husband might look a little askance upon receiving intelligence that his betrothed is having an affair with a woman."

"There's no need to make it sound so sordid Nicky."

Nicole shrugged. "Well just be thankful that there's not likely to be anybody from the Toggenburg at your engagement party. After last night's debacle your infidelities are hardly a local secret."

"That's enough Nicole! I've been spanked enough for my conduct last night thank you."

Nicole held up her hands. "Ok, ok! But you are going to have to deal with her Sarah. You have to let her

213

go. You can't get engaged and still be conducting an ongoing relationship with her."

"It's not as easy as that."

"Why for fuck's sake?"

Sarah swallowed. "Because I love her." She whispered.

"What? What did you say?"

Sarah took a deep breath. "I said I love her Nicky. I mean it too. I *do* love her!"

"Oh Sarah...."

"Don't have a go at me Nicky. I don't understand it any more than you do. I've never fallen for a woman before but I have now. She means the world to me right now. I think about her all the time. I... I didn't think I was lesbian but maybe I am after all. All I know is that every time I think about Alan my stomach turns over and every time I think of her the world seems a brighter place. I didn't want to fall in love with her Nicky. It just happened and even I don't know how. Don't ask me to rationalise it or justify it. It's just the way it is. If I was going to Ticino to marry *her* I'd be on the train tomorrow."

"Oh God! Have you told her this?"

"Not in the same words perhaps but yes I've told her I love her."

"And her?"

"She's told me she loves me several times Nicky."

"Christ! What a mess!"

"I can't just let her go Nicky. I love her."

"Sarah! It's impossible. You know it's impossible."

"I know Nicky but what can I do? I can't help my feelings. It would be simple if I had never fallen for her but I have and I can't put the genie back in the bottle." Sarah wrung her hands dejectedly. "I've... I've never even made love to her. Oh God there were times we came awfully close and it wouldn't have taken her much persuasion but it never happened. Every time she touches me it's like somebody setting a bomb off in my libido. I know she wants me but I've managed to stave it off until now. Thank God I've resisted her. It's bad enough as it is. I hate to think of the complications if we were actually lovers. There's still a part of me that regrets never becoming her lover. I've never made love to a woman. I don't even know what it would be like really. Now I guess I'll never know. I might spend the rest of my life wondering. Each time that Alan is attending to Daddy's grandchildren duties I know I'll lie back and wonder what it would have been like to lie in bed in *her* arms. Oh God! Why did this have to happen?" Sarah buried her face in her hands and wept bitterly.

For all her disapproval of Sarah's conduct Nicole was essentially a compassionate girl and she stepped around the table to take a seat beside Sarah and hug her. "Sarah I don't know what to say." she breathed. "Until this summer I thought I knew you. Now I don't any more. You were always the one with your head screwed on; everything all sorted out and a clear path into the future. Ever since you came back from uni though, you've been a mess. I put it down to your anxiety about getting married. I thought you'd get your head back together and just get on with things as you always do. Then this thing with Daniela happened and now I hardly recognise you anymore. What's happening to you Sarah? I don't think I ever even saw you cry until this summer but now you're on the sort of emotional roller coaster that I thought was my prerogative. What happened to the Sarah I thought I knew?"

"Oh Nicky! Help me! In the name of our years of friendship, help me now. What am I going to do?"

"I don't know if I *can* help you Foxy. I don't understand what's happening to you. I never even thought about you being lesbian before. It never occurred to me. If somebody had told me that I'd have told them that they were talking crap. Are you sure about these feelings for Daniela? She's a pretty overwhelming woman Sarah. She might be taking you for a ride.

215

Suppose she had her way with you and then just ditched you. You'd be left with nothing. I mean it's not as if she couldn't get all the little star struck sweethearts she wanted. You could be just a plaything for her."

Sarah shook her head vigorously. "No Nicky. You're wrong. Oh I know that's what people will say but she's not like that. I know. Don't ask me how but I do. She's going through a tough patch with this too. She's had her share of rocky relationships as well. Did you know that she has a child?"

"You're kidding me!"

"It's true. She told me at Bollenwees. She has a daughter that lives in America."

"You mean she's not lesbian after all?"

"It was you Nicky, as I recall, that pointed out that the word lesbian is pretty relative and that people don't necessarily fall into simple categories such as straight and gay. You said that up at the Schwendisee, the day we went sunbathing."

"Well yes I know but sheesh... a daughter!"

"Yes she was married for three years too."

"Well I've heard about that."

"So you know that it's not as simple as her being some lesbian seductress out to trap some naive little girl then?"

Nicole shrugged helplessly. "Hell I don't know. I mean I don't like what this is doing to you but I don't dislike her as a person. God why did she have to set her cap for you? She could have had anybody."

"But she wants *me* Nicky."

"Hell I don't know what to advise Foxy. Ok you could just say to Alan that you're lesbian and that you don't want to marry him but you'd be risking throwing your life away over what might be just an infatuation."

"Or I could throw my life away by finishing with a woman I love to marry a man which I do not."

"Oh hell! This is going to end in tears. You've never even made love to her Sarah. You don't even know if you'd like it."

"I know. So what am I supposed to do? Drag her into bed just so I can see whether it suits me or not, risk it and end the relationship? I lose every which way."

"Sarah sweetheart listen. Are you sure, I mean absolutely sure that this thing with Daniela isn't something to do with your misgivings about marrying Alan? I mean, at first, when you came home, you were unhappy about this marriage so you set your cap for Peter. Then, when that went tits up, you throw all your affections onto Daniela. Are you looking for a get out clause here?"

Sarah shook her head. "No Nicky. Oh I know that's what it must look like but honestly no. Daniela came as a complete surprise to me. I never expected anything like that to happen. Why should I have done? I didn't even think I was attracted to girls."

"Are you? I mean attracted to girls; apart from Daniela of course."

Sarah frowned. "I don't really know Nicky. I mean I always used to like to see a pretty girl but then I like to see a pretty flower too and I don't particularly feel like having sexual relationships with a sprig of Alpine Bastard Toadflax."

"You made that name up!"

"*Thesium alpinum;* look it up."

"God what does Daniela see in a geek like you." Nicole giggled. "It could be worse. At least you haven't fallen for a bloom of Stinking Hellebore."

Sarah grinned tearfully, "Or Beakless Red Lousewort."

"Austrian Hogweed."

"Creeping Lady's Tresses."

"Narrow Leaved Wormwood."

Sarah smiled; some of her humour returning. At least Nicole wasn't being beastly to her any more.

"Anyway," she asked, "Why do you ask that? About being attracted to girls?"

"Because it's important Foxy. Look if you're just attracted to Daniela then this whole thing could just be a one off; a sort of mad aberration if you like. You could be just fundamentally heterosexual but have the one mad crush on a girl. That happens to everyone."

Sarah shook her head. "I have had crushes on females before Nicky. I know what a schoolgirl crush is like but I'm a little beyond pubescence now Nicky!" Sarah sighed. "Anyway it's not as if I spend my time looking at good looking boys either. I mean I can appreciate a handsome man but to be honest I find most young men mildly irritating. The only man I've ever really been attracted to is Peter and he's gay and I'm forced to admit that his boyfriend is a bit of a dish too. Quite frankly I seem to like gay men. You can read whatever you want into that. But this isn't just a one off Nicky. I don't have a passing crush on Daniela. When I'm with her I feel just so alive. It's like she pushes all my buttons and lights up all my screens. I've never felt like this about anybody before. When she touches me I feel dizzy. When she kisses me I feel faint. Nobody ever made me feel like that before."

"Yes but are you truly gay?"

"To be honest Nicky, I think this is the first time in my life that I've actually really confronted my sexuality. Sex was never a thing I was much interested in."

"Oh come on Sarah! I know where you keep your bedtime toys."

"It's true Nicky. To be quite frank masturbation is about the only sexual gratification I have had. Alan is more or less the only boyfriend I've ever had and sex is a bit of a let down with him. I thought perhaps that it was always that way. They say that married people hardly ever make love with each other after the first year or so anyway. I thought as well that maybe it was my fault that sex wasn't great because Alan seemed to enjoy

218

it. I was always worried about getting pregnant as well and, say what you like about safe sex, there's something fundamentally unromantic about having to halt proceedings to open a pack of bloody condoms. So I never really bothered much about making love. I never went out of my way to be attractive for Alan; I never took the initiative or anything. Somehow he just didn't turn me on. I thought I was just a prude. Everybody else thought he was absolutely gorgeous and envied me for him. He is a fine looking man, there's no doubt about it, but somehow he doesn't do anything for me physically. I know that there's more to marriage and everything than just sexual attraction but surely that's got to be there too. Is it because I'm lesbian that I'm not attracted to him? I don't know. All I know is that Daniela only has to stand next to me and my pulse rate goes off the scale. She's been really noble about it actually Nicky. I know you think that she's some awful seductress but in fact she's been extremely understanding and gentle with me. She could have had me a dozen times Nicky but she's always held back because she knew I was frightened to make that step and not ready for it. But she knew and I knew that I was there for the taking. If you hadn't thrown that party for me last night and I'd walked home with her then you would have come home today and found us in bed together. That's the truth Nicky. Maybe that party saved me. Maybe I've pulled back from the brink at the last moment. I can marry Alan with a more or less clear conscience. I just wish I didn't feel so wretched about it."

"If you really are gay Sarah then marrying Alan is about the worst thing you could do."

Sarah nodded miserably. "I know. What do I do?"

"You have to be sure. You have to be *absolutely* sure. If you're going to go to that party in Ticino to tell Alan to take his engagement ring and stick it where the sun don't shine then you have to know exactly what you are doing. You have to be certain about your feelings.

219

You have to be if you're going to tell him that you have feelings for a woman and that it is impossible for you to marry him."

"Oh God! I can't. It would be bad enough if I were to leave him for another man but to announce to one and all that I'm lesbian.... Oh God! It doesn't bear thinking about. My family would never forgive me."

"Well I wouldn't like to be in your shoes Sarah but that's the reality of it. At that party you choose; Alan or Daniela; a respectable, prosperous married life with your family's approval to a good looking man with great prospects that you don't happen to love or a dangerous lesbian affair that will alienate you from your family, possibly drag your name into the tabloid papers and liable to end in tears with a famous and notorious pop star that you're dotty about."

Sarah pulled a face. "If you put it that way then there isn't really any choice at all is there?"

"I wouldn't like to make that choice Sarah."

"What do you mean?"

"I mean it's a bitch of a choice Sarah. It's like you lose either way."

Sarah groaned. "Don't I know it." She paused. "What would you do if you were me?" she asked.

"I'd probably go with the dangerous option but that's me. I always jump in where angels fear to tread. Undoubtedly it would be a disaster but a scandalous relationship with a famous pop singer sounds a shed load more exciting than being a respectable housewife in a Zurich suburb."

"Are you telling me now that you *approve* of my relationship with Daniela?"

Nicole shrugged. "I'm just saying what I'd do. I'm not giving you advice."

"This is too bad Nicole! You've been down on my seeing Daniela for weeks now. You've been giving me all sorts of moralistic bullshit and spanking me for my scandalous behaviour and now you turn around and tell me that you'd have done exactly the same. What kind of bloody consistency do you call that?"

Nicole sighed. "Ok maybe I was a bit harsh on you but I was shocked Sarah. I'd never seen you like this before. It seemed to go against everything I thought I knew about you. I thought you were making a terrible mistake. I thought Daniela was leading you up the garden path. I was scared Sarah. Hell I'm still scared. You're one of the most important people in my life. I couldn't just let you throw it all away for what seemed to be some crazy infatuation. I thought you were making a fool of yourself."

"So why the sea change now?"

Nicole shrugged helplessly. "I don't know. Just talking to you I suppose. Maybe I'm starting to see that things aren't as simple as I thought." Nicole laughed shortly. "You know what's crazy? I actually *like* Daniela. I keep trying to paint a picture of her in my mind as the pampered rich super bitch; the odious witch that's got her claws into my Sarah and it doesn't work. She's actually a really nice person... damn her eyes! Things would be so much easier if I despised her but I can't. There's an honest part of me that even understands why you fell for her."

"Do you mean that?"

Nicole nodded numbly. "Yes I suppose I do. I couldn't accept, to begin with, that you were gay. I thought you'd just gone off your trolley or something but now I'm not so sure. I think this thing goes deeper than just some wild assed rush of hormones to the brain. You looked awfully happy with her last night. You didn't seem to care that everyone could see you. God... a few weeks ago you thought you were creating a scandal just by wearing a bikini in public. Now it's full speed ahead and damn the torpedoes."

It's a mess isn't it Nicky?"

"Yes! Yes it is. I suppose coming out as gay usually is."

"God Nicky I can't even believe I'm doing this. I've never even thought about being gay before."

"And now?"

"I don't know. It's weird. Since I've known Daniela I've started to look at other girls and it's not been purely aesthetic either. I've started to wonder what their skin feels; like how their lips taste... all sorts of things. God there was this girl at Bollenwees the other night with really long thick brown hair and I felt the urge to stroke it. I can't even believe I'm talking like this."

"What would Daniela say about this wandering eye of yours?"

"Oh she'd just laugh. She doesn't have a jealous bone in her body. She often points out pretty girls and even nice looking boys sometimes. I think she'd be quite pleased if I admitted that I find girls attractive."

"Can I ask you a question Sarah?"

"Go ahead."

"Do you find *me* attractive?"

Sarah sat bolt upright in surprise. "Why Nicky! What a thing to ask."

"Answer the bloody question!"

Sarah blinked in confusion. Nicole was looking at her levelly; her face serious. It was no trivial or flirtatious question. Sarah recalled the odd conversation she'd had with Daniela about Nicole the night before. Sarah took a deep breath. "Yes Nicole. I do. You're a beautiful girl. I've always thought so. Oh I'd prefer it if you changed that bloody hair colour and started wearing a bit more grown up clothes but yes you're an attractive girl."

"Would you sleep with me?"

"Nicky!"

"It's just a rhetorical question Sarah. If you didn't already have a girlfriend would you sleep with me?"

Sarah bit her lip, flustered and feeling she was losing control of the conversation. "I... I have slept with you Nicky... lots of times."

"Don't be bloody pedantic Sarah! You know exactly what I mean."

"But Nicky the situation would never arise. You would never want to do anything like that with me."

"How do you know? Have you ever asked?"

"It wouldn't occur to me to do so."

"Would you kiss me?"

"*What?*"

"Kiss me now; just one kiss."

"Nicky! You've come adrift of your marbles."

"I'm just asking for one kiss Sarah, not a major infidelity."

"I've kissed you thousands of times."

"Yes but not properly. Just sisterly kisses, not as if you mean it. Will you just kiss me once; properly; the way you'd kiss Daniela?"

"Oh Nicky!"

"Please Sarah. Just one kiss. It would mean a lot to me." Nicole's eyes were wide and serious.

Sarah swallowed. "Do you really want to?" Nicole nodded. She seemed to be holding her breath. "Well come here then." Nicole squirmed into Sarah's arms and turned her face to receive the kiss. Sarah tried to keep the embrace light but she was shocked as Nicole fastened herself like a limpet into her embrace. Their lips met in a fierce engagement and Nicole moaned softly as she teased apart Sarah's lips with her tongue and her hands held Sarah close, stroking her back and the back of her neck. She pressed close to Sarah and Sarah felt the heat of arousal in her friend and her own body responded in kind. She caressed Nicole's back and felt her shiver under the touch.

Suddenly; abruptly Nicole broke the embrace. Her face was flushed and she was breathing heavily. "Thank you Sarah." she whispered hoarsely.

"Nicky..." Sarah paused not knowing what to say.

Nicole smiled ruefully but there was a tear in the corner of her eye. "Well now you know."

"Know? Know what?"

"Know why I was really mad about you and Daniela. I was jealous."

"But Nicky..."

Nicole held up a hand. "It's ok Sarah. Honestly it is. I understand. Really I do. She's an amazing woman. I could never hope to compete with her."

"Nicky! What are you trying to say?"

"I've loved you as long as I can remember Sarah. You've always been the one for me. All those years I thought you were just straight and that it was impossible. Now I find that you could fall in love with a girl after all. The trouble is that the girl's not me. I couldn't help it Sarah. I was jealous. Daniela took away the woman I'd always loved."

"Oh Nicky! I'm so sorry. Is this why you have a picture of me on your computer?"

"I've got lots of pictures of you Sarah. I save them. I've even got a nude one of you. It was last summer when we had that heat wave and you slept in my room and threw your nightie off because you were too hot. You fell asleep on top of the bed and you looked so beautiful that I had to have a photo of you. I'm sorry. I'll destroy it if you want."

"Oh God keep it if you want Nicky."

"I've even got a lock of your hair Sarah. I pinched it when Gisela came around to cut your hair the summer before last. I keep it in a little locket with a picture of you. How sad is that?"

"Oh Nicky! I don't know what to say."

"You don't have to say anything Sarah. I cried last night. I've done a bit of that recently. I guess I'm just going to have to get used to it."

"Oh Nicky! Why have you never told me this before?"

"Because I was scared of losing you. I thought that you'd never want to know me any more if I felt like that about you. How ironic is that? The last thing on earth I was worried about was losing you to another woman."

"But you'd lose me to Alan anyway."

"I know but that was different somehow. If you married Alan you were still the impossible dream you'd always been. But Daniela was different. When you fell for her it showed me what might have been. It showed me what might have happened if I'd had the guts to tell you how I truly felt years ago. I couldn't lose you to Alan because in a sense you were never really mine if I had. I could lose you to Daniela however. I have lost you. That's why I was such a bitch about it."

"You know Nicky Daniela knew all about this. She figured it out straight away. She told me last night at the party. I didn't believe her. She was actually really sad about it. I... I was mad with you because I thought you were being mean to her and she defended you. She told me to have more sympathy for you; said that this would be hard on you."

"Oh God! I didn't want her sympathy."

"I think you've got it anyway. She likes you and it hurts her to see you so sad."

Nicole bit her lip sadly. "I knew she'd sussed me out Sarah. It was something she said to me last night. Bloody typical; her being so fucking noble about everything. If she'd been a bitch to me I could have handled it."

"I don't think she could be a bitch to anyone Nicky. It's not in her nature."

"Will... will you still be my friend Sarah?"

"I'll always be your friend Nicky. Always!"

"You can't marry Alan now."

"It comes back to the same problem Nicky. What option have I got?"

"But you're gay."

"I thought we were still trying to establish that. I thought you were not convinced."

"I am now."

"Since when?"

"Since you kissed me Sarah. You couldn't hide it then. I knew then. God if I had half the sense of a bloody sparrow I'd drag you upstairs to my bedroom and the devil with the consequences. It wouldn't do though would it?"

"Please Nicky! You know I couldn't."

"Yes sadly I do. Ok I'll say one more thing. I still think that it'll all end in tears Sarah but I'll not oppose you again. Take your girl with my blessing. I'll not fight it any more. You can count on my support and just remember that I'll be there when you need someone to pick up the pieces when it all goes pear shaped."

"Oh Nicky! I still can't see me going against my family and not marrying Alan."

"The hell with your family! What are you going to do? Marry a man you don't love and condemn yourself to a life of misery just so as not to upset your parents? You can't do it Sarah."

"How am I supposed to avoid it?"

"Alan hasn't formally asked you yet Sarah. Tell me this; tell me this honestly. When Alan goes down on bended knee pulls out a bloody ring and asks you to be his wife what are you going to be thinking? Will you be thinking that this is what you wanted all along or will you be thinking how to squirm out of it? If the answer is even remotely approaching the second then how are you going to look him in the eye and say yes? You can't do it. At that moment you'll know that you can't go through with it."

"Oh God I don't know Nicky. The whole thing's just a nightmare."

"You could just not go Sarah. Run off with the girlfriend somewhere. I'll stay and fight the rear-guard action with your parents."

"I have to go Nicky. I've promised. I have to face this thing."

"Your sense of duty and responsibility could trap you into a loveless marriage Sarah."

"I know Nicky. I suppose that is what my parents are counting on. I have some hard thinking to do. At the end of the day I can't tell my family that I'm foregoing the marriage on which they've placed such hope because I'm in love with a woman. That's just not an option. I can't do that to them."

"This is going to be the longest ten days of your life Sarah."

Sarah gazed out of the kitchen window. The Santis was gleaming in the afternoon sun. She wanted to run to its embrace and hide among its rocky slopes forever. "I know Nicky." she said. "I know."

Chapter Nineteen

Nicole had to work the following day and Sarah, for reasons that she was at a loss to explain to herself, spent the day in Winterthur. She had a vague idea about doing some shopping since after all she had barely touched the generous allowance her father had given her and her account was further fleshed out with the wages she had earned at the Toggenburg Hotel. Really however, she just wanted some distance from the valley for a day; a place to be, if not alone, at least anonymous with her thoughts. And Sarah had some hard thinking to do. There was another, somewhat odd reason, for her to choose to go to Winterthur. She had a new persona to try out in public. She wanted to see if she was gay.

This odd consideration was nagging at her mind. It was in fact crucial to any decision she would have to make although she was tending not to emphasise its importance too much. Nevertheless the conversation she had had with Nicole had brought the question into sharp focus. Discovering that she had feelings for another woman was bad enough but finding out that the girl she shared a house with had feelings for her well beyond the usual requirements of platonic friendship had shocked her to the core. Then there was Peter and Simon. All her closest friends it seemed were gay albeit in Nicole's case of a rather limited variety. Sarah needed to have some understanding about just what that meant. Somehow it seemed fundamental to her to understand what was happening to her.

She wanted to try some tentative experiments with her newly discovered sexual identity. She wanted to look at pretty girls and ask herself if she was attracted to them. She wanted to see if she could spot other lesbian girls or if they could spot her. She wanted an insight into the sub-culture of gay people the better to understand it and whether or not she fitted within its framework.

Of course such a mission would have been unthinkable in the Toggenburg but Winterthur had a small, but active gay community and, in the relative anonymity of the city, she was unknown and able to proceed with her careful probing without fear of discovery. Of course she hadn't told Nicole about this ulterior motive to her day in Winterthur and, although she carried her mobile phone in case Daniela called, she certainly hadn't informed her either.

In fact the only person Sarah had consulted about the adventure was Simon who was becoming her ally in her struggle with her new sexual awareness. After Nicole had gone to work early that morning she'd phoned him, blessing the foresight that she'd taken his card the previous day. Simon had been bemused by her request. "Why the hell do you want to know that?" he asked. "I thought you already had a girlfriend."

"I do Simon. I just want to know what it's like... to see how other girls like... well like me are. I'm still trying to come to terms with all this. I don't know what it's like to be gay. I've never met any gay girls before except at uni and I've never gone to the sort of places where they hang out. I need to see what it's all about."

"Jesus Sarah! Does Danny know you're off gadding about in Winterthur trying to pick up girls?"

"I am not trying to pick up girls Simon. I just want to see what gay girls are like."

"You know what gay girls are like. You *are* one."

"That's what I'm trying to find out Simon. I want to see if other gay girls are like me or if I fit the role."

"Oh Sarah! Of course they're not like you. You're unique Sarah. There's *nobody* like you. Don't be too ready to assume roles Sarah. Your sexual preferences don't determine your character. Don't try to be a gay cliché."

"I'm not Simon. I just want to see other gay girls. I'm here in the Toggenburg and it's a pretty lonely place to be different. I want to see somewhere where people are openly gay and where I can see what it means to them."

Simon chuckled softly. "Well you won't find much of a roaring gay scene in Winterthur Sarah but there are a few places where gays hang out. You'd be better off in Zurich but I'm damned if I'm going to allow a sweet little innocent like you to expose yourself to the predatory vampires there. Danny would have my balls as grill decoration on her Ferrari."

"Well just tell me where they hang out in Winterthur then."

"You might be disappointed Sarah. I mean a lot of gay girls don't actually meet in bars or anything. They meet at school or work or at sports clubs or whatever. Most gay bars are pretty much male, I'm afraid, although there are a few where lesbian couples go so they can hang with their girlfriends in a safe environment. You will get places that cater for gay girls but you'll get a few older butches in them that'll try to hit on any young unattached girl. There's one place in Winterthur that's quite mixed; gays of both sexes. Be careful though because quite a few straight people use the place too and you've got to be aware of the fag-hags as well."

"What the devil is a fag-hag?"

"Sorry Sarah. It's a derogatory name for women that are attracted to gay men and tend to hang around in gay bars. Nearly every gay bar has its quota of such women."

"I was once attracted to Peter, Simon and I think you're good looking too. Does that make me a fag-hag?"

Simon laughed hugely. "Good God no! If your Danny was around you wouldn't look twice at either of us. Stick with what works Sarah. Don't make your life even more complicated by taking a fancy to gay men."

"Advice taken. So where do I find this place?"

"Look Sarah do you want me to come with you as a chaperone?"

"I'm a big girl Simon. I can look after myself."

"No you're not Sarah. When it comes to this you're a complete novice. This is something new to you. You're out of your depth here."

"I'll be careful Simon I promise."

"Well ok look there's this cafe bar in the city centre where a lot of gay people, male and female, hang out in the afternoons. It's not really a pick-up place but quite chilled, very chic and I think you'll be safe enough there. It's a nice enough little place and the people are friendly so you won't come to too much grief. Just promise me you won't let some old dyke drag you away. I don't fancy being Ferrari road kill."

"Don't tell Danny if you see her."

"You're joking aren't you? Do I look like a man with a death wish?"

"Ok give me directions to this dive." Sarah noted down Simon's instructions. "What should I wear?" she asked at last.

"What?"

"What's the normal dress code for places like this?"

"How the fuck would I know? I'm not a lesbian."

"Well what would I wear to blend in?"

"You're not *going* to blend in Sarah. You could walk in there in old rags and you'll stand out. You could dress up like a bag lady and every warm blooded dyke in the place will be crawling all over you. Have you the faintest idea how beautiful you are?"

"Well do I dress up in a more masculine way?"

"God no! For one thing you couldn't manage it. Lesbians can be pretty derisive of girls that try to look butch unsuccessfully. Just look natural and if anybody tries to hit on you tell them you've already got a girlfriend and to get lost."

"Danny likes to see me in very feminine clothes. Maybe I should go for that look."

"Oh God Sarah! You're scaring me to death here. There's no way I'm letting you go on your own."

"I'll be alright!"

"Like hell you will! I'll pick you up at that bar and drive you home at five o'clock sharp ok? You stay there until I arrive ok? Promise?"

Sarah smiled bemused by Simon's sudden fraternal sense of protection for her. "Ok I'll be there."

"Don't get lured away mind. I'll bring a cattle prod to clear the crowds away."

"I'm sure you're exaggerating Simon."

Her conversation with Simon had put Sarah in a fine mood and she had to admit that it was comforting to know that he would pick her up in Winterthur. She felt protected, as if she had a big brother to look after her if she got into any scrape she couldn't handle. She began to look forward to her adventure in town. In the end she decided to opt for the kind of clothes she knew Daniela would love to see her in. Resurrected for the occasion was the lovely gold cocktail dress that Sarah had bought in Buchs. The dress had cost her five hundred francs and she had only worn it the one time to go to the disco in Unterwasser with Nicole. It had been residing in her wardrobe like a guilty secret ever since. Sarah pulled it out and agonised over it. It was perfectly ok for a day dress but it was dangerously alluring. She stroked the material lovingly and then her good sense got the better of her and she placed it firmly back in the wardrobe. Thirty seconds later she pulled it out again and held it up biting her lip. "No! I can't!" she said and thrust it determinedly back from whence it had come. She held up another dress and regarded it critically. It seemed a little drab. Shortly after she hauled the gold dress out again and glared at it furiously. "I can't possibly wear this." she told herself. She held it in front of her before the mirror. "No! Absolutely out of the question. What would Danny think?" Well the answer to that, of course, was that Daniela would have whistled in appreciation.

"No really..." Sarah told herself. With a sigh she started to replace it. It never got there. "Oh the hell with it!" she snorted and a minute later it was adorning her body as she preened in front of the mirror in it. She twirled narcissistically and smoothed the material over her thighs. "Well," she said to herself, "Simon did say this bar was a chic establishment so it wouldn't do to dress drably. Suddenly she giggled. "Anyway... I've got a rock and roll star as a girlfriend so I can't appear in public looking like a tramp. I've got appearances to keep up."

Still giggling to herself she donned her moissanite earrings. Her emerald necklace was by now almost a permanent adornment. She fussed over her hair and make-up, agonised over her shoes, and, once satisfied, she picked up her handbag and tripped out of the house almost merrily. The Ticino and its looming doom could wait. Today she was out for fun.

In the end she didn't even have to walk all the way to Unterwasser for her bus, which was a hazard in itself in her high heels. One of her neighbours in the Alpli stopped her up on the roadside to give her a lift and showered embarrassing compliments on her appearance all the way to Unterwasser. Mounting the bus in Unterwasser gave her some moments of doubt because her stunning appearance drew a number of stares from the other passengers but she ignored them. Less easy to ignore was an old woman Sarah knew well who dragged her into conversation and openly admired her dress. Sarah groaned inwardly. Now undoubtedly it would be all over the valley that she'd gone flouncing off to town dressed like a tart. Her morale recovered in Nesslau where the platform conductor ushered her onto the train for Wil with exaggerated gallantry and she felt quite a star at his obsequious attentions. With her ego flattered, Sarah jumped on the Inter-City train in Wil and went straight to the restaurant car. It only took about twenty minutes for the train to get to Winterthur but Sarah felt it commensurate with her appearance to demurely sip a small glass of wine for the duration of the journey. The waitress that brought her the wine smiled in a friendly fashion and, because this was a day for testing her new sexuality, Sarah smiled back and held eye contact. The girl lingered to chat a little longer than was professionally necessary and Sarah wondered with a thrill whether the girl was attracted to her. Maybe she was just being friendly and reacting to a friendly smile but Sarah dismounted at Winterthur tingling.

She went shopping. That alone was enough to suggest that Sarah was in a dangerously frivolous mood. As has already been noted, she was generally not the most enthusiastic of shoppers and only her heightened sensuality can account for her sudden decision to look for pretty clothes. Of course she had other justifications for going shopping. It was only about half past ten in the morning for one thing and far too early for her to begin her tentative exploration of the Winterthur gay scene. Also she had to buy some things just to justify her trip to town to Nicole. Then again, she was conscious of the fact that she needed some good clothes for her engagement party in just over a week and to satisfy her mother that she wasn't entirely a fashion disaster. For once, however, obligation was not the main motivation behind her shopping. For once she was shopping for pleasure. The day was a hot one and, dressed in the lovely gold dress, she felt daringly sensual. She wanted to look pretty. She had not the slightest doubt for who she was shopping. She wanted to look pretty for Daniela.

There was another, somewhat more surprising, reason behind her shopping spree. The town centre of Winterthur was well supplied with fashionable boutiques and clothing outlets along its pedestrian precincts and wherever you found lots of clothes shops on a sunny day you were going to find girls; lots and lots of girls. Sarah had a mind to do a little girl watching.

She spent an obscene amount of money by her standards. Even the madness that had gripped her in

Buchs just a few weeks ago paled into insignificance against the spree she went on this day. It was an insanity founded on rebelliousness, for her father had, after all, sent her twenty thousand francs to buy some clothes for her engagement and the social obligations that went with it. She now just had nine more days of freedom to blow it in. She was damned if she was going to save the money to buy new net curtains and a dishwasher for her marital nest in Zurich. If they were going to offer her up like a fatted calf to cement an alliance with Alan's family then she'd make sure she was the fattest calf in the market. She had nine days of freedom left and she was going to live them. They might think that she was suddenly blossoming into a well-dressed young lady for Alan's benefit. Let them! The truth was that the only person that Sarah wanted to look her best for was Daniela.

Every item therefore, that Sarah lifted from a rack, was subjected to a single demanding criteria; "Would Daniela find me attractive in this?" From a beautiful day dress in white with colourful abstract swirls about the skirt and hem that cost her a hundred and fifty francs the spree went out of control. In the space of only three hours she bought no less than five dresses, two skirts, three new pairs of elegant shoes, three tops, two ridiculously frivolous blouses and a matching short skirt and jacket. She even bought expensive sexy stockings with seams running down the back, a new handbag and a number of costume jewellery accessories. So far did the madness extend that she even visited a lingerie store. Underwear to Sarah had always been a totally functional item of her wardrobe and you would have looked in vain for frivolity and provocation amongst her collection of plain knickers and sensible bras. Well now her underwear had another function to perform. It had to be the sort of wispy alluring little bits of nonsense whose only purpose was to make Daniela want to tear them off her.

Sarah was appalled at the price of high class sexy lingerie. Her normal underwear purchases consisted of economy packs from large retail outlets where you paid twenty francs for five pairs of knickers in a box you picked out of a bin in the middle of the store. She lifted some diaphanous creation from a rack, that couldn't have weighed much more than a few grams or covered a midget with any decency, which was retailing at three hundred francs. She took a deep breath and waded in however. Her voluminous shopping bags were quickly augmented by five pairs of knickers, three frilly and utterly unnecessary bras, a matching camisole and French knickers in silk whose price took her breath away, a long negligee whose powers of concealment were effectively zero, a little baby doll and matching thong, a long chemise and a perfectly lovely teddy and matching jacket in silk that cost her a cool three hundred and fifty francs. Even her defiant rebelliousness sobered mightily when the final bill came to over a thousand francs. She doubted if she'd spent that much on underwear in the last ten years. The girl at the cash desk packed her acquisitions for her carefully and winked. "Looks like the boyfriend is in for a treat." she noted mischievously.

Sarah blushed and stifled a giggle. "Er actually I'm getting married shortly."

"Ah! Stocking up for the honeymoon eh? Well Miss you've got the figure for it and I'd say your hubby is going to drop one wing and run around in circles crowing when you model this little lot for him." She giggled helplessly. "It seems a lot of money to pay for something you're only going to be wearing for about five seconds after he sees it."

Sarah laughed, enjoying the pretty girl's banter. "Well that's the whole point isn't it?"

"It is indeed! Give me your card honey and take a good strong pinch of snuff while I put a dent in it."

Sarah watched the girl as she processed her card and admired her. She was very pretty. Sarah wondered if she liked the sort of lingerie she sold in the shop. She pictured the girl in some of the more daring creations on sale and she found the thought stimulating. She hoped the shop gave discounts to its employees. The girl surely couldn't afford this kind of stuff on a shop assistant's salary otherwise.

The girl handed Sarah's card back with the receipt. "There you go Miss." She said with a warm smile. "Tell your husband he's a lucky man."

Sarah looked at her straight in the eye. "Actually I'm not marrying a man. I bought these for my girlfriend's benefit."

The girl's eyes flew open in surprise. "Oh! Oh I see. I'm sorry Miss."

Sarah smiled. "That's perfectly all right." She placed her card back in her purse and picked up her new purchases. "Thank you very much. You've been most helpful." With that she turned on her heel and walked to the door. She could feel the girl's stare at her back all the way out of the shop.

Out in the street Sarah leaned against a wall laughing and hardly daring to believe her own audaciousness. She'd just told a complete stranger that she was a lesbian. The girl's face had been a picture. The poor girl hadn't known what to say. Composing herself Sarah picked up her bags and staggered off down the street. In one sense her plans had gone awry. It was difficult to maintain her desired appearance of feminine allure whilst struggling along under the weight of a dozen shopping bags.

But she still had one more shop to visit. It was a little jewellers shop and she'd seen something earlier she really wanted to have. It was a white gold edelweiss pendant with a cluster of little diamonds around a sapphire in the centre on a white gold chain. It was beautiful and Sarah wanted to hang it around Daniela's neck. It cost nearly a thousand francs. Sarah didn't even flinch when she handed over her card. She was in love.

237

Sarah deposited her purchases in a hired locker in the nearby railway station not wanting to be encumbered by them for the next part of the day's itinerary. She made adjustments to her appearance in the ladies room and gazed at herself in shock in the mirror. The lovely face that gazed back was one that had just thrown away the cautious habits of a lifetime and frivolously blown nearly six thousand francs in the space of three hours. Sarah couldn't believe it was happening to her yet she felt curiously liberated at the same time. At least her conscience was clear in one respect. She had followed her father's instructions to use his money to augment her wardrobe to the letter. She even had receipts to prove it. Only the pendant and chain she had bought for Daniela did not fall under that mandate and Sarah had determined that that expenditure would come from her own money. Whatever might be the outcome of the looming doom, which she could still see no way of avoiding, she was determined that Daniela would have one thing at least to remember her by. She grinned to herself and with a last toss of her hair strode out to prowl the streets of Winterthur in earnest.

Chapter Twenty

Back on the streets, Sarah began her appraisal of the womanhood of Winterthur. It was strange that a person who was such a gifted observer of nature as Sarah was so unskilled in the arts of people watching. It was just something she never did. She was generally uncomfortable in crowded places and usually far too polite to observe people closely. Today, however, she had a direct mission; a purpose to her observations. She wanted to look at girls. If she was supposedly gay then she wanted to look at girls and decide whether she found them attractive and to ask herself why they were attractive. Would she prefer blonds or brunettes; slim willowy girls or well curved ones? Would she find boyish girls with short hair and masculine attire more appealing or be more drawn to very feminine girls in softer female garbs? Would her senses be more taken by confident looking, strong girls or would she find shy, vulnerable looking girls the more beguiling? She really had no idea. She had never really looked before.

At the outset of the exercise, she decided that she had to lay down one basic starting premise. She knew that the girl she found most attractive in the world was Daniela. It would negate the whole point of the experiment however if she simply compared all the girls with Daniela. That simply wasn't fair for one thing. Daniela was such a strikingly beautiful woman that not one in a thousand other girls was even going to come near her. Also to merely compare other girls to Daniela would run the risk of proving that Sarah's newly discovered sexual orientation was merely centred around a single woman and that the charge of atypical infatuation was well grounded. If she only found Daniela attractive among the approximately three billion women in the world it was hardly conclusive evidence of her homosexuality was it? Well all right there was Nicole as well but that was a complicated subject upon which she didn't desire to dwell for the moment. No... she had to regard a broad range of girls and judge her reaction to them. Pompously she told herself that she needed to regard them dispassionately. No that wasn't right. She had to look at them *passionately.* She had to look at them as if they were potential lovers. Would this girl please her? Would she like to kiss this girl? Would the thought of this girl in her arms give her pleasure?

Sarah roamed the crowded shopping streets with her senses finely tuned. The men on the street she ignored completely although they certainly didn't ignore her. The beautiful girl drew many an admiring glance, the occasional whistle and raucous remark. Sarah was hardly even aware of them and, when she was, she was mildly irritated by their distraction. She was focussed on the girls and quickly became quite fascinated by them.

It was impossible, she realised after just a short while, to place the girls on the streets into any categories of attractive or unattractive. Anybody who had spent a lifetime in dedicated research into the enigma of female beauty could have told her that of course. Women just came in such a bewildering variety of forms, shapes and identities that they simply defied logical categorisation. Daniela was blond so Sarah thought perhaps she must prefer blonds but, after covertly looking at two or three breathtakingly lovely brunettes, that theory was discarded. There were plenty of blonds, in any case, that she found cheap and artificial looking. Then again she spied one girl with gorgeous natural blond curls that she could not take her eyes off. Just to complicate matters, a minute later a girl with waist length jet black hair came around a corner who was so stunning that Sarah came to a grinding halt in the street. After coming to several bewilderingly differing conclusions regarding the colour of hair Sarah decided it didn't really matter what colour it was as long as there was lots of it. Sarah had become fond of Daniela's luxurious mane of hair and she knew how much she loved to stroke it. She was forced to admit that long hair she found attractive. The stuff was gorgeous. She walked behind one girl with such a riotously perfect shiny cascade of chestnut hair that it was all she could do to prevent herself reaching out to caress it. But it wasn't quite that simple. She spied another girl with a short haircut that seemed almost the perfect adornment to an exquisitely lovely pixie face.

Then there was the question of build. To be honest with herself, she could find no preferences in this area at all. She preferred slim girls but that quality of slenderness was not confined to rakishly thin or boyish figures. She found that she liked to see girls with curves to them. For the first time in her life Sarah began to notice women's breasts. She had heard endless tedious conversations from men about women's breasts and, like many a girl, had assumed that men liked them big. She quickly decided that it wasn't the size of a girl's breasts that made them attractive; it was the appropriateness of them. A thin girl with overly large breasts looked grotesque and equally a girl of generous curves in other areas seemed inadequate if her breasts were small. It was a question of balance she realised. You couldn't just look at a girl's breasts in isolation. They were a part of the overall harmony of her figure. Things had to be in proportion. She liked to see shapely breasts; firm and well formed.

She enjoyed the sight of nipples too. There were enough girls in the hot weather that wore thin enough tops that their erect nipples were easily visible and Sarah had to stop herself staring. In her curiously elevated sensual mood Sarah was aware that her own nipples were standing pertly away from her breasts. She knew that when she was very aroused her nipples became so hard they almost hurt and she took the sight of erect nipples for a signal of sexual arousal. It sent a shiver down her whenever she saw a girl whose nipples

241

protruded at her top and she allowed her mind to wonder what it would be like to draw a languorous finger over them. She remembered the morning when she had awoken to find Nicole suckling at her nipples in her sleep and she had to pause a moment to catch her breath.

Legs she enjoyed too. The hot weather was perfect for the display of female legs for numerous young ladies were abroad in dresses and shorts that exposed acres of them. Sarah found herself examining the musculature of the legs almost as if asking herself how they would fare on the mountains. The thing that most enticed her though was the skin on them. When she had shared blankets or duvet with Daniela on the mountain Daniela had huddled so close to her that her bare legs had come into contact with her own and Sarah had marvelled at the smoothness of the skin on them. In fact any bare flesh caught Sarah's eye. She had had enough, just enough, experience of the feel of Daniela's body to know just how softly velvet was a woman's skin. Daniela had hugged her when they were both naked on the path down from the Altmannsattel and Sarah could still feel the intoxicatingly sensual feel of her flesh against hers. It was quite unlike the rough texture of a man. There was a warm silkiness to it that begged to be caressed. The sight of a girl exposing a generous amount of soft skin of enticing complexion could arrest her stride and walk more slowly and languidly behind them yearning to feel that skin against hers.

The most arresting feature she noted however were the girl's faces. It almost came as a surprise to Sarah when she understood why girls spent more time decorating their faces than almost any other part of their body. It was the face you looked at first. It was the single most important item in any girl's appearance. The most exquisitely lovely and perfect body could be ruined by an unappealing face and, conversely, a girl, with indifferent assets otherwise, could be transformed into an attractive young lady simply by the possession of a pretty face. But what made a pretty face? Again there was no easy answer. They came in such a variety that it was impossible to single out any one distinguishing feature. Sarah was sure that Daniela with her artist's eye could have pointed out the salient features that were particularly fine in any girl's face and she was sure that there were some sorts of artistic rules that defined the beauty of the female face. Doubtless it was not any specific thing but a combination; a harmony of differing features that had to blend proportionately to create the aesthetic affect. A nose that might be too large on one girl was just perfect when set among the features of another. Generous lips might look disproportionately large on one girl yet beg to be kissed on another. Sarah found she liked high foreheads which she associated, possibly erroneously, with high intelligence and she admired high, well-formed cheekbones that seemed to speak of character and vivacious personality.

If Sarah had to pick out one particular feature, however, it was the eyes. Sarah found pretty eyes irresistible. In fact the whole face was where you looked for the personality and humour of the girl you were looking at and there were few better indications of that than the eyes. The eyes were the precious gemstones set into the jewel of a girl's beauty. If her hair was her crowning glory and her lovely face a masterpiece of natural design those features only served truly to form a background for the display of her eyes. No other part of her body, with the possible exception of her hair was given more care and attention than a girl's eyes. Her cheeks might be satisfied with a little foundation and the application of rouge; her lips could pass muster with a coat of lipstick but her eyes required the most delicate and fussy of treatment to enhance them; eyeliners and mascara, eye-shadow and the whole gamut of cosmetic eye make-up as if a girl knew instinctively that the jewels in her crown were the two little organs set in her face through which she viewed the world. Women worldwide spent billions, *billions,* every year to show off their faces, the settings for their eyes and the most obvious outward projection of their souls.

It was that latter consideration that really made the face the most important part of the body Sarah decided. You could admire a pair of shapely legs, be titillated by a firm high bosom or a pair of well-rounded hips. You might even find your eye caught by a pair of pretty feet or elegant hands. A long and shapely neck was deliciously inviting and a curvaceous bottom needed to be patted. But ultimately you looked at the face to find out where the girl was really coming from. Every expression of her character, her warmth or lack of it, her invitation or rejection, her joy or sadness, her mood, her intelligence, her sweetness or hardness; they were all there to be read in the features of her face. A lovely face could be ruined by an ill-humoured expression and yet a plain one could light up with a dazzling smile. It was the one most important erogenous zone of any girl. The face was where you made your opening gambit for her seduction. You could touch a girl's hand or even her leg without the immediate sense of intimacy that a caress to her face or a kiss to her lips would bring. If you touched her face you were signalling your intentions and desires in the most fundamental and undeniable of ways.

Sarah thought of Daniela and how Daniela loved to stroke her face and kiss it. She would often pause in conversation to lay a hand on Sarah's cheek or to lift away a rebellious lock of hair the better to look at it. Daniela adored Sarah's face Sarah knew; could not drink her fill of the sight of it; was magnetically drawn to it and could not tear her eyes from it. In return Sarah had gloried in the chance to openly stare at a woman's face without fear of appearing rude. It was quite a face to look at as well. The creator must have tired of mediocrity the day he fashioned Daniela's face for he had excelled himself that day. It was gift not only to see that lovely face but also to be able, without inhibition, to examine it and admire it at such close quarters. It could so easily belong to her; be hers to kiss; hers to stroke, hers to enjoy in all its captivating radiance. It was a face to change a person's life and, if it could launch a thousand ships, it could lead them into perilously rocky shoals indeed.

Girl watching was not without its hazards, Sarah discovered. Simply looking at girls was relatively straightforward if all you required was a covert glance and a fleeting glimpse of them. To subject them to the sort of searching examination that the exercise required, however, was far more dangerous. Then you ran the danger of staring at them and, if they became aware of your gaze, the risk of their interpretation of your interest. For instance Sarah wanted to know the colour of their eyes and that meant making eye contact as often as not. Swiss people with their innate courteousness did not stare openly into a stranger's face when not addressing them and it was difficult to hold their eyes for a moment or two. It was necessary to invent a ruse to hold their attention and Sarah found a relatively safe one by simply asking directions. She'd sight a girl at close quarters that she found generally pleasant to look at and then approach them with an innocuous request to be directed to some arbitrary destination. The Swiss were far too polite not to respond and nearly every girl would pause to assist her and look directly at the person she was addressing.

It became quite a game for Sarah and she began to enjoy the little encounters she engineered along the shopping streets. One or two girls were apparently hostile under the veneer of their civility. Sarah couldn't understand that. She simply couldn't grasp the fact that she was a sensationally beautiful girl, expensively dressed and that some girls would instantly see a rival. Sarah didn't possess an envious bone in her body. Mostly however she encountered anything but hostility. Her beauty was, after all, based largely upon her warm open friendliness and natural charm and it usually disarmed even the most suspicious of temperaments. Daniela had long been aware of Sarah's irresistible charm. People just instinctively liked Sarah. She was not one of the most popular girls in the Toggenburg without reason. Even a girl solidly heterosexual would find her day brightened by a minute's conversation with Sarah and even the most dour of humours could be tempted into a smile by her gentle radiance.

Sarah loved it and her enjoyment began to make her more daring. She stopped one girl to ask where she could find a certain boutique. The girl was wearing a lovely floral dress and Sarah complimented her on it and asked her where she had bought it. The girl blushed with pleasure and told her. Sarah thanked her and told her that the dress suited her very well and the girl preened visibly with the compliments. Another girl she stopped to ask directions to a shop wore a pair of beautiful earrings. Sarah exclaimed, apparently impulsively, how lovely they were. The girl was obviously proud of her ear adornments for she seemed pleased by Sarah's admiration. When Sarah asked politely if she could look at them closely the girl turned her head to one side to afford a better view and allowed Sarah to reach out and hold them gently on her fingertips; her hands perilously close to the girl's face. The touching little intimacy was a minor triumph and the pupils of the girl's eyes widened as Sarah leaned close to look at her jewellery with the aroma of her perfume in her nostrils. The girl seemed slightly reluctant to part and she said goodbye with a warm smile. Sarah felt like dancing with pleasure at the little victory.

After two hours of this, Sarah was convinced. She liked girls. More than that, she found them absolutely fascinating. She could have spent all day observing them. Almost sadly she wondered why she had never taken the time to look at them properly before. They were intriguing, beguiling, astonishing in their infinite variety.

In her enlightened mood she saw a story behind every pretty girl's face and a promise in every bewitching smile. In truth she had never closely examined men before either but it didn't matter today. Today she wanted to see girls. In a real sense it made her suddenly aware of her connection to the stream of femininity; to feel a part of the collective sisterhood of womankind. It was almost a paradox that her interest in women coincided with the burgeoning of her own femininity. It was almost as if she had needed to become a woman herself in order to truly appreciate them. For the first time in her life she could truly thank God that she had been born a woman. They just seemed so superior to men in every way and she adored them.

But did they like her? This was the secondary object of the day's experiment and Sarah's antennae were out and waving for any reaction to herself. If she was lesbian then could any other girl with similar tastes recognise the fact? She'd heard gay people refer to a sixth sense they called "gaydar"; a sort of intuitive detection device built into them to know their own or, to put it more bluntly, it took one to know one. Sarah had no idea of what signals to look for to spot other gay girls but she wondered idly if she was unconsciously signalling her own inclinations. Certainly the girl with the earrings might have found her attractive and there was another girl that had stopped to chat with her for over five minutes, well beyond the requirements of common civility, that Sarah marked down as a possible. In only one case however was Sarah aware of an overt sexual attraction for her.

A slightly older woman was lounging in the doorway of an expensive boutique smoking a cigarette. She was obviously an employee of the boutique and had slipped outside for a break and a dose of nicotine. She was a beautiful and alluring lady with soft brown hair, inviting eyes, a sultry pair of lips and she carried her sensuality around like a barely concealed bomb. Sarah caught her eye as she walked past and noted that the

247

woman's eyebrows rose markedly at her appearance. Sarah smiled daringly at her and was rewarded by a warm and inviting smile in return. The woman fixed her eyes on her and took a long sensual pull at her cigarette; her eyes never wavering from Sarah. Sarah felt her dark brown eyes on her like a physical shock wave and she slowed her gait deliberately as she wandered past the shop knowing that the woman followed her every move. She almost trembled with excitement but she dared not return to the shop under the pretext of examining the goods on offer. The woman was a powerful sensual force and likely a dominating seductress. Sarah was out of her league.

It was this encounter that caused Sarah to consult her watch. It was nearly half past three and Simon was picking her up at five. She hadn't even begun to move toward what promised to be the most challenging of the day's tasks; the perusal of a known location for gay people. Hastily she fumbled in her handbag for the directions Simon had given her to the gay cafe bar. Fortunately it wasn't too far away. Taking a deep breath she endeavoured to locate it. It was the one place for which she dared not ask for directions.

Chapter Twenty-One

It took her only five minutes to find the bar's location on a broad boulevard that was traffic free and lined with little cafes and bars. It took her a further ten minutes, however, to muster the courage to enter it. She might not have made it at all if not for the fact that it possessed a sunny inviting terrace out on the street where at least she could maintain some pretence of having walked in purely by accident. The place was full. The interior of the bar was packed with well-dressed people and these spilled out onto the terrace in front. It was obvious that Simon was right for many of the customers were quite clearly overtly gay. The men were most obviously gay for the most part, many of them effecting the camp mannerisms and speech of the classic queen. Not all of them were so aggressively gay but most of them were well dressed with a far greater sense of fashion and appearance than you would have expected among straight men.

The women seemed more problematical. It was true that there were women present that were garbed in such masculine fashion that they appeared more male than their fellow customers with XY chromosomes. Oddly, Sarah found them peculiarly unattractive. Somehow she liked her girls to look like girls and not surrogate men. She found the more effeminate young men more attractive than the more butch girls. But not all the women were so determinedly masculine however. Most, in fact, were decidedly feminine and often very pleasant to look at.

Sarah took one of the few free tables on the terrace with her heart pounding. It was just too noisy and lively in the bar's interior. The sound system was belting out a collection of old disco hits from the seventies and eighties; Donna Summers, Amanda Lear, the Pet Shop

Boys, Boys Town Gang, Madonna, Abba, Gloria Gaynor, The Weather Girls, Shirley Bassey and Divine and interspersed with more up to date songs by Melissa Etheridge, Lady Gaga or, to Sarah's shocked surprise, Daniela Devin. Sarah sat at her table for nearly fifteen minutes before she realised that nobody was going to serve her. The place was evidently bar service only. She had to face the interior if she wanted a drink.

The walk to the bar inside sorely tested Sarah's courage. Now she finally found eyes upon her and they were somewhat disturbing. A lot of the men seemed to regard her suspiciously and one or two of the more butch women regarded her with openly predatory looks. It was quite shocking inside the bar for several men were openly holding hands and even kissing. Sarah had never actually seen two men kiss before and she found the sight strangely odd. There was a tiny dance floor at the back of the bar and several people were dancing together to a slower number. She blinked as she saw a very muscular man clad in leather clutching a frail looking young man in tight jeans to him hungrily and pawing at his bottom. Several girls were dancing as well and Sarah watched in fascination two short haired girls dancing closely and quite obviously lost in each other's embrace, oblivious to their surroundings. They looked terribly in love.

Sarah had to squeeze through to the bar and push up to it alongside a middle aged woman, perched on a barstool, dressed in a masculine cut suit complete with a tie, who gave Sarah such a frankly sexual appraisal that Sarah was glad when the bartender attended to her requirements and she was able to escape with her small beer. As she wended her way outside, she noted two girls on a settle together, locked in each other's embrace and kissing so passionately it was a wonder the management hadn't turned a fire extinguisher on them. Sarah couldn't help but stare. They were quite attractive. Another girl took her attention. She was a pretty young girl sat alone and looking quite scared, holding a glass of wine in front of her protectively. Simon had said that quite a few straight people used the bar too and Sarah wondered if the girl had wandered in by mistake and was regretting it. It wasn't the whole story though for Sarah caught her eye as she passed and smiled sympathetically. The girl smiled back gratefully and her face lit up. It was an instant contact and Sarah knew that if she had asked to join the girl at her table the response would have been immediate and enthusiastic. She was the one girl Sarah would have liked to have talked to. Somehow Sarah knew that here was a girl as confused about her own sexuality as she was. This was her kindred sister. It would have been instant rapport. But Sarah was not about to make advances on other girls on her first foray into a gay bar. For one thing she was terrified of doing so and, secondly, she already had a girlfriend.

She battled her way outdoors again breathing heavily. Gladly her table was still free and she seated herself gratefully, not sure what to do next. There were a lot of pretty girls sat around the terrace in the sunshine or under the shade of the big parasols but Sarah was having difficulty separating them. How could she tell the gay girls from the straight ones? Her "gaydar" didn't seem to be working. And now she was in a gay environment she felt awkwardly shy and less inclined to make eye contact with other girls. There was a sensationally beautiful girl in a short skirt a few tables away that Sarah refused to believe was gay. She was just too girly. But then again, Sarah remembered ruefully, she was looking pretty feminine herself. Maybe the other clients of the bar were thinking exactly the same thing as she was.

Did gay girls have private symbols that advertised their sexual orientation to each other? She had no idea. She'd heard that gay men often wore items of jewellery; rings on certain fingers or earrings that let other gay men know they were of the same ilk but she had heard of nothing similar among gay women. Perhaps it had been

251

a mistake, after all, to dress in such a feminine fashion. Perhaps she was sending out confusing signals. But what signals did you emit? She herself liked girls in feminine attire. Was there a sort of lesbian gender role that determined that feminine girls paired off with butch girls? If she liked feminine girls was it incumbent on her to assume a more masculine attire? That couldn't be right she thought. Daniela was the most elegantly female of women and Sarah knew that she loved to see her and dress her in softly feminine clothes. There was no butch and femme in their relationship, just a solid appreciation of female beauty and the decoration of that beauty. Were they atypical? She couldn't imagine two butch girls together. Two feminine girls together however excited her senses. It was all very confusing. In bewilderment Sarah took a sip of her beer.

"Hi there!"

Sarah jumped in surprise. A tall slender girl of about her age was stood by her table looking at her. She was pretty in a somewhat boyish fashion. Her hair was cut short but her face was lovely and she wore little earrings above a shapely neck. She was dressed in an open necked shirt and a pair of tight fitting jeans. She held a glass in her hand and a cigarette in the other and her smile was friendly if touched with a hint of nervousness. Sarah, caught off-guard in her musings, was momentarily flustered. "Oh! Er hello."

"Er I haven't seen you here before."

Sarah swallowed. "That's probably because I've never been here before."

The girl seemed suddenly at a loss and deflated. "Oh er right." She ploughed on bravely. "I... er... I just wondered if you'd like a drink and some company."

"I've already got a drink." Sarah pointed out.

"Yes! Right..." the girl looked utterly defeated. "I... er... I'm sorry to bother you Miss." She started to turn away.

Sarah smiled, taking pity on the girl. "I could do with the company though."

The girl's face lit up with renewed hope and she turned back. "Really?"

"Yes. Do take a seat if you wish." Sarah held out her hand. "My name's Sarah."

The girl took the hand with a grin. "Pleased to meet you Sarah. I'm Charlie."

"Charlie?"

"Well Charmaine actually but people call me Charlie."

"I think Charmaine is a lovely name. Please sit down Charmaine."

The girl blushed but obeyed and with shock Sarah realised that she was more nervous than she was. She ran a hand through her short hair agitatedly. "Oh God! You must think I'm a complete retard Sarah. I couldn't have made a bigger balls up of that if I'd tried."

"Of what?"

"Coming up to you and saying something dumb like I've never seen you here before. God! Of all the limp opening lines I could have thought of."

"I thought it was very friendly of you Charmaine."

"I was wetting myself trying to pluck up courage to come over and speak to you."

"Then you were very brave. But why?"

"Why was I wetting myself?"

"No! I mean why did you want to come over to speak to me?"

Charmaine looked uncomfortable. "Oh! I'm sorry Sarah. Maybe we've had a misunderstanding. I'm Sapphic."

"Sapphic?"

Charmaine groaned. "You know.... lesbian.... gay. Oh God! Why doesn't the ground open up and swallow me now? I'm so sorry."

Sarah laughed at the young girl's discomfiture. "Please don't apologise. I think you're sweet."

Charmaine looked at her disbelievingly. "Are you gay too Sarah?"

Sarah blushed. "Yes. Yes I am."

Charmaine's face was a picture of delight. "Oh wow! I... I wasn't sure. Oh Brilliant!"

"But why did you want to talk to me Charmaine?"

"I beg your pardon."

"Why me? There're lots of gay girls here surely."

"You're joking surely."

Sarah frowned. "No I'm not. I just wanted to know why you picked me out in particular. Or do you just like to talk to all the girls here."

Charmaine regarded Sarah as if she had just landed from Mars. "I've actually never done that before Sarah!"

"Done what?"

"I've never gone up to a complete stranger in a bar before and tried to pick them up. I've spent twenty minutes trying to pluck up the courage to do it. Oh hell I know lots of gay girls but that's different. I've never tried to pull a stranger before."

"You were trying to pull me? Why Charmaine? I mean am I attractive?"

"Now you're definitely pulling my leg."

"No seriously Charmaine. I'm not. I'm very new to this. I don't know if girls find me attractive or not."

Charmaine blinked and stared at her. "You're serious aren't you?"

"Yes Charmaine. I'm sorry. I've no idea if girls find me attractive. I mean I know, or at least I know a little bit, what I find attractive in a girl but I don't know if... well gay girls think the same as me. I'm saying this all wrong. I mean I am gay but do other gay girls have the same tastes? Oh Hell! I don't know what I'm trying to say."

Charmaine shook her head in disbelief. "You're well screwed up aren't you honey? You're one of the most beautiful girls I've ever seen. When you walked in that bar every dyke in the place came to a grinding halt.

You can't honestly be sitting there and telling me that you've no idea how beautiful you are."

"I've never really thought about it before Charmaine. My girlfriend tells me I'm beautiful but I've never really thought myself beautiful before."

Charmaine's shoulders slumped resignedly. "Oh Hell! You've got a girlfriend. I might have known."

Sarah looked sympathetically apologetic. "Oh I'm sorry. Perhaps I should have said before."

Charmaine shrugged. "It's ok Sarah. It wasn't exactly rocket science to figure out that the best looking girl in town would be already spoken for."

"Would you stay and talk to me anyway? I mean if you have the time that is. I wouldn't want you to feel you were wasting your time talking to me."

Charmaine smiled ruefully. "Oh hell no! You're the best looking girl I'm going to get to talk to all day. Anyway if I get brushed off this quickly those bitches in there will never let me live it down. They told me I didn't have a hope in hell."

Sarah laughed. She was beginning to like her new friend. "Well how about if I change my mind about that drink Charmaine?"

Charmaine grinned hugely. "Coming up lady!" she leapt from her seat and disappeared indoors before Sarah had even a chance to tell her what she wanted to drink. Sarah glanced around nervously. The first thing she noticed was that the beautiful girl in the short skirt she had noticed before was regarding her with clearly invigorated interest. Sarah had called that one wrong. With surprise Sarah realised that the girl must have thought she was heterosexual until Charmaine had made her apparently successful move on her. Now she was looking at Sarah intently and with the worried look of someone who has realised that they have just made a major error of judgement. Charmaine returned to the table looking triumphant. She was carrying an ice bucket with a bottle of good quality wine in it and two glasses.

"Ha!" she declared exultantly. "That shut those dykes up."

Sarah regarded her exasperatedly. "I wanted a glass of beer Charmaine."

"No way sister! I can't have a gorgeous babe like you drinking beer. Besides I want to get you drunk and entice you away from that girlfriend of yours."

Sarah giggled. "You've no chance Charmaine. I'm sorry."

Charmaine poured two glasses of wine. "So what's she like this girlfriend of yours Sarah; some awful bull dyke or something?"

"I'm sorry?"

"You know bull dyke or diesel dyke; some big butch built like a brick shithouse who weight trains every day, has a black belt in karate and cracks walnuts in her eyelids."

"Oh God no! Danny's anything but butch. She's the most feminine girl I know. She's far more beautiful than I am."

"I don't believe you."

"It's true. If she was sat here you wouldn't even notice me."

"So she's femme then?"

"I'm not really familiar with the accepted terminology Charmaine but I'd guess that was probably correct."

Charmaine laughed. "God I can't get used to you calling me Charmaine. Only my mother calls me that any more. I'm Charlie to everyone else."

Sarah looked at her seriously. "I like calling you Charmaine. I think it's a beautiful name. But if you feel more comfortable with Charlie I'll call you that."

"Hell call me what you want honey. Actually it's kind of nice you using my proper name. I like hearing you say it. Makes me feel quite girly. Mind you, you could call me bag lady and it would be beautiful from you."

"Charmaine means charming. You're well named Charmaine."

Charmaine laughed. "You must bring out the best in me. So anyway where's this girlfriend of yours today?"

"Oh I don't know. I think she's probably home but I know she went away on business yesterday and she hasn't phoned so maybe she's not home yet."

"You don't share digs then?"

"Oh no. Danny has her own house in the Toggenburg."

"You live with your folks then?"

"No I share a cottage with a friend in the Toggenburg."

"A girl friend?"

"Well yes but not a girlfriend if you know what I mean. She's just a housemate."

"So if you're an item with the girlfriend and she has her own house why haven't you moved in? I mean you know what they say about lesbians don't you?"

"Er not what do they say?"

"It's an old lesbian joke. What does a lesbian bring for wheels on a second date? Answer; a removals van. So you and the girlfriend haven't moved in together then. How come? She's not married or some bullshit is she?"

"Oh heavens no. No she's not. She's just well...." Sarah pulled a face. "Actually it's all pretty new and I guess we're not up to the living together stage."

Charmaine grinned. "Well that's encouraging news."

"Stop it Charmaine! I have not the slightest intention of being unfaithful to her."

"But you've slipped the leash today." Charmaine pointed out.

"I suppose I have, but only to do a bit of shopping and looking around."

"Well I'm on offer at a reduced price and my flat is just around the corner if you feel like looking a bit closer."

You're a bad girl Charmaine."

"Yep! Come on have some more wine. You're not nearly drunk enough yet." Charmaine plied the bottle. "So what's this business that keeps your girlfriend out of town then?"

"Oh she's a singer."

Charmaine raised her eyebrows. "Really?"

"Yes."

"Anybody famous is she?"

"Well yes I suppose so but please don't ask me her name because it wouldn't be discreet of me to tell you."

Charmaine laughed. "I already know it Sarah."

"Impossible!"

"But I do. Here you are, a beautiful girl, expensive clothes and you tell me that your girlfriend is a famous singer that lives in the Toggenburg. I don't need to be a deductive genius to work that one out honey. I'm a musician myself and I know which famous singer with a reputation for liking pretty girls lives in the Toggenburg Sarah. Hell you even called her Danny." Charmaine laughed ironically. "God and I thought I could woo you with a bottle of cheap wine."

Sarah clamped a hand to her mouth. "Oh God! Have I said too much?"

"Don't worry about it Sarah. I'm not running to the paparazzi. It's your business honey."

Sarah groaned. "I thought I was being discreet."

"Like I said don't worry about it. Just ask your girlfriend if she knows anyone with a job for an out of work bass guitarist."

"You play the bass guitar?"

"Yes. I played in a band for two years but it split up in April and I've just been playing the odd gigs since."

"What was your band called?"

"Weisse Stern. We were pretty good."

"But I know you! I saw you play last summer in Wil. My housemate took me along. I thought I recognised your face from somewhere."

"Did you like the set?"

"Yes I did actually. It's not usually my kind of music but I thought it was very good."

Charmaine ran a hand through her short hair and grinned. "Well thanks Sarah. That's praise indeed from Daniela Devin's girlfriend. I saw her concert last year in Zurich and it was brilliant."

"Well it's more than I've done. I've never seen a full live concert from her."

"You're kidding!"

"No really. I've seen her sing the odd song for people and I've seen bits of televised concerts from her but I've never been to one of her concerts."

Charmaine frowned. "Just how long have you been together with her Sarah?"

Sarah bit her lip. "I've only been seeing her for a few weeks. This is all a bit new for me."

"But you had girlfriends before right?"

Sarah shook her head and blushed. "No it's the first time I've ever had a girlfriend. Before this I was in a long term relationship with a man." Sarah was hedging the truth somewhat.

"So you've just come out?"

Sarah looked puzzled. "Yes but only to do some shopping as I said."

Charmaine threw back her head and laughed uproariously. "Oh my!" she said at last. "You really are a newbie aren't you? I mean you've just "come out" as gay. You know; declared yourself lesbian."

"Oh I see what you mean. Yes I suppose it is. Actually today is the first time I've actually told anyone else, apart from the people who know I'm seeing Danny, that I'm gay. It was quite challenging."

"Jesus! Do your folks know?"

"Oh God no! I wouldn't dare tell them."

"Well you've picked a hell of a high profile girlfriend if you were thinking of trying to keep it under wraps. Your girlfriend's just like one of the most drop dead beautiful gay chicks in Switzerland and you ain't hardly pig ugly yourself. You'll be like the lezzie couple of the month when DIVA gets hold of the story."

"DIVA?"

"It's a magazine Sarah; the biggest lesbian magazine in Europe. Ask your girlfriend. She was on the front cover last year."

"Oh Christ! I never knew." Sarah smiled wryly. "Hopefully it won't be on my mother's subscription list."

Charmaine grinned wickedly. "Hey what's she like? I mean in bed."

Sarah shook her head sadly. "I don't really know. I've never made love with her."

"What?"

"I said I've never made love with her. We... we've shared a bed and so on but we've never done anything much more than kiss really."

"Oh God! Now you really *are* kidding."

"No honestly. I suppose I've been holding back somewhat."

"Are you mad? God every dyke in Switzerland would love to jump into bed with Daniela Devin. Does this mean that you've never actually made love with a woman?"

"Yes. I'm kind of scared about it. I mean I wouldn't know what to do!"

Charmaine reached out and touched Sarah's hand. "Well darling if you want some practical instruction then, like I said, my place is just around the corner."

"Stop it Charmaine! It's serious. This is new to me. I'm confused and I don't know what to do. It's the first time in my life I've ever had to face up to being lesbian. I came to this place today on the advice of a gay friend because I wanted to see other gay girls and try to understand what it's all about. My life's turned on its head Charmaine. I'm supposed to be marrying my boyfriend at the end of summer but now I'm faced with this. I'm in love with a woman and she's in love with me. What the hell am I supposed to do?"

Charmaine grew serious seeing that Sarah was genuinely upset. "But you've never actually had sex with her?"

"No."

"Don't you want to?"

"Yes I think I do. But if I do that then there's no going back is there? Things will get messy very quickly."

Charmaine nodded seriously. "They usually do Sarah. When my folks found out I was gay when I was sixteen they went loopy on me. They never spoke to me for six months. Things have a way of working themselves out in the end though. Your parents kind of remember that they love you after all in the end and they come around. It's always going to be a shock to them. They think they're never going to have grand kids and all that." Charmaine paused to take a sip of wine. "Hell that's no problem these days. Most lezzie couples in stable relationships want to have kids now and, since we've got now got legally registered partnerships in Switzerland, we've got most of the rights enjoyed by heterosexual marriage."

"Do they adopt children then?"

Charmaine shook her head. "No we still don't have the right to jointly adopt children in a same sex union but theoretically single people can adopt. Also the law forbids medically assisted procreation for same sex couples. There're all sorts of ways around that though. AI is available in most countries and there are even laws protecting anonymity in some of them so nobody has to know where the sperm donation came from. You even get fertility tourism. Lots of people go to Denmark for instance where the law is more liberal but that can get expensive because it may take you several visits. In Switzerland full anonymity for sperm donors is forbidden. Still if you peruse any gay mag you'll find plenty of adverts for sperm banks and private donors and so on. Some gay couples even resort to NI to get around the problem."

"NI?"

"Natural insemination; the old fashioned way."

"Oh! I see."

"I don't know if I'd fancy that but some gay men offer sperm donation by NI which as you might imagine is going to be mighty weird. If one of the women in a same sex union has a kid by AI I suppose she's legally speaking a single mother in a gay union. I mean, if you go abroad and get knocked up, who is to say where the kid came from? If you go to a country that allows anonymous sperm donation I suppose you could just say "Sorry Milud. I just fancied seeing how the other half lived and I met this guy in a bar on holiday whose name I can't for the life of me remember." Theoretically there's no way the law can stop you bringing up the child together with your partner. The big minefield is with adoption. Now you can't adopt children jointly with your partner but what is the law when the child is the biological offspring of one partner? In Germany the partner can legally adopt that child as a stepchild. That means that should the mother die then full custody devolves on the step parent i.e. her partner. That's not the case in Switzerland though. It's a messy issue. In the states for instance there have been custody battles over the children of the dead partner between the surviving partner and the deceased's grandparents. Things would be a lot easier if the government would stop fanning about and grant full legal marital status to same sex couples."

Sarah blinked in surprise. She had underestimated Charmaine. She had regarded her as a very pleasant but generally fairly shallow young woman flirting with her. The more she spoke to her the more she realised however that here was an intelligent girl who took the issues of her sexual orientation seriously and thought about them deeply. "I'd no idea things were so complicated." Sarah told her.

"Oh hell yes! We've made a lot of progress but there's still a long way to go. Will we be seeing you at next year's pride?"

"Pride?"

"The Gay Pride Festival in Zurich; it's the big annual event for all gay people in Switzerland to stand up and be counted and to demand gay rights. It's at the beginning of June. You ought to come. It's fun."

"Heaven's I'm only just trying to get used to being gay. I don't know whether or not I'm ready to be proud of it."

"Well maybe you should be honey. You say that today is the first time you've ever told someone you were gay. Well it's not so many years ago Sarah that you'd have been arrested for that and risked jail. Gay Pride Festival used to be called the Christopher Street Day. Know what Christopher Street is?"

"No. I've never heard of it."

"It's a street in the Greenwich Village district of New York City. There was this sleazy gay bar run by the mafia on it in the late 1960s. Well the Mayor of New York was running a campaign to rid the city of its faggots so he had the police raiding every gay bar they could find, beating gay people up and arresting them. It was easy work for the police. Gay people were pretty timid and unlikely to put up any fuss. Well in June 1969 that all changed. The police raided this bar called the Stonewall Inn on Christopher Street. It was a dump by all accounts and some of the poorest and most socially isolated gays used to frequent the place. The only reason the police hadn't hit it up until then was that the mafia were paying them off to leave it alone. Well they must have missed a payment because the police raided it on the 28th of June. It seemed easy enough to begin with; just a bit of routine fag bashing. Then it all went wrong. Some of those gay people that used that bar had no place else to go and nothing left to lose. It erupted into a riot. The riots went on for days and the police were literally forced off the street. It wasn't the first time gay people had stood up for their rights but it was the most visible manifestation of it yet especially since it happened in Greenwich Village which was a hotbed of political activism anyway. It radicalised the gay rights movement. Gays were no longer just willing to sit back and take it. When the riots occurred there were maybe fifty or sixty gay rights groups in the whole of the United States; within a year afterwards there were fifteen hundred and a year after that two thousand five hundred. It was really the starting point for the explosion of the gay movement and the fight for our rights. You can sit here on this terrace today and tell me that you're gay without the fear of being arrested Sarah because a bunch of poor gays, street kids, drag queens, dykes and transsexuals suddenly said, "Enough is enough. Gays are through with being invisible. The time for fear is past. Now we'll march on the street, tell everybody who we are and won't be ashamed of it." Those people in that bar weren't middle class whites Sarah. They were whites poor and rich, black people, Hispanics, Asians... you name it. There was no racial segregation in the gay world. They were segregated from society enough as it was but they all collectively stood up and stated who they were. That's why we call it "Pride" Sarah."

"Goodness! You're pretty passionate about this aren't you?"

"Yes I am. Being gay isn't just about the kind of person you prefer sleeping with Sarah. It's a whole cultural identity too. There's more to it than just having preferences. You've only taken the first step to becoming gay. Just saying you're gay is I admit a big step but there are responsibilities that come with that too. Now you say that you'd never tell your parents and you're probably scared to death of some of your friends finding out. Coming to a gay bar is a soft option. There you can still hide your sexuality from the world at large. The real test Sarah is if you can stand up and declare yourself gay to the world.

"Your girlfriend has done that. She's openly out and she's even performed at the Gay Pride. She's had the bottle to stand up and say, "Look I'm gay what are you going to do about it?" It's important she does so Sarah because she's a well-known, popular artist and a beautiful high profile personality. Every time somebody like that comes out and declares them self then it's another blow to declare the normality of homosexuality and an in your face statement that we're here and here to stay. Your girlfriend has my admiration. Now I don't know just what relationship you have with her but if it's a serious one you're not going to be able to hide much longer Sarah. If you try to hide you're just back to being a little baby dyke, pre Christopher Street, cowering in the shadows and scared that someone's going to find out about you and punish you for it."

Sarah lowered her eyes. "I *am* scared Charmaine. I can't help that. Give me time. You've had years to come to terms with it. I've had a few weeks."

Charmaine nodded sympathetically and grasped Sarah's hand. "I'm sorry Sarah. I shouldn't have gone off like that on you. Yeah I know it's hard. I shouldn't lecture you. You're a sweet girl Sarah. I think maybe your girlfriend's going easy on you. Do you really love her?"

"Yes I do."

"And this guy you're supposed to be marrying?"

"I don't know if I ever did." Sarah was close to tears.

"Well that's easy then isn't it?"

"I wish it was!"

"Ahem!" Sarah turned around in shock. Simon was standing over her shoulder. She'd completely lost track of time. Hastily she snatched her hand away from Charmaine. "Oh! Hello Simon."

"Hi Sarah."

Charmaine grinned. "Hey Simon! How are you keeping?"

"Hi Charlie. Fine thanks. You?"

"Couldn't be better. How's the boyfriend?"

"He's fine Charlie."

"You know Sarah here?" Charmaine asked.

"She's an old friend of Pete's Charlie."

"Oh right!"

Sarah stood up awkwardly. "Er where is the ladies Charmaine?"

"Back through the end of the bar. You can't miss it."

"Thank you. Do you want a drink Simon while on my way back?"

"Just a coke please Sarah. I'm driving." He was looking at her peculiarly.

Sarah vanished hastily and Simon took a seat looking grave and addressed Charmaine seriously. "Charlie! Back off! The girl's spoken for."

"Chill Simon! She already told me. I was just being friendly and sympathetic. She seems pretty messed up."

"She's going through a patch."

"Is she really together with Daniela Devin?"

"Did she tell you that?"

"No I sort of figured it out and she didn't deny it. Is it true or is she just having fantasies?"

"It's true Charlie and that is classified information. Don't you dare start spreading it around."

"Hey, it's not my business. Is it serious though or is she just La Devin's little playgirl?"

"It's serious Charlie; very serious."

"The lucky bitch."

"Which one?"

"Both of them."

Simon smiled but grew serious again. "Seriously though Charlie, Sarah's a sweet girl and pretty mixed up about things right now. She doesn't need the world and its grandma to know she's having an affair with Danny Devin."

"She isn't going to keep that secret for long."

"Give her a bit of space and time Charlie; time enough to figure out what she's doing."

"Simon you've known me long enough. I'm no gossip. How come you're so protective of her anyway?"

"She's one of Pete's oldest friends and he worries about her Charlie. Anyway I like her and I don't want to see her hurt."

Charmaine looked thoughtful and glanced in the direction Sarah had departed. "You could be on a hiding to nothing there Simon. I think she's in for a rocky ride."

"She's well-loved Charlie. There'll be people to help her."

Charlie smiled. "Well I'm sure Miss Devin's money will be a comforting compensation."

After Sarah returned with a drink for Simon they stayed and chatted with Charmaine a little while longer before Simon somewhat brusquely announced that it was time to head back to the Toggenburg. Sarah rose and politely thanked Charmaine for her company. Charmaine in her turn produced a small card. "Hey that's my card with my number on it Sarah. If your girlfriend hears of any openings for a bass guitarist let me know. Then again if things don't work out Sarah or you need a friendly shoulder to cry on then just give me a buzz."

Sarah blushed and thanked Charmaine once more and swapped her own telephone number before Simon whisked her away. Simon had parked his car not far from the cafe and Sarah was unsurprised to discover that Simon's tastes in automobiles were on the sporting side. His car was an old Porsche 911 convertible, lovingly maintained although appearing as if it had experienced a certain degree of modification over the years. Sarah squeezed into the passenger seat. The 911 model was not known for the roominess of its interior. Simon let the hood down for it was baking hot in the car under the hot sunlight. "I've got to pick up my shopping Simon." Sarah told him "I've left it in a luggage locker in the station."

Simon nodded and pulled out. It was only a short drive to the station and Simon placed the car in a short term parking space as Sarah scuttled into the station to retrieve the products of her morning's retail insanity. He was leaning casually against the car smoking a cigarette as she emerged from the station bearing her numerous bags. He pushed himself away from the car and blinked in astonishment. "Christ have you bought the damn town?"

"It feels like it."

"Hell Sarah! By the looks of things your luggage is going to exceed in price the second hand value of the car carrying it."

"I'm just helping my father offload some of his disposable income Simon. Will there be room for all these bags?"

"We'll squeeze it in somehow. Come on."

They drove away from Winterthur in silence. Simon seemed to be very serious and thoughtful. Sarah glanced at him nervously. "Are you mad with me Simon?"

Simon shook his head slowly. "No not mad Sarah, just worried. What the hell was all this about? I mean why did you suddenly decide you wanted to go cruising the gay bars for a day?"

"I just wanted to see what it was like Simon. I've never experienced the life that gay people have. If I'm gay I needed to understand it. Anyway I was hardly out "cruising"! I spent a little over one hour in one bar. That's hardly a wild night out on the town Simon."

"Yes and picking up the first thing with a pretty face that comes along Sarah!"

"I did *not* pick her up. I was just sat at that table when *she* approached *me*. I *told* her I had a girlfriend. I behaved myself impeccably."

"I wonder if Daniela will see it in that light."

"Simon I'm not even sure if I'm in a relationship with Danny. We're not even lovers. If I spend an hour talking to another gay girl quite innocently it hardly constitutes unfaithfulness in any case."

"Well maybe not." Simon looked unconvinced.

Sarah smiled to herself. Simon was like a big protective brother at the moment. "I'm surprised you know Charmaine." She commented.

"I'm *from* Winterthur Sarah. I know nearly every gay person in the town."

"Oh of course. She... she seems like a nice girl."

"Oh Charlie's ok. She's got a bit of a rough history though. She was in a relationship with a married woman ten years older than she is for two years. I think the woman was just using her as a toy girl really; a way to spice up a pretty loveless marriage. Anyway the hubby found out about it and that was that. Charlie was pretty cut up about it."

"Oh God! The poor girl. She never told me this."

"Yeah well it was a couple of years ago now. Charlie was just a teenager. She's got over it by now and she's pretty radical about being gay."

"She seems to know a lot about it... the gay movement I mean."

"Oh yes. She's quite politically minded."

"What happened to the other woman? Did it end in divorce?"

"No. They stayed together. They had kids and everything. They moved away shortly afterwards. I heard they live near Interlaken now but she's not been back to Winterthur since."

Sarah sighed profoundly. "That could be me in a few years Simon couldn't it; sneaking away from my lonely Zurich suburb when my husband is out to meet some girl for a few hours in the afternoon?"

"Your life will be what you make it Sarah. I think you've got some hard decisions to make about just what kind of life that is going to be."

"I'm running out of time to make decisions Simon."

"Then make some time. Just don't do it by going off on clandestine little adventures in gay bars or I'll save Daniela a job and put you over my knee and spank your bottom for her!"

Sarah laughed shortly. "Don't do that Simon. Who knows? We might both enjoy it and then things will be *really* complicated."

Chapter Twenty-Two

Nicole had commented that Sarah was on a roller-coaster of a ride that summer and any critical examination of Sarah's mood the following day would have conceded the justification of that analysis. The word "gay" is a sadly misappropriated word in the English vocabulary for, since its hijacking and reinterpretation as a label for homosexuality, the language had lost a very useful word indeed. There was no other word quite so apt and to the point to describe a mood of frivolous pleasure and vivacious happiness; just the sort of mood, in fact, that had possessed Sarah in Winterthur. Yesterday Sarah had been gay in every meaning of the word. Today she was anything but.

It was as if she had drunk too much champagne and whilst the bubbles effervesced in her bloodstream she had ridden a giddy height of fantastical illusion; a fairy story through which she had stepped lightly without a care; danced along a yellow brick road far from the drabness of Kansas. Yesterday the world had seemed bright, carefree and full of strange promise. Yesterday the girls had looked pretty. The clothes in the shops had been like jars of tempting sweets to a child and their price tags irrelevant. Yesterday there had seemed to be another road through life; one which did not include the looming trip to Ticino and the sealing of her fate in matrimony, as if she had dared to step along a new path at a fork in the journey of her life. It had been exciting; thrilling even, and wildly liberating.

Today, however, the bubbles had burst. Sarah sat on the edge of her bed and gnawed at her knuckles in uncertainty and gripped with foreboding. Scattered across her bed were the purchases that she had made in Winterthur. Yesterday she had regarded them with pleasure but today she was horrified by them and racked with guilt. She was at a loss to understand what madness had overcome her in Winterthur. She had carelessly thrown away six thousand francs in three hours; an insanity that defiled everything that a lifetime of common sense and prudence had stood for. Her purchases lay about like accusations resembling the vague memories in a hangover when you know that you were drunk last night, had said something unspeakably rude to the vicar and made a pass at your best friend's partner. She almost felt like throwing all her new clothes away except that that would offend her sense of prudence even more.

She shook her head in disbelief. What was happening to her? Daniela! It was Daniela, like some siren perched upon a shoal of perilous rocks, who had lured her away from the straight and sensible into dangerous currents. Since Daniela had come into her life things had changed beyond recognition. She was unstable, throwing caution to the wind, daring to contemplate the unthinkable and risking every foundation upon which her life was founded. She cringed as she recalled yesterday's lunacy. She had even publicly declared herself to be a lesbian; had told complete strangers that. She had ogled girls on the street. She had even inadvertently revealed that she was the girlfriend of a famous celebrity. And to top it all she had squandered her money on the entirely frivolous purpose of making herself attractive to that girlfriend. It was madness.

Why was this happening to her? Well the simple answer to that was that she in love. The trouble was that Sarah had virtually no experience of the consuming passions of romantic love. Of course she loved the people in her life, and with devotion too, but she had never truly felt the rush of emotions and physical impacts that obliterated one's sense of reason under an enveloping wave of irrational passion. Sarah was caught in a classic dichotomy. She was a sensible, level headed girl and love was anything *but* sensible and level headed. Love itself was a form of madness. Life had been a lot simpler before it had reared its head. Cupid's arrows were tipped with poison.

In the cold clear daylight, alone in her room, Sarah asked herself the question of what loving Daniela would mean. That it would mean immediate scandal and outrage among her family was a given. The logical expression of her love was to reject Alan's suit in marriage. For that she would have to give a reason. The first thing that would occur to both her family and Alan was that she had found somebody else. How long could she hide the fact that that somebody else was a woman? It wasn't just any woman either was it? If she had merely discovered her lesbianism with some obscure girl of no particular note then she might have concealed the relationship for a long time and simply found another pretext for not marrying Alan. Paradoxically, she realised, it would have been easier to have a lesbian relationship with Nicole. After all she had shared a house with Nicole for years without incurring any suspicion of her sexual orientation. They might have continued for years without anybody assuming that they were anything other than just close friends.

It was too late for that however. Daniela was an entirely different matter. Sarah had learned things about Daniela yesterday. For one thing she had not realised just how high a profile Daniela had as a gay icon. She had previously had some nebulous view that there was perhaps a little scandal attached to Daniela founded on rumour and tabloid gossip but the pertinent facts were that Daniela had been married and indeed had a child. Perhaps there were indications of bisexuality but they were largely speculative in the public eye. It was somewhat of a shock therefore to realise that Daniela was quite open about her sexuality publicly. Charmaine had told her that she had even appeared on the front page of an international lesbian magazine and performed live at a gay festival. Now of course Sarah was inevitably linked with her in the Toggenburg and there was now the real possibility that the knowledge of their affair had spread into the Winterthur gay community. It was easy to see that knowledge coming to the notice of predatory journalists hunting for stories. How long would it be before their names were linked together on the pages of some awful tabloid? Sarah had lived her life in contented obscurity outside of her valley. She quailed at the thought of her name becoming public property; being dogged by paparazzi; of losing the privacy of anonymity.

Love again! It led you into the most foolish of indiscretions. Why had she so publicly embraced Daniela at that stupid party at Gamplut? Perhaps she had been drunk but in truth she had been drunk on Daniela; intoxicated by her presence. When she was there to be held and kissed you thought nothing of the consequences. Fools rushed in as the saying had it and Sarah had been the most foolish of infatuated girls.

Sarah looked at the clock on her bedside table. It was ten in the morning. Nicole was out at work and Sarah had been sat on her bed in an agony of indecision since shortly after eight. The clock was ticking too; marking down the seconds relentlessly to the time she was obliged to pack her bags and head south to the Ticino and a date with destiny. Her father had phoned her last night on her mobile. Sarah had got home late for she had felt curiously unwilling to go straight home after returning from Winterthur. Simon had bought her dinner in a little restaurant in Wildhaus and listened patiently as she agonised over the decisions facing her. Her father's phone call had not helped. She had wanted to delay until the last minute her arrival in the Ticino but her father had insisted that it would be bad form if Alan was to arrive home from America and find her not there. It was best that she arrived as soon as possible. He'd wanted her to set off tomorrow or, at the latest, the day after. Sarah had protested that she had things to do that precluded such an early arrival. Her father had been quite sharp with her. He could not see that there could possibly be anything of greater importance than her forthcoming engagement. It was time to get serious about things. Eventually they'd compromised. The party was on the Saturday and Alan would be there for then. Sarah would arrive on the day before. Sarah had lost two days. The clock was ticking faster.

Daniela had texted her. The message was loving but brief. She was evidently busy and absent from the valley. Sarah was almost relieved. She needed to marshal her thoughts before she faced Daniela once more. She picked up a new dress she had bought and regarded it in exasperation. It was a sensational strapless maxi dress in pure silk in aquamarine and an ocean-themed print of corals, starfishes and seahorses that she had spent five hundred francs on. In her incapacitated lunacy she had wanted something to wear when Daniela took her to dinner and to remind her of her promise to show her the sea. She grimaced as she grasped the material of the lovely dress but as her thoughts drifted to Daniela her hands became sensuous and caressing. She laid it down with a sigh, sure she would never wear it for Daniela now.

For it was impossible wasn't it? It had never after all been anything more than a beguiling dream. How could she ever have thought herself to be the lover of a pop-star? How could she ever throw herself into that uncertainty of a world? She loved Daniela but it was surely an impossible love. In the end she would do what was expected of her after all. She would go to the Ticino and hear Alan's proposal of marriage. Perhaps it would not be too bad after all. She had been, if not perfectly content, then at least satisfied with her man for three years. Perhaps it would be a relief not to surrender to the dangerous passions of love. They only led you into irrationality. Most people seemed perfectly happy with the mundane trappings of ordinary marriage. There was more to marriage than love after all wasn't there. There were such things as duty, responsibility and commitment. Perhaps her father was right after all and it was time to grow up. Perhaps her besotted love for Daniela was just the final fling of her adolescence; her way of escaping the realities of impending adulthood.

She looked at her lovely new clothes again. Her father would be proud of her in her new finery and Sarah knew that, deep down, it was one of the most important things in the world that her father was proud of her. She pictured that pride shining in his eyes as he escorted her in her wedding dress down the aisle and knew she could not bear to lose that. It would break his heart if she rejected Alan for a woman; to know that his beloved little Sarah was lesbian and involved with a pop singer of dubious reputation.

She forced herself to think of Alan. He was not so bad was he? In three years of their relationship he had never really caused her any real reason to complain. True he had been absent for large parts of that time and they had rarely spent a great deal of time together but he had always been considerate and respectful to her. It was also true, as her father had pointed out, that you could not fault his depth of commitment and responsibility to the marriage. He had quite selflessly pledged to establish himself financially before taking on the burden of marriage so as to be able to assure Sarah's parents that their daughter would not be marrying a pauper. He was hard working and diligent. Certainly she would never have any cause to complain about his laziness and lack of ambition. He was highly regarded by all that knew him for his energy and drive. He would forge a fine career. He was handsome too and his faithfulness and loyalty were not in doubt. Most women would have regarded him an excellent catch.

Perhaps she could learn to love him. Sarah had once heard someone say that you always marry a stranger. Maybe it was Daniela that had said that to her. But there was truth in that statement. However well you thought you knew someone you would not really know them until you lived every day with them. The passionate love that drove people into hasty conjugality was perhaps a lie after all. When the bubbles in that particular champagne burst there had to be something left upon which to found the grounds of a marriage. Most married people didn't swoon as their spouses entered the room, flush with excitement at the mere thought of them or quiver helplessly at the merest brush of their lips. Marriage wasn't the fantasy world of lovers. It was the daily partnership of mutual respect and cooperation; a joint venture based on good sense and prudent utilisation of resources. Husbands weren't starry eyed romantics. They were solid, reliable and dependable providers. You didn't blow all your money on frivolous clothes. You invested it wisely in a new sofa and chairs for the living room; new lampshades for the hallway or to furnish the children's bedroom. You didn't make love under the stars and walk naked in the meadows. You redecorated the bedroom or mowed the lawn. That was the reality of marriage wasn't it? The rest, the romantic stuff, was just the fairy story; the illusion of love; ephemeral and insubstantial; as wispy and tenuous as the flimsy items of lingerie that Sarah had bought the previous day to titillate her girlfriend's fancy.

The sensible Sarah, the cautious Sarah, the Sarah that always did the right thing was on the ascendancy once more. She would not forget her dreams. She would simply relegate them back to that inner place where they belonged; locked in a private world only to be seen by her. She hoped that Alan would admire her in her new wardrobe. Then at least there might be some point to it. The fact that she had bought them for somebody else other than he would be her own secret.

She would tell Daniela. That much courage at least she must find. She would tell her that in a few days' time she would be engaged to be married. She would tell her that she loved her and in some secret part of her heart that she always would. But she would also tell her that it was impossible. Romantic love was not for her. Hers was the steady and predictable route of conjugal marriage. She wasn't cut out to being a rock and roll singer's lover. She didn't understand what it was to be lesbian. Marriage to Alan wasn't, after all, a madcap dash into the unknown. It had been expected for nearly three years. She would do what was expected of her. She hoped they could remain friends for she had come to admire Daniela enormously but she would understand if that was not enough. It would be heart-breaking for her but at least she could carry the sweet memories of their short time together for the rest of her days. If they could remain friends then that would be wonderful but if not then they must kiss one last time and say goodbye.

Steeling herself to her new resolve Sarah packed away her new possessions in her wardrobe pausing only to stroke them a last time sadly. Now that her course was set she couldn't bear to stay in the house. After the coming week it might be the last time she time she ever lived here. The memories of the house were too much for her to bear. She wanted to be out in the open; to tread the land of her Toggenburg while she still could. She pulled on an old pair of jeans and trainers and donned an old favourite lumberjack shirt and walked from the house, her head bowed in sadness.

She paused on the terrace of the Alpli restaurant and took a disgracefully early glass of wine but it did not lift her melancholy. She tried to focus on Alan; her future husband. She had once fancied she'd loved him but that was before the volcanic eruption of Daniela had shown her how very different was that emotion when it really came to mess up your life. Was there she wondered another sort of love? One that, if it didn't seem to tear the world apart, was nevertheless a sort of growing thing; something that you only found in time and would prove more lasting and stable than the fiery torment that grasped you when your hormones went off the scale? Could she learn to love Alan sometime? She remembered the words of an old Carol Carpenter song,

"Love, look at the two of us
Strangers in many ways
Let's take a lifetime to say
I knew you well
But only time will tell us so
And love may grow for all we know."

Somehow the words gave her comfort. Perhaps there would be happiness unforeseen beyond the seeming gloom of her marriage. Perhaps she would one day look back and smile at herself for her foolish youthful dreams and acknowledge the wisdom of her parents in forging this marriage for her. There were huge tracts of the world where marriage was arranged by the families. Perhaps they were right after all. How could young people at the mercy of their emotions be possibly expected to make wise decisions concerning the rest of their lives? Perhaps it took wiser heads to see what was best for them in the long run. She'd gone slightly crazy for a few weeks now because she'd been carried away by her own emotions. Perhaps this was the time she needed a steadying hand to direct her back onto the path of wisdom and sense. Perhaps there was sadness in that but then there was sadness in the day when you realised you were too old to play with your dolls any more. Growing up was a sadness.

She drifted down into Unterwasser for no other reason than she felt she wanted to walk. Her steps felt leaden and laboured and the joy of another beautiful day in the Toggenburg passed her unseen. She dreaded having to talk to Daniela but now she knew she must. She took the short cut around the old hostel across the meadows and dropped down the steep track that led to the Thurwasserfalle. The scents of the meadows were strong in her nostrils but for once they couldn't lift her gloom. At the bottom of the hill she turned aside and walked up the little hidden gorge to the Thurwasserfalle. This waterfall was one of the Toggenburg's hidden treasures. It was concealed up a tiny gorge, a few hundred metres long, where it fell in two steps into a deep churning pool. It was a magical little secret spot you would not have known the existence of had you not known exactly where to find it. One man had spent a lifetime of dedicated love to opening the gorge to access so that people could find this extraordinary sequestered waterfall. It crashed down into an almost circular cavity in the cliffs completely surrounded by rock faces. It was a place for the imagination where you could envisage goblins perching on the rocks above or water nymphs disporting in the pool below. Sarah paused on a little steel bridge constructed over the pool and let the spray from the fall moisten her face and dilute the tears from her eyes. She had stood here more times than she could recall in her life and the thunder of the water had always brought her tranquillity until now.

With a sigh she turned away and retraced her steps along the gorge feeling almost as if she had left that other Sarah; that strange romantic one with impossible dreams she had barely known until now, to linger among the spray of the falls and be lamented in the songs of the sirens as they brushed out their hair on the rocks below the cascade. She emerged in Unterwasser by the Hotel Sternen but the sunny terrace at the front of the hotel was filling up with people for the lunchtime service and it didn't tempt her to linger for she wanted solitude. Instead she crossed the broad base of the valley, skirting the marshy meadows where the pretty little Goldfinches were feeding on the thistles and walked up the valley until at last she came to the small rustic restaurant at Eggenwaldi which lay at the bottom station of the chair lift which led up to Oberdorf. Here she paused for the restaurant was obscure and off the beaten track and virtually empty. There were a few tables outdoors for her to sit at in the sunshine and she lowered herself sadly onto a bench at one of them. The waiter at the restaurant knew her well but he divined at once that Sarah was in no mood for conversation so he served her a glass of wine and left her to her thoughts.

Sarah watched a family walking to the chair lift. The man was laughing at the antics of his pretty young daughter no more than four years of age whilst his wife fussed over the little girl's elder brother who had seemingly had some misadventure in the boggy ground on the way across from Wildhaus. He had managed to coat himself fairly liberally with mud and his mother looked fondly exasperated with him as she plied handkerchiefs in a futile attempt to make him more presentable. The little boy was submitting to his mother's ministrations with barely concealed impatience and looking sulky so she released him with an affectionate pat to rush ahead in excitement for the adventures ahead.

Sarah regarded the mother carefully. She was still pretty although obviously the cares and burdens of parenthood had taken their toll. Her clothes were old and generally practical and her brown hair was tied back in a pony tail. She wore no make-up on her face and her hands were the hands of a working mother although, Sarah noted, she still painted her nails in deference to her fading youthful beauty. She carried a large bag on her shoulder quite obviously full of the emergency requirements that two young children were liable to generate. Sarah saw a teddy bear poking out of the bag and realised that the mother had been assigned the task of transporting the children's toys. She was obviously worried about her children on the chair lift and she scolded her daughter for rushing about and told her to take her father's hand.

There was nothing remarkable about the woman. She was just another harassed mother concerned about her children like countless millions of her spiritual sisters. She had probably been a great beauty when her husband had asked her to marry him. Sarah wondered if he loved her still and decided that he probably did even if their former passion had long been subsumed under the day to day practicalities of raising a young family. What was her story Sarah wondered. Had she too once had dreams? Were there times, when she faced another day of toil in the care of her family, when she wondered what had happened to all the dreams she once had? Did she sometimes pause over the kitchen sink and catch a reflection of her fading appearance in the polished worktop and feel a sorrow for her lost youth and the dreams that could never be now? Perhaps after all she was happy. Perhaps her life and her children gave her a contentment that compensated for the nebulous fairy stories she had once harboured in her imagination. This was real life after all; mortgages, electricity bills, babysitters, school runs twice a day, new shoes for growing feet, tension filled encounters at nursery, vaccinations and dentist visits, daily crises with petulant youngsters and all the other burdens of raising the new generation to carry the torch of humanity into the future. There was no place for romance in that daily labour except perhaps just the odd moment of sweetness; a fragmentary occasion for tenderness when the kids had been put to bed or away to their doting grandparents for an hour or two.

"I will be that woman in a few years." thought Sarah wistfully. "It'll be me trying to keep my children in one place as we take them out for an afternoon and a trip up to Oberdorf on the chairlift." She wondered just how big a logistical exercise it must have been to bring the kids to the Toggenburg; all the food for the kids, drinks, their toys, packs of paper handkerchiefs for the inevitable mishaps, band aids, dry clothes because you just knew one of them would fall in a stream, hairbrushes, maybe the little girl's medicine, clean shoes for the little boy because he would invariably find some mud to paddle in. Then they'd have to pack them all in the car and endure their bleating at the length of the journey and deal with carsickness and them fighting over the play station. They'd have to keep good hold on them as they parked in Wildhaus so they didn't dash out into the busy road and then somehow shepherd them across the valley to the chairlift.

Oberdorf was about as far as their ambitions would allow, Sarah thought. Mum and Dad could relax for a few minutes after feeding the kids at the restaurant there for there was a little playground at the restaurant the children could play in. Sarah placed herself in the woman's shoes. Would she sit and watch her children play and perhaps look about at all the mountains around and tell herself "This once was all mine. Now we can barely make it to Oberdorf and that only after a hazard fraught journey grasping the kids tightly on the chairlift." Perhaps one day in some distant future she would recover the old freedom of the mountains but she would be much older then and perhaps the magic would have faded and her physical energy jaded and she would quail at the goal of the high peaks. Maybe she would be like those people she and Daniela had seen on the Santis who had done nothing more strenuous than climb aboard a cable car and the aura of the mountain would be lost forever.

The parents managed to place their children on the chairlift and Sarah could hear the young girl giggling as they set off up the hill to Oberdorf. Oberdorf! Daniela lived near Oberdorf. Perhaps some future Sarah would take her children to Oberdorf and know that there were other mountains apart from the one's visible in the panorama that were lost to her now. Sarah wondered idly if she should take the chairlift herself and seek out Daniela at Oberdorf. She didn't actually know exactly where Daniela's villa was although she guessed that it wouldn't take much finding. Nearly anybody in Oberdorf would be able to tell her. She had never been in Daniela's house. Somehow it had never happened. Even in the days when they had spent their afternoons together when she worked at the Hotel Toggenburg and they'd had time to visit Daniela's house they had never gone there. It had been almost as if it were forbidden territory; as if the act of entering Daniela's house was an intimacy for which she had not been ready. Daniela had invited her enough times but Sarah had always resisted knowing that to step into Daniela's house was to step into Daniela's arms and onto dangerous ground.

Curiously Sarah wondered what Daniela's house was like. What did a pop star's house look like? Was it expensively furnished in modern style or did Daniela favour simpler and more rustic surroundings? With a shock Sarah realised that she didn't know. It was a part of Daniela's private life she had not seen. Sarah knew that Daniela shared her house with her cats which suggested that the house was cosy. She guessed that it was tastefully furnished for Daniela had an artist's eye for fine things and was embarrassed by the ostentatious. It would be simple and artistic, Sarah thought, and not flamboyant; gently comfortable without being overly luxurious. Daniela was a sensual woman. It was likely she enjoyed soft furnishings, warm thick carpets and soft bedclothes. Sarah wondered what her bedroom must look like. She was certain that Daniela liked to sleep in a big bed even if she only shared it with her beloved cats. Sarah envisaged warm, soft colours and gentle drapes.

Sarah imagined her bathroom. Daniela had told her that she loved to luxuriate in a big bath tub. There was something of water about Daniela. She loved water. Sarah remembered her dabbling her toes in the Fahlensee. The stuff delighted her. She had wanted to show Sarah the sea; amazed that Sarah had never seen it as if it was incomprehensible to her that somebody would not be driven by some deep urge to stand on its shore. She was a person that would wallow in hot soapy suds and pour the liquid of life through her fingers and across her body and never tire of it. There was a fluidity about her; even her music had a liquid quality to it. Her caresses felt like the flow of water on you as if you were a stone protruding from a river bed or a mountain whose harsh edges were softened by the ceaseless erosion of gentle rains upon your flanks. Her deep blue eyes were like the profound depths of an alpine lake and her laughter the singing of a careless brook as it bubbled over the stones on a high meadow. Where most people stumbled through life from one stone to another Daniela flowed, irresistibly aqueous, around the shoals, restlessly impatient as if searching out the final tranquillity of the ocean depths. She was a water nymph; a siren of the stream of life; a mermaid chanting her haunting melodies by the side of the sea.

Sarah felt a great sadness. How close she had come to truly knowing this extraordinary woman. How bitter it was that fate denied her this knowledge; that it was forbidden for her. How cruel it seemed that Daniela would not now take her by the hand to the water's edge, where the land surrendered its domain to the mastery of the sea, and whisper her words of love to the accompaniment of the cries of the gulls on the foreshore. It was as if Sarah had picked Daniela up in her cupped hands like the crystal waters of a mountain stream only to watch her trickle away through her fingers and vanish into the currents of life.

In despondency Sarah took her mobile phone from her bag and opened Daniela's number in her phone book. She stared at the number for a long time before she keyed it and waited for a response. Daniela sounded excited on the phone. "Sarah! I just tried to call you at home. I only got back a few minutes ago. Where are you?"

"I'm at Eggenwaldi."

"Hey that's at the bottom of the chairlift up to Oberdorf isn't it?"

"Yes.... yes that's right."

"Can we meet?"

"Yes Danny. I... I have to talk to you."

Daniela paused detecting the melancholy in Sarah's voice. "Sarah is something wrong?"

Sarah swallowed hard and felt a tear on her cheek. "Yes Danny. I'm sorry. I'm afraid there is."

Chapter Twenty-Three

"I am so, so sorry Danny." Sarah said as she regarded Daniela's haunted face. They were sitting on the terrace of the restaurant at the top of the Oberdorf chairlift. Sarah had made the journey up after all and Daniela had walked across to see her, her heart full of foreboding. She had been expecting this conversation. Sarah's resolve had faltered when she had seen Daniela approach. Daniela was dressed in the simply yet elegantly soft style which was characteristic of her and became her so well. Her dress fell to her knees, the soft fabric clinging to her thighs in the breeze as she walked, as blue as her eyes and clasped at the waist in a simple white leather belt. The dress had a halter neck and Daniela's lovely golden hair fell about her naked shoulders begging to be lovingly lifted aside to bare her long slim neck for the bestowal of a kiss. She was so beautiful that it brought a lump to Sarah's throat.

Daniela nodded slowly. "I understand Sarah. Really I do. I had the feeling that this would happen." Daniela had listened sadly as Sarah had told her that she was going to the Ticino in a few days to become engaged and that she could no longer delay that or be deflected from it. She had told Daniela that she loved her and always would but that it was impossible. She was fated to become Alan's wife. Duty and familial responsibility dictated it so. She could not give that up for an impossible dream with Daniela. She was going to the Ticino and that was that. Daniela understood that Sarah saw; even respected it. She seemed calmer about it than Sarah was; her inner tranquillity accepting the inevitable. But the light had gone out in those clear blue eyes and it tore Sarah's heart to pieces.

In some strange way Sarah felt disappointed. There was a demon inside her that had wanted Daniela not to

287

be so gently understanding; had wanted her to rail against her decision and fight for her. It wanted her to grasp her and tell her, "You're mine! You don't belong to Alan! You don't love this man you love *me*. You're not going to the Ticino. You're staying here! How dare you throw away our happiness together to marry a man you do not love?" But Daniela hadn't. She seemed almost broken, resigned and her resistance at an end. The irrefutable logic of Sarah's decision had defeated her. For the first time since Sarah had known her, she seemed small and vulnerable.

"Do you really understand Danny?" Sarah whispered.

"Yes I do Sarah. I should have known that this would happen. I was foolish to think otherwise. You are who you are Sarah and I am who I am. I was foolish to think that you could abandon your life for a person like me."

Sarah stared at Daniela. "What's wrong with a person like you? I think you're a wonderful person."

"I'm a rock and roll singer Sarah. That's a hard life for a girl like you. Rock and roll's a world of dreams; ephemeral and insubstantial. Rock and roll singers live fast and die young. You're an earth child Sarah; as solid and firm as the mountains you live amongst and I'm away with the fairies. I'm just a dreamer Sarah. You need more substance than that. I realise that now. I was wrong to have even tried to become part of your life. All I did was disturb you and upset your balance. You were perfectly content until I came along. I couldn't help it Sarah. I loved you from the minute I saw you. I wanted nothing more than you in all the world. Perhaps this will teach me humility. I have wealth and fame and the adoration of more people than I deserve but I cannot have the one thing I truly desire. I have more money than I will ever spend in a lifetime but I feel truly impoverished now." To Sarah's shock there were tears in Daniela's eyes. She had never seen Daniela cry before.

"Danny! Stop it! Please don't cry."

"I can't help it Sarah. I'm sorry. You know I had dreams that I could give you the stability you wanted. I dreamt we could somehow make a life together; our own house; a place of love; our own garden; maybe even children. Was I so stupid to dream that Sarah? Will that always be something forbidden to me? I never harboured dreams of fame and fortune Sarah. I just wanted to make music and they happened by the way. How did I let that happen Sarah? How did I let the illusions of fame and wealth deny me the true happiness I wanted? Why couldn't I have been just an ordinary girl you fell in love with? I'd have been perfectly happy for the rest of my life if the only person that listened to my music was you. I want to make you happy. I want your love. I don't want this fame." Daniela buried her face in her hands.

"Danny stop it. You've made *millions* of people happy through your music. You belong to them as well you know. You're loved by millions. I talked to a girl, a lesbian girl, in Winterthur yesterday and you are an inspiration to her. You can't take that from her. People *need* you Danny."

Daniela raised her tear stained face and gazed at the distant mountains. "Don't you ever wish you could rewind your life Sarah? Don't you wish you could go back to the place where it all went wrong and start afresh from there?"

Sarah took her hand. "Danny you can't go back. Why would you want to? Your life has been so important to so many people."

"But not important enough to you."

"You will always be important to me Danny. If you rewound your life then perhaps you would never have come to live in Switzerland and we would never even have met. Whatever happens in the future my life would be poorer if I had never met you."

"That might have been better Sarah. If I had never met you then perhaps I would not be so tormented by that which I cannot have."

"Stop torturing yourself Danny. There'll always be somebody for you. You're one of the most amazing people I have ever known. I don't believe that there is nobody else you can love."

"There's only one *you* Sarah. A Sarah only comes along *once* in a lifetime."

"That's not true Danny. Please don't be sad. There will be somebody for you. You deserve somebody Danny; somebody better than me; somebody with more courage than I've got. Do you want to know really why I can't be yours Danny? It's because I'm a coward. I'm too frightened to become your girlfriend; too frightened to go against my parents' wishes; too frightened to give up the predictable course and jump into an uncertain life with you. There! I've said it! I'm a pussy Danny. I'm scared of being lesbian; scared of being the girl in a rock and roll singer's life; scared of my father being disappointed in me; scared of what people will think of me; just scared. I found out yesterday that you've appeared on the cover of a lesbian magazine; that you've played live at a gay pride concert and I haven't even the guts to stand up and tell the people closest to me that I love you. How miserable is that Danny? How would you like a girlfriend who is too ashamed to admit that she loves you? You deserve better Danny. I'm going to marry Alan because I'm too frightened to do anything else. I'm not proud of that Danny but I can't do anything else. Please forgive me. Maybe if things had been different or if I'd been a different person then it might have worked."

"Will you be happy Sarah?"

"What?"

"Happy. Will you be happy with Alan?"

Sarah shrugged helplessly. "I don't know. How can you ever know if your marriage is going to be a happy

290

one? I'd like to have children. I like children and I want my own. As to my marriage... well I don't know. I'll try to be a good wife and a good mother. That's all anybody can do. Most people seem perfectly happy with that."

"Can we still be friends Sarah?"

"Of course we can. This isn't a goodbye Danny. I'd be devastated if I thought we'd never talk to each other again. I'll always be your friend. I didn't want to ask you because... well because it's awful when you tell someone that you can't be their girlfriend but you still want to be their friend but yes, of course I still want to be your friend. I just can't be your.... well your lover."

"But it's dangerous Sarah."

"How do you mean?"

"I mean Sarah that I might still seduce you. I might not be able to help myself. I love you Sarah. Every time I see you I want to...." Daniela shook her head with a tearful smile, "Well you know what I want to do."

"I... I can't Danny!"

"How much would you resist if I tried Sarah?"

"Please don't Danny! I don't trust myself."

Daniela smiled sadly. "Then I won't Sarah. I promise you that I will not seduce you. You have nothing to fear. I will control my desires. You have my sincere promise that I will not seduce you. Is that fine by you?"

"Yes. Yes thank you."

"I want to stay your friend though. Do you have any problems with that?"

Sarah shook her head vigorously. "No! No of course not. I want that too!"

"Then let's leave it at that. I just wish you all the happiness possible in your marriage Sarah. Your husband is a very lucky man. You will be a fantastic wife. I just wish you were mine."

"Oh Danny...."

Daniela raised her hand. "It's all right Sarah. I'll be fine. Perhaps you're right. Perhaps it was only an impossible dream." Daniela took a tissue and wiped her eyes. Sarah had never seen her look so fragile. "What are you doing now Sarah?" Daniela asked at last.

"I don't know really. I was going to take the chairlift back down and walk to Wildhaus because I've got to get some things for the house in Migros."

Daniela rose slowly. "Well I'll leave you to your shopping then Sarah. I have some things to do as well and I hope you won't be offended but I'd like a little time on my own."

Sarah jumped to her feet. "But of course. I... I understand perfectly."

"Thank you. Can we meet before... I mean before you go to Ticino?"

"Yes. Yes I'd like that."

"In that case I'll call you." She leaned over and kissed Sarah swiftly on the cheek. Sarah wanted to grasp her tightly and smother her in kisses but Daniela stepped out of range. "Until then, then Sarah." She turned and walked away slowly. Sarah flopped down on the bench and watched her walk across the little alp that led to the restaurant until she turned around the cow sheds at the end and vanished from view. Sarah had everything she wanted. She could go to Ticino with a clear conscience, knowing that she had not been unfaithful. Daniela had promised not to endanger that conscience and had agreed to remain her friend. Everything had returned to normal. So why did she feel so miserably wretched?

Chapter Twenty-Four

Daniela had been less than truthful when she said she had things to do. In fact there was nothing requiring her immediate attention other than the deep sadness in her heart. The day before, she had been in Zurich with her band and agent. There were big plans for the release of her new album; a new tour to plan and promote. Her agent was very excited. He was foreseeing an enormous success. The new album was her best yet. The single release off it was already in the European charts and almost certain to climb to the very top. There was more. He had American promoters on the phone every day and even Asian promoters. Daniela was about to go global. She already had some success in the United States but with the projection of a major tour there she could name her own price. The Chinese and Japanese had discovered her and there were huge initiatives for her expansion into Asia. Her last single was number one in Russia, storming the charts in that most discerning of nations Britain, ubiquitous in Australia and making modest progress in India. Her agent was talking of world tours, television appearances, live televised concerts, film appearances and new albums to record to ride the wave that was carrying her to global super-stardom. Her European fan base was rock solid and about to expand enormously. Daniela's career, already stellar, was on the verge of something extraordinary. It was the moment at which Daniela would emerge as one of the most popular singers and musicians in the world. Her remarkable virtuosity was on the brink of global recognition. People were clamouring for this rising star. Everybody wanted a piece of her. It was a phenomenon in progress; a superstar in the making. Daniela had listened to her agent's plans with growing trepidation. She could not have wished for a greater culmination of her musical ambitions nor, at this moment, a greater sadness at their fulfilment.

She wandered sadly from Oberdorf, cursing the success that led her to such grief. She was a lonely figure in the green meadows of the road to Schwendi. Sarah had told her she was loved by millions and she would be loved by millions more but it was scant consolation to her now. She wanted Sarah's love. Perhaps Sarah had truly believed that a woman as remarkable as Daniela would have her pick of extraordinary people to love her. Sarah could never really understand Daniela's complete dedication to her. She could not see that Daniela's love for her was absolute and all-consuming. Perhaps she had bought into the perception that a famous singer with the world at her feet might dally with her, perhaps take her as a casual lover but never really consider her as a partner for life. Sarah didn't understand the intensity of Daniela's love for her or realise the extent of the devastation she would cause by her rejection of that love. All Daniela's fame; all her wealth and the glittering promise of the future was meaningless now. She had lost her Sarah.

Her footsteps brought her to the Schwendisee where she had passed such sweet hours with Sarah. She walked around the two little lakes numbly, her heart broken. She saw the last of the little Early Purple Orchids fading in the marshy meadows and her tears fell freely. She remained for a long time by the side of the lakes; seeking peace and reassurance in the gentle beauty of the scene. Her blue dress and the gold of her hair were splashes of colour in the verdant pastures around the lakes but her spirit faded and she melted into the background and those who walked about the lakes that day saw only a slight figure huddled by a dry stone wall and knew her not. Later, much later, she would rise and walk to the Hotel Toggenburg, there to take a drink and bid farewell to her love in her mind.

In the meantime Sarah went to Wildhaus. For a person who had gained everything she had set out to achieve this day, Sarah's footsteps could scarcely have been more leaden or filled with gloom. After the short chairlift ride back to Eggenwaldi, the walk across the broad base of the valley and the climb back up to Wildhaus Sarah was about as miserable as she could recall ever being. The light peck on the cheek she had received from Daniela by way of parting had been like a knife to her heart. She was used to Daniela's effusive and affectionate embraces; the tiny kiss had been a seal of doom on their nascent relationship; stillborn before it had time to mature; a full stop before the story had truly begun. Daniela was not the only one with tears in her eyes this day. In a fundamental way Sarah knew that she had just lost something very precious indeed.

In Wildhaus, ever the practical one, Sarah went to the Micros supermarket and purchased household necessities; fresh bread, milk, eggs, fruit juice, butter, two packs of noodles, toilet roll, a bag of sugar, a plastic bottle of washing up liquid, a tube of tomato puree, five hundred grams of minced beef, four large onions, three hundred grams of Appenzell cheese, a fresh lettuce, a small bottle of olive oil, a pack of fresh coffee, four chicken breasts, some shower gel and, because she thought that it would make a pleasant variation to their diet, a small jar of capers and a pack of lightly smoked salmon filets. Sarah normally enjoyed these domestic interludes when she shopped for household provisions for Nicole and herself. It had always been a part of their togetherness; something solid in their life together; a continuity symbolic of the steadfastness and security of their enduring partnership. Today however the process left her feeling deeply sad.

It had not escaped her that this might be one of the last times she would shop for a household including Nicole. In the future she may have to visit the local supermarket to provide the provisions for her husband.

She hardly knew what Alan liked or what to buy for him for his evening meal. She had never cooked for him. They had normally eaten out in restaurants. She had no idea what her domestic budget would be or how to spend it to satisfy Alan's requirements. Alan had always poured eulogies on his mother's cooking; declared her to be the best cook he knew. Sarah was not an incompetent cook but she suspected that she would fall far short of the high standards Alan had come to expect from his mother. Did he like vegetables or was he a red meat man and high on starchy foods and high protein? Nicole liked the way that Sarah prepared salads. Sarah bit her lip wondering about whether Alan had ever eaten a salad in her presence.

Men were funny like that. Men would consume a high carbohydrate meal, which would have any woman blanch at the thought of, without blinking. They seemed to burn off calories effortlessly that a woman would consider herself ruined by. Even if they didn't, they seemed totally unfazed if they got fat. A man would pat his beer paunch with something approaching pride whilst a woman would blanch with shame if her youthful figure lost its willow like proportions and bordered on the rotund. It was so unfair. Men seemed to consider it their masculine prerogative to grow fat and ugly whilst expecting their womenfolk to remain slim and attractive as long as the ravishes of time would allow. Sarah had an awful vision of Alan some twenty years hence; his athletic figure degraded into paunchiness, his hair receding dramatically; lying on the sofa before the television with a can of beer in his hand and too tired or apathetic to make love to her.

Sarah saw herself in that distant future; perhaps before the bathroom mirror staring at her reflection and perhaps just discerning the distant echo of the girl that had once captured the heart of one of the most beautiful women in all Europe. One day she might perhaps be a grandmother and totter across to her dressing table there to take from a secret drawer the dusty emerald pendant and the moissanite earrings that spoke of a different way her life might have turned. Sarah felt a deep loss that it was not to be and she cried bitterly at the unfairness of it all.

The Micros supermarket was just across the little square in Wildhaus from the Hotel Hirschen where Nicole worked and Sarah staggered across with her shopping bags to flop down at a table on the veranda. The hotel was busy with the warm weather and Nicole was soon out carrying a tray full of drinks for the guests. Nicole saw her immediately and gave her a wink before dipping into the purse around her waist to furnish her customers with change. As soon as she could Nicole made her way across to Sarah's table. "Hi Foxy! What brings you here?"

"I've got the shopping in Nicky. I wondered if I could leave it with you to bring home in the car. I can't carry it all that way on my own."

Nicole regarded her shrewdly. "Yeah sure. What's up Foxy?"

"Nothing Nicky."

"Bullshit! You've got a face like a slapped arse. What's the matter?"

"I.... I'm just having a bad day ok."

"Girlfriend problems right?"

"I.... I just finished with Daniela Nicky. I'm going to marry Alan after all."

Nicole rolled her eyes to heaven. "Oh God! Sometimes I just don't believe you Sarah."

Sarah swallowed. "It.... it was the best thing to do Nicky."

"What are you doing now?"

Sarah blinked. "I... I don't know. I was going to leave the shopping with you and walk home I suppose."

"You're doing nothing. I'm off in about one hour. You keep your fanny rooted to that chair until I'm free. You go nowhere understand? As soon as I get free we'll talk ok."

"Nicky I...."

"Shut up Sarah! This has to be sorted. Don't move until I can get out of this place alright?"

"All right Nicky."

Sarah waited patiently watching the world pass by on the street adjoining the hotel terrace with eyes that blurred with tears. At last Nicole emerged, clutching her handbag, and took Sarah's hand firmly leading her across the road to a small guest house with its own restaurant. They took a drink on the veranda at the back of the guest house. It was on the other side of the building from the main road through the valley and quieter while its elevated position on this side of the valley afforded a fine view. Sarah could look down at the path she had traced all the way to Eggenwaldi and the chairlift up to Oberdorf where the restaurant in which she had talked to Daniela earlier was easily visible. Sarah stared at the distant building with a terrible feeling of loss.

Nicole did not seem interested in the view. She was thoroughly exasperated by Sarah. "What the hell is it with you Foxy?" she demanded to know. "Yesterday it's all sweetness and light and you're in love with this woman and now you walk up and tell me you've finished with her. I swear I can't keep up with your bloody vacillations any more. I've no sooner got my head around the fact that you are in a relationship with a woman than you turn around and tell me you're not. Why have you done it Sarah; for God's sake why?"

"It was you, as I recall, that advised me to finish with Danny in the first place."

"That was before Sarah. That was before we established that you were gay. That was before I told you how I feel about you. That was before you told me that you love her. Was all that bullshit Sarah? Do you love her?"

"Yes I do."

"Then why, for fuck's sake, have you finished with her?"

Sarah lowered her head sadly. "Because it was impossible Nicky. I'm not cut out to be a famous pop diva's girlfriend. Look at all the madness that's come over me since I knew her. Yesterday in Winterthur I spent over six thousand francs on clothes and jewellery for heaven's sake. I've never done anything like that before in my life. It was lunatic!"

Nicole whistled appreciatively. "Whee! Yep that's one serious shopping binge. Was it fun?"

"It was madness Nicky. I have never spent so much money in such a short time ever and only because I wanted to be pretty for Daniela. I still can't believe I did it. When I woke up this morning and realised what I'd done I was mortified. I knew then that this had to stop."

"Why? Just because you went a bit mad shopping? For fuck's sake Sarah you're not the first girl to blow a blasted great hole in her bank balance on a day's shopping and you won't be the last. Most girls do that sometimes you know."

"I don't."

"Well I'm proud of you that you finally did. Welcome to the sisterhood."

"How can I justify spending so much money on vanity Nicky?"

"Female vanity is one of the largest economic sectors in the world Sarah. You were just dutifully making your contribution to the stability of the global economy. There'll be people all over the world in the textiles and fashion industries that owe their jobs to the fact that you want to look pretty for your girlfriend. What's wrong with that?"

"You're being flippant."

"Oh come on Sarah. What are you worried about? It wasn't even your money. Your dad gave you twenty grand to buy new clothes and so on. It sounds as if you were following his mandate to the letter."

"He gave me that money to buy clothes and things for my forthcoming engagement and the associated social engagements that come with it not to preen in my vanity in front of my girlfriend. It was dishonest of me Nicky. How can I face my father knowing that I've been so deceitful?"

"So you've finished with Daniela just because of a guilty conscience?"

"I've deceived everyone Nicky. I've cheated on my boyfriend and lied to my family and even used their money for my own mendacious purposes. I never lied before Nicky. You know me. I don't lie. I can't live dishonestly Nicky. I have to go to the Ticino and do the right thing. I'll marry Alan. I'm through with living a lie."

Nicole stared at her. "That is the biggest load of unmitigated bullshit I have ever heard Sarah Fuchs."

Sarah glared at Nicole. "I presume I'm about to receive a lecture."

"Yes you fucking well are! Sarah I love you to bits although God knows you've got your faults. One fault I've never seen from you before though is moral hypocrisy."

"Are you calling me a hypocrite?"

"Yes I am! You're sitting there bleating about doing the right thing and your moral obligations at the same time as you plan to do the very worst thing you could. Living a lie Sarah? You say you're living a lie? You haven't even started. You're about to go to Ticino and look a man in the face and tell him that you love him so much that you agree to be his wife when inside you know that you're gay, don't love him, in fact love another woman and the only reason you're allowing yourself to be Shanghaied into marrying him is because you haven't got the moral fibre to turn around and tell your parents the truth. Not only that but you have probably deeply hurt the person you *do* love because of your cowardice. I know where you're coming from

300

Sarah. All this is about your father and mother. You daren't oppose your mother and you can't bear your father being disappointed in his little baby girl. Well sorry Sarah but you're a grown woman now. There are consequences to your actions. If you can't think of yourself, then at least think of Alan."

"But Alan stands to gain."

"Like Hell Sarah! He's about to be lumbered with a wife that doesn't love him, is secretly gay in any case and is only marrying him because she's too scared of her parents. Not exactly the basis for a future happy marriage is it?"

"I... I'll try to be a good wife. He's a good man. I can learn to love him."

"Crap! What are you going to be thinking on your wedding night Sarah? Who will you be thinking you really want next to you in bed? What are the chances that you'll always feel regret that you threw away the person you love for the sake of your parent's approval? You'll end up resenting Alan; hating your cosy little suburban life; staring at your reflection in the mirror and wondering why you threw it all away in a loveless marriage because you hadn't the guts to stand up and tell the truth."

"I... I can't Nicky!" Sarah brushed a tear from her cheek. "I just can't."

"You have to Sarah or you'll live a lie for the rest of your life. I didn't have the courage to say what I felt either Sarah and it cost me you. Don't make the same mistake my love."

"Nicky I'll lose everything."

"No Sarah. You'll lose everything in Ticino. Your life now revolves around what you're going to say when Alan pulls that ring out of that box and asks you to be his wife. If you make the wrong decision there then you ruin more lives than your own. Think about it."

"I... I spent six thousand francs of my dad's money." Sarah was floundering helplessly.

"Well give him it back if it worries you. I know for a fact you've got enough brass squirrelled away. Anyway, just in case you've forgotten, your girlfriend is a millionairess. She probably spends more than six grand on one of her stage costumes."

"I can't use Daniela's money Nicky. Anyway she's not my girlfriend any more. I've finished with her."

"Then do something sensible for a change; do the *right thing*. Go straight back to her and beg her to forgive you. Go down on your knees if necessary and tell her that you're just a crazy bitch who doesn't know her arse from her tits at the moment and that you spoke in haste and that you want her back. A little bit of humble pie won't hurt you. It might do you a bit of good."

"Nicky it's not that simple. She's a pop star. They're not noted for the longevity of their relationships. I could be throwing it away for just a temporary affair. I don't know what it would be like to be the lover of somebody famous. It could be messy. I could have my name dragged through the newspapers. I'm in unknown territory."

"That's the risk you take Sarah. All you've got to lose is a life you know you're going to hate anyway. Sure it could all go wrong. If it's any compensation there's always one thing to come back to."

"What's that?"

Nicole swept a hand around the vista from the terrace. "This Sarah! Your valley. You know you're going to hate it in Zurich. This is where you live. There's always a place for you in the Toggenburg. This is where you belong. There'll always be happiness for you here. There're people who love you here Sarah." Nicole lowered her eyes sadly. "I'm one of them."

Oh Nicky...."

Nicole lifted her eyes and looked Sarah steadily in the face. "I know it's not much Sarah but there's always me. If it all goes tits up with your marriage, your family and Daniela I'll still be here. I'm always here."

Chapter Twenty-Five

During a quiet moment at the Hotel Toggenburg, Frau Fritzl took a minute to survey her domain; walking out into the restaurant to assure herself that her rigidly high standards were being maintained on behalf of the paying public. She spotted Daniela almost immediately. Daniela was sat at her customary table out on the terrace, her hands clasped in front of her and her head bowed. Frau Fritzl frowned. Daniela must have entered unobtrusively and without drawing a waitress's attention for she had no drink in front of her. Making a mental note to chide her waitresses for their lack of diligence in that such an important customer should go un-served, Frau Fritzl walked out onto the terrace. "Daniela! How nice to see you. I'm afraid Sarah's not working today but can I get you something anyway?"

Daniela raised her head and Frau Fritzl saw to her shock that she had been crying. "Thank you Mein Frau." Daniela choked. "Perhaps a small glass of wine."

"Good God girl! What on earth is the matter with you?" Frau Fritzl blurted out.

"I... I'm sorry Frau Fritzl. I... I'm a little distressed today."

Frau Fritzl lifted her eyebrows dramatically. "Has this anything to do with Sarah?"

Daniela nodded slightly. "Sarah has decided to go to Ticino and marry her boyfriend Frau Fritzl. I understand of course but I'm a little upset about it. Forgive me."

Frau Fritzl regarded Daniela in shock. "Are you saying that Sarah has finished with you?"

"I don't think we really started Frau Fritzl."

"Bullshit!"

Daniela looked at Frau Fritzl in melancholy puzzlement. "I beg your pardon."

"Sarah's loopy about you Daniela; has been since the moment she clapped eyes on you. You two are an item. What's the matter? I thought you loved her."

Daniela lowered her eyes. "I do Frau Fritzl. I truly do."

"Then what's all this crap about her going off and marrying her boyfriend?"

"I think Sarah wasn't ready to... to well have a relationship Frau Fritzl. It's very difficult for her you must understand. She has the expectations of her family to consider and well I don't think they're going to be impressed if she tells them that she's abandoning the man they expect her to marry because she's met a woman with a dodgy reputation she hardly knows. She's not going to throw it all away because of me."

"Are you letting the barmy bitch get away with this?"

"I really have no option Frau Fritzl."

Frau Fritzl stabbed a finger at Daniela. "If that was the case then you're not the woman I think you are and I refuse to believe that." Frau Fritzl caught the eye of her waitress. "Carrie! Fetch us a bottle of that '97 Chateaux Rieussec white Bordeaux and two glasses honey." Frau Fritzl planted herself firmly into a chair opposite Daniela. "Right Daniela let me ask you one question. Do you want this girl?"

"I've never wanted anything more."

"Then you can stop turning belly up and waving white flags. You're going to have to fight for her. Don't take any bullshit from her. She needs a firm hand. She doesn't know what the hell to do. You're going to have to make the decisions."

"I'm not the sort of person to force somebody to do something against their will Frau Fritzl."

"It won't *be* against her will. She's crazy about you. She just needs a good slap and taking firmly by the hair and dragging off to your cave. She'll soon see what it is she really wants."

304

"I think it's a little too late Frau Fritzl. She leaves for the Ticino in a few days."

"Then we'll have to move quickly." Frau Fritzl paused in thought. "The weather forecast isn't too good for the next few days I see."

Daniela blinked. "Er isn't it?"

"No. Where's your car Danny?"

Daniela's mind struggled with Frau Fritzl's oblique line of thought. "It's at home Frau Fritzl. I walked over here."

"You have an *Italian* car right?"

"Well yes. It's a Ferrari but what on earth has this got to do with the situation?"

Frau Fritzl stroked her chin with a thoughtful smile. "Let's just say I might have a cunning plan."

Chapter Twenty-Six

Daniela didn't call Sarah for the next few days and her silence compounded the deepening gloom and sense of loss gripping Sarah. It was an uncomfortable atmosphere in the house as Sarah half-heartedly prepared for her departure to Ticino. Nicole seemed almost as depressed as Sarah and even her usual optimism failed her as the fateful day approached. The two girls were close during this period of impending doom but it was a togetherness of mutual misery occasionally punctuated by those heart stopping moments when the telephone rang.

The telephone rang frequently but it was never Daniela. Sarah's mother, now sensing triumph within her grasp, was a frequent caller, bombarding Sarah with a seemingly endless stream of trivial prattle concerning the upcoming festivities and copious reams of advice on the question of Sarah's wardrobe. She seemed to be under the impression that, without continuous micro-management, Sarah was liable to turn up for her engagement party dressed and coiffed in the kind of style one normally associated with people that lived on park benches and drank cheap cider. Her long and tedious monologues were liberally sprinkled with news of assorted items that she had seen in various boutiques that would suit Sarah eminently. It was obvious that she was going slightly mad with anticipation of the forthcoming social events and probably driving the shop assistants in Ascona and Locarno Boutiques dotty with her attentions. It sounded as if barely a day went by without her augmenting Sarah's collection of haut couture with half a dozen new additions. It made not the slightest difference that Sarah protested that there was no need for her to buy her clothes or that she had perfectly suitable things to wear already. Her mother seemed simply unable to believe her. At least it put Sarah's shopping madness in Winterthur into perspective. Her mother, with a daughter to dress for a wedding, a crowded social calendar to contemplate and a platinum credit card at her disposal, could put all of Sarah's best efforts to shame. Six thousand francs was peanuts. Sarah had known her to spend nearly that amount on a pair of shoes and a handbag. When it came to squandering money in the name of vanity, Sarah wasn't in her mother's league.

Her father called several times as well and, whilst his calls were usually just quietly encouraging, he left Sarah in no doubt that the time for procrastination was past. She was under parental orders and only life threatening illness, natural disaster or the outbreak of war would excuse her from presenting herself in the Ticino at the appointed hour. There were even two brief calls from Alan in America who was presumably being continually updated on events. He was looking forward to seeing her and enthusiastic about their reunion. He never mentioned the words engagement or marriage but they hovered in the background like the Sword of Damocles. Sarah felt herself blushing guiltily whenever she spoke to Alan and was grateful that the telephone did not allow him to see that guilt on her face. Of course, in a few days, that obscurity would not be an option but thankfully Alan was not the most sensitive of men when it came to the observation of subtle nuances.

There was a surprise call from Sarah's older sister Jessica. This, at least, was a pleasant call for Sarah adored her sister and Jessica was one person in her family who was never judgemental about her. Jessica was a thoroughly self-determined woman and if she possessed something of her mother's stubbornness it was at least ameliorated by her father's tolerance and balance. She was astute as well and, while she was not the sort of person to press advice upon anybody, her opinion was always worth seeking for it was always well considered and usually to the point. Jessica it seemed had been invited to Sarah's engagement party as well. The invitation had come from their mother and, Mrs Fuchs being the person she was, it had been tantamount to an order.

In the normal course of things Jessica would have instantly bristled at anything she perceived to constitute a direct order from her mother for she had rebelled against her mother's dominance from an early age to an extent that Sarah never had and there was still a tension between the two strong willed women. Jessica, however, loved her little sister and cared a great deal about her. She was prepared, if not to bury the hatchet, then at least to keep it out of sight for a few days on behalf of her younger sister's engagement party. Jessica was setting off for the Ticino early and she was phoning to see if Sarah wanted a lift. She lived near Luzern and it was only a minor deviation for her to drive to the Ticino by way of the Toggenburg to pick Sarah up. Sarah declined the offer because Jessica was setting off two days before her planned departure date and Sarah resented any further loss of the small amount of time left to her in the Toggenburg. She was pleased though. Jessica's presence ensured that she had at least one ally present in the Ticino.

The one person who didn't call was Daniela although every time the telephone rang Sarah rushed to it in eager haste or each time her mobile sounded she fumbled desperately for it in her bag. It was never Daniela and her mother's interminable trivial conversations became unendurable torments as they blocked the line from the more desirable possibility of Daniela's call. Of course Sarah could have telephoned Daniela at any time but she lacked the courage to do so. It is true that she started to call Daniela on at least three occasions but each time her resolve failed her and she aborted the call before making the connection. She understood Daniela's reticence in phoning her. She knew that Daniela had been deeply upset by their conversation in Oberdorf and the fact that Daniela had excused herself in order to be alone was indicative. Daniela obviously wanted to place some distance between them and Sarah decided to respect that wish. Nevertheless it tore her heart apart and the longer the silence continued the more desperately miserable she became. It occurred to her that it was now a very real possibility that she would depart for the Ticino without ever seeing Daniela and then it was anybody's guess when they would ever meet again. The very thought opened a gaping chasm in her soul.

Nicole tried to lighten the gloom around the house by being thoughtfully considerate to Sarah but her efforts were somewhat spoiled by her own melancholy. Nevertheless she made the effort. She took Sarah out for a few drinks at the Alpli one evening but the pair of them became so maudlin after a few drinks that they both ended up in tears. Nicole was eager to see just what Sarah had spent six thousand francs and made Sarah model some of her purchases for her. She was enthusiastic about Sarah's new clothes but her praise fell on stony ground for the sight of the garments that Sarah had bought with Daniela in mind brought another flood of tears. Sarah packed the clothes away in her bag for the Ticino reflecting that at least they might as well justify their existence by proving to her mother that she did have some dress sense.

Nicole for her part was devastated by the course of events. She cajoled Sarah to phone Daniela continuously but Sarah remained resolute. Nicole was now aware that Sarah was on the brink of making a huge mistake and she seemed to be walking towards the edge of the chasm almost fatalistically. She was frantic with worry. Sarah seemed almost suicidal in her determination to marry Alan. The one person who she might have called upon as an ally in deviating Sarah from such a course was Simon and he was away for some days. Peter wouldn't have done. He had never approved of Sarah's relationship with Daniela in the first place. In point of fact Nicole did have one remaining ally left had she but known it. Frau Fritzl was about to re-enter the game in decisive fashion.

To add to the general sense of foreboding, as the days crept nearer to Sarah's departure, the weather took a turn for the worse and the valley was clogged in under a large depression, filling the sky with leaden clouds and soaking the valley with gloomy drizzle. Sarah stared out of the rain streaked windows of the house feeling that even the elements had conspired to ruin her final days in the Toggenburg. The forecasters were predicting rain for the rest of the week. It was the final blow but it was the blow that gave Frau Fritzl her chance.

In point of fact Sarah could not have been more wrong in assuming that Daniela's silence was in any way a deliberate attempt to maintain distance between them. The separation was just as heart-breaking to Daniela as it was to Sarah and, had it not been for Frau Fritzl's continual reassurances, Daniela would have broken the silence long ago. Frau Fritzl however had insisted that Daniela leave the means of reunification up to her. Frau Fritzl was playing a cagey game knowing that a period of enforced deprivation would be just about driving Sarah crazy. She had to time the thing to perfection. If she left it too late then all hope would be gone and resignation would reign. On the other hand, if she moved too early, then Sarah's misguided dutiful resolution would not have cracked under the pressure of division from her beloved Daniela.

With two days to go before Sarah was obliged to depart for the Ticino Frau Fritzl made her move. Sarah was pottering about the house alone in a desultory fashion when the telephone rang. "Gruezi Sarah! Elke here."

"Oh..." Sarah hesitated before remembering. She was still unused to calling Frau Fritzl Elke. "Oh yes of course. What can I do for you?"

"Well are you busy tonight Sarah?"

"Well not particularly so Frau Fritzl. I was going to stay in because the weather's rotten."

"Well I know you're going to Ticino in a couple of days and I hate to impose upon you just before you leave Sarah but I could really use you tonight. Two of my girls have had to go away on urgent business and I'm short-handed. Is there a chance you could help me out in the restaurant this evening?"

"Why yes I'd be delighted to." Sarah was telling the truth. Nicole was at work all evening and the thought of remaining in the house on her own to ruminate on her woes was not a pleasant prospect. It was just what she needed; to get out of the house and do some honest work.

"Thanks Sarah! You're an angel. I'll see if I can find someone to give you a lift home after work because they're saying it's going to really piss it down tonight."

"That's kind of you. Thank you."

"Ok. Can you make it in around five o'clock?"

"Sure."

"Ok until then. And thanks again Sarah."

Frau Fritzl put the phone down in satisfaction. "Childe Roland to the Dark Tower came!" she murmured to herself. With a grin she picked up the telephone once more.

Chapter Twenty-Seven

Sarah set off early to walk to Schwendi for the weather was awful and getting worse by the minute. She wrapped a rain proof coat about herself and carried an umbrella which proved a struggle in the high wind. In the end she quite enjoyed the walk. It was refreshing to feel the wind in her hair and the cool rain against her face. She didn't even have to walk the whole distance for, no sooner had she crossed the floor of the valley and started on the steep road up to Schwendi on the far side, than an acquaintance of hers passed in his car and, with the civility which was endemic in the Toggenburg, stopped to give her a lift. She arrived at the Toggenburg Hotel early to be greeted effusively by Frau Fritzl. "Thank heavens you've come Sarah." she told Sarah with a hug. "The hotel is full and with this horrible weather most of the guests will be dining in. We're going to be busy! We're looking at eighty or ninety covers at least."

"I hope we'll be able to cope Frau Fritzl. If you're missing two staff members I'm not sure I'll be able to pick up all the slack."

"Oh don't worry I've got somebody else to come in and help."

"Oh good!" Sarah tied her apron on in a business like fashion. "So what prep needs doing?"

"I've already laid most of the restaurant but we've got fresh flowers to put down on the tables, napkins to fold and the menus to change. You can be getting on with that if you like while I go and sort out the bar."

Sarah busied herself making the final preparations for the evening dinner in the restaurant. She enjoyed this part of the job for she took a great pride in a beautifully laid table. She examined each table critically. To her eye every item of cutlery had to be in exactly the right place, the condiments full and carefully placed and menus displayed perfectly. She found herself dissatisfied with the laying of the table cloths on two of the tables and so she stripped them and started again. She examined every item of cutlery to reassure herself that they were all polished correctly. She hated to find knives or spoons with watermarks on them. Every wine glass was subjected to the same searching appraisal and she corrected any flaw in their lustre with the aid of a tea towel and a pot of steaming hot water. Then she started to fold napkins.

This was the time consuming part but she had over one and a half hours before the first guests were due. Sarah took pride in her napkin folding. She knew over thirty different ways to fold a napkin and was always looking out for new stylish designs. She noted, with pleasure, that the laundry consignment of napkins was well starched and stiff which gave her a greater range of possibilities. Impulsively she decided to utilise one of the most difficult and elegant folds in her repertoire. It was called a "Bird of Paradise" fold and to create it perfectly she borrowed an iron from the housekeeping department and set up a small production line in one corner of the restaurant. Once up to speed she could make a Bird of Paradise fold in under thirty seconds. She needed to as well for there were just short of a hundred settings in the restaurant. Soon the service station at her side was filling up with her creations and she was humming to herself happily. She would miss this she knew. Of the many things in her life she would have to sacrifice in marriage it was perhaps only a small thing but she had a professional pride in her skills as a waitress and it somehow seemed a shame that they would be consigned to the obscurity of the marital dinner table when guests were expected.

She was well advanced in her labours when the promised reinforcements arrived. Frau Fritzl ushered in the extra help with a flourish and Sarah's efforts came to

313

a grinding halt. Shedding a long raincoat and divesting herself of a sodden umbrella was Daniela. She shook the rain from her hair and smiled. "I hope I'm not too late Frau Fritzl." She said. "It's getting really wild out there. I thought I was going to do a Mary Poppins all the way over to Wildhaus."

"Not at all Daniela." Frau Fritzl assured her. "I'm just so pleased you could help us out at such short notice."

"Er.... what... I mean.... just what...." Sarah was having trouble articulating.

"Oh Daniela offered to help us out tonight Sarah since we're so short-handed." Frau Fritzl explained.

Sarah blinked. Daniela was dressed in a frilly white blouse and a black skirt and, as Sarah watched with growing astonishment, she donned a spotlessly clean, white pinafore and tied back her hair with a ribbon. Sarah swallowed. "You.... you mean... you're actually going to wait on tables?"

Daniela grinned. "That's right. Now do I get a kiss and a hello?"

Her mind reeling Sarah pecked Daniela on the cheek. Frau Fritzl clapped her hands. "Great! Now I've got loads to do in the bar so can I leave you two girls to it?"

Daniela nodded. "I'm sure we'll be alright Frau Fritzl. You carry on."

"Fine. We've still got loads of time. I'm not expecting the first bookings until seven o'clock but we need to be up and running by half past six. Can you show Daniela where everything is Sarah?" Sarah nodded numbly. "Good. Well I'll leave you to get on." Frau Fritzl departed flamboyantly leaving Sarah staring at Daniela.

Daniela smiled and looked at her. "Ok boss. What needs doing?"

Sarah shook her head perplexedly. "What the hell are you doing here Danny?"

"I'm helping out Frau Fritzl in a crisis Sarah. She... she's been kind to me. It was the least I could do in return."

"But... but you can't!"

"Why not Sarah?"

"Well... because... because of who you are. You... you're Daniela Devin. You're... you're a famous pop star. You can't wait on tables."

"Why Sarah? Do you think it's beneath me? Do you think I'm so high and mighty that I can't do an honest day's work? Do I look down on you because you get your hands dirty in honest labour? I don't think so Sarah."

"But...."

"But nothing Sarah. Just for once forget about what I am Sarah. Stop looking at me as a pop star. Look at me as the woman I am Sarah and, right now, that woman is your junior waitress and we have a restaurant to run tonight."

"Is... is Frau Fritzl *paying* you?"

"I don't give a crap if she is. I'm not doing it for the money and neither are you. You're not so impoverished that you need to work tonight in Frau Fritzl's restaurant. We're doing it as a favour; a favour to somebody who has been a good friend to us."

But... but can you do this?"

Daniela laughed heartily before putting her head on one side and raising and eyebrow. "How do you think I paid my way through drama school Sarah? How do you think I made ends meet when my first band and I were practising in an old disused warehouse and doing weekend gigs in pubs? I wasn't born rich Sarah. I've known what it's like to keep house on noodles and leftovers too Sarah. I'm not too proud to work Sarah. I've even cleaned lavatories before. I've worked in a burger outlet, I've served pints in a bar and I sure as hell have waited on tables before."

"Oh God I'm sorry. I... I didn't want to sound as if I was demeaning you." Sarah rubbed her head in consternation. "Oh God! What are the customers going to think being served by one of the most famous stars in Switzerland?"

"Hmm that's a point. Maybe you'd better take all the money. They might look at me and think "she's a millionairess" and feel un-obliged to leave a tip! I'd hate to think that any punter was leaving the establishment without being divested of the maximum amount of his or her disposable income."

Sarah laughed. "You're terrible."

"Come along sweetheart. Let's work. What do you want me to do?"

"How are you at flower arranging?"

"It's my speciality."

Good! Then you'll find fresh flowers and all the vases in the still room. One vase to each table but two to the three big tables we've got booked. Can you do that while I finish the napkins?"

"I'm on it."

Daniela had told the truth. Her artist's eye was perfectly suited to the task assigned. Her simple floral arrangements on the tables were exquisite and combined with Sarah's elegant napkin designs the restaurant had rarely looked more aesthetically pleasing to the eye. Frau Fritzl whistled her approval when she took a last minute inspection. "Beautiful girls! It looks good enough for a wedding party." Frau Fritzl grimaced. "Oops! There's me and my big mouth." She laughed. "Seriously though girls it's lovely. Those napkins are amazing Sarah. Rebecca Waltemath would have been proud of you."

"Who the blazes is Rebecca Waltemath?"

"The lady that invented the napkin Sarah. She was the first to utilise the napkin in her school for etiquette for Formal Women in eighteenth century London. Those flower arrangements are lovely too Daniela. I'm guessing that you've had some experience in floristry."

"I've taken evening classes in it Frau Fritzl but it's just a hobby really. I'm really into Ikebana at the moment. I find it beautiful."

Sarah made an exasperated noise with her lips. "At the risk of sounding completely ignorant and uncultured may I be permitted to ask what the hell Ikebana is?"

Frau Fritzl answered. "Japanese flower arranging Sarah. Japanese flower arranging goes back to the sixth century and the rituals of offering flowers in Buddhist temples but the formal art of Ikebana was introduced around the fifteenth century from the school of Ikenobo in the Rokkakudo Temple in Kyoto."

"You are very well informed Frau Fritzl." Daniela observed.

"Hell I've been in this business for over thirty years Daniela. I know a bit about putting flowers in vases by now." Frau Fritzl glanced at her watch. "Ok we've still got a good fifteen minutes before our first booking so let's grab a coffee and then we'll hit the ground running."

Chapter Twenty-Eight

Sarah had never known an evening in the simple service of restaurant guests like it. There were four of them to serve in the restaurant and it was a significant four. Frau Fritzl was everywhere and she was joined by Angelica who, Sarah now knew, was Frau Fritzl's partner. Angelica was a warm hearted friendly soul who Sarah had always liked. She was perhaps ten years younger than Frau Fritzl and had a soft feminine beauty and an inner tranquillity that perfectly matched her older lover's extrovert nature. Then there were Sarah and Daniela. Sarah was bemused by the composition of the team. It was almost as if Frau Fritzl had designed her serving team around two female couples. By working alongside her own partner she was emphasising in some subtle way that Daniela was Sarah's partner. Frau Fritzl was openly affectionate to Angelica in a way that Sarah had never seen before; frequently pausing to kiss her in the kitchen, before carrying plates out to the guests, or patting her bottom in passing. It was obvious that Frau Fritzl loved her Angelica dearly and the sentiment was clearly reciprocated. Sarah found herself touched by the obvious devotion between the two older women which, had she known it, was entirely the point.

Frau Fritzl was manipulating the situation deviously. Both she and Angelica were treating Sarah and Daniela as equal partners and tacitly assuming that the two younger girls were as intimately involved with each other as they were. Angelica was particularly overt in this assumption and, whenever mentioning Daniela to Sarah, rarely used her name, preferring to refer to her as "your girlfriend" or "your young lady". Sarah felt disinclined to put the record straight largely because it would have taken far more time than was available in the short interludes in the service. Also Sarah found herself secretly pleased to have Daniela designated as her girlfriend. She was deeply proud of Daniela this evening.

Daniela was enjoying herself. It was such a bizarre change of circumstances for her that she was amused by the novelty of it. It was true that she had waited on many tables before but that had been in the days before she was a recognisable celebrity. It was deliciously funny to observe the reactions of the guests when she attended upon their tables. Many people seemed to recognise her but put the recognition down to some sort of uncanny resemblance since they were unable to believe that the real Daniela Devin could possibly be serving in a hotel restaurant. Others, mostly local people, recognised her at once and were thrilled by her presence if not a little puzzled. Daniela explained to them that she was helping out Frau Fritzl during a temporary crisis and her reputation, already in high esteem locally, was greatly enhanced by the discovery that, for all her fame and fortune, she was a down to earth girl, after all, and not above rolling up her sleeves and pulling on a pinafore to help out a friend.

Sarah could have watched Daniela all night. She seemed to sparkle in the novel situation and she lit up the restaurant with her vivaciousness. She was also, Sarah observed, a damn good waitress. By now even the doubtful among the clientele had realised the identity of the beautiful woman serving them and Daniela found herself in the ludicrous position of having to autograph her customers' bills. At one point Sarah returned to the kitchen still room with an armful of dirty plates to find Daniela laughing with Frau Fritzl. "Do you believe it Sarah?" Daniela asked. "That guy on table eleven gave me a twenty franc tip. Does he honestly think I need the money?"

Sarah laughed. "Well don't spend it all at once."

Frau Fritzl guffawed. "What an absolutely brilliant evening." she declared. "I've never seen the restaurant so animated. Even old Herr Gunther is gawping at

Danny like a love struck schoolboy. He was dribbling his soup down his chin while she was pouring his wine for him."

"Is he the old guy on table seven that keeps patting my hand?"

"There's more than your hand he'd like to pat I'll wager. God if you ever want a full time job, Danny let me know. With you on service we'd pack this place every night." She was interrupted by the chiming of a small bell. "Ah that'll be the desserts for table nine." She dashed off to see to the matter.

Sarah stacked her dirty dishes on the dishwasher station and turned to look at Daniela who was updating the orders board. "Busy huh Danny?"

"Yes. It's fun."

"You're really enjoying this aren't you?"

"Of course and anyway..." she gave a little twirl, "don't you think I look cute in a waitress's uniform?"

"You look gorgeous."

Daniela stepped over and put a hand around Sarah's waist. "God I've missed you Sarah."

Sarah swallowed. "I missed you too Danny. Why didn't you phone?"

"I didn't think you wanted me to."

Sarah shook her head. "I've been sat by the phone all week Danny."

The kitchen bell chimed once more and Daniela sighed blissfully. "No rest for the wicked sweetheart. We'll talk later."

At last the final guests had been fed and the kitchen staff had finished for the night. Lots of guests still lingered in the dining area over drinks for the hotel bar stayed open long beyond the evening meal. The volume of work was much reduced however and, since Frau Fritzl and Angelica were more than able to cope with it, Sarah and Daniela's services were no longer required. As a thank you for their efforts Frau Fritzl insisted upon them sitting down with her and Angelica for a drink.

"You've both been wonderful!" she told them. "Come on what are you drinking?"

"I'll just have a beer." said Sarah.

"The same for me." was Daniela's response.

Frau Fritzl brought beers for all of them and they eased around a table next to the bar where Frau Fritzl could keep an eye on the remaining guests should they still require more drinks. "Well that was just fantastic." she noted with gleaming eyes. "I don't think we've ever had such a glamorous waitress here before Daniela. We've certainly set chins wagging. The punters will never forget *this* dinner."

Angelica giggled. "God those Japanese tourists even asked for *my* autograph. I think they thought they'd better be on the safe side just in case I was somebody famous too."

Frau Fritzl chuckled warmly. "They were probably trying to look into the kitchen as well just in case we had a Hollywood movie star on pot wash. Did you see the faces on the Mannsteins when Danny brought them the wine card? I thought Frau Mannstein was going to choke on her amuse bouche."

They all laughed. Everybody had a funny story to tell about the evening. "Those Japanese wanted my autograph as well Danny." Sarah told her. "I didn't know that your music was well known in Japan."

Daniela sipped her beer. "Our last single is at number three on the Japanese charts Sarah and I think the album was pretty solid in place eight last week. We have a big market there. The agency is bugging me to do a Far East tour."

"My God!" said Angelica, sounding impressed. "Global super-stardom no less."

Daniela smiled modestly. "Oh not quite Angelica. America's the big mountain to climb. We've only had modest sales there so far. We're touring the States next year all being well. I'm dreading it."

"Well you were certainly a star tonight." Frau Fritzl remarked warmly. "And you too Sarah. I can't thank you girls enough."

"It was our pleasure!" Daniela assured her.

"Are you all right for tomorrow Frau Fritzl?" Sarah asked.

"Well we'll be ok for breakfast but I could use the help at lunch if either of you girls can spare the time. Angie has to go to town straight after breakfast and my girls won't be back until the evening."

"We'd be delighted." Daniela affirmed.

Sarah looked doubtful. "I... I'm not sure I can work tomorrow evening Elke. I... I'm setting off for the Ticino the day after."

This information was a cold dash over the camaraderie around the table and there was an awkward silence. Frau Fritzl nodded soberly. "Oh I won't need you tomorrow evening Sarah. The girls will be back by then." She peered out of the window. It was an unprepossessing sight. The spruces in the garden were swaying alarmingly in the high wind and illuminated by the lights on the veranda. Beyond the small pool of light the night was as black as ink and rain spattered against the window. "God it looks ugly out there." She observed. She turned to Daniela. "Listen Danny, Angie and I have to stay here and run the bar so do you think you could run Sarah home?"

Daniela frowned. "I wish I could Frau Fritzl. Unfortunately my bloody car is hors de combat; broken down. God knows what the matter with it is. Typical Italian; all very sleek and chic but downright temperamental and doesn't always work when you need it to."

Frau Fritzl swore. "Damn! Maybe you could borrow my car to run Sarah home."

Daniela looked dubious. "I don't think I could do that Frau Fritzl. I've never driven a big four wheel drive before and on a night like this down that road I don't think I'd trust myself. I'd be scared to death."

Frau Fritzl pondered agitatedly. "Well we've got to do something! We can hardly let Sarah *walk* home on a night like this."

"Oh I'm sure I'll be all right." ventured Sarah hesitantly although in truth she didn't relish the prospect.

"Nonsense!" asserted Frau Fritzl firmly. "I'm not letting you walk home in this." She ran a hand through her hair. "I can't even give you a room for tonight because the hotel's full and it'll be at least another three hours before we can close up and drive you home."

"Sarah could always stay at my place." Daniela volunteered innocently.

Sarah started violently and glared at Daniela but Daniela's face registered only helpful consideration. Frau Fritzl smiled in relief. "Now that's a good idea Danny. It's not too far to your house is it?"

"Oh no. It's only about twenty minutes' walk. It'll be a bit of a dash in the rain but it's not too bad."

"I think that's a fine idea." Angelica observed. "That way, Sarah won't have far to come tomorrow for lunch as well."

"Well then that's sorted thank heavens." stated Frau Fritzl determinedly. Sarah closed her mouth firmly, aware that it had been hanging open for several seconds. Frau Fritzl drained her glass. "Well then let's have a last beer and then we'd better let the girls get off Angie." She glanced up. "Angie see to that couple on table three while I'm getting the beers will you. I think they need serving."

With Frau Fritzl away at the bar and Angelica absent to attend to the customers Sarah found herself alone with Daniela. She turned to Daniela agitatedly. "Danny! I... I can't stay at your place."

"Why ever not Sarah? I don't live in a mud hut you know. There's plenty of room."

"But... but..."

"But what Sarah?"

"You *know* what."

"No I'm sorry. I'm not following you."

"Well where..." Sarah blushed crimson, "Where would I sleep."

"At the last count I had six bedrooms in my villa Sarah. I don't think we'll be pushed to find a place for you to crash out."

"I... I'd have my own bedroom?"

Daniela sighed. "I'm disappointed in you Sarah. Do you really think I'm so bad? Do you doubt my word?"

"Well no but..."

"Sarah I promised you at Oberdorf the other day that I would never try to seduce you. Is my sworn oath so meaningless?"

"Well no but..."

"No buts Sarah. I have promised faithfully that I will not seduce you and I will remain true to that promise. You have nothing to fear from me. You'll have your own room. You can even lock the bloody door if it makes you feel any safer."

Sarah blushed. "Oh God I sound horrible Danny. I didn't mean to sound as if I didn't trust you."

"Listen Sarah you'll be quite safe from me I swear. We can just go home, have a bath, have some nibbles and curl up on the sofa to gossip and watch some mind numbingly, escapist, sentimental trash on the DVD. Just a girl's night in. Your chastity is safe with me."

Sarah smiled sheepishly. "It sounds lovely."

Daniela's smile was dazzling. "I've missed you Sarah. You're going off to the Ticino in two days. You can't deprive me of the pleasure of your company for one teeny weeny little night."

Sarah stared into the big blue eyes she so loved and felt suddenly very happy.

Chapter Twenty-Nine

"We are going to get wet!" declared Sarah firmly. It was a fair analysis as she and Daniela stood huddled in the doorway of the Hotel Toggenburg, contemplating the wretched weather before them. It was still raining heavily and the wind was blowing the sheets of rain around in a bewildering variety of directions. Umbrellas promised to be hazardous accessories rather than being of any use in affording protection from the elements. Beyond the pool of light surrounding the hotel there was only forbidding darkness and the hiss of the wind and rain in the tops of the trees.

Daniela squeezed Sarah fondly. "Well we'd better make a dash for it although how the hell we're going to see where we're going in this muck I've no idea."

Sarah, ever the practical one, produced a large, heavy duty torch with the smugness of a person who has come prepared for every eventuality. "Frau Fritzl leant me this Danny. We'll be all right. Come on let's do it." They dashed out into the darkness and the powerful beam of the torch was a godsend in the wild night. There were no other illuminations on the tiny little road between Schwendi and Oberdorf and without something to light their way it would have been almost impossible to orientate themselves in the darkness. The wind whipped at their skirts and lashed their sodden hair about their faces as they struggled along picking out their way in the light of the torch. Within a few hundred yards they were both soaked and staggering in the high wind. It should have been almost unadulterated misery but somehow it was nothing of the sort. They were both gripped in a madness of exuberance, exulting in the howling wet gale that threatened to lift them bodily from the narrow road. They clung to each other laughing helplessly as they battled across the flank of the hillside high above the valley bottom. There seemed no spite of the weather that could break their unity or dampen their exhilaration. Their spirits were as wild as the night and the most vicious gusts of wind only made them whoop and laugh the louder. It was a crazy night to be abroad on, absolute madness to be out in and enormous fun.

Daniela's villa was set back some way beyond Oberdorf and they passed through a small belt of woodland before they reached it. The villa was set in a little glade that afforded some shelter from the storm but the tiny stream that skirted the edge of its gardens was swollen with water. Daniela led Sarah to the front of the house and in the relative shelter under its eaves fumbled in her bag for her keys. The hallway of the house was a warm sanctuary after the conditions outside and the two young women looked at the wreck of each other's appearance after the battering of the storm and broke into giggles. Sarah looked at Daniela's glorious golden locks reduced to a wasteland of saturated chaos dripping water on the tiles of the hallway and burst into laughter thinking that she had somehow never seen Daniela look so beautiful. "You look a mess." she told her fondly.

Daniela laughed merrily. "You're not exactly a picture of haut coiffure yourself Miss Fuchs. Come on for God's sake. Let's get these wet clothes off and get into a hot bath." They were interrupted by the sudden presence of two cats that greeted them with purrs and a determination to entwine themselves about their ankles. Daniela laughed and bent to pick one up and hold it to her face affectionately. The cat closed its eyes ecstatically and rubbed its head against her face purring loudly. "Let me introduce you Sarah. This is Lady; short for Lady Gaga, and she *is* gaga too." Sarah grinned and stooped to stroke the head of the big tabby tom that was apparently trying to make the intimate acquaintance with her thighs. "That's Tom." Daniela told her. "Tom Jones formally but Tom to his mates."

"Do you name all your cats after singers?"

326

"Well this gang anyway. I suppose Stevie's probably asleep somewhere and Roddy will, most likely, be out in the old barn at the back chasing mice. He's an unrepentant predator. Come on give me your coat and let's get inside properly."

Daniela ushered Sarah into the living room and then rushed off to run a bath for her. For a few minutes Sarah was left to examine Daniela's domain alone. She was gratified to note that Daniela's house was much as she had imagined it. The living room was huge and tastefully furnished although not ostentatiously so. The large veranda windows were covered in long rose coloured drapes that matched the cream of the walls and the cream and pinks of the deep pelted carpet strewn liberally with thick rugs in cream and magenta. The furnishings were simple yet luxurious; a pair of enormous soft leather cream couches and two large armchairs in matching colours around a large open fireplace and a huge coffee table carved out of the bole of what must have once been a magnificent tree. Daniela liked the contrasting hues of modern styles and rustic harmony it seemed for she had retained the old wooden beams that were a part of the infrastructure of the house and blended them perfectly into the more modern fittings. The fireplace was magnificent in stone and cast iron and clearly ancient. It was obviously hardly necessary for heating purpose for the house was well provided for with radiators and under-floor heating but it leant a cosiness to the overall room. This was a room to relax in and to lie around at your ease in. It spoke of sensual informality and languid hedonism.

Although the furnishing was simple it was not austere. There were deep cushions on the couches and large poufs for one's feet on the floor. One wall was taken up with a large bookcase that reflected Daniela's character for there were volumes of books on music, fine arts, high literature, philosophy and poetry. They were not only for show either for they were obviously well thumbed and loved. Sarah saw books on gardening and decorating nestling alongside Tennyson and Wordsworth. She spotted a biography of Mozart flanked on one side by an imposing looking treatise on Buddhism and on the other by a well-worn copy of Tolkien's "Lord of the Rings". She found a full anthology of Shakespeare's works sharing bookshelf with the complete Penguin collection of Arthur Conan Doyle's Sherlock Holmes. There were volumes of written music too but Sarah noted that Daniela had a fondness for old P.G Wodehouse novels of which she had a formidable collection. Art fascinated her too for there were reams of books on the subject; Impressionists, Surrealists, Modern Art and classical art. There were at least three books on Dali alone, two on Turner and three more on Van Gogh. But Daniela seemed to love the period of the Renaissance the best for she had shelves of books on Titian, Rafael, Michelangelo, Da Vinci, Botticelli, Tintoretto, Caravaggio and the like. The whole book collection bespoke of a woman with a profound love in all things beautiful from music through the visual arts to the glory of the written word. It was a telling insight into the complex character of the remarkable woman Sarah was beginning to discover.

Another set of shelves contained a collection of DVDs and that these were well used was evidenced by the enormous plasma screen television, the biggest Sarah had ever seen, that nestled close to the fireplace. Here Sarah saw that Daniela had special tastes too. She obviously loved old musicals. Some of the great classic musicals of all time resided among her collection; The Sound of Music; The wizard of Oz; Singing in the Rain; The Jazz Singer; West Side Story; My Fair Lady; Mary Poppins; Chitty Chitty Bang Bang and many more; Daniela loved them all it seemed. There were newer musicals too such as Chicago, The Phantom of the Opera, Mama Mia and even Bollywood productions from Mumbai. Daniela loved old classic Hollywood films.

There was Citizen Kane there and Breakfast at Tiffany's; venerable old westerns and Gone with the Wind; Casablanca and Mutiny on the Bounty. It was an archive of some of the greatest films in the history of the medium. There were also newer films as well though and filmed concerts of modern and classical artists were well represented. Daniela seemingly had a weakness for Walt Disney cartoons; Jungle Book, Snow White, Cinderella, Fantasia, Alice in Wonderland, Peter Pan, Sleeping Beauty, One hundred and one Dalmatians, Pinocchio and such.

Another set of shelves held a formidable collection of CDs and the stereo system was large and obviously expensively state of the art. Music held a place of importance in this house. It was not untidy but also not without its clutter for two guitars and a set of keyboards reclined carelessly about the room and several sheets of musical scores were scattered about on the coffee table. There was even a harmonica and a small amp and speaker pushed aside into one corner. Three CDs lay on the coffee table. They were interesting. One was Beethoven's violin concerto, another was the Beatles "Sergeant Pepper's Lonely Hearts Club Band" and the other was "I am.....Sasha Fierce." by Beyonce. It would be hard to categorise Daniela's musical tastes.

The room was green in many ways for Daniela loved her plants. At least a dozen large pot plants occupied the room including an exquisite little bonsai holding a place of honour on a small side table to a large Rubber plant taking up much of one corner. There were also two or three beautiful arrangements of wild flowers which bespoke of Daniela's interests in this floral art. Here was a woman who liked to surround herself with beauty.

In nothing was this more illustrated than in the pictures hanging on the walls. The voluminous space in the big villa had acres of wall space and Daniela had set to determinedly to utilise that space for the display of her collection of art. It was mostly watercolours and oils although there was the odd pencilled drawing and the subject matter was the simple things that Daniela found beautiful, landscapes, paintings of wild flowers, still life, animals and portraits. It occurred to Sarah after about five seconds that the pictures showed a single characteristic style. They were all painted by a single person and the identity of that person was revealed by the large picture over the fireplace. It showed a beautiful young woman squatting among the meadow flowers by the Schwendisee. It was Sarah. Daniela must have painted it from the sketches she had made of Sarah on their afternoon walks during Sarah's free hours at the Hotel Toggenburg. The picture was beautiful and lovingly crafted. Sarah felt her eyes fill with tears; touched to the point of heartbreak that Daniela had put such loving into the picture and then hung it in pride of place in her living room above the fire where she could gaze upon it every evening. So intent was Sarah on the picture that she never heard Daniela re-enter the room. "It's not very good I'm afraid."

Sarah spun guiltily at the sound of Daniela's voice, almost as if she'd been caught in a discretion. Daniela was stood by the doorway eyeing her quizzically. "It's beautiful Danny!" Sarah exclaimed at last. "I can't believe you painted this."

"Do you want it? You can have it as a wedding present if you wish."

Sarah shook her head vigorously. "No! Never! I could never take this Danny. It... it wouldn't be right. This belongs to you."

Daniela lowered her eyes sadly for a brief moment before smiling at Sarah. "Come along Sarah. I've run a big hot bath for you. Let's get you out of those wet clothes."

The bathroom was enormous and the bathtub was appropriately huge and full of steaming foamy water deliciously scented with rose and apple. Daniela handed her a bathrobe and showed her a set of towels hanging luxuriously on a heated rail, shampoos and scented soaps. "Are you sure you don't want to bath first?" asked Sarah.

"Oh I'll take a bath in my own bathroom while you soak Sarah."

"Good God! You mean this is just the *guest* Bathroom?"

Daniela laughed. "I have *three* bathrooms altogether Sarah."

"My God!

Daniela looked at her with a wicked smile. "I'm a wealthy woman Sarah; probably much richer than your current fiancée. Your parents would never be able to claim that I was unable to keep their daughter in the manner to which she was accustomed."

"Danny! You promised."

Daniela laughed mischievously. "I'm not seducing you Sarah. I'm just pointing out economic realities. Come on.... get in the bloody bath." With a last laugh Daniela swept out.

Bemusedly Sarah undressed and laid her damp clothes on a chair before sinking into the enormous bathtub. Daniela presumably had a heat resistant hide for the water was very nearly scalding and Sarah eased herself into it gingerly. Once immersed among the suds, however, she lay back languidly and luxuriated in the warm soapy water. She soaped herself all over and giggled at the imposing array of shampoos and perfumed gels around the tub. She tried them all frivolously and closed her eyes ecstatically; cocooned in the heat of the bath and her nostrils full of warm scents. She washed her long hair until it squeaked as she ran her hands through it and rubbed a sponge sensually over her body until she tingled. She could have laid there for hours and indeed she lingered long; almost dozing with the suds rising to her chin.

Sarah was startled from her revelry by the bathroom door. Daniela walked in clad in a bathrobe and her hair

331

wrapped in a towel. Suddenly feeling shy Sarah folded her arms over her naked breasts. "You might have knocked Danny." she protested feebly.

"I've seen you without your clothes on before Sarah" Daniela picked up Sarah's clothes from the chair. "I was just coming to put your things in the wash with mine."

"Oh! Oh er thank you."

"I've put some night clothes on your bed. When you've finished your bath I'll show you your room then I'll make us a bit of supper and we can eat in the lounge."

"Oh er... good."

Daniela smiled and walked out but, as Sarah noted wryly, not before giving Sarah such a long look of appraisal that it made Sarah shiver and caused her hormones to send urgent messages to the relevant parts of her body. Fully awake now, Sarah eased out of the bath and took one of the deliciously warm scented towels and rubbed herself dry. Her body was glowing pink with the stimulation of the bath, her nipples stood erect, her pupils were dilated and her nostrils flared as she drank in the aromas of her body; dangerously aroused. Daniela's promise was all that separated her from complete ruin. It would have taken but a single offer to scrub her back Sarah knew. With her heart beating powerfully in her chest and her breath deep Sarah took a long look at herself in the bathroom mirror before folding her damp hair in a towel and wrapping the bathrobe around herself. Daniela had left her an unopened toothbrush and toothpaste by the washbasin and she carefully cleaned her teeth and rinsed her mouth with mouthwash before setting out to find Daniela.

Stepping from the bathroom she ran straight into Daniela who was carrying some plates through from the kitchen. Daniela smiled at her warmly. "Feeling refreshed?"

"Yes thank you. Much better."

"Good. Come on let me show you your room. There's a drier in there for your hair."

The room was large and comfortable decorated in warm creams and pink and dominated by a huge bed with cream satin drapes over the duvet and enormous pink and cream pillows. The bed looked invitingly luxurious and sensual. It seemed almost a desecration not to share it. Decorating the walls were several watercolour studies of pink and red flowers and they had been so meticulously executed that Sarah could identify the species; Fringed Pink, Red Campion, Ragged Robin and Sweet William. They complimented the decor of the room perfectly. Daniela showed her to the other dominant item of furniture in the room; a huge ornate, white dressing table in a French design with an enormous arched mirror flanked by two side mirrors and illuminated with its own lights. Sarah stared in bewilderment at the vast array of scents, powders, creams, implements and cosmetics half of which she had not the faintest idea of the function of. At least she could recognise the hair brushes and hair-dryer.

"I don't know what you normally wear to sleep in Sarah," Daniela was saying, "so I've laid you out a selection of the sort of nightwear I usually go to bed in and you can take your pick as to what you'd be most comfortable in. There's a dressing gown hanging up on the peg there."

"Thank you. I'm not used to this sort of luxury."

Daniela grinned. "If you're not too tired, join me in a glass of wine and a bite to eat in the lounge after you've dried your hair."

"Yes of course."

"I'll leave you to it then. The cats are bugging me to be fed."

After Daniela had departed Sarah lowered herself onto the stool in front of the dressing table and shook her hair loose. She was quite unused to such an altar to female vanity. At home her dressing table consisted of a mirror propped up against some books on a sideboard and some rudimentary accessories. This shrine of indulgence felt almost decadent. She dried her hair carefully, brushing it until it gleamed under the soft lamps on the dressing table and admired its burnished sheen as she stroked her fingers through it. She undid her bathrobe and cast it aside to sit naked before the mirror and drew breath at the sight of herself glowing in the gentle illumination. Experimentally she examined the other items on the dressing table. She found a bottle of expensive body moisturising cream and she worked it into her skin loving the softness of her skin under the ministrations. She hesitated over the cosmetics on the table. For some reason she wanted to make herself look beautiful but putting make up on before going to bed was a dangerously overt signal. Only tarts went to bed with their make up on she told herself. She did however pick up a bottle of ludicrously expensive perfume and applied two tiny sprays of the scent to her torso.

Finally she rose from the stool and walked to the bed to peruse the nightwear that Daniela had left her. This precipitated the major crisis of the night so far. Daniela was unabashedly sensual and her nightwear collection reflected that. She'd left half a dozen outfits for Sarah's approval and there wasn't one of them that didn't make Sarah tingle with strange feelings. Sarah picked up a tiny, pink, sheer sleeping vest and matching G-string in pink that tied with a single bow at the breast and otherwise lay open and would just about fall to the bottom of the buttocks even if its transparency did a wretched job of concealing them. It was obviously expensive and decorated in sequins and artificial pearls and with Venetian trimmings but it was so overtly sexy you might as well have worn an advertising board around your neck. Sarah rejected that out of hand. She groaned as she regarded the other items on offer. Normally during the summer Sarah wore a vest and a pair of knickers to bed or a pair of old cotton pyjamas during the colder months. Until her recent purchases in Winterthur she had possessed nothing of a particularly inviting nature as night attire.

In confusion she sat down heavily on the bed. It was ironic that but a few days before she had deliberately gone in a shop in Winterthur with the express intention of buying some titillating lingerie and night wear for Daniela's benefit but now she was hesitant to the point of embarrassment in wearing any such thing. Despairingly she picked up a short silk nightdress in violet with semi-sheer lace cups and a low cut back. It was gorgeous and the material so enticing that she couldn't help herself from holding it against her cheek. There was also a long soft pink nightdress of such seductive silkiness that it took Sarah's breath away. It was another creation with sheer cups and Sarah rejected it on the grounds that she felt she wanted more than a token gauzy film to conceal her breasts behind. There was also a matching set of silk cream camisole and French knickers, a lovely lacy chemise with matching briefs in pale green and a pink baby-doll.

In the end, Sarah bottled it. She picked out the one costume that could decently be described as modest. It was a pair of silk pyjamas in classic style; ivory in colour and deliciously soft on the skin. Even these failed in the chastity test however for they were sensually luxurious and the material felt like a caress against Sarah's skin. Over these Sarah donned the pink silk robe Daniela had left her and left the bedroom in search of the lounge.

Chapter Thirty

Daniela was sat on one of the big couches with a short silk robe in aquamarine tied loosely over pale blue knickers and camisole. Her hair was brushed and shining gold in the subdued lighting as she bent over her foot, perched on a low stool, to paint her toenails, biting her lip in concentration. "Everything ok?" she asked.

Sarah nodded numbly. Daniela looked so radiantly beautiful she robbed Sarah of speech momentarily. Sarah felt suddenly overdressed. "Yes er fine." She breathed at last.

Daniela nodded to the coffee table. "I put out some munchies for us. Only cold stuff I'm afraid. I couldn't be arsed to cook anything."

Sarah gazed at the food. There was good country bread, a selection of cheeses, pickles, big green olives, a plate of cold meats and salami, sticks of celery, slices of honey melon, green grapes, slivers of smoked salmon garnished with onions and capers, a tomato salad drizzled with olive oil and balsamic vinegar, a bowl of pasta salad in mayonnaise and a plate full of chocolate truffles liqueur stangeli. Sarah blinked in pleasure. "Well I don't think we'll go hungry." she remarked.

"Would you pour the wine sweetheart?" Daniela asked. A bottle of fine Rioja Alta Gran Reserva 1997 was open on the table accompanied by two crystal goblets. Reverently Sarah took the bottle and poured two glasses full of the rich deep red liquid. Daniela replaced the cap on her bottle of nail varnish extending her foot to examine her labours critically and wriggling her toenails. Pointedly she made no comment on Sarah's dress choice but took the glass from Sarah with a smile. There was soft music playing from the stereo. Sarah recognised the music. It was Beethoven's Pastoral Symphony; one of her favourites. She racked her brain to think whether or not she had ever told Daniela that. Daniela had also lit a fire in the fire place and a pair of logs were crackling merrily casting dancing reflections into the soft light of the lounge and filling the air with aromatic scents. Two of Daniela's gang of felines were curled up contentedly on the rug in front of the fire. "Cheers." Daniela raised her glass in salute. "Take a seat Sarah and let's eat."

Sarah lowered herself into an armchair opposite and began to fill a plate with tasty titbits. The food was simple but delicious and they picked at it in silence. Sarah spread a wafer thin slice of smoked salmon onto a piece of bread and smeared sweet horse radish on it before conveying it to her mouth with pleasure. She watched Daniela in fascination. Daniela always seemed to eat so delicately yet there was a true delight in the flavours of the food which belied the dainty manner in which she ate. She could pop an olive into her mouth with the tiniest of movement but her eyes would close in something approaching ecstasy as she savoured the oily saltiness of it on her tongue. You had the feeling that she was greedy but far too fastidious to gobble her food. Her eyes fixed on the food before her with a gleam of satisfaction and from a tiny morsel of cheese she would extract the maximum amount of enjoyment. It was sensual, hedonistic; it was the indulgence of a woman that was enslaved to her senses; drugged on the sensations of life.

Daniela lay back on the couch as she ate and the short robe she wore fell away from her shapely legs. Sarah could not tear her eyes from those silky limbs. Neither could she divert her attention from the glorious golden locks that fell across Daniela's shoulders. The robe was loose about Daniela and it fell from her right shoulder to reveal the perfect skin of her slender neck and the inviting curve of the nape. Sarah longed to caress that soft skin; lift the hair away and bestow soft kisses. It suddenly seemed so terribly, terribly wrong that this loveliness was denied to her. She felt the hot flush of mounting arousal but Daniela seemed oblivious to her urgently growing interest. Daniela pushed her plate away with a sigh of satisfaction and sipped her wine delightedly; rolling the rich Rioja around in her mouth and dabbing away the tiniest trickle at the corner of her lips with a napkin. Sarah was transfixed; mesmerised by the vision of loveliness before her. With a sudden awareness of her physicality and passion, Sarah knew then that she wanted this woman more than anything she had ever wanted in her life before.

Daniela brushed a hair from her face. "So what do you want to do Sarah? Shall we watch a movie?"

Sarah could hardly breathe. "Er... well maybe..."

Daniela raised an exquisite eyebrow. "Maybe what?"

Sarah blushed and lowered her eyes. "I... I don't know."

"What's the matter Sarah?"

Sarah swallowed and took a breath. "You er... well you had a poor record of keeping your honour as a girl guide didn't you?"

"Are you impugning my honour Sarah?"

"No! No. I... er just well hoped... well I mean... well that your honour... wasn't so... well honourable."

Daniela frowned with an ironic smile. "I'm not following you Sarah."

"You know bloody well what I mean."

Daniela shook her head. "Nope. Completely fuddled at this end Sarah. Please elucidate."

"You... you promised not to seduce me."

Daniela held up her hands in innocence. "And I have been true to my word Sarah. I have done nothing whatsoever to endanger your celibacy."

"Oh Right! So trying to dress me up in the sort of clothes more commonly associated with a high class bordello and plying me with food and fine wine in front of a log fire to the accompaniment of soft music had

338

nothing whatsoever to do with your amorous intentions then?"

Daniela shook her head indignantly. "Absolutely not Sarah. My sole intention was to make you feel comfortable and at home. I swore that I would not seduce you and I remain faithful to that oath. I have no amorous intentions on you and I will not make any move to seduce you at all."

"None at all?"

"Absolutely none. You have my word."

"You mean this?"

"Sarah! I'm not used to having my honour and sworn word questioned in this fashion. I am upset that you have so little trust in me."

Sarah bit her lip. "I'm sorry Danny. I... I didn't want to doubt you or anything."

"Good. I'm gratified to hear it."

"It's just that...."

"Just what?"

"Well I might be open to negotiation."

"*Negotiation?*"

Sarah cringed and clasped her hands tightly. "Well yes. I mean I won't think the worse of you if you were to break your word."

"Break my word?"

"Stop repeating everything I say Danny. You know what I mean."

"Well let me make a shrewd guess Sarah darling. Do I assume by this oblique line of reasoning that you wish to release me from my sworn word; that in fact you wish me to seduce you after all?"

Sarah gulped. "Well yes.... I suppose so."

Daniela laid down her glass decisively. "Absolutely out of the question."

Sarah blinked. "What?"

"I said Sarah that it was out of the question. For the past few weeks you have resisted every effort I have made to seduce you into an intimate relationship with me.

Furthermore you have extracted the most solemn of oaths from me to the effect that I respect your purity and have pointed out repeatedly that my advances were unwelcome to you. In deference to those stated rules I will therefore make no attempt whatsoever to seduce you."

"Oh!" Sarah was deflated.

"Absolutely not. It is unfair of you to place such restrictions on me and then expect me to come running the minute you change your mind."

Sarah was chagrined. "I'm sorry Danny. I... I didn't want to offend you."

"I'm not offended Sarah just... well just a little disappointed."

"I'm so sorry Danny. I just well... I just thought.... Oh God I'm stupid."

"For what Sarah?"

"I... I thought you wanted me. I'm sorry."

"I *do* want you Sarah."

"Eh?"

"I want you more than anybody I've ever known Sarah but I'm not going to seduce you."

"I don't understand."

"Don't you? It's like this Sarah. I want you; God I want you! The question is do you want *me*?"

"I... I'm willing to let you seduce me Danny."

"But I'm not going to."

"But... but..." Sarah shook her head in bewilderment.

Daniela sighed and lifted a lock of her hair. "Tell me Sarah what colour is this?"

"Well it's a sort of honey gold..."

"In other words it's *blond* right?"

"Well yes I suppose so..."

"And your hair is what... dark chestnut brown... or shall we say brunette?"

"Ok but..."

"So please tell me Sarah, why you are the one being so *blond* at the moment?"

"I'm sorry?"

"Let me spell it out for you Sarah. I am refusing to seduce you, correct?"

"Well yes..."

"I have also indicated firmly that I desire you. Am I still correct?"

"Yes but..."

"You have intimated that a sexual contact between us would not be disagreeable to you as well I believe."

"What are you trying to say?"

"Namely this Sarah; I have vowed not to seduce you but I've left a hole in that vow you could throw one of Messalina's orgies through."

Sarah bit her lip in puzzlement. "I'm not following this."

"Sarah, in my vow that I would not seduce you, did you, at any time, hear me say that it was forbidden for you to seduce *me*?"

Sarah sat bolt upright. "*What*?"

Daniela held her hands out. "I've done all the running up until now Sarah. If you truly want me and you truly love me, well here I am. It's *your* turn to go the distance."

Sarah was in shock. "How... how am I supposed to seduce you?"

Daniela shrugged. "Well you've wined me and dined me; got me barely dressed by the light of an open fire; half the work's done already. I'm sure I won't put up too much of a fight."

"This is ridiculous."

Daniela slumped. "Oh well, if you don't want to, I suppose we can always see if there's anything good on the telly."

"Stop it Danny. I... I don't know the first thing about how to seduce a girl."

"Well that much is obvious since you're making such a pig's ear out of the thing."

"Well... well what am I supposed to do?" Sarah's voice sounded shrill with agitation.

"Hmm, just a suggestion you understand, but it often helps to compliment the person who you want to have your wicked way with. You know; tell them that they're beautiful and desirable."

"But you already know that you're beautiful."

"Way to go Sarah. That's right. Just tell me that I'm conceited and vain. Not exactly a major step forward to relieving me of my drawers is it?"

Sarah snorted in exasperation. "All right then bugger it! You're beautiful all right."

Daniela feigned indifference. "Well thank you for the compliment but you could have couched it in more romantic terms, I think."

Sarah took a deep breath. "Danny you know that I think you're the most beautiful woman I ever saw. I've told you that before! You are sensational; I've never seen a woman to match you."

"Getting better Sarah. Anything else you'd like to add?"

"What else should I add?"

"I think an Early Purple Orchid is beautiful Sarah but I don't want to sleep with it."

"Ok, ok! You're not only beautiful but you're desirable too. Does that make you happy?"

"Not quite."

"Oh God! Now what?"

Daniela simpered comically and rolled her eyes theatrically. "I just want to know that you want me for more than just my body."

Sarah gripped her forehead and resisted the temptation to throw the olive bowl at Daniela. "So you're a blushing virgin now."

"I'm a sweet young lady being stalked by a predatory seductress with dishonourable intentions on my innocence. I need reassurances that you don't just

342

want to have your wicked way with me and then abandon me, a ruined woman."

"My arse!"

"Is very pretty but not sufficient at this juncture in time to lure me into your lair. I am requiring romantic cajoling not vulgar language expressing a disbelief in my veracity."

"I'll slap you in a minute."

Daniela inclined her head thoughtfully. "That *might* work but I'm not at all certain that you're experienced enough to carry off the domineering mistress role just yet. I'd recommend that you leave that part of the proceedings until after you've laid a little more groundwork."

"What groundwork?"

"Well money is often regarded as the universal aphrodisiac but that won't hack it in this instance because I happen to be considerably richer than you. Flowers are a good standby but that isn't an option either because of your lack of foresight and the fact that you're unlikely to be able to arrange an Interflora delivery at this time of night. So, if I was you, I'd fall back on the old tried and trusted methods and try telling me that you love me."

"You *know* that I love you."

"That is exactly what I *don't* know Sarah. I hope you love me. I desire above all that you love me but I don't *know*. What I *do* know is that in two days' time you are travelling to the Ticino to see a man who you have stated that you have every intention of marrying. Now forgive me Sarah but that is hardly compelling evidence that I am the light of your life or the star in your firmament. It would be possible, with every rational and sober analysis, to argue that I am merely a dalliance; a good time for a night. Naturally, therefore, I am suspicious of your intentions. So, if you want to drag me down onto that carpet, you're going to have to do better than that."

"Is this what this is about? Are you mad at me because I'm going to Ticino to get engaged?"

"That's still two days away Sarah. A lot can happen in two days. People in love are always hopelessly optimistic. That's your window of opportunity. It is still possible to persuade me that it's really *me* you love; that there is still hope for me. I'm so desperate I'll clutch at any straw. A few little lies and you've got me halfway to the bedroom already."

"But I don't want to lie to you Danny."

"Honest people spend a lot of time sleeping alone Sarah. The wheels of love are greased with pork pies."

"Is that why Muslim marriages are usually arranged?"

"Don't change the subject by using my choice of Cockney rhyming slang to make flippant remarks and cast slurs upon our Islamic brothers and sisters Sarah. I'm sure that the same is true in Islamic society too. The prophet himself had at least eleven wives, if not more, as well as any number of slave concubines and what have you. I'm sure even Allah would have forgiven his prophet the odd little fib to keep that lot happy in the name of domestic harmony."

Sarah frowned. "It doesn't seem right to tell lies just because you want to sleep with someone."

"Do you play backgammon Sarah?"

"Yes. Why?"

"Well because a game of backgammon is about the most exciting a prospect that this evening holds for us if you persist in holding a philosophical debate on the virtues of veracity in human sexual relationships."

"I'm sorry. What should I do?"

"God Sarah! I'm not an instruction manual. Try reading men's magazines. They're usually full of useful tips on how to get women into bed."

"Well I could use some now."

"Alcohol."

"Eh?"

344

"Alcohol. It's almost universally praised for its efficaciousness in lowering inhibitions and female resistance." Daniela pointed to the coffee table. "My glass is empty."

"Oh I'm sorry." Hastily Sarah plied the wine bottle to replenish their glasses.

Daniela took a sip and leaned back on the couch twirling her wine in the glass. "Now then. Let's recap shall we. Where were we before we got side-tracked into a discussion of the moral dilemmas of romantic mendacity?"

"You said you wanted me to say I love you."

"Ah yes! Of course. Pretty much standard operating procedure if you want to get to base camp one. Well?"

"Well what?"

"Well are you or are you not going to declare your undying love and devotion to me or shall I get the backgammon board out you muppet?"

"I love you Danny."

"Better."

"Danny I love you more than anybody I've ever known. I know I'm going to Ticino but the person I love, the person I truly love isn't there. She's sat right in front of me now."

"Much better! I love you too Sarah. Now that wasn't so hard was it?"

Sarah blushed and pulled a face. "That wasn't a lie Danny."

"I believe you."

There was an awkward pause. "Now what do I do?" asked Sarah at last in some desperation.

Daniela pursed her lips. "Well the neutral observer would probably remark that you have a spatial problem Sarah."

Sarah blinked. "What do you mean?"

"Well it's a recognised fact that sweet nothings are best whispered at close range and preferably in close physical contact. Our hypothetical neutral observer would doubtless point out that there is going to be little mileage in bellowing endearments at each other from opposite ends of the room."

"You mean I should join you on the couch?"

"It's worth trying Sarah. If I don't leap up, dash off screaming and lock myself into my bedroom you may consider it an incremental victory."

"You're impossible."

"That is yet to be ascertained Sarah. You certainly have no grounds as yet to believe it. I'm not giving you negative signals. It's not as if I'm yawning or passing the tedium of the conversation by browsing through the television channels on the remote or flicking olive pips at you. There are still considerable grounds for optimism."

"All right. I'll come and sit on the bloody couch!"

Daniela sniffed haughtily. "Well if you don't want to..." Sarah gave a little growl of exasperation and moved to the couch. Daniela raised an eyebrow and regarded her. "It's an awfully big couch Sarah. I'm pleased that you appreciate its generous spaciousness by utilising all of it." Sarah groaned and moved up alongside Daniela. Daniela held up a hand palm upwards. Feeling increasingly foolish Sarah took the hand in her own. Daniela rewarded her with a dazzling smile and lowered her voice. "Well, well. We're making progress. This is cosy isn't it? Now then tell me again; what was it you were shouting at me from the other side of the room earlier?"

"I said I love you, you barmy bitch!"

"Shall we try that again, only this time sweeter and without the vulgar aspersions?"

"I love you."

"Try whispering it softly in my ear." Daniela brushed her hair out of the way and inclined her head. "Go on. Just try it."

With a sigh Sarah leaned forward. Daniela's scent was intoxicating at close proximity. "I love you." she whispered. She sat back once more. "Was that better?"

"No. It was rubbish."

"Why?" demanded Sarah indignantly. "I did what you said."

"Which only shows that you're listening. What you're not doing is watching."

Sarah shook her head in confusion. "You're not helping me here Danny."

"I couldn't be helping you *more* Sarah. I'm giving you signals all the time and you're just not seeing them. Good God Sarah even *men* are usually sensitive enough to spot overt invitations. If they were all as myopic as you then we'd be a seriously declining species."

"So what am I missing?"

"Look Sarah I moved my hair out of the way right?"

"Ok."

"I leaned slightly away and I even let my robe slip off my shoulder. I exposed a huge area of naked flesh from my shoulder to my ear with your lips two inches away and you haven't got the common gumption to kiss me on the side of my neck. It's one of a woman's most erogenous zones Sarah and I laid it out on a plate for you. A few kisses there and you'd have had me quivering like jelly. Shape up and start watching my body language! Do I have to provide cue cards or something?"

Sarah laughed, beginning to enjoy the absurdity of Daniela's coaching. "Can I try again please?"

"Ok but don't mess it up this time."

Sarah leaned forward and kissed Daniela in the nape of her neck. Daniela shivered perceptibly and her hand squeezed Sarah's. Glorying in the triumph Sarah continued to bestow soft kisses to the side of Daniela's neck. The texture of Daniela's skin seemed to change under her caresses. It was an indefinable sensation; a sort of warm glow combined with a suddenly silkier feeling.

347

With a shock Sarah realised that Daniela was aroused. She had never known that a person's skin felt so different under arousal. She glanced down and saw that Daniela's robe had come adrift from the waist, and her face and the cleavage of her bosom were suffused in pink. Daniela's free hand was gripping her leg and her breathing was suddenly deep and laboured. "Is this better?" whispered Sarah.

"Yes." Daniela's voice sounded hoarse. "But I'm sure you could use your tongue for more useful purposes than to ask for further instructions."

Sarah ran her tongue the length of Daniela's neck and delighted in the little gasp that emitted from Daniela's mouth. She became bolder licking the side of the neck and face and nibbling at Daniela's ear. Daniela was almost panting and rewarded Sarah's effort with cute little moans and squeaks. With a profound sigh Daniela turned her face to Sarah and opened her lips. "Oh Sarah!" she breathed. Sarah did not make the mistake of ignoring this invitation and she fastened her lips to Daniela's. Daniela reached up to grasp Sarah's head and hold it to her, her tongue urgent inside Sarah's. Sarah was almost shocked by the intensity of Daniela's passion. In bemusement she realised that Daniela was so much putty in her hands. She had always felt the subservient one in their relationship. Now she realised that she was calling the shots; stoking the fires in Daniela. She felt wonderful. She stroked her hand over Daniela's bare shoulder marvelling at the softness of the skin beneath her touch. She reached around to touch the other shoulder but inadvertently brushed Daniela's right breast. Daniela stiffened sharply and Sarah withdrew her hand hastily. "Oh er... sorry."

"For what darling?"

"I er... I didn't mean to... I mean I didn't...." Sarah groped for words uncomfortably. Daniela gave a muffled squeak and buried her face in Sarah's shoulder. She was shaking. After a few seconds Sarah realised that she was laughing helplessly. "What the hell's the matter?" she demanded.

"Oh Sarah you're just priceless. You're the most adorable little do-nut I've ever come across."

"What have I done now?"

"Give me your hand." Sarah obeyed and Daniela lifted it to her breast and clasped it around the orb firmly. "There now. Is that better darling?"

"Er... yes..." Sarah's voice sounded unnaturally high and squeaky to her.

"You're getting up the mountain Sarah. Any sixteen year old lad worth his salt will tell you that if she lets you put your hand on her tit you're half way there to getting her knickers off."

Sarah grinned. "Shut up talking and kiss me."

"Yes my lady." The kiss went on interminably it seemed until Daniela broke for air. "I noticed on the Santis when you roped us up you were good with knots Sarah." she breathed hoarsely.

"Now what are you blathering about?"

"Do you think you could manage the bow knot on my robe?"

"I don't think that will provide any real technical difficulties." Sarah unfastened Daniela's robe and smiled as Daniela seemed almost indecently urgent in divesting herself of the encumbering garment. Eager to feel Daniela's skin with her hands Sarah lifted her camisole over her head. Daniela was co-operating admirably; even enthusiastically. Bare to the waist Daniela was so beautiful that Sarah abandoned any inhibitions and greedily indulged herself in the unfamiliar novelty of exploring another woman's breasts. Daniela panted desperately as Sarah kneaded her breasts with her hands and groaned almost comically as Sarah bent to kiss her nipples and nibble them with her teeth; grasping Sarah's hair so tightly that it hurt. Daniela was almost incoherent with lust and she grasped Sarah's hand determinedly and thrust it beneath the elastic of her knickers. Sarah felt the damp silkiness of Daniela's sex with her fingertips and stroked it experimentally. Daniela arched her back and cried out softly. From there it was an easy stage to sliding the last vestige of Daniela's modesty over her ankles and taking the now naked woman in her triumphant arms. Daniela was pawing at her dressing gown and fumbling at the buttons on her pyjamas. Soon they were both naked in each other's grasp on the carpet before the fire and Daniela's cats rose disapprovingly, twitched their tails austerely and sought out a less disturbed environment for their slumbers.

The next hours passed in a whirl for Sarah. She could never remember such a night of unalloyed joy. Once the two girls had possessed each other, they became greedy for each other. Sarah was beguiled by the experience of squatting between Daniela's open legs and observing her sex at close quarters. Sarah had never had the opportunity to examine another woman's vulva at close range before and she found herself fascinated by it. She parted the lips with interest and stroked a finger around the labia majora and the labia minora experimentally; almost academically whilst Daniela moaned in frustration and begged her to stop teasing her. Detachedly she inserted a finger into the vagina and parted the labia minora to uncover the external manifestation of the clitoris; the little "man in the boat" and noted with interest how Daniela's convulsions and wailing became more frantic by the second as she rubbed a finger across it. She leaned down to kiss it and Daniela's hand clasped to the back of her head as she writhed in what appeared to be exquisite agony. Sarah found to her surprise that she liked the taste. Better still she liked the manic shrieks and violent shudders of Daniela as she licked her to orgasm. Daniela had her revenge for the sweet torment. Sarah could not tear her eyes from the golden locks draped across her lap as Daniela buried her face in her crutch and brought her to

350

such a scalding climax that Sarah thought she would faint.

They made love on the carpet before resuming operations on the couch. They cleared the dirty dishes from the coffee table and tried it out in the kitchen as well. Their exertions left them so sweaty and soiled that they ran another bath and shared it, getting suds all over the bathroom floor, and performing acts with a shower-head that would make a sailor blush. Finally Daniela dragged Sarah to her bedroom and they sated themselves on her enormous bed collapsing at last into a blissful revelry that was not yet sleep but that dreamy half way stage of exhausted content and sleepy giggles. It was nearly five o'clock in the morning.

Sarah looked down at the ruined figure of Daniela on the pillow beside her and felt an upwelling of love that took her breath from her. "Oh Danny. I love you." she murmured and there was no doubt in her mind of her deepest sincerity.

Daniela reached up to stroke her face. "I love you too Sarah. What are we going to do?"

"I don't know Danny. I really don't. I still have to go to Ticino you know."

"I know darling."

"I don't know what's going to happen. But I have to go. I can't get out of it. What the hell am I going to do now?"

"I can't advise you my love. I just want you to know that I'm here; I'll always be here. In the end it'll be your decision my sweet. I love you. There's no going back from that. Whatever happens you're my Sarah."

Sarah glanced at the clock. "God! It's gone five o'clock. We might have to work today."

"Only for lunch sweetheart. We can have the rest of the day together."

"I... I have to pick up my bags to go to the Ticino."

"That's not a problem. We can drive down to your place after lunch and pick up your things and you can

351

stay here the night. I'll drive you down to the station in Buchs in the morning."

"Yes ok..." Sarah paused. "Just a second! Just one bloody second Miss Daniela Devin! You told me that your car was broken. That was the reason I had to stay here tonight because you couldn't drive me home because your sodding car was broken."

Daniela chuckled deeply and pulled Sarah down onto the pillow beside her. "I lied!"

To be continued:

Afterword

While the characters in this novel are entirely fictitious, the Toggenburg is a real place. The beautiful alpine valley known as the Toggenburg can be found in North Eastern Switzerland in the Canton of St Gallen. Every feature or location described in this story is true to life. This includes all of the features negotiated by Sarah and Daniela on their hike over the Santisgebiet. The only invented places are the house that Sarah shares with Nicole, Daniela's house at Oberdorf and the gay bar in the town of Winterthur. Even the Hotel Toggenburg at Schwendi exists although, of course, my fictitious Frau Fritzl bears no resemblance to the owners of that establishment.

The cover of this novel shows a view from Schwendi high on the southern side of the valley. The little lake in the foreground is the larger of the two Schwendiseen; the little lakes where Sarah and Daniela liked to take a walk around in the afternoons in the first book of the series. The Hotel Toggenburg lies a few hundred metres away and Oberdorf, where Daniela lives, is some twenty minutes' walk to the east. The large mountain in the distance is the Santis; the highest peak surrounding the valley at just over two and a half thousand metres high and the mountain that Sarah and Daniela scale on their excursion.